MR. DARCY AND THE ENCHANTED LIBRARY

A PRIDE AND PREJUDICE VARIATION

MONICA FAIRVIEW   ABIGAIL REYNOLDS

VICTORIA KINCAID   SARAH COURTNEY

MELANIE RACHEL   LARI ANN O'DELL

MAGICAL AUSTEN PRESS

Cover design: Monica Fairview

Written by: Monica Fairview, Abigail Reynolds, Victoria Kincaid, Sarah Courtney, Melanie Rachel, and Lari Ann O'Dell

Published by: Magical Austen Press

Edited by: Victoria Kincaid

❀ Created with Vellum

INTRODUCTION

This novel has been a fun collaborative project in so many ways, and I'm so thrilled that it's finally been published. It has not only been a collaboration between six Jane Austen fantasy authors, but it also involved our readers, without whom this novel would never have been possible.

Ever since I participated in the collaboration *The Darcy Brothers* with several other writers [remember Theo Darcy, anyone?] I've been wanting to do it again. There's something intensely challenging about writing with other writers who are all good at what they are doing. It pushes you in directions you would never have expected.

So when I set up the Magical Austen website with Abigail Reynolds, one of the first things I proposed was writing a novel together as a group and setting up weekly chapters on the blog. After some discussion, we decided to leave it up to our readers to decide what they wanted the story to be about. Obviously, it was going to be *Pride and Prejudice* based, and we wanted it to be magical.

We were delighted by the response from our readers, who quickly entered into the spirit of the things by taking part in a series of polls and coming up with ideas. There were lots of wonderful back-and-forth conversations before our readers narrowed down the elements of the story that they wanted, which included second-chance romance and magical familiars (later more specifically griffins).

I can tell you, when the authors sat down and looked at the list of requirements the readers had given us, we realized it was going to be a lot more daunting than we expected to pull everything together. Each author had different ideas about how the story should go, and it took us a while to finally reach the writing stage.

Once we got started, though, it was a blast. We still had to iron out so many things along the way, but it was such an enjoyable experience to read what each of our fellow authors came up with each week.

Now, at last, we have a final version of the book we'd love to share with you, as we shared it with our readers along the way. Your comments were immensely helpful to us on our journey, so I'd like to dedicate this book to you, the readers, and to thank every one of you who voted and commented and helped us along in our journey.

Monica Fairview

Note: To participate in future projects like this, make sure to sign up on the **Magical Austen** website
https://magicalausten.com/
and join our group on Facebook:
https://www.facebook.com/groups/fantasyjaneausten

CHAPTER 1

*D*arcy straightened as the doctor emerged from Georgiana's sickroom. Before the maid closed the door, he caught a glimpse of his sister's wan, thin face resting on her pillow, her eyes closed in exhaustion.

"Well?" Darcy demanded.

The man shifted his bag from one hand to another. "There is no improvement, as you are no doubt aware. I have given her a sleeping remedy to make her more comfortable, but there is no cure I can offer for a magical malady. Have you consulted a medical mage?"

"Yes." Every single one he could bribe or threaten to make the journey to Pemberley to examine Georgiana, and they had all said the same thing – that this was beyond their abilities.

"I am sorry, sir." The doctor bowed and left, taking Darcy's last scrap of hope with him.

He rubbed the back of his neck as the doctor's footsteps faded away. Surely there must be something he could do! But Georgiana would need time to recover from the doctor's visit before he could sit with her again, and he had exhausted his last lead. No amount of brooding would help her.

All that was left was for him to distract himself. He might as well be useful, so he headed to his study and the long-neglected pile of mail his secretary had left him.

The first few were invitations which he pushed aside. As if he had any desire to be entertained! Then he spotted the familiar spiky handwriting of Lady Catherine de Bourgh on the next envelope. With a groan, he broke the seal.

MY DEAR NEPHEW,

I will waste no time in coming to the point. The Patronesses of Magic have met, and we are in unanimous agreement that you must marry immediately. We are well aware of your objections to the idea, but now that Georgiana cannot produce an heir to Pemberley, it is time for you to give up your stubbornness and do your duty. Anne is awaiting your proposal —

WITH AN OATH, he crumpled the letter and threw it into the fire. Devil take her! How dare she assume that Georgiana would die! And he was not a breeding stud to answer to her demands.

His fingers reached out to stroke the left-hand drawer of his desk in the familiar spot where the finish was shiny from all the times he had undertaken the same action. Everything he had left of Elizabeth Bennet was in that drawer – the few notes she had written him, the sketch her sister had drawn of her. Five years, and the wounds were still fresh.

And the damnable thing was that his aunt was right. For Pemberley's sake, he did need to marry, intolerable as it might be.

A voice whispered inside his head. Hespera, his griffin

familiar. *There is important news afoot. The Great Library has reappeared at last.*

It took a moment to sink in, but then Darcy jumped to his feet. *Are you certain? It is open?*

I just received word. It is certain.

The Great Library, home to the spell books that just might hold the answers to Georgiana's illness. It had been inaccessible for half a dozen years, since the death of the last Librarian. And now it was open again.

Excitement filled his throat. At last, a ray of hope! *We will leave for Oxford immediately,* he told her. He had no intention of allowing Georgiana to suffer for a minute longer than necessary.

DARCY TOLD Hespera to circle three times before gliding down into the square in front of the Great Library. He could feel the griffin's annoyance at the extra effort after the long flight, but the people of Oxford needed the advance warning. Even on the first high circle, he could see people looking up and starting to run at the sight of the griffin.

He shook his head in annoyance. He would never have brought the griffin into a city if the Library did not require the presence of his familiar.

The square was almost empty by the time Hespera's paws touched down on the cobblestones. Her eagle's head turned from side to side, and she spoke in his head. *What an interesting place, even if the inhabitants are cowards.*

He swung his leg over her back and dismounted. *Those who have never seen a live griffin before are naturally in awe,* he told her. He needed her to be on her best behavior today, and that meant placating her vanity.

That building has statues of griffins. There is something odd about them, though.

They guard the library with magic and are the first test we must pass, Darcy said. The two stone griffins held crossed swords which barred entry to the great metal doors. *Come.*

He drew in a deep breath before leading the griffin to stand in front of the imposing statues. This should be the easiest of the tasks he would face, but it was magic far beyond his understanding, and so much depended upon it. Steeling himself, Darcy said, "We beg leave to enter the Great Repository." No one ever called it that in this modern age, but the tests relied on using the library's proper name.

At first nothing happened, but then a grinding sound began. The doors swung open, and the two statues raised their stone swords to allow Darcy and Hespera to pass.

It was uncanny to see, even though he had known what would happen. Mages had been arguing for centuries over how it worked – both how the statues moved and how they knew to admit only those with magical familiars. Not to mention how this relatively small building could possibly contain the hundreds of rooms that comprised the Great Library. If the fae who had built the Library knew the answers, they were not sharing them with mortals.

A prickle went down Darcy's spine as he walked between the stone swords. Hespera trailed a few steps behind him. She disliked being indoors, but he had promised her a new gold chain for her cooperation.

Beyond the doors was a courtyard paved in cobblestones. On the far side of the courtyard was another set of double doors that opened to reveal a long columned room that would not have looked out of place in a Roman palace, its marble walls lined with portraits of elderly women, some dressed in the manner of medieval times. A few men, too, but mostly women. It was completely unfurnished apart from a desk where sat a dark-skinned man in an embroidered cap. In front of him lay a closed ledger and an inkwell.

Darcy approached the desk. "I wish to see the Librarian," he said firmly. "I am Fitzwilliam Darcy of Pemberley, and my familiar is Hespera."

The scribe gave him the barest glance and opened the ledger to a blank page with two columns. "Welcome to the Gallery of Librarians. Your name does not matter here, only your motives and actions. Why do you wish to see the Librarian?"

"My sister is deathly ill from an unknown magical malady. We believe that the cure may lie in the Library's spell books."

The man made a careful check mark in the right-hand column. "Your concern for your sister is laudable, but the world is full of people who are deathly ill. Why does your sister deserve to be saved?"

How dare he ask such a question? But with Georgiana's life at stake, Darcy had no choice but to answer. "My sister is responsible for many lives. She and her seal familiar sail with the Navy, and her magic has saved hundreds of sailors from drowning."

The scribe dipped his quill in the inkwell but hesitated over the ledger. "She has saved British sailors." He sounded dubious, leaning forward enough to reveal pointed ears beside his embroidered hat. A fae!

Darcy swallowed hard. "Yes. A great many of them."

The fae man studied the ledger with a frown, and then placed a tick in the left-hand column. "The Great Library takes no sides in wars. Why else does she deserve to live?"

Darcy's breath caught in his chest. If Georgiana's work was not enough, what hope could there be? But he had to try. "She has a rare talent for music. Her playing often brings tears to people's eyes." And he might never hear her play again. "She is but twenty years of age and is all that is generous and kind."

The fae made a tiny tick in the right-hand column. "What else?"

Fitzwilliam Darcy of Pemberley, Griffin Keeper, never had to beg for anything, and to do so now gave him a sickening sensation. "I love her dearly. She is my only remaining family, and I would be bereft without her. I would give my own life to save hers."

But it earned him another check in the right-hand column, so it was worth it. He would beg all day to get inside the library if that was what it took.

"You say she is your only family, yet is that not your own doing? Is there a reason you have not married and expanded your family?"

Darcy's stomach churned. It had to be magic, that this stranger could so quickly narrow in on his most painful vulnerability, something that he never spoke of. But if it would save Georgiana, he would humiliate himself utterly. "Some years ago, there was a woman I wished to marry, but I was persuaded against the match owing to her lack of magic," he said in a clipped voice. "I would have been neglecting my duty and harming my family if I married her. But I wish most dearly she could have been my wife."

The fae's expression did not change. "If that was years ago, you have had plenty of time to marry another, more suitable woman."

A surge of bile rose in his throat. "Do you think it is acceptable to marry one woman while my heart belongs to another? I do not, and I will not. They said I would forget my first love quickly. Perhaps someday I shall, but that day has not come yet. And so my sister is all I have. I will do anything for her."

A check in the right-hand column. Thank God!

The scribe closed the ledger. "You may present your case to Abraxas. I will take you to the courtyard, where you will await him."

He had done it, made it past the first line of questioning! But it was only one step, and everyone said that gaining the Librarian's approval was the hardest part. "I thank you."

~

FORTUNATELY FOR DARCY'S SANITY, the next test proved embarrassingly easy, which gave him time to regain his shattered equilibrium. Even after all these years, speaking of Elizabeth hurt.

This, in comparison, was nothing. True, it would be a severe trial of most men's courage to face the full-grown griffin at close quarters, but not for a Griffin Keeper like Darcy. Not to mention that he had his own griffin by his side.

The griffin Abraxas seemed far more interested in Hespera than Darcy in any case. After briefly asking Darcy to state his business, he engaged in a long silent conversation with Hespera, one which left her tossing her head in annoyance.

Finally Abraxas spoke to Darcy, *This way. You must go alone; your griffin will remain here.*

Darcy followed him through a winding stone corridor with deep-set closed doors to each side. At the foot of a narrow circular staircase, the griffin lifted his front paw. "You will find the Librarian in the room above."

But when Darcy reached the top, there were three doors. Only one of them was open, so he chose that one and stepped inside.

The room was surprisingly lofty and large. Sunlight filtered in through high arched windows, illuminating bookshelves that lined each wall, rising at least twenty feet, if not more. The air was redolent with the dusty vanilla scent of old leather-bound books, and a hint of lavender teased his senses with its familiarity.

But there was no Librarian to be seen, only a young woman perched atop a ladder replacing a book on a shelf. Perhaps she could give him further directions.

He cleared his throat. "Good afternoon, Miss. I wonder if you could assist me–"

His stomach dropped as she turned to face him. It could not be. He blinked his eyes twice, as if that could change his vision.

"Elizabeth," he whispered.

CHAPTER 2

*E*lizabeth had been deeply immersed in urgent research involving the weakening wall between Faerie and the mortal world when the Library griffin, Abraxas, mentally interrupted to announce that a supplicant had arrived.

So soon? Opening the Library could not have come at a worse time. Strange unnatural events were occurring all across the world, and they had to be dealt with. Now was not the time to start meeting with supplicants.

Still, it was what she had been training to do, and she intended to do the best she could.

"Good afternoon, Miss. I wonder if you could assist me—"

There was no mistaking the husky timber of that voice. It had haunted her dreams for so many years, but Elizabeth had never expected to hear it again. Surely Mr. Darcy could not be here, in the Library?

She twisted around quickly to make sure it was him, and her foot slipped on the rung of the ladder. She tumbled downwards, her arms flailing. Instinct took over, and she called on magic to stop the downward descent. A cushion of air formed beneath her, buoying her up and holding her steady as she carefully regained her footing on the ladder.

She felt like a fool for reacting so strongly, but at least her dignity was intact. Feet firmly planted on the wooden step, Elizabeth was now able to focus her attention on her visitor. The man – Mr. Fitzwilliam Darcy – was standing under the ladder, arms outstretched. He had formed a floating carpet of feathers, closely clustered together to break her fall.

She stared at him in disbelief. Did he really think a Librarian would not have enough magic to save herself? That she would require his assistance? Was there no limit to his arrogance? He had clearly not changed at all.

She schooled her thoughts and waited for him to acknowledge her magical power, but he did not show any sign of it. The alarm on his face simply faded and his expression turned neutral. All too neutral. He released the feather spell and stepped back, putting a clear distance between them.

Yes, that was the Fitzwilliam Darcy she knew. Always concealing his emotions. The same man who could easily cast her away when she was inconvenient, whose declarations of love meant nothing at all. She remembered that blank face with its tight expression. It had been five long years, but it was etched deep into her memory. It was the last thing she had seen before he turned his back to her and walked away, his footsteps hollow echoes as he broke her heart.

"Miss Elizabeth Bennet? Are you assisting here? I am sorry. I must have come the wrong way. I asked to see the Librarian."

How could the powerful mixture of human and fae magic that surrounded her escape his attention? He was so single-minded; he barely acknowledged her presence. His only concern was meeting the Librarian. Miss Elizabeth Bennet was beneath his notice. Towards her, he was silent, grave, and indifferent.

Elizabeth was glad she was still perched on the ladder, because at least she was looking down at him.

"Did you, indeed?" She turned to face him and crossed her arms, setting her back against the ladder. "How did you trick the scribe into allowing you to come in? Are you here to gather information that would give you even more power in society?"

She could hear the bitterness in her voice. She was supposed to be the Librarian. She was not allowed to judge the supplicants. In this case, though, it was impossible not to recall how easily he had cast her aside when she did not prove useful to him. She could not imagine that he had a good reason to be here.

"That is hardly fair—" He stepped towards her and started to extend his hand, then dropped it to his side. "As you know very well, no-one is allowed to enter unless they have a good reason. I need to speak to the Librarian. I am afraid the Library griffin misdirected me. He suggested I would find the Librarian here."

Should she keep Mr. Darcy in the dark about her identity and send him away? She would rather not deal with him. Besides, it would serve him right for not even entertaining the possibility that she could be the Librarian. How very typical of him to underestimate her.

Elizabeth? Do you wish him to leave? I do not blame you. His griffin is the most arrogant familiar I have ever encountered.

It was likely that Abraxas could sense her turmoil, though he would never eavesdrop unless she deliberately opened her mind to him. Elizabeth almost agreed with the griffin's assessment of Hespera, but she held back. She had met Darcy's familiar twice, and both times she had been unapproachable. However, she did not want Abraxas to know that she and Darcy had once been close.

If only he had given her a few minutes' warning, she could have prepared herself. *Why did you not tell me that our visitor had a griffin familiar? If you had, I would have known who he was. Mr. Darcy is the only Griffin Keeper in the Kingdom.*

Apart from you. Abraxas sounded pleased with himself.

Of course. That goes without saying. She felt a surge of affection for the old griffin.

Were you well acquainted with him?

So much for trying to hide things from him. *It was a long time ago.*

Was it only five years? It seemed like a lifetime.

Abraxas was too wise to be fooled by her dismissal. *Is he the one who cast you off?*

The griffin knew the sorry tale of a love that had splintered her heart into a thousand little pieces. He had witnessed her grief.

I would be happy to expel him, along with his familiar, and bar them from the library if you wish. Abraxas sounded like he would relish it.

It was tempting. Very tempting. Mr. Darcy's arrival had unsettled her profoundly. She did not want to work with him. But she did not wish him to be barred from the Library on a whim, either.

No. There is no need for such measures. I just need more time.

She turned back to Mr. Darcy, whose impatience was almost palpable. "Unfortunately, sir, you have come at the wrong time. The Librarian is not currently available. If you would like to return in a day or two, perhaps?"

"It is of the utmost urgency. I *must* see the Librarian immediately."

It was out of the question. Elizabeth was too shaken to work with him today, and she did not want him to know it.

She could not refuse to help him. It was what she was here for, after all, and she would not abandon her duty simply because she did not like Mr. Darcy.

"Why not return tomorrow morning?"

At least that would give her one night to compose herself.

Mr. Darcy looked as if he might object, but then he nodded. He did not want to risk the ire of the Librarian.

He already had. Five years ago.

"Will nine o'clock suit?"

"That would be acceptable," said Elizabeth, relieved at the temporary reprieve. "I will let Travinius know that you are to be admitted. I am certain you have no wish to go through all the questions again." She gave him a small smile. This would all go more smoothly if they could find a way to be civil at least.

"I would not." There was no hint of an answering smile, only tension. So much for trying to make things easier.

She wanted him to leave, and soon – before she broke down and asked him the question that had tormented her for so many months after he had walked away. *Why did you betray me?*

Instead, she inclined her head. "Until tomorrow, Mr. Darcy."

He bowed stiffly. "A pleasure to see you again, Miss Bennet."

She was glad she was on the ladder because she had an excuse not to curtsey and give him her hand.

She watched as he turned on his heel and walked away. Then she made her way down the steps onto solid ground and took several shaky breaths. She had thought her heart was healed. Why should the sight of Darcy rattle her like this? She had believed the bitterness and the pain buried inside her a long time ago. Instead, here she was.

She would not allow him to affect her this way. She was a

different person now. She was the Librarian of the Great Repository, connecting the human world with the fae with access to the knowledge of centuries. She was not helpless Miss Bennet anymore, at the mercy of some unwritten rule established by society. The nightmarish events five years ago no longer had the power to hurt her. She had found her place in the world. She belonged here, and she would not let Mr. Darcy ruin that.

She rose to her feet. Abraxas was standing in the doorway.

He has upset you. His voice in her head was kind. It reassured her that her world was not going to be torn away. She had no intention of allowing a gentleman who had no place in her life to grind everything she had accomplished under his heel.

True, she replied to Abraxas' query. *But only because this was our first encounter. Next time, I will face him with complete indifference.*

I am relieved to hear it. Then let us resume our tasks.

MR. DARCY PRESENTED himself just as the clock struck nine. This time, Elizabeth was ready for him. She examined him closely. Yesterday, she had been too busy avoiding eye contact to judge whether he had changed. But now, in the harsh morning light, she could see that those five years had left their imprint. The passage of time was etched into his skin. He looked thinner, more careworn. His arrogant demeanor was the same, but he seemed – diminished, somehow.

She wondered if he saw her the same way. Or if he even saw her at all. She could not tell. He was avoiding her gaze.

"I thought the Librarian had agreed to meet me at nine. Time is of the essence."

He was here for the Librarian, not for her.

Impatience was written all over his body. To him, Elizabeth was nothing more than a means to an end, just as she had always been. At least this time she knew he was just using her. He was barely making an effort to be civil. Why should she be surprised? He had been uncivil the first day they had met at the Meryton Assembly. He had been uncivil when they parted. Why should it be any different now? And why should it matter that it had not even crossed his mind that Miss Elizabeth Bennet might be the Librarian?

"We cannot make it too easy to access the Librarian, can we now?" There was an edge to her voice.

She wanted him to look at her properly, to see what she had achieved, who she had become. It might be wrong to hold back the truth, but she wanted him to discover it on his own.

He frowned at her words and finally turned to examine her. His gaze was disconcerting, his dark eyes intense and deep.

Her heart tilted at the intensity of his expression, and she braced herself for his verdict.

"You look different."

She tried to make light of it, now that she had what she wanted. "I hope you mean to compliment me, not to tell me I look old."

"Old?" She was vain enough to be glad he dismissed the idea at once. "No. You look – radiant. You were always lively, but this is more than that. It is difficult to describe. I have encountered it before." His eyes suddenly sharpened. "It is the glow of magic. Fae magic. How is that possible?"

Behind him, Abraxas made a sound, something between a sniffle and a snort. *He took his time working that out.*

Finally! "It is a long story," Elizabeth replied. "Are you prepared to hear it?"

Darcy's mouth tightened. "Much as I would love to hear how you were able to connect to fae magic, and how you came to work in the Library, I am here to consult the Librarian."

She was growing more vexed by the minute at his willful blindness. This is why they had parted. He had accepted Lady Catherine's verdict that Elizabeth's powers were too weak. Now he was standing before her, seeing what she was capable of and yet stubbornly refusing to alter his perception. Was he really so set against her that he could not see what was in front of his very eyes? Did he think so little of her?

Her bitterness at his betrayal increased twofold and she reached out to Abraxas. *His mind refuses to accept I am the Librarian.*

Shall I tell his familiar who you are? I would like to see the expression on her human's face when she communicates it to him.

I would rather inform Mr. Darcy myself.

If he refused to see it, she could not put off the revelation any longer. Clearly she needed to bash him on the head with it.

"You wish to speak to the Librarian, Mr. Darcy? Very well. You have your wish."

He gave a nod of acknowledgment. Even now, he was too intent on his purpose – whatever it was – to notice that she was the one granting him the permission.

"Before you do, you must swear an oath that you will not do harm to the Library or to the Librarian, or you and your descendants will be cursed forever."

"I swear." Again, he was chafing at the bit to get started.

"You must speak the words, Mr. Darcy. Three times. They

have binding magic. They will give you access to a wealth of knowledge and information, if you know how to find it."

She waved her hand, and words appeared in the air, the letters glowing brightly.

He read them out. "I promise that I will do no harm to the Library or to the Librarian. If I do, my descendants and I will be cursed forever." He intoned the words solemnly, in the manner of someone who knew words had the power to build and destroy.

She listened as he repeated the oath two more times. For better or for worse, she was bound to help him now, whatever his request.

As the Library accepted his oath, the sensation of fae magic prickled on her skin. She took a deep breath while the words of the oath swirled around her, faster and faster, creating a whirlwind. The air began to glow and expand. The bookcases moved backward, and the illusion of the neatly arranged shelves disappeared.

Elizabeth opened herself up to the ancient wisdom of the library and to all the knowledge passed down through the generations.

"Tell me what you wish to know, Mr. Darcy, and I will do what I can to fulfill it. How may I help you?" She spoke the ritual words in the Librarian's voice. It was her own voice, joined with the voices of many others, whispers of the past and the present, of everyone that had come before her.

Mr. Darcy was looking as if he had seen a ghost. In a way, that was who the Librarian was: voices from the past. Elizabeth had stood where he was standing now, and she still remembered how it felt. The presence of the Librarian was overpowering. Everyone reacted strongly to this moment, and Mr. Darcy had even more reason to be shocked than most other people.

After a moment of stunned silence, he managed to rally his thoughts enough to bow to her. "Your Eminence."

Abraxas' voice whispered somewhere in the back of her mind, among the other voices. It sounded muffled and remote. *He has been coached well. He knows how to address you.*

Elizabeth smiled wryly. Of course. Mr. Darcy would never leave anything to chance.

"How may I help you?" she repeated, her voice echoing through the vast chamber. "Choose your request well. There is a limit of three requests for the lifetime of each person admitted to the Library. Please do not forfeit one of them by requesting something trivial."

"I can assure you I will not. I have come here, Your Eminence, to ask you to save my sister Georgiana's life. Without your help, I—" he stopped and swallowed, then forced himself to go on. "I believe she will die."

Librarians were supposed to show compassion, but they were not meant to feel anything towards the supplicants. Elizabeth had met Georgiana. She had once believed they would be sisters. Even at the young age of sixteen, Georgiana's magic had been strong. Elizabeth could only imagine how powerful she should be now, five years later. What could possibly have happened to that young lady to bring her close to death? Elizabeth was gripped by a strong sense of melancholy. She had never had the opportunity to grow closer to Georgiana.

In response, the voices around her swirled with agitation, and the light around her began to flicker. The air grew suddenly ice cold. Blinking, she looked around her in alarm. Everything around her was coated in frost, including Mr. Darcy.

He was on his knees, scrunched over, blowing on his hands, and trying to stay warm. He was shivering violently, his lips blue. He looked as if he was about to topple over.

"Your Eminence? Miss Bennet? What is happening? Have I said the wrong thing?"

She could barely see him through the snowflakes on her eyelashes. What had she done? Her emotions were always amplified when she was connected to the Library, but this was the first time she realized it could have material consequences. If she did not do something quickly, she could kill him.

She was appalled that she had let this happen. In response, the temperature dropped even further. The only way to control what was happening was to change the direction of her feelings. Blaming herself would only make matters worse.

She forced herself to think of happy things. Running up Oakham Mount with her sisters, their bonnets in their hands, feeling the wind against their faces. The ridiculous Mr. Collins and his studied compliments to the ladies. The first time Mr. Darcy had held her hand.

Slowly, the ice began to melt.

Mr. Darcy straightened up and came to his feet. His color started to return to normal.

"What happened?" His voice was hoarse, and he looked bewildered.

She had allowed her emotions to get the better of her, despite all her training. She was not supposed to be Elizabeth Bennet. As Librarian, she was expected to maintain complete control. Any thoughts, any personal feelings could seep into the magic surrounding her.

When Abraxas had taught her the importance of detachment, she had not understood the power of her thoughts. She could have killed Mr. Darcy.

How on earth was she going to work with him? She could only do it if she clamped down on her feelings so hard she would snuff them out.

He was still waiting for a response.

"There are some unexpected difficulties." Her voice rang out, her own, but not her own. The voices of the other Librarians were pressing in on her. "I am not sure I will be able to help you, Mr. Darcy."

He looked devastated, as if she had taken away all his hope. "But Georgiana—?"

She pushed down the impulse to feel guilty. It would only make matters worse.

"I am not saying I *will* not help you. Only that I do not know if I *can*."

Because, in order to help him, she would have to forget she had ever known him.

CHAPTER 3

*I*t was another caprice, another delay.

Miss Bennet had sent him away again. He was to return in the morning.

Darcy collapsed on a chair near the hearth and laced his fingers behind his neck. Good God, would Georgiana still be alive in the morning?

Never had he wanted something so fiercely and been forced to overcome so many obstacles, to exercise so much patience to achieve it.

He sat up and rubbed his hands together near the fire as he waited for the bath to be filled. Normally he would not put the innkeeper to this sort of trouble for what he had intended to be a one-night visit, but he was still nearly frozen through.

There was some difficulty with the Great Library, apparently, or perhaps even with the Librarian herself. Was it possible she had not been the Librarian long enough to anticipate its moods?

No, the process of approval for the Librarian was an arduous one. More likely it was her way of exacting a punishment from him for ending their engagement. He had once been in love with Elizabeth Bennet and was well aware of her excellent character, but among her many fine qualities was mixed a rather sharp temper.

The laugh was bitter on his tongue. Had *once* been in love? He was in love with her still. He had never stopped.

Darcy shut his eyes, recalling Elizabeth's question, nay, challenge. Had time treated her well?

Far better than it had treated him.

He had always been healthy, even vigorous, and there was yet strength in his limbs. But the countenance in his looking glass was worn further each day with the debts of sleepless nights and joyless living. He had thrown over his only chance at happiness to do his duty, and this was the result.

Darcy's spirits had never really recovered from his disappointment. He made a good enough show of it, he supposed. He had found that when he drowned himself in work, it was easier. Each morning he awoke before everyone else, and each night he slipped into bed only when exhaustion was already overtaking him. Only in that way could he avoid dreaming of a life from which he had walked away and avoid the certainty that if he had it to do over again he would make a different choice. He would defy the Patronesses, including his own aunt, if he could only have Elizabeth. Not even the prestigious position of Griffin Keeper, the only one in all of England other than the Librarian herself, was worth the cost he had paid.

He had faced a harsh truth today. The sacrifice he lived with, had lived with every minute for five long years, had been entirely for naught. The Patronesses had been wrong somehow. Elizabeth did have magic. Elizabeth was eminently worthy of marriage to Darcy.

Unfortunately, Darcy had proven, definitively, that he was not worthy of a marriage to her.

Miss Elizabeth Bennet was the Librarian now. She had no more use for him and every reason to distrust him. Had he been braver, had he been stronger, had he stood beside her – facing down the Patronesses and forcing them to accept his choice – he might have been spared the agonies he had suffered.

He might have spared them both.

What improbable series of events had resulted in Elizabeth becoming the Librarian? The Librarian required a magical bond with the Library griffin. How had she accomplished such a thing when she had failed at the much lesser test of bonding to a familiar? Not only failed, but done it in so spectacular a fashion?

He undressed, throwing his clothes at the bed with more violence than he ought and leaving them there to wrinkle. Bickerstaffe would be appalled.

Good.

Finally, he lowered himself into the bathtub, a rather luxurious one for an inn, though still too short for a man of his height. The hot water eased the tremors that still plagued him. What to do about the chill around his heart? That he could not say.

His soak was interrupted by Hespera's prim voice. *Mr. Bickerstaffe is inquiring whether you have had any success.*

Darcy grunted. *Some.*

This recalcitrance was received with a small huff and wheeze that signified a griffin's laughter. *He asks for more detail.*

Darcy sighed. His valet always wanted to know everything. He had been with the family a long time, and Darcy felt obligated to indulge some of his more harmless eccentricities.

There was a small boy named Martin among the tenant families at Pemberley who could speak to the griffin by way of his own familiar, a squirrel. It was a rather laborious system and prone to error in translation, but it was better than an express rider in situations such as these.

Darcy's response was terse. *I have passed the tests. I must return to the Great Library in the morning. How does Georgiana fare?*

There was the usual delay as he waited for the griffin to speak to the squirrel, the squirrel to Martin, and then Martin to Bickerstaffe.

She is no better but no worse.

Hespera inquired whether there was a message for Bickerstaffe, and Darcy said no. Truthfully, it was a relief to be beyond the man's reach, beyond his judgment and disapprobation.

Darcy closed his eyes and leaned his head back against the edge of the tub. He must think of his sister, not Bickerstaffe, and certainly not the very powerful, very comely Librarian. Yet she was all he could think about.

It was because his shock at seeing her had been so great, that was all. When in her presence, he had to shut down all his roiling emotions. He was not here for himself but for Georgiana.

How had Miss Elizabeth Bennet from Hertfordshire ever come to the attention of those who chose the Librarian? It made little sense.

Even five years ago, Elizabeth had always known the most intriguing things—the name of a flower he had never seen, the location of the Kee Monastery in India, the composition of the bricks used to build the Egyptian pyramids. Even which ancient crops had been favored by the Ñanchoc people in Peru. In that sense, her selection was not a surprise. But in other ways . . .

Miss Elizabeth had said she was not certain she could help him. She had the power of the Librarian, but given what had happened today, he wondered whether she could control it.

Was this why she kept delaying? Was she truly ready to be the Librarian? And what would happen to Georgiana if the answer was no?

He rose when the water cooled, wrapped a towel around his waist and took another to dry his hair. He reached for his wrinkled clothes.

Hespera, he said, almost desperately, *shall we fly?*

The griffin's golden tones rang in his head. *Of course.*

THE FOLLOWING MORNING, Darcy tended to his ablutions with care and arrived at the entrance to the Great Library promptly at nine. He was met by the fae clerk, whose name he could only recall began with a T, before being ushered past the desk and up the stairs.

Miss Elizabeth was there to meet him, in the same room where they had met before, though she was standing on the far side, near a window and not on the ladder. The clerk retreated at her nod and closed the door behind him.

Darcy stepped towards Elizabeth, but she held up a hand. "Please remain where you are, Mr. Darcy."

He halted. She lowered her hand.

"Let us begin," she said, speaking with the Librarian's voice. "Abraxas has explained the nature of Georgiana's illness. Thank you for sending that information so that I might begin to conduct my research. It is an ailment of the heart, I understand."

Darcy hesitated for a moment to quell the anger that rose into his throat. "Yes. I believe you recall Mr. Wickham."

A frosty mist filled the air and Darcy flinched. Was the

freezing cold about to descend again? In the next moment it disappeared.

"Yes," the Librarian intoned. "I remember."

"He wishes to take by force what he could not by consent. It was a love potion, polluted with more than one dark spell of coercion and seduction. He managed to slip it into Georgiana's food, and she strives to resist." Darcy's voice broke a little as he recalled her battle to retain control of her own heart. "The spell itself is not designed to kill but enslave. However, if she resists...."

The expression upon her countenance was hard, as though it had been sculpted in marble. "How do you know it was Mr. Wickham's spell? I presume he has left no signature upon it."

"Because not long after my sister took to her bed, he arrived on Pemberley's doorstep, humbly offering his services to break it."

"I presume that by "services," his intention is to bed her?" The room grew colder before it warmed again. She was striving to keep the power she wielded under control. It was something he understood well.

"Yes," he replied, biting back his fury. "Bed her and wed her, in that order. According to Wickham, it is the only way to break the curse. You can see why I require the Library's assistance."

Miss Elizabeth's eyes were dark and angry. "This is why love potions are forbidden," she said through gritted teeth. "They are too easily used to forward such schemes, with disastrous outcomes."

Darcy agreed. "I have collected additional evidence of Wickham's involvement, but the life of my sister must be my first duty."

"Yes," she said thoughtfully. "You have always been a man of *duty*." The emphasis on the final word was a cynical one, and it did not suit her.

His eyes sought hers out. "It does not follow that I take pleasure in it."

The admission only made her lips draw into a tight straight line, though the stoic mask upon her face did relax a bit. "When you say spells of coercion and seduction, do you know which ones, precisely?"

"No, though we believe he has used the Scottish Word."

She stared at him in disbelief. "Your sister is resisting the Scottish Word?"

He nodded once.

Again, her countenance did not alter. It was an odd thing to witness such stoicism in a woman who had once been so very expressive. "Your sister is a very strong woman."

"She is indeed," he agreed. "Georgiana did not know what Wickham was when she was fifteen, but now she would rather die than submit to him."

Elizabeth did not appear to be listening to him, and he was both affronted and unsurprised. He closed his eyes until a warm breeze ruffled his hair.

"What was that?" he asked in a whisper.

There was a large book in Miss Elizabeth's hands, or a magical representation of one. She set it upon a lectern that had suddenly appeared before her and opened it. After a moment, she turned the page, read, and then turned another.

And another.

And another.

The wait was excruciating. "Have you found anything?" he asked after she turned her fifth page.

"Patience, Mr. Darcy," she said. "Had I known we were confronting the Scottish Word I might have been better prepared."

"I am not certain . . ."

"Better to research as though we are. It is important that

we find the proper course of action. It would not do to waste time and one of your three requests on the wrong cure."

He was so tired. "Of course, Your Eminence."

"This is not the correct tome," she announced at last. With a sweep of one hand, it disappeared, and she had another book to place before her, this one even larger than the first.

Elizabeth leafed through at least twenty pages without another word, and each time it was as though a dagger was being plunged into his chest.

He detested waiting. Unfortunately, that was all he could do. He had no power at all in this situation, with Georgiana's life in the balance. And he hated that most of all.

"Hmm. Newt and toads, hummingbird feathers, no, no. White moss, sumac leaf, red seaweed . . . no."

She was reading to herself. This at least, had not changed. He had almost forgotten how fond of it he had been. Darcy focused on the sound of her reading instead of his wait, and the tightness in his chest eased. They would find a way to defeat Wickham's spell and then they would find a way to deal with him. Preferably one that would not put Darcy himself in irons.

"Oh dear," Miss Elizabeth said, breaking into his thoughts.

"What?" He knew his question sounded more like a demand, but he could not help it.

"Breaking the hold of the spell will require a journey." She shut the book, and it vanished in a small burst of light. "In order to affect the Scottish Word, Mr. Wickham must have traveled to a specific site north of here. To undo it, you must be there."

His heart sank. "How far away?"

"Rather far, I am afraid, and your griffin cannot take you there. Listen." She tossed her hands out wide and a mysterious voice intoned.

. . .

At the mouth of the faerie kingdom,
Where the lily lovell grow
In the shadow of the grotto,
Those who seek must enter slow.
Never bring what is familiar
Lest the magic be brought low.
Deep into the darkness burrow,
Two speak the word the fae do know,
When spoken true, both pain and sorrow
From the heart away will go.

"I MUST TRAVEL TO FAERIE?" he asked. Without Hespera's assistance it would take days! He could trust Hespera to keep Wickham away from Georgiana as long as she did not weaken and call out for the blackguard. If she capitulated, there would be no saving her.

Elizabeth appeared to be listening to something he could not hear. Eventually, she nodded solemnly, her complexion whitening to an almost ghostly hue.

"Are you well?" he inquired. It seemed a foolish question, for what would he do were she ill? It was not as though she would allow him to aid her in any way. He was answered with one more somber, solitary nod.

"Your Eminence, I thank you. May I write down the instructions?" He recalled them perfectly, but this was too important a quest to leave to chance.

She offered him a sickly smile. "You may."

They waited a moment in silence before the fae clerk arrived bearing paper, ink, and a quill.

"Thank you, Travinius," Elizabeth said calmly.

Travinius! He knew it had started with a T. He glanced around. "May I use your lectern?"

She crooked one finger. The quill dipped itself in the ink and wrote out the words she had spoken.

"Thank you," he said when the ink had dried, and he held the document in his hands. He read the words over.

"This must be a mistake," he said, glancing up at the woman for whom his heart yearned. She arched a single eyebrow in the way that always made him want to kiss her.

"Perhaps you ought to have said as much five years ago, Mr. Darcy, but I am pleased that you have at last learnt how."

He ignored the sudden sharp pain in his heart and the insult that was its cause. Given current circumstances she was, after all, correct. "But this says, 'two speak.' Two, as in the number. Ought it not be 'to speak'?"

Elizabeth laughed at him. "Very good, Mr. Darcy," she said. "The spell requires two to trigger the counter spell. Therefore, as much as you disdain me, you have no choice."

Hope and terror flamed to life in equal measure. "What do you mean?

"I mean, Mr. Darcy, that you will not travel alone." She brushed her hands against her skirt and straightened her back, casting a defiant glare directly at him. "I am coming with you."

CHAPTER 4

*M*r. Darcy was staring at her, mouth agape. It was a diverting expression on such a solemn, serious man. "Why?" he asked at last, his brow furrowed.

"My reasons are my own," she said simply.

If only they were.

The moment she had read those fateful words, "Two speak the words the fae do know," she had felt the Library nudge at her. She had finished the poem before questioning it. In response, the Library had reminded her of the *Mabinogion*, specifically the tale Culhwch and Olwen. She closed her eyes, allowing the memories of other Librarians to fill her with knowledge. Yes, she knew the story now.

Elizabeth opened her eyes, bemused. She was accustomed to deciphering the Library's thoughts by the books it suggested, but this one still stumped her. Was it implying that Mr. Darcy would have to complete a number of apparently impossible tasks as Culhwch had had to? Lost in contemplation, she had barely heard Mr. Darcy's inquiry as she questioned the Library herself.

This time it answered with exasperation and another

Arthurian story, Yvain, the Knight of the Lion. And it prodded her into remembering the handmaiden, Lunete, who helped him with his task. This time, she understood. And she wished she did not.

The Library meant for her to go on the quest with Mr. Darcy. No. No, that was a horrid idea. She could not travel for days alone with Mr. Darcy. She could not!

But I am needed here, she had reminded it silently. She had only just completed her training, and the Library had not been open for long at all. There might be many people who wished to seek its aid.

And even more importantly, there was her work sustaining the Faerie wall. Despite her and Abraxas's efforts, it seemed to be growing worse, and her reinforcement was nothing more than patching holes. Yet she could not give up. If the wall were to falter entirely . . . the very idea made her shudder.

To her surprise, she had felt the Library's deep rumbling laughter. The Library then reminded her of its oldest book, the *St Cuthbert Gospel*, immediately followed by *On the History of the Great Library*. Its message was clear. The Library had survived long before her and would survive long after her. And for some reason, it wanted her to make this journey.

Wait. The quest would require them to travel to the Faerie Realm, where the wall would be the easiest to see – from both sides – if she traveled into the fae lands. Perhaps the Library had a quest of its own. She would go, then, and do what she could. Maybe there were answers to her struggles with the wall that could only be found where the bounds of the Faerie Realm were the closest.

"Are you well?" Mr. Darcy had asked at last, and she had managed a shaky nod before continuing their conversation. She could not resist holding back the information that she was coming until the very last moment. She might have told herself it was to irritate Mr. Darcy, but really, she could not help hoping the Library would change its mind.

It had not, and now she was walking with Mr. Darcy towards the front door.

"A moment, please," she said, leaving him there while she returned into the depths of the Library. She would have to prepare for a journey.

Despite all of her travels with the Library to lands near and far, she had always been in its care. But now she would be leaving it behind to go on a quest with the one man she both longed and feared to be alone with.

Her time in the Library had been good for her. She had learned so much. And the Library itself had become like a friend, almost a familiar.

Abraxas. Was he coming with her?

But no, of course not. The poem had been very clear that familiars could not travel to seek the cure.

Besides, Abraxas said with a smirk she could almost hear, *I am needed here to protect the Great Library in your absence.*

Elizabeth raised an eyebrow. She had not realized that he would stay in the Library itself. *You will guard it?* she asked.

Somebody must.

"I must not take long in packing," Elizabeth said aloud, thinking wildly. She would need clothes at the very least. Perhaps Mr. Darcy's people could supply the food and other things they would need.

She called several of the assistants to her and set them to work. She had a great deal to arrange and would have to do it quickly. A message was sent to her ladies' maid, Price, to have her things packed and brought to the Library's entrance.

Abraxas would guard the Library in her absence and could call her if there were any urgent requests. Most requests could wait until her return, but she spoke to the clerks about what information to procure from any applicants. Lord Elkins could wait to speak with her about his research until her return, but she would have several of her people collecting information for him while she was gone.

Finally, Price appeared with a large satchel. Elizabeth would not let her discomfort about leaving the Library delay them from their departure.

She found Mr. Darcy still waiting by the door, poorly hiding his impatience. She nodded to him. It was time.

"Miss Bennet," Mr. Darcy said as they reached the doorway. He was holding out his arm, and for a moment, she stared at it in confusion. Of course. He meant to offer her his arm. She had been here for so long that she had almost forgotten that nicety.

Before she could take it, she felt the Library nudge at her. "A moment, please," she said.

The Library reminded her of yet another book, *A Magical Reference Manual*. She frowned, not comprehending. She called forth the memories of former Librarians again, and her mind was filled with the details of the book. Yet she still did not understand what the Library wished to tell her.

Impatiently, the Library pushed the book to her, and a magical representation appeared before her. But before she could open it, the ghostly book closed itself and pressed itself up against her chest.

Elizabeth smiled. It wanted her to take the book with her. Very well.

"Travinius," she called. The fae hurried up to her, and she directed him to fetch the book.

"It seems that we will be bringing at least one book along on our journey," she said to Mr. Darcy.

The book was soon in hand and then in her satchel, and Elizabeth could no longer put off the moment. She was on Mr. Darcy's arm.Tthe door opened, and she was outdoors.

Elizabeth squinted in the sun and marveled at the sights and sounds of the busy street, wrinkling her nose at the smell.

When she had been chosen as the Librarian years ago, the Library had insisted upon taking her on a tour of the world – especially its books. Every morning, one of the Library's many doors had opened into a new land. This door led to Rome, that door led to Constantinople, but tomorrow this one might lead to Tenochtitlan and that one to Cuzco. Some of the places it opened were not in the ordinary world, but places where only those like the fae, pegasi, and dragons roamed. She had been to Faerie a number of times. Each time felt like the first thanks to the fae glamors that tricked and teased the eye and mind.

Thankfully, the Library had also understood her need for quiet and to take long walks. There was one door that always led to some gentle path between a meadow and a wood, and she was free to slip outside that door whenever she needed to feel the sun on her face and the fresh air. Of course, sometimes the path was in Scotland, sometimes China, and occasionally Upper Canada, but it was always a safe, peaceful place to ramble.

There was only one place the doors never led – to England. Not until the Library had deemed her training complete and allowed her to declare the Great Library open.

A touch on her arm startled Elizabeth out of her thoughts. Mr. Darcy placed her arm on his. She inhaled a deep breath and allowed Mr. Darcy to lead her forward onto the pavement. She had been so lost after he left her. Well, she had been lost at first. Then, she had been furious.

She had known, absolutely known, that she had magic powerful enough to bond with a familiar, powerful enough to be Mr. Darcy's wife. She could not explain just how she had known it, but she could feel the deep well of magic within herself and knew it as a certainty. There had to be an explanation.

She had never found the explanation, exactly, but she had proved them all wrong. The Library had chosen her. She had bonded with Abraxas, and she had found a new purpose in life after her first dreams had been torn away.

As the Librarian, she had been consumed with excitement over her wonderful connection to Abraxas, the Great Library itself, the books it was constantly thrusting at her, and the world it had opened at her feet. It had not entirely kept her from the misery that wet her pillow at night, but she had allowed herself to find joy again.

There was a great pounding of wings as Mr. Darcy's griffin familiar dropped to the ground in front of them. Hespera was still as beautiful as she had ever been. Elizabeth remembered Abraxas's opinion of her with amusement and wondered, fleetingly, if he had ever seen her fly. Her landing was a thing of beauty.

Matchmaking? Abraxas asked, amusement in his mental voice.

It was an idle thought, Elizabeth sent back.

Abraxas's deep laugh reverberated along their familiar connection. *Is that not a human saying? Idle hands are the devil's workshop? Perhaps it applies to thoughts as well?*

Elizabeth's grin faded when Mr. Darcy gestured for her to climb on.

"We cannot," she said, surprised that Mr. Darcy had forgotten so soon. "We must not take our familiars on the quest. Do you not remember?"

"I had thought . . . that is, I hoped we might ride to Pemberley first. It is mostly on our way, and I . . . I would like to see my sister before we continue." His words were stumbling. It was strange to hear him struggling to defer to her as the Librarian. There were so few whom he had to defer to, with his position as master of Pemberley.

Elizabeth considered. "Very well. And I do believe my reading served a further purpose. I can make something that will help Georgiana's health hold a little longer. Or, rather, you will make it."

"I?"

"Yes. Because you love your sister. The best counters to love potions gone awry must be created in love."

She curtsied to the griffin. *Do you remember me?* she asked. *I am Miss Elizabeth Bennet, the Librarian.*

Of course I remember you, although you were not the Librarian then. Hespera cocked her head, looking disconcertingly chicken-like for a moment. *You are welcome to ride with us, Your Eminence.*

Mr. Darcy held out his hand to Elizabeth, and she allowed him to boost her onto the griffin's back. Elizabeth had become accustomed to the feel of Abraxas, but Hespera was unfamiliar, and the disconcerting feeling reminded Elizabeth of her first, frightening ride on a griffin's back –when the Great Library had claimed her for its own and sent Abraxas to retrieve her. She took a deep breath to calm her racing heart.

Mr. Darcy climbed up behind her, and Hespera launched herself into the air.

Elizabeth clung to Hespera as the griffin soared upwards, gaining height quickly. Mr. Darcy was wrapped around her as he clutched the griffin, all propriety quite literally lost to the wind.

When Hespera eventually leveled out, Elizabeth was able to sit up a little and flex her stiff, sore fingers. It did not help. She could still feel Mr. Darcy pressed against her, his entire front against her back. He was warm, and she could feel the muscles under his shirt shift as he changed his hold on

Hespera. He had not changed so much, then, during the years they were apart. Had she?

Elizabeth tucked her head low against Hespera's feathers, as the sun still felt too bright.

Did he miss her, the Elizabeth Bennet he had once known? The girl who loved to walk miles every day? The one who teased him about his pride and arrogance?

She was no longer that Elizabeth Bennet. She had been ripped apart and made anew. That Elizabeth Bennet was gone.

Hespera's speed was extraordinary. Abraxas rarely had cause to carry her far, since the Library had doors to take Elizabeth anywhere she wanted to go. He had had little occasion to gain so much speed in flight. This was terrifying. The countryside, villages, towns, and even cities sped by at rates beyond her imagining, but all Elizabeth could do was to hold on.

It felt endless, but it could not have been more than an hour or so before Hespera began to drop. And there it was.

Pemberley.

She had never seen it, of course, but Mr. Darcy had described it so many times in those halcyon days of their courtship that she could recognize it easily.

The beautiful gray stone manor stood proud in the distance, just as she had always imagined. Elizabeth could already see the small pond in front of the house. Hespera swooped just above the trees before landing neatly on the circular drive before the main entrance.

Mr. Darcy dismounted first. He turned to offer a hand to Elizabeth. She swallowed and accepted it, just as she had done on their last day together. But there was Georgiana to think of now. She could not stay lost in her memories.

A woman came bustling out of Pemberley, practically wringing her hands when she saw Mr. Darcy. "Mrs.

Reynolds!" Mr. Darcy drew Elizabeth to his side. "Miss Bennet, this is Mrs. Reynolds, the housekeeper at Pemberley. Mrs. Reynolds, Miss Bennet is the Librarian of the Great Library."

"Your Eminence," Mrs. Reynolds said as she curtsied.

The older lady turned to her master. "We did not know when to expect your return. I was just seeing to Miss Georgiana."

"Of course. Thank you for taking care of my sister so diligently. How does she fare?"

Her face drooped. "Not well at all, sir. She sleeps most of the time, but she seems almost delirious in her rest."

Mr. Darcy bowed his head. "Miss Bennet has suggested a temporary remedy that might alleviate some of Georgiana's symptoms a little while we travel to find the cure."

"We will need stinging nettle leaves, red currants, and gooseberries," Elizabeth told Mrs. Reynolds. "Mr. Darcy will need to boil them into—"

"Mr. Darcy, make the tea! Oh, goodness, dear, I hope you do not think I am unwilling to see to a special tea for the young lady.

"I am afraid that will not do, although I thank you for your help." Elizabeth accepted Mr. Darcy's arm as they hurried into the hall, Mrs. Reynolds following them anxiously. "Mr. Darcy must prepare the draught himself. He will supply the most crucial ingredient."

The housekeeper looked puzzled but was clearly used to dealing with the eccentricities of magic.

As she led the way down to the kitchens, Mrs. Reynolds assured them that Georgiana was sleeping, so they opted to wait until the tea was ready before going to see her. They would need her to stay awake long enough to drink the tea.

The draught was surprisingly easy to make, even in Mr. Darcy's unskilled hands, which were probably further hampered by the women watching him work and offering instructions. Once it was ready, they visited Georgiana.

Her room was dark, the drapes pulled to keep as much daylight out as possible. The fire had been stoked to blazing, making the room overwarm. Movement from the corner revealed a seal, which perked up its head at their arrival and regarded them with serious eyes. Not just a seal, then, but Georgiana's familiar. He lowered his head but remained watchful as they approached.

Georgiana tossed and turned in her bed. But when Mr. Darcy pushed the draught into Elizabeth's hands and hurried to the sick girl's side, calling her name urgently, her eyes flew open.

"Fitz!" she cried. She struggled to sit up in the bed, and Elizabeth's heart hurt to see her so weak. Mr. Darcy had to arrange the pillow and prop her upright.

She was thin and pale, but she gave him a grateful look as she accepted the draught and drank it obediently. When she caught sight of Elizabeth, though, she blinked in surprise.

"Miss . . . Miss Elizabeth?" she rasped.

"She is the Librarian," Mr. Darcy said simply. "We are to travel together to get the cure for you."

It was a pleasure to see Mr. Darcy so gentle with his sister. He spoke to her softly, telling her about their quest to retrieve the cure and assuring her they would return quickly. Elizabeth listened with half an ear as she looked about the room, from the table of medicines and basins to the seal who still sat so still on his own chair. A tub of water in a corner puzzled Elizabeth for a moment – had they interrupted an intended bath for Georgiana? – when she realized that it must be for the familiar.

Georgiana turned bleary eyes on Elizabeth. "May I . . . May I speak with Miss Elizabeth, please, brother? Alone?"

Mr. Darcy stiffened. "Miss Elizabeth?"

Georgiana gave a slow nod.

He looked from Georgiana to Elizabeth, his face unreadable. Then he stood and walked out quickly.

Georgiana sighed. "I did not mean to hurt him," she said quietly. "It is just . . . there are some things you cannot say in front of your brother."

Elizabeth gingerly sat at a chair next to the bed.

"I was very angry at him, you know," Georgiana whispered. "When he ended things with you. I thought . . . I thought you were to be my sister."

"I did, too." Elizabeth took her hand.

Georgiana coughed. "I had best not waste my words. It is so hard to stay awake these days, but you must know I try. I try so desperately. My dreams . . ." She looked down at their entwined hands. "My dreams are so frightening."

Elizabeth nodded, although her heart ached for the younger woman. The dreams of the Scottish Word were notoriously terrifying.

"He comes to me in my dreams." Georgiana's words were barely audible. "Sometimes we are walking on the beach at Ramsgate. Sometimes we are shopping together or dancing. And always, always, I am falling for his charms. He says the sweetest and most romantic things, or sometimes . . ." Her voice faltered. "Sometimes sultry things, too, but I am always intrigued, eager for more."

The seal made an odd little grunting squeal and left its place by the fire to waddle towards them, thumping its head against Georgiana's hand. Did Georgiana receive the same comfort from her familiar that Elizabeth did from Abraxas? She hoped so.

Elizabeth squeezed the girl's pale hand.

"But then there is always something." Georgiana squeezed back, her slight smile giving Elizabeth hope. "I do not know how to describe it. But his tone will sound a little strange, as if he is reciting his words from rote or distracted or simply insincere. Or he touches his hair a certain way. And as soon as he does, I am reminded of the real Mr. Wickham and the kind of man he truly is."

The seal barked, and Georgiana reached out to stroke its silky head.

"That is the moment you fight loose from the spell," Elizabeth guessed.

Georgiana lifted one thin shoulder. "And then it becomes a nightmare. His face transforms into something that I cannot describe. And he grabs me, squeezes me." Keening, the seal leaned into Georgiana, who kept her eyes on her familiar as she continued. "Sometimes he kisses me. Still, it is not about love but power. It is terrifying. And that is when I wake up."

Elizabeth leaned over to embrace her, and Georgiana leaned into her. "I cannot tell my brother. He would never look at me the same way again. But what can I do? I cannot control my dreams!"

"They are not your dreams, not entirely. The Scottish Word influences your thoughts and memories to trick you into its false love. And I believe you are wrong about your brother. He loves you, and he knows about the mistake you made. But it was years ago when you were barely more than a child. It is not your fault that that potion attempts to exploit those feelings you briefly had for that fiend."

And if Georgiana succumbed to Wickham in her dreams, she would be a hair's breadth from falling into his grasp. But Georgiana was no child. She knew what she fought against.

Georgiana lowered her arms and leaned back against her pillow. Her breath was shallow. "I cannot stay awake much longer." Her voice cracked. "What can I do? I do not know how to be sure I will not give in! I cannot control my dreams!"

The seal nudged Georgiana's arm so that he could press against her, his whiskers brushing her face as he wriggled his way into her bed. She gave an audible sigh of relief and closed her eyes, resting her cheek against his head.

Elizabeth would not have cared to have a seal in her bed – the smell of fish was rather pungent – but she knew well the comfort a familiar could bring, so she said nothing. If the seal brought the poor girl some peace, then the maids would just have to deal with the odoriferous sheets.

The Library nudged at Elizabeth, bringing to mind a book she had once read about how to control one's thoughts when they strayed improperly. At the time, she had relegated the book as being as dull as Fordyce's sermons, but perhaps there was something of use there.

"You may not be able to control the dreams well," she said slowly, "but during your waking hours, perhaps you might think over the things Mr. Wickham has done to show you his true colors. Remember his lies being exposed, the revelation of his vicious propensities, the cruelty he showed Mr. Darcy. Anything you can think of. Mrs. Reynolds may have stories to tell."

The girl nodded, her eyes narrowing. "You think that will make such things come more easily to mind when I am on the verge of succumbing?"

Elizabeth shrugged. "The Library thinks it might help. And, I hope, so will the draught your brother made you."

It occurred to her suddenly that the Library had communicated with her despite the miles between them. Was it always able to do such things?

Her satchel felt suddenly warm at her side. The book, then. Perhaps it, as the Library's history, was somehow connected to the Library? It would be a comfort if she could bring the Library's reassurance and expertise along with her.

And me, another voice broke in.

Abraxas! she called out to him in relief. *I did not know you could speak at such distance.*

I will guard the Library, and the Library will assist you, he sent firmly.

"There was one time when I watched Mr. Wickham sharpen his knife on his favorite whetstone," Georgiana said softly, her eyes drifting shut. "It seemed fascinating and beautiful at the time —when I thought I was in love. But now when I close my eyes, I see him like that, only it all feels different. Mr. Wickham did always keep his knife sharp and ready." She shuddered without opening her eyes.

Elizabeth squeezed Georgiana's hand. "We will protect you. You need not fear him." She hesitated. "But in your dreams . . ."

"I will stay strong," Georgiana whispered, her words barely audible. She sighed, her eyes drifting shut and her arms going still around her seal familiar.

So little time. Georgiana had so little time to be awake between dreams that turned into nightmares and trapped her in a never-ending game of avoiding seduction. Elizabeth and Mr. Darcy had so little time to return with the cure before Georgiana finally lost her battle with Mr. Wickham.

She could only pray the draught would help. According to the book she had found, it kept the victim from falling as deeply into their dreams. That should help Georgiana to remember who Mr. Wickham was . . . she hoped.

Elizabeth opened the door and almost stepped right into Mr. Darcy.

"My apologies, Miss Bennet." He bowed. "I was returning to inform you that my stable master will have the horses prepared for us tomorrow morning."

Elizabeth bit her lip. "I do not usually consider myself a horsewoman." What little experience she had was from over four years ago.

He gave her a look of sympathy. "I am afraid I see no other option. You know we cannot take Hespera, as the poem itself forbade familiars. A carriage will take far longer, and it will not be able to travel the most direct route, nor the final portion at all."

Elizabeth nodded reluctantly.

Dinner that evening was quiet. Georgiana was still sleeping, although Mrs. Reynolds promised to look in on her. Colonel Fitzwilliam – no, General Fitzwilliam now – Georgiana's other guardian, was expected to arrive any day to watch over her. But Mrs. Reynolds had a rotating shift of maids to make sure someone was with the woman at all times.

They woke early so they could be on their way just after sunrise. Elizabeth let out a startled squeak when Mr. Darcy unexpectedly lifted her into her side-saddle, but thankfully he did not comment as he mounted his own horse.

She checked to be sure that her own saddlebag contained the Library's book. If the Library was offering aid along their way, it would be foolish not to accept it.

As they rode through the gates of Pemberley and turned north, Elizabeth shivered. The quest suddenly felt more real – and more dangerous – than it had in the Library or even at Pemberley.

Where was Mr. Wickham? Did he know that Mr. Darcy had gone to the Library? Was he in a position to watch them depart on their quest?

He must have traveled to Faerie to obtain the Scottish Word. Did he know that they would have to do the same in order to get the cure? And if so . . . how far might he go to prevent it?

CHAPTER 5

They had only been riding a few yards when Darcy heard the sound of hooves behind them. He signaled Elizabeth to rein in her horse and turned around to learn who was following them. It was Bickerstaffe, mounted on one of Pemberley's more placid mares.

Darcy scowled at the man. "What are you about?"

Bickerstaffe made a show of being affronted. "I will accompany you, of course. You cannot travel without the assistance of your valet."

Darcy ground his teeth. There was no chance that Bickerstaffe's presence would make the journey more pleasant. "We are not taking a trip into town or sea bathing at Brighton," he told the man. "This is a quest which is likely to be arduous and dangerous."

Bickerstaffe squared his shoulders. "You should not be required to face such dangers without a freshly laundered cravat."

Elizabeth rolled her eyes.

"But your gout?" Darcy asked.

"It has hardly been bothering me these past days, Mr. Darcy," Bickerstaffe responded.

Darcy sighed. It was difficult to say no to the man who had served his father so faithfully before Darcy himself.

Elizabeth regarded the valet skeptically. "What value will you bring to our endeavor?" Do you provide particular magical skills?"

Oh no. Darcy covered his mouth to conceal a smile. He knew what was coming.

"I am particularly talented at locating water," Bickerstaffe said finally. "On a long journey it is always important to find sources of water." Noting Elizabeth's skeptical expression, he closed his eyes as if in concentration and then opened them, pointing triumphantly to his right. "We can find water right there!"

Elizabeth and Darcy both turned their heads. As Darcy had expected, there was indeed a small muddy puddle at the edge of the road. He choked back a laugh and a corner of Elizabeth's mouth quirked upward. "Truly we would be lost without you," she said. "Do you possess any other talents?"

"I believe that is sufficient." He stuck his chin in the air. "Besides, you and Mr. Darcy cannot travel together alone without doing irreparable harm to your reputation."

Damnation! Bickerstaffe was actually right about something. In the throes of his concern for Georgiana and the relief of finally having some hope for finding a cure, Darcy had completely lost sight of the impropriety of traveling with an unmarried single woman.

"I am the Librarian, sir," Elizabeth said sharply. "Our reputation is always above reproach, and we never marry."

It was like a punch to the stomach. The Librarians never married? Darcy had not known that. Of course, it did not matter; she would never agree to wed him. But he was disturbed by how distressing he found the thought of Elizabeth living the rest of her life alone.

"But any scandal that attaches to your name would fall upon your family," Bickerstaffe retorted in a sly, insinuating voice.

Elizabeth frowned.

"Bickerstaffe is right," Darcy conceded with a sigh. "Having a servant on the trip will help avoid any hint of impropriety and will lend the journey greater legitimacy."

"By that token we should have a female servant as well – if my 'reputation' is to be protected," Elizabeth said with some asperity.

"Excellent idea!" Bickerstaffe said. Before they could stop him, he had turned his mare and was trotting back to Pemberley.

Elizabeth rolled her eyes at Darcy. He could only shrug. Fifteen minutes later, Bickerstaffe returned with a donkey in tow. Perched on top of the donkey was Polly, one of Pemberley's scullery maids. She looked uncertain about the entire endeavor.

"Polly," Darcy said. "Did Mr. Bickerstaffe explain why we wanted you to accompany us?"

"He said it would be a privilege to go with you on an adventure to protect the lady's reputation," she said with a pronounced north country accent.

Darcy sighed. "I suppose." He had no desire to further delay their departure to find a more suitable lady's companion. "I assure you that you will be well compensated for the journey."

She stared at him with a blank expression.

"You will be paid extra."

"Oh." She almost smiled. "Well, that's all right then."

With these auspicious words ringing in his ears, Darcy

turned his horse and led the way to the road, hoping everyone would follow.

∼

THEY RODE in silence for nearly an hour. Elizabeth's muscles were already protesting the unaccustomed activity, but she refused to acknowledge her discomfort to Mr. Darcy or his servants. Eventually, he brought his horse closer to Elizabeth's. "I must confess that I am very curious to know how you became the Librarian – if you are free to share the tale."

"Librarians do not usually provide such information to outsiders," she said.

He flinched at the coldness of her words, but then spoke again. "If the Library allowed you to accompany me, then surely it follows that this quest relates to that institution."

Elizabeth stared at the road before them. His words made sense, but that logic warred with her desire not to give him any satisfaction. Still, she needed to maintain civility during the journey.

She stole a glance behind them at Bickerstaffe, who was following them too closely. He was watching with avid curiosity, not even pretending not to eavesdrop.

Elizabeth raised her hand to sketch magical words in the air. They glowed an eerie blue for a few seconds before breaking apart like small pieces of confetti, carried by the wind to flutter around Bickerstaffe and Polly.

As Elizabeth watched, Bickerstaffe's horse and Polly's donkey immediately slowed and they soon fell several yards behind.

When Elizabeth faced forward again, Mr. Darcy asked, "What did you do?"

"I encouraged their beasts to slow down so they cannot

overhear our conversation." Indeed, she could hear the valet alternately muttering to himself and shouting at his horse to go faster. Apparently Polly did not care about the pace of her beast.

"Does that mean you intend to answer my question?"

"Yes. However, I must warn you that what I tell you is not common knowledge and would endanger the Library if it is widely known. As such, the information is bound by the oath you swore."

Mr. Darcy nodded. "I understand. Proceed, Your Eminence."

Elizabeth sighed. The first time he had addressed her by that title, it had been thrilling. But now it seemed faintly ridiculous. "I do not insist that my friends use the honorific."

He raised an eyebrow and smiled. "Are we friends, Miss Bennet?"

Was he flirting? Well, it hardly mattered. "I would hope that we can at least be amicable," she said in a quelling tone. "Since I intend to tell you some of the Library's secrets."

He gestured for her to proceed.

Because Mr. Darcy had played an inadvertent role in the story, Elizabeth had hoped she could avoid telling him. But he might have need of the information. "I...was shocked when I failed to summon a familiar during the patronesses' ritual."

"I remember your reaction," Mr. Darcy said. She was surprised to see sympathy rather than disdain in his eyes.

"There is strong magical lineage on both sides of my family. My father summoned a land eel familiar."

"Yes." The man managed not to grimace, but it was a near thing. Elizabeth could not blame him. Land eels were one of the less...appealing varieties of familiars.

"I showed early magical aptitude, and my family had always assumed I would summon a familiar if I made the attempt. I still do not understand why the ritual failed." She was pleased her voice did not wobble. Even now, when her magical ability had been definitively proven, the memory still had the power to hurt her. In a single day she had lost both the man she planned to marry and the magical future she had envisioned for herself.

For weeks, even simple things like rising from her bed in the morning had seemed pointless. Food lost all flavor, and she could barely bring herself to speak with her family. At night she had sobbed herself to sleep. She refused to admit this to Mr. Darcy, but she could not forget.

"A few months after the ritual, I went in search of answers." Her family – her father and Jane in particular – had been quite concerned about her. Elizabeth now suspected they had simply hoped that travel would cure her melancholy. "My Aunt and Uncle Gardiner took me in their carriage to Land's End in Cornwall."

Mr. Darcy's eyes widened. "You met the fae oracle?"

"Yes. Of course, we did not know if she would grant me an audience, but my uncle had spoken with her before. We discovered she had been awaiting me, which surprised us at the time. But she *is* an oracle." Elizabeth gave him a wry smile. "She told me that I did indeed have magic, powerful magic. Although she could not tell me why the familiar ritual had failed, she said it was my destiny to be the Librarian. Fae from the Library were present to collect me."

"She gave you no choice?" Mr. Darcy's expression was horrified.

"I did not mean to suggest such a thing," Elizabeth said hastily. "I was given a day to decide if I would choose the Library or return to Longbourn and live as I had."

Mr. Darcy regarded her intently. "Did you consider refusing?"

Did he have any inkling how his rejection had influenced her decision? "Of course," she responded. "I knew that the training would require long years away from my family, and I love them very dearly." She pushed away an accustomed sense of melancholy. "But, I could not possibly turn down such an opportunity for learning. You know how I much love books. The idea of caring for a whole building full of books was quite appealing."

"Do you know what criteria the fae used in selecting you for this honor?" Mr. Darcy asked.

"They sought a Librarian of great integrity. The Librarian who preceded me had betrayed the Library – although I do not know the particulars. This is one of the reasons it was closed for so long."

"Were there other criteria?"

"I know that the position requires a human who is capable of bonding with Abraxas. Few mages can summon griffin familiars."

"Then why could you not call a familiar during the ritual?" The words exploded from him almost angrily.

"I do not know, Mr. Darcy," she responded rather coldly. "I can assure you that I tried my hardest."

"Of course," he said hastily. "I did not mean to imply otherwise."

Elizabeth was not sure she believed his denial. Certainly he had seemed to blame her in the immediate aftermath of the ritual's failure.

They rode in a tense silence for a few minutes. Then he asked, "What occurred after you accepted the position of Librarian?"

"Abraxas flew me to the Library, where my training commenced." Her first griffin flight had been quite overwhelming – as she had worried constantly whether she had made the right decision.

"That is fascinating." Mr. Darcy's face was lit with wonder. "What did the training consist of?"

"Ah, that I cannot reveal."

"I must say that I consider that most unfair. Now that you have aroused my curiosity, you should satisfy it." The shadow of a smile played about his lips. Was he teasing her? She nearly smiled back before recalling that this was the man who had broken her heart.

"Have I answered your question to your satisfaction?" She kept her tone cool.

The smooth mask settled over his features once again. "Yes. I thank you."

Elizabeth gave him a curt nod and encouraged her horse into a trot quick enough that she soon left him behind.

PEMBERLEY'S COOK had packed a small luncheon, which they ate under the shade of a tree by the side of the road. Polly huddled miserably near her donkey and said nothing. Elizabeth spoke with distant cordiality about the weather and the state of the roads to Darcy and Bickerstaffe. However, the amiability Darcy had momentarily glimpsed as Elizabeth told her story did not return. Darcy could not help mourning its loss.

He knew it was impossible for them to rekindle their romance, but he hoped at least to be her friend. On the other hand, he was unsure if he was worthy of her friendship. Perhaps it would be best to deal with her in a distant and disinterested manner.

In the afternoon, his thoughts turned to where they would spend the night. He recalled a suitable inn along the route, but it was small. If it accommodated many travelers, they might only have two rooms available. Elizabeth would share with Polly and Darcy would be forced to share a room with Bickerstaffe. Perhaps Darcy could send him to sleep in the stable and ignore the complaints about his gout.

His thoughts had just turned to Georgiana's illness when he felt a ripple of magic on the road ahead of them. Elizabeth reined in her horse as abruptly as he did. "Did you sense something?" he asked her.

She nodded gravely. "Someone used magic very near to where we stand."

"I did not sense anything," Bickerstaffe said rather belligerently.

"It was rather subtle," Darcy said, peering ahead anxiously. They could see only a few yards ahead before a bend in the road obscured the view.

He heard a muffled thud coming from around the bend. And then another. Something rather large was walking in their direction. Darcy looked around wildly, but potato fields lined both sides of the road – offering no concealment.

Thud. Thud. Thud. The pace of the footsteps was increasing. Darcy swore he could feel vibrations in the ground. "Wh-What is happening?" Bickerstaffe's voice quavered.

"It must be some variety of magical creature," Elizabeth said. "I believe that was a surge of portal magic – a gate opened and brought something to our vicinity."

"That should not be possible," Darcy said.

"Agreed. The holes in the Faerie border must be growing quite large."

"Wh-What kind of a cr-creature could it be?" Bickerstaffe asked.

"What if it's the kind that e-eats people?" Polly asked.

"A b-brownie perhaps?" Bickerstaffe suggested. "Or a gnome?"

Thud. Thud. Trees vibrated with the force of the approaching footsteps.

Darcy gave Bickerstaffe a sidelong glance. "That does not sound like a gnome."

"Something big might really eat people!" Polly cried.

Darcy kept his eyes fixed on the road. "I would imagine the creature only hunts me and Miss Bennet since this is our quest."

"Good point." Bickerstaffe said. Without any warning, he wheeled his mount around and galloped back along the route they had come.

"Some servant," Darcy muttered.

Elizabeth muffled a giggle. *We might be about to die*, Darcy thought. *But at least we agree on something.*

"Fighting is not good for his gout," Elizabeth murmured.

"You may leave as well," Darcy said to Polly.

"Will I still get extra pay?" she asked.

Darcy managed not to roll his eyes. "Yes."

"Even if you are eaten?"

"Yes!"

Polly wasted no time turning her donkey around and hurrying away.

The thudding footsteps had become more like crashes. Whatever approached was massive. It would be visible in a few seconds. Darcy positioned his horse across the road – in front of Elizabeth.

She sighed in exasperation. "I am not defenseless!"

"I have been trained in combat magic. I doubt it was part of your training – unless you plan to hit the creature with a book."

Before Elizabeth could reply, a large tree was uprooted from the side of the road and flung into the nearby potato field. Only then did Darcy glimpse the creature they faced.

A troll.

ELIZABETH STEELED herself as the troll strode into view. It was at least eight feet tall and very broad. Shaggy black hair hung over a sloping forehead. It wore nothing but an animal skin around its waist and Elizabeth had to stifle the missish impulse to avert her eyes at its immodesty.

Mr. Darcy moved first, drawing arcane symbols in the air. They instantly ignited into blue flames and floated toward the creature, forming a circle of fire around it.

"That was well done," Elizabeth said, genuinely impressed.

In the next moment, the troll strolled through the ring of fire like it was circle of daisies.

"Damnation!" Mr. Darcy cursed. "That was a powerful spell. Elizabeth, you must flee!" he shouted without taking his eyes from the creature.

"Nonsense. I can help!"

"Fae magic will be of no use here!"

Elizabeth gritted her teeth against a tart rejoinder. What did he know of fae magic?

As the troll stomped toward them, she considered what kinds of spells might be effective. Fae magic was not designed for combat, but undoubtedly some spells could be adapted. Perhaps air magic; librarians received extensive training in air spells.

Drawing power from the surrounding environment, Elizabeth gathered a gale force wind, blasting the troll with the force of a hurricane. The gust flung the creature onto the road several yards away.

Mr. Darcy gasped. "Was that air magic? I have never seen the like!"

Elizabeth did not respond, but inwardly she preened.

The troll roared as it struggled upright, and it soon clomped toward them again. Elizabeth sent another gust of wind toward it, but this time the creature's progress barely slowed. She allowed the wind to die down and considered which spell to attempt next.

The horses rolled their eyes in fear as the troll drew closer. Elizabeth fought to keep her mount from bolting.

"You must retreat! Air magic is not sufficient!" Mr. Darcy shouted.

Elizabeth declined to point out that their spells had been equally ineffective. "I will not leave you alone," she said through gritted teeth.

She could sense Mr. Darcy gathering magic for another attack. He hurled his next spell not at the troll, but at the dirt at its feet. That patch of road immediately turned into quicksand, sucking the creature's enormous feet into holes that had not existed moments before. This arrested the troll's forward momentum as it bellowed its frustration. Elizabeth breathed a sigh of relief. Hopefully, the dirt would hold the creature long enough to allow an escape.

Before she could suggest such a thing, the troll gave a loud cry, more deafening than a hundred church bells and pulled first one and then the other foot from the confining dirt, leaving behind immense craters in the road. It lunged forward with unexpected speed and grabbed Mr. Darcy by the neck, pulling him off his horse.

The troll effortlessly held up him with one arm, exerting pressure on his neck while Mr. Darcy gurgled horribly, twisting his body and grabbing futilely at the creature's enormous hand. Elizabeth's stomach lurched sickeningly. She might be angry at Mr. Darcy, but she had no desire for his death. How long could he survive when he was deprived of breath?

Her mind froze, choking on the enormity of the situation. What spells would possibly be effective against such an adversary? If only she could summon help! Then she recalled that she had been able to communicate with her familiar even at Pemberley.

Abraxas! she screamed.

Elizabeth? Anxiety tinged his mental voice, no doubt a reflection of her panic. *How can I help?*

Rather than waste time on a long explanation, she sent a mental image of the troll holding Mr. Darcy aloft. *What spells work against trolls?* she asked.

Abraxas paused for a second, which felt like an eternity to Elizabeth. *They are impervious to most spells*, he said finally. *But you can try air shaping or air hardening. Those are sometimes effective.*

Elizabeth did not like the sound of "sometimes," but she had no other options. She sketched symbols for a quick air shaping spell and hurled it at the troll, blasting it with the force of a sledgehammer. It fell backward onto the dirt of the road, releasing its hold on Mr. Darcy who fell like a rag doll, hitting his head against a stone with a loud crack.

Before the creature could regain its feet, Elizabeth ordered the air to harden around it, creating a box which was extremely strong despite being invisible. The troll roared in frustration and pounded its fists against the top of its transparent cage but was unable to even rise to a sitting position.

That worked! She told Abraxas.

Elizabeth wanted to collapse in exhaustion, but Mr. Darcy needed her help. She raced to his side, relieved to see his chest rising and falling with shallow breaths. Purple bruises were forming on his neck. Kneeling in the dirt of the road, she leaned over him. She lifted his head and felt a lump forming on the back of his skull. Her fingers came away with blood on them.

"Mr. Darcy? Are you well? Can you hear me?" When she received no response, she brushed the hair from his forehead. "Please speak to me! William?" Fear held her heart in an iron grip. He could not die on this deserted country road!

If only she knew healing magic! Tears sprang to her eyes. She did not want to watch him die.

Just as she was about to call on Abraxas again, Mr. Darcy's eyelids fluttered open, and his eyes focused on her. She had forgotten their rich cobalt color, a shade unlike any she had ever seen.

"Elizabeth..." he murmured as his hand reached out and brushed his fingertips along her cheek. Her breath caught in her throat. "Elizabeth, you saved me."

His eyes were fixed on her lips. Was he about to kiss her?

CHAPTER 6

*I*nstead, Mr. Darcy's eyes closed, and Elizabeth felt strangely disappointed. The disappointment quickly passed, replaced with worry about the man's health.

Elizabeth heard a squeal and turned around to see Mr. Bickerstaffe staring at the sight of his master collapsed in an inelegant heap. Of course he would only choose to return the moment the danger had passed!

"What have you done to him?" Mr. Bickerstaffe cried as he practically fell from his mare in his attempt to make it to Mr. Darcy's side. The valet glared daggers at her before checking his master's pulse.

Elizabeth felt prickles of heat at her fingertips. The man had no right to assume the worst of her. It was her magic that had saved Mr. Darcy from being crushed by the troll. "I saved your master while you were hiding like a coward. And Mr. Darcy does not seem to be the only one you abandoned. Where, pray tell, is Polly?"

Mr. Bickerstaffe glared at her. "On her way back to Pemberley, I expect. She said extra pay would do her no good if she did not survive the journey."

Elizabeth forced herself to take a few calming breaths. She could not allow her magic to spiral out of her control. Polly would be fine. It was Mr. Darcy who needed her assistance. "He will need a healer. But first we must figure out how to safely move him."

"It appears Her Eminence is not in possession of every answer," muttered Mr. Bickerstaffe.

Elizabeth suppressed the heat that was trying to pool in her fingertips. Setting Mr. Darcy's servant on fire would not help the situation. Mr. Bickerstaffe had offered no helpful solutions, despite his insistence on accompanying them on the journey for that very purpose.

Abraxas?

You sound troubled. How may I assist you?

Mr. Darcy was injured by the troll. He needs a healer, but I do not know the best way to move him safely.

There was a stretch of silence as Elizabeth waited for the griffin's reply. Mr. Bickerstaffe was doing nothing to disguise his contempt for her as he paced back and forth along the road.

Perhaps I can suspend him in the air. It should be simple enough, she suggested.

Elizabeth, that may not be the best use of the Library's magic. Perhaps you should move him by non-magical means.

If Elizabeth waited, Mr. Darcy might suffer further injury. As the Librarian, she was honor bound to fulfill his request to retrieve the necessary objects to save Miss Darcy. Surely she could use the Library's magic for the sake of fulfilling her mission.

We cannot wait, Abraxas.

If you insist. You must first immobilize his body. Then you must use a hovering charm and make your way to the nearest village.

Elizabeth nodded resolutely before drawing several links

in the air, creating a glowing chain. The chain settled across Mr. Darcy's broad chest before disappearing. Elizabeth then spoke the words of the hovering charm and watched with satisfaction as Mr. Darcy's form rose three feet in the air, perfectly rigid and safe from being jostled.

Elizabeth was pleased to see the look of shock on Mr. Bickerstaffe's face. The insufferable man had always doubted her abilities. "There is a market town three miles down the road, Your Eminence. I will take the horses ahead and search for a healer, if this meets with your approval."

Finally, a useful idea from Mr. Darcy's meddling servant. Elizabeth nodded. "That will do very well, Mr. Bickerstaffe. I shall keep him safe. You have nothing to fear."

If Mr. Bickerstaffe did not appear entirely convinced, at least he offered no protest as he returned to their horses.

Elizabeth glanced over her shoulder, only to see the troll, still trapped in her air magic.

Abraxas?

Yes, Elizabeth?

Is there a spell to return creatures from whence they came?

Abraxas told her the page number and Elizabeth opened the book that kept her connected to the Great Library. She recited the incantation and watched with satisfaction as the troll disappeared through the shimmering portal.

Under normal circumstances, a distance of three miles would be trivial to Elizabeth, but keeping Mr. Darcy safely suspended in the air was more than a little tiring. Her pace was slow. It would be disastrous if she became overtired and dropped him.

Elizabeth could not deny the satisfaction she felt in using magic to save the man who had set her aside because of her supposed lack of magic. He never should have doubted her or her abilities.

At long last, Elizabeth spotted the thatch of several

cottages lining the road. Further still, was the welcome sight of an inn.

"Your Eminence!"

Elizabeth looked up upon hearing Mr. Bickerstaffe's voice. He was accompanied by a mage dressed entirely in shades of blue, from her cap to her half boots. Her apron bore an image of Hermes's staff embroidered with golden thread. So Mr. Bickerstaffe had found a healer. Perhaps he would not be entirely useless after all.

Two young boys followed behind, carrying a litter. Elizabeth lifted the hovering charm, and Mr. Darcy landed gently upon the litter.

The inside of the healer's cottage was stifling. The space was dominated by an enormous fireplace that held a large cauldron. The walls were lined with shelves, each crammed with dozens of herbs, potions, books, and magical baubles and trinkets. A sweet-smelling smoke wafted lazily from the cauldron, and Elizabeth felt her worry for Mr. Darcy retreat to the edges of her awareness.

Tread carefully, Elizabeth. I can sense the effects of magic upon your mind.

The echoing call of Abraxas shattered the effect of the healer's brew. She watched as the healer settled Mr. Darcy upon a table and began gesturing and reciting words of ancient healing spells.

Mr. Bickerstaffe's eyes were glassy; blessedly the healer's potion had calmed the man's nerves.

"It is a useful trick for the weak willed," the healer said. "Or those who come to me to heal their loved ones and can do nothing but worry."

Elizabeth looked up at her, surprised to be addressed at all.

"You, madam, are very magically gifted. I could sense it the moment I saw you. And then the little man addressed you by your title. Tell me, what business does the Librarian have with Mr. Darcy of Pemberley?"

"I am aiding him with a request."

"It must be serious indeed," the healer said. "The Darcys of Pemberley rarely lower themselves to ask for help."

"Believe me, I was quite surprised to be approached. But now our mission could be compromised," Elizabeth said. "Will you help me? I can ensure that you are paid for your service."

"It would be my pleasure to help the Librarian." The healer studied her as she mixed several vials of herbs and brews. "My mother is Lady Dalrymple. I know all about the Great Library, Your Eminence. Years ago, I failed to bond with a familiar. The Patronesses of Magic declared I was unfit to maintain my position in society, but they could not deny that I had enough magic to help others. Because I was the daughter of a Patroness, I was not sent away to join a group of spellcasters. But I could not stay and be a black mark upon my family's reputation."

"You are the eldest Miss Carteret?" Elizabeth asked with astonishment. The failure of Lady Dalrymple's eldest daughter was a cautionary tale used in the schoolroom to scare young ladies into focusing on developing their magic.

Miss Carteret nodded. "My younger sisters still had a chance to make good marriages and it was unlikely to happen if I stayed with them. My mother sent me to Derbyshire because no one knew me in this county. I have lived a life of anonymity since my failure to bond with a familiar."

Elizabeth could understand the need to protect one's family, but to be so heartlessly banished by one's own mother was beyond the pale.

"I am sorry for what you have suffered, Miss Carteret. You appear to be very gifted, despite what your mother believes. The Patronesses' judgment is clearly not infallible. I, too, failed to bond with a familiar." Elizabeth said the last with no small amount of bitterness.

Miss Carteret transferred her concoction to a vial, appearing resigned to her fate. "I believe that we all end up where we are meant to be. The Patronesses were wrong about you as well. You have risen higher than any of them, Your Eminence."

Miss Carteret tipped the vial of amber liquid into Mr. Darcy's mouth.

Elizabeth watched, waiting for something to happen. A wave of relief washed over her as Mr. Darcy stirred. His eyes opened and immediately sought hers. The expression upon his handsome face was part amazement and part disbelief. "Elizabeth?"

"I am here, Mr. Darcy. You passed out after we defeated the troll. We are in a market town. This kind lady has healed you." Elizabeth decided it was for the best not to reveal the healer's true identity to Mr. Darcy. Miss Carteret deserved peace after all she had endured at the hands of the Patronesses.

"Well, I have done what I can. Mr. Darcy will need to rest," the healer said. "Whatever quest you are on shall have to wait until morning. He suffered a minor head injury and is in some danger of adverse effects. You will have to watch him closely until morning for any signs of dizziness, headaches, or confusion."

Miss Carteret helped Mr. Darcy off the table. Elizabeth withdrew a coin from her pocket, but the healer shook her head. "I am honored to assist the Librarian. I wish you luck in your endeavor. Do all that you can to prove your worth."

Elizabeth nodded, silently agreeing to do her best to prove the Patronesses wrong. She took Mr. Darcy's arm, despite Mr. Bickerstaffe's sound of protest.

When they stepped out of the stifling cottage, Mr. Darcy turned to Elizabeth and said, "I assure you, I am perfectly capable of resuming our travels."

The statement was belied when he swayed wildly as he tried to mount his horse. Elizabeth shook her head. Why did Mr. Darcy always have to be so stubborn?

"Mr. Darcy, you will be no help to your sister if you fall from your horse. We can resume our quest at first light, but now the best course of action is to spend the evening at the inn."

"Mr. Darcy, the Librarian may be correct," Mr. Bickerstaffe said, surprising them all.

Mr. Darcy looked from Elizabeth to his valet, clearly wishing to protest more, but at last he conceded. Elizabeth rewarded him with a smile and took his arm to steady his steps as they walked to the inn.

DARCY KNEW The Griffin and the Gorgon by reputation. It was a handsome stone building with comfortable rooms and excellent fare. It was small, though, only half a dozen rooms. When they entered the inn, the common room was crowded with a troupe of spellcasters, recognizable by the silver badges pinned to their identical green kerchiefs. The spellcasters, mostly young ladies with a few older chaperones, were surrounded by a crowd of men, young and old.

Darcy pulled Elizabeth closer to him, as some of the patrons appeared rough and rowdy. One of them even whistled crudely at the sight of Elizabeth. Darcy steered her to the bar to speak to the innkeeper.

"I am in need of three rooms for the evening," Darcy said.

The innkeeper shook his head. "I am sorry, sir, but I only have one room available at the moment. Yesterday, we were visited by a group of spellcasters. They are servicing the wells and fields which have been neglected since the travails of last year." While the innkeeper undoubtedly appreciated the work of the spellcasters, he did not appear pleased with the assemblage of their admirers, laughing and hooting over games of dice and cards near the roaring fire in the common room.

"You and your wife may take room three, and your man can sleep in the stables," the innkeeper offered.

Both Elizabeth and Bickerstaffe opened their mouths to protest. Darcy silenced Bickerstaffe with a look, and to Elizabeth he asked, "What say you, Mrs. Darcy? This may be the last inn we come across for some time. We could ride on if you wish."

Elizabeth's eyes narrowed at this address, but she caught his meaning. It was either pretend to be his wife and share a room for the evening, or Darcy would ignore the healer's advice.

"Very well, we shall take the room," Elizabeth said. Her concern for him was touching.

Darcy paid the innkeeper and asked him to show Elizabeth to the room. Once she had disappeared up the stairs, Bickerstaffe said, "Sir, you cannot share a room with the Librarian. It is most improper."

"As far as anyone in this establishment knows, she is my wife. There will be no whispers and no hints of impropriety." He sent Bickerstaffe away to deal with the horses and baggage.

As far as sharing a room with Elizabeth went, it was a decision solely made from practicality. Though it had given him a great deal of pleasure to refer to Elizabeth as his wife, the ruse was only to preserve their reputations. There could be no future between them, but Darcy would enjoy this time spent with her. Despite the troll attack, the daunting quest ahead of them, and his hindering valet, ever since reuniting with Elizabeth, Darcy finally felt whole again.

Darcy climbed the stairs and pushed open the door to the room. Elizabeth was sitting in front of the small toilette table shoved in the corner. She was studying her reflection and did not appear to have noticed his entry. Darcy took a moment to drink in her appearance. Her lovely curls were mussed, some of them falling out of the careful arrangement she had worn before their encounter with the troll. Not for the first time, Darcy wished to run his fingers through them as he had done five years ago.

Darcy closed the door softly, not wishing to startle her. Elizabeth turned at the sound, her pert lips forming a cautious smile. "Ah, Mr. Darcy, or should I call you William in deference to our married state?" Her tone was light and teasing, but there was a hardness in her fine eyes.

"I apologize for the ruse. It was the only way to avoid awkward questions," Darcy said. The last thing he wanted to do was upset Elizabeth. They would be in each other's company for the next several days at least.

"It was a sensible story," Elizabeth agreed. "The Librarian is not always known in small countryside villages. I would not want any hint of scandal to affect my family."

"Nor would I wish to harm Georgiana further than I already have," Darcy said.

Elizabeth looked at him, a strange expression on her lovely face. Darcy had not meant to give voice to the guilt he had been harboring. Georgiana's illness was as much his fault as it was Wickham's.

"Mr. Darcy, what happened to your sister was not your fault."

It was nothing he had not heard before from Georgiana herself, but Darcy knew better. "Georgiana fell victim to Wickham when she encountered him while at port. Had she stayed at home with me, I could have kept her safe." He confessed to Elizabeth, secretly wishing for her to reaffirm that his guilt was justified.

Elizabeth, though, rarely did as he wished. "Mr. Darcy, believe me, Mr. Wickham would have sought out your sister wherever she went. You cannot protect her from everything. She is a grown woman with her own familiar."

"I am her brother. It will always be my duty to protect her," Darcy said.

"Georgiana is very fortunate to have you for a brother. As a Librarian who can draw on centuries of past experiences, it is rare to see a supplicant make a request with such pure intentions. We will succeed in our quest to find her cure."

Darcy could only hope that Elizabeth was correct.

ELIZABETH SAT CURLED in a chair by the fire with a book, having convinced Mr. Darcy that he needed rest to recover from his injuries. He had conceded only out of civility, and he had been watching her from the bed with barely concealed irritation for much of the time since.

Elizabeth looked up from her book. "Are you well, Mr. Darcy? Does your head hurt?"

The clock on the mantel had just struck seven. Mr. Darcy had not experienced any of the symptoms that the healer had warned about. Or if he had, he had not owned them for fear of appearing weak. Stubborn man!

"I am well. We could have ridden further," Mr. Darcy said.

"You may be cavalier with your own health," Elizabeth said, "but I am not." Elizabeth did not want to dwell on the feelings that seeing him attacked by the troll had evoked. She was the Librarian. Once she was done with this quest, she and Mr. Darcy would part ways as indifferent acquaintances.

"I appreciate you worrying over my safety," Mr. Darcy said, "but I am well enough."

"Well enough to join me downstairs for dinner?" Elizabeth asked. She was itching to get out of this room, and perhaps stretch her legs in the cool night air.

"I do not believe that would be wise. The inn is filled with spellcasters and their admirers. Magic and drink do not mix well."

Elizabeth only laughed. She did not balk at the presence of spellcasters, though she could understand why Mr. Darcy might disapprove of them. After all, every spellcaster was a young lady with magical power insufficient to impress the Patronesses of Magic. "Come now, Mr. Darcy, would you have us spend the entire evening alone in the bedchamber? Where is your sense of adventure? I promise we can retire early if the crowd becomes too raucous."

In the happy months of their courtship, Mr. Darcy had never been able to refuse her. She was pleased when he consented to join her in the taproom. She took his arm.

The fire was blazing merrily in the hearth. The taproom was still crowded, but Mr. Darcy and Elizabeth managed to find two places at a table in the corner. Mr. Darcy went to purchase their meal, and Elizabeth viewed the spellcasters' games with interest. It was strange to think that this might have been her fate if not for becoming the Librarian.

The young ladies were playing charades and using all manner of simple spells to convey their chosen word or phrase. The chaperones sat at the edges of the crowd, casting austere looks at any of the men who dared get too close to their charges. One steely-haired woman even swatted a drunken lout with her fan after he tried to kiss the hand of a ginger-haired girl no older than Lydia.

Elizabeth was quite amused when a pair of players reenacted Don Quixote and his fight with the windmills. One spellcaster swung her arms rapidly, gusts of wind bursting from her fingertips, while her partner conjured a sword and mimicked charging forward on a steed.

The players bowed, their silver badges glinting in the candlelight. They seemed happy enough with their lot in life, but Elizabeth was grateful she had been chosen by the Great Library.

Mr. Darcy appeared, holding two tankards, as the spellcasters began a new round of charades. Elizabeth raised an eyebrow.

"It is only small beer," Mr. Darcy said. "We must make an early start in the morning."

Elizabeth nodded. They spoke of insignificant matters when the innkeeper appeared with the food. Elizabeth had rarely had such a fine meal at an inn. She supposed Mr. Darcy was accustomed to only the finest establishments. After dinner, Elizabeth said, "Will you join me for a stroll down High Street?"

"Certainly," Mr. Darcy said, gallantly offering his arm. They walked down the street for several minutes in companionable silence before Mr. Darcy finally spoke. "Thank you for saving me this morning. Without your intervention, I do not believe I would have survived the encounter."

"You do not need to thank me. I have pledged to help you on this quest. It goes without saying that I will do whatever I can to keep you safe," Elizabeth said.

"Your magic was most impressive, but is your pledge as the Librarian the only reason?"

Elizabeth looked away for a moment. She had once loved this man. Despite the way he had jilted her, he would always hold a place in her heart. She wanted him to live a long and happy life, even if it had to be without her. "I have no wish to see you harmed," Elizabeth finally said.

"I will do all I can to protect you as well, even without the oath I made at the Library. You must know that," Mr. Darcy's expression was genuine, but Elizabeth could only think of how he had given up his right to protect her when he had set her aside. Even after all these years, his abandonment still stung. During her training, she had done her best to bury those feelings deep, but now that she was forced into his company again it threw into sharp relief all that she had been missing.

"Elizabeth, are you well?"

They had stopped their progress, and Mr. Darcy was looking at her with concern.

"I am perfectly well, but we should retire. As you said, we have to make an early start." It was better to lie than to speak the truth about feelings that would amount to nothing.

Mr. Darcy looked as if he had more to say, but he simply nodded and escorted her back to the inn.

He did not immediately follow her to the room, to give her privacy for her nightly ablutions.

Abraxas? She called the griffin.

I am here. How are you faring?

I do not know if I have the strength to treat Mr. Darcy as an impartial acquaintance on this journey. What will happen if I allow our history to distract me from our quest?

You are not made of stone, dear one. The quest you are undertaking is one that is meant to banish pain and sorrow for Miss Darcy. Allow it to do the same for you.

It was sensible advice, but easier said than done.

All will be well, Elizabeth. You have the courage and strength of a Librarian. There is nothing you cannot do.

Thank you, Abraxas.

When Mr. Darcy returned to the room, she would face him with courteous equanimity.

∾

"WHAT ARE YOU DOING?" When Darcy entered the room, it was to find Elizabeth resting upon a crudely constructed bedroll before the fire.

"You need to rest, Mr. Darcy. A night spent on the floor is not conducive to adequate healing," Elizabeth said, her tone casual, almost deferential.

"That is nonsense. It would be ungentlemanly for me to force you to sleep on the floor," Darcy said.

"I am not delicate. I can spend an evening on the floor without breaking," Elizabeth said. Her expression was resolute, and Darcy suspected she would not be gainsaid.

"Very well, but you will take the bed should we find ourselves in this situation again."

"We have an accord," Elizabeth said.

Darcy went behind the screen and removed his coat, cravat, and boots. Bickerstaffe would be furious with him for rumpling his clothes, but he could not sleep in only his shirt – as he was accustomed to. The valise he had packed was not very large; they had to travel lightly out of necessity.

As Darcy settled into the bed, his eyes fell upon Elizabeth. It had quite escaped his notice before, but she had taken her hair down and tied it in a sloppy plait, some of the curls had already fought themselves free. Her nightgown was modest, but Darcy could see the outlines of her shapely legs as she lay curled in front of the fire.

"Goodnight, Elizabeth," he said as he waved his hand and extinguished the half a dozen candles in the room.

"Goodnight, Mr. Darcy," Elizabeth said.

But sleep did not come easily for Darcy. His traitorous mind kept conjuring images of Elizabeth in bed beside him, soft and warm in the circle of his arms. Had he not followed the advice of the Patronesses all those years ago, Elizabeth would be his wife.

At length, the clock struck midnight. Elizabeth was fast

asleep, and Darcy was nowhere near slumber. He rose from the bed and crossed the room. Elizabeth should have the bed. He would sleep on the floor. Carefully, he took her in his arms and carried her back to the bed. She did not stir as he pulled the bed clothes over her sleeping form.

Against all reason, Darcy pressed his lips against her forehead. "Sleep well, Elizabeth."

CHAPTER 7

*A*s the first light of morning streamed through the window, Elizabeth awoke to the same mortifying thoughts and meditations which had at length closed her eyes. She could not yet recover from the surprise of what had happened, and her cheeks burned at the recollection. There she had been, in the bedroll by the fireplace, feigning slumber rather than acknowledging that sleeping in the same room as Darcy – in front of him! – was impossible.

And she had been caught in her deception when she heard his footsteps and felt his arms go around her, lifting her into the air and carrying her to the bed. She should have just opened her eyes and demanded to know what he was doing, but it seemed easier to continue to pretend to be asleep. Especially since that meant she could enjoy the brief feeling of his embrace, a warmth she had despaired of ever feeling again, a closeness that filled her heart. Was it so wrong to steal that moment for her memories? Even if it was only Darcy giving into his gentlemanly beliefs that the lady should have the comfort of the bed.

And then she had felt his soft lips against her forehead

and the warmth of his breath flowing over her skin as he had whispered, "Sleep well, Elizabeth."

That kiss could not be explained away as the result of ingrained good manners.

What did it mean? Did he still feel some affection towards her?

She could still feel his touch, and it made heat rise deep within her, making her want more. But it could never be. She was the Librarian, and that meant she could never marry, even if he would have her. And there was no reason to think anything had changed in that regard. But, oh, how she longed for just one more moment of closeness, one where she did not have to pretend to be unaware!

She sat up and gazed at Darcy's sleeping form by the fire-place. Perhaps it was just that sleeping in the same room made it hard to avoid tender feelings towards him. Or perhaps it had been the result of fighting for their lives side by side.

Or perhaps she was lying to herself. How did a woman ever forget her first love?

But she needed to remember she was on a mission, not here for her pleasure. Should she wake him so they could get started? No. The healer had said he would need rest. And she needed the time to collect herself. She quietly gathered up her clothing and slipped behind the screen to change into her day dress, mentally thanking the Library servant who had taken care to pack clothing with fastenings down the front which she could put on without assistance.

Then her rebellious mind insisted on presenting her with a different image, one where Darcy was doing up the buttons on the back of her dress. A surge of desire rose inside her, her skin prickling with desire as she imagined him standing close behind her, his deft fingers moving slowly up her spine

—

No. This was no time to allow romantic fantasies into her head. Especially not ones about the man who had already betrayed her once.

Discipline. She needed to remember the years she had spent learning the self-control necessary to hold the Librarian's power. These free moments should be used to study, to prepare herself for their quest. Her task was to help him perform a quest, nothing more, and that should be her focus. But she could not resist the temptation to steal a glance at his profile, the chiseled lines softened in sleep, as she hefted her spell book onto the desk.

Settling herself in the chair, she opened the cover, and her breath caught in her throat at the sight of a completely empty page. What had happened to it? The ornate illuminations and words of the spells had vanished as if they had never existed.

In shock, she turned one page after another, faster and faster. All blank. She squeezed her eyes shut and opened them again, but it made no difference.

Abraxas! Something is wrong. All the words have been erased from my book!

She could feel the griffin's presence in her mind, but he said nothing.

Abraxas? What is the matter?

The griffin sighed. *You drained the book. Where do you suppose the energy for your rescue efforts was coming from?*

She drew in a sharp breath, her cheeks growing hot. *The Library has always been the source for my spells.*

A feeling of heaviness came from her familiar. *That is for necessary magic, like fighting the troll. Unnecessary use of magic damages the Library.*

But it was necessary! He was injured and needed help.

You could have sent for a cart to carry him. The amount of magic you used to transport that man could have built a new Library entrance or saved a dozen lives.

Her throat grew tight. *How can I fix it? Should I pour my own magic into the book?* It might take years to replenish it, but she would do it.

It is not so simple. The book is destroyed, its contents lost to us.

A spell book that had existed for centuries, gone. Forever. At her hand. Elizabeth's stomach churned.

She felt the loss like part of her own body. Irreplaceable. And what of the immediate implications for their quest? She would have no ability to look up spells, or to connect to the past Librarians! How could she continue without their support? And Georgiana's life depended upon it. *Must I return to the Library, then?* Defeat tasted bitter on her tongue.

The Library set your task, you must complete it.

But if I cannot access the Library...

And you must do it on your own, with only your own magic and knowledge.

She licked her dry lips. It had been years since she had worked on her own, and even then, she had only common magic, those weak powers available to people without familiars. Not until she called Abraxas to her could she use her full abilities, and after that she had the Library at her disposal.

Oh, how she hated feeling Abraxas' disapproval! *I did not know what else to do. I was afraid he might not survive.*

Possible, but he is just one man. The Library serves the entirety of the human world and the fae. We cannot favor a single individual.

But this one individual had been dear to her. She had loved him.

She did not intend Abraxas to hear that thought, but apparently he had, and his response was sharp. *Have you forgotten what he did to you?*

It was like an icy bucket of water dumped over her head. Her body remembered for her, that worst day of her entire life. The sick, crushing mortification as she had walked out of her meeting with the Patronesses of Magic, having failed to call even the weak familiars they offered her. She had known from the moment she walked in the door that they intended to humiliate her. She had not expected to be offered the sort of lofty magical creatures a highborn young lady might get, but there was not even a typical cat or bird. No, the Patronesses had set out a rat, an old badger, a turtle with a scarred shell, and an earthworm for her. An earthworm! But she had swallowed the insult, having no other choice, and did her best to call the creatures, never imagining she would fail.

After all, her magic was strong. Her father had said she would have no difficulty bonding to a familiar, but he had refused to arrange for her testing by the Patronesses. Unlike Darcy, who had first insulted her, and then later, after seeing her magical abilities, courted her assiduously, vowing his love and promising to announce their engagement as soon as she had a familiar. And he had personally requested the test.

After that meeting, she had thought nothing could make her feel worse. Except then Darcy had appeared, with that blank, unapproachable expression that still haunted her dreams. The cold, crisp words had come from the same lips that had kissed her so tenderly only that morning, telling her an engagement was no longer possible. And then, after a perfunctory wish for her future felicity, he had walked out of her life. His words of love, his tender touches, they had all been meaningless, mere tools for winning a magical wife. And when she failed to bond to a familiar, she was useless to him.

She ran her hand over her mouth, swallowing the nausea rising in her throat. And she had sacrificed her magical book for his sake! What a fool she was!

For his sake, or for your pride? Abraxas nudged her mind.

Abraxas knew her better than anyone in the world,

including all her weaknesses, and his words cut like broken glass. She buried her face in her hands, hot tears stinging the corner of her eyes.

The griffin was right. Ever since Darcy had appeared before her in the library, she had not been able to resist rubbing her new powers in his face, displaying her magic to the man who had once rejected her for having none. How gratifying it had been to magically transport him for three miles! Oh, her pride, her cursed, misplaced pride!

Have you given even a thought as to why you were attacked by the troll? Abraxas asked. *Someone is targeting you, and you have been too preoccupied with that man to consider the significance of that.*

She straightened abruptly. That cut to the quick, that she had allowed Darcy to distract her from her duties.

"Is something the matter?" Darcy's voice, still rough with sleep, came from behind her. The same deep, resonant voice that had once tempted her, the same voice that had broken her heart five years ago.

He was only being pleasant to her because he needed her Librarian powers – those same powers that were now out of her reach. She could not tell him, either of her failure or her new weakness.

Blinking back her tears, she lowered her hand and turned to see him standing behind her. In her iciest voice, she said, "Merely a little headache. I will thank you to return to the bed. The healer said you must rest."

His smile faded, to be replaced by that dreaded blank look. "Have I offended you? I only thought to make you more comfortable."

"I will not have this quest endangered because you will not listen to advice. Now pray excuse me. I will have breakfast sent up to you."

He reached out his hand. "Elizabeth, wait!"

Fury burning in her chest, she spat out, "You gave up the right to use that name the day you rejected me."

He took half a step backwards, as if she had slapped him. "It was never a rejection of you. I had responsibilities, duties, that left me no choice."

"Of course you had a choice! You chose your so-called duty and your precious family name over the promises you made to me." She saw him flinch, but she could not stop, not after having this argument inside her head for hundreds of sleepless nights. "But it cost you nothing, did it, to charm the gullible country girl on the chance she might win a familiar? You could always walk away if she failed."

His face grew pale. "It was not like that. I meant every word I said to you. But I could not marry a non-magical woman, no matter how much I wanted to. I always knew that, and I never would have courted you had I not believed so certainly that you had magic."

"How lovely for you, to be so utterly blameless for all the harm you did to me! Did you ever think about that, even for a moment?"

"Every day." The words were barely audible.

She did not believe him. "Did you ever think of what would have happened if you married me anyway? The world would still have turned on its axis. Your wealth and lands would still be yours. You would still be received by the *ton*, even if a few of them sniggered about your non-magical wife. But that would be intolerable, would it not? Better to destroy my life than for you to have a wife who was anything but the best!" Her voice was shaking, along with her hands.

He gripped the bedstead, as if he needed its support to stay upright. "You seem to be doing remarkably well for someone whose life was destroyed, Your Eminence."

"No thanks to you!"

But there it was: he did not care that she had been hurt

and nothing she could say or do would ever change that. The only thing he cared about was his own needs and desires. There was nothing for it but to complete this quest and leave him behind. Forever.

Clutching the now useless book to her chest like a shield, she stormed from the room, slamming the door shut behind her. She did not stop moving until she reached the public room where she would be safe from pursuit, or at least from any chance at private conversation.

Through her pain and fury, one thought became clear. It was a fortunate thing she had been cut off from her Library powers, or her rage might have caused the entire inn to be enclosed in a giant block of ice.

She would never, ever forgive him. Or herself, for allowing him close again.

CHAPTER 8

ired, dusty, and severely windblown from his hasty trip across the Channel, General Richard Fitzwilliam handed off his mount to a Pemberley groom. For a moment, he stood in the drive, hands on his hips, staring up at Pemberley's great entrance.

The doors remained firmly closed.

He had been in Vienna for the past few years, offering advice that was routinely ignored and supervising the protection of British diplomats, partly from enemies to the peace and partly from their own excesses. It almost made him long for his days on campaign. Almost. For his soldier's instincts were being pricked just now, and he did not enjoy the sensation.

He was briefly diverted by his familiar's complaints. *Why is this boy touching me? I am not a child, to require leading strings.*

"You need not use the reins," he told the groom without looking away from the doors. He used them himself only to remain on her back in the air. "She will follow you."

He will take you to the stables, Maor. We are guests here. Please try to be mannerly.

Maor was unimpressed. She flapped her great wings and reared back a bit on her hooves. *Why, when I shall be required to sleep out of doors while you are welcomed inside?*

Nothing inside Pemberley is built for hippogriffs, he reminded her. It would not be comfortable for you. He had been afraid of this. Maor had been given her own indoor quarters in Vienna, where the hotels were more accustomed to serving more diverse visitors.

And why is that I must wonder? Why must the soft beds, good food, and pleasant rooms be only for humans?

A flash of Maor's wings brushing priceless portraits from the walls or her hooves cracking the marble floors made Fitzwilliam groan. *I do not know. I am neither an architect nor a cook.*

The hippogriff sniffed disdainfully. *It smells like griffins here.*

Do they not smell better than a hoard of ape-drunk politicians?

Maor grumbled but did not reply.

Fitzwilliam pinched the bridge of his nose. *I must see to Georgiana, Maor. Would you be so kind as to repair to the stables?*

The hippogriff hummed disapprovingly. *I do this for Georgiana. We have met but once and still I can say that she is the best of you.*

He could not argue that. *You are correct.*

Maor huffed out a knowing laugh. *I am always correct.* She shook her great body a little harder and the saddle slid to one side. *Take this thing off me.*

Fitzwilliam sighed and grabbed the saddle, removing it quickly and handing it over to the groom. It had cost him a great deal of blunt to have the special saddle made by a master craftsman near the end of the peninsular war. It had been a present to thank Maor for taking him on after he had mourned two other familiars who fell in battle.

The saddle was designed to be beautiful, to appeal to

Maor's pride, as well as light and comfortable for her to wear, but his recalcitrant familiar hated it anyway. He was not even sure she liked him all that much, come to that, but they had survived Waterloo together. That sort of loyalty earned her a great deal of latitude to be . . . herself.

"Maor has run and flown far in the past days to aid Miss Darcy," he said to the groom. "You are to offer her every consideration."

The boy nodded vigorously. They were very used to griffins here. Despite Maor's haughty remarks, hippogriffs were not that different. "This way if you please, Miss."

As Maor half flew, half trotted away behind the groom, Fitzwilliam again regarded those closed doors. He had not been to England in some time, but in the past when he arrived at Pemberley, he had always been met by family. Darcy's uncharacteristically frantic message had told him that Georgie was ill and Darcy was leaving to attempt to reverse the curse placed upon her. But the fact that none of the household staff were outside to greet him gave him pause.

"Well, nothing for it," he said to no one in particular and bounded up the outdoor steps.

He tossed open the front doors, for they were unlocked. The entry hall was dark and empty. As his eyes adjusted to the dimmer light inside, they focused upon two footmen who were laid out flat at the foot of the stairs, their eyes glazed as they stared up at the ceiling.

Fitzwilliam pulled his sword from its scabbard and stepped over to render assistance. They were alive, but unable to move. He had seen it before, an energy absorption spell. It would wear off in a few hours.

He moved up the staircase quietly. More bodies littered the hallway, but he could not stop, for their path led to Georgiana's chambers and her door was ajar.

"Galon," he heard someone groan. The voice was pained, haggard, and female. A bolt of recognition struck him hard. It was Georgiana.

He pressed himself against the wall and snuck a glance inside, where a male figure with jet black hair was slumped on the floor, one hand thrown out wide. Fitzwilliam did not recognize him, but he had not been to Pemberley in some time. A new servant, most likely. He had been hit with the same spell as the others.

"Where is it?" a man cooed. "Come, Georgie, you know where he has hidden it. Tell me, love, tell me what I wish to hear, and this can all be over."

If the timbre of Georgiana's voice had shocked Fitzwilliam, this sound infuriated him. *Wickham.*

Who is Wickham and why are you interrupting me? Maor was vexed.

There is an intruder in Georgiana's room.

He could feel Maor's pique fall away. *Where is it?*

He did not want the hippogriff breaking through the window. Yet. *Let me find out what he wants before you come in after him.*

Do not wait too long.

"No," Georgiana whispered with such pain that Fitzwilliam's own heart ached for her. "Never."

Wickham was approaching the bed. "You must kiss me, my sweet, for we are to be wed. And then you will tell me."

Fitzwilliam slipped noiselessly into the room. Wickham closed his eyes as he bent towards Georgiana. Fitzwilliam used that moment to slip the broad side of his blade between the scoundrel's mouth and his cousin's. Wickham's eyelids flew open when his lips touched not Georgiana's but the cold steel of a sword.

Fitzwilliam slid the blade down to Wickham's neck and tutted, stepping forward and forcing Wickham to back away from Georgiana. He held it there, the tip shining bright with magic and pressed lightly against Wickham's skin. He continued to walk forward, forcing Wickham to scamper backwards, towards a window. "Now really, Wickham," Fitzwilliam said. "After all these years, have you still not learned that a proper invitation is required to enter a gentleman's home?"

"Georgiana invited me," Wickham replied as the corners of his mouth turned up slowly. "She is violently in love with me, you know."

"No," Georgiana said, slurring the word as she attempted to sit up but failed. It was all she could do to rasp out three words. "Wants. Galon's. Skin." Her body fell limply back to the pillows.

Fitzwilliam stared wordlessly at Wickham, turning the blade up just so. A tiny drop of blood fell upon the sword with a brief sizzle. Galon was Georgiana's seal familiar, but why would Wickham want his skin?

Unfortunately, Georgiana was in no condition to enlighten him.

Maor, is there a bird or horse or any sort of animal waiting along the north side of the house to provide a quick escape? Wickham is attempting to seduce Georgiana. We must cut off any means of escape should he attempt to abduct her.

He dares? It was almost a howl of rage. This was followed by silence for a moment as Maor did as she was asked. *It is a thunderbird.*

Fitzwilliam had never heard of it. *A what?*

Maor sighed. *A thunderbird. From the northern colonies or perhaps Lower Canada. But it is not his familiar for they do not speak. The bird has been spelled into obeying. I do not like this Wickham.*

Nor do I. Fitzwilliam stepped in, pressing the edge of his sword more firmly against Wickham's neck and decided to pretend he knew what was happening. "What do you want with Galon's skin, Wickham?"

Wickham shrugged rather nonchalantly, given his current situation. "I want to sell it. I am rather rolled up, as it were."

Ah. His experience with Wickham told him that this, at least, was true. It must have cost the man a small fortune to buy the curse he had laid against Georgiana, a curse he could ill afford. He had undoubtedly intended to use Georgiana's funds to pay for it, for her fortune had only grown in the years she had been at sea.

He felt a swell of pride in his youngest cousin. For in fighting as she was, she had put Wickham in a perilous position. Wickham owed money to a curse maker yet did not have the wherewithal to pay the debt. That was a precarious position to be in. He must have gone further into dun territory to purchase a compelling spell for the thunderbird and the energy absorption spells. As Wickham had not attempted to throw such a spell at him, Fitzwilliam presumed that they had all been spent. Georgiana's funds would have paid for it all and still left him a wealthy man but instead, he had run into more resistance than he had expected. The debt he owed must be increasing apace, and he had failed to gain any means of paying it.

It would make him desperate. Desperate men could be dangerous.

Wickham would be frantic if he realized that the curse could be broken without his help. He was counting on using their fear for Georgiana's safety to bring the Darcy and Fitzwilliam families to heel. Darcy and the new Librarian were even now on their way to destroy the curse, but though Fitzwilliam had great faith in Darcy's abilities, it was possible that they, too, might fail. No, he could not run Wickham through as he might wish, but he could not allow the villain to leave either.

Yes, he would play this game. Allow Wickham to believe he had won. For now.

Fitzwilliam addressed Georgiana. Though she slept now, likely exhausted by her exertions, he pretended to believe she could hear him. Indeed, perhaps she could. "Shall I kill him, Georgiana?"

The blackguard only smiled. "If you kill me, you shall lose your precious little cousin forever. For she will not be restored until I lift the curse."

He allowed a little fear to creep into his response. "She has become as much a soldier as I, and would clearly rather die than wed you, Wickham. If it is money you are after..."

Wickham lifted his eyebrows. "Georgiana has come into her fortune now. There is no need to convince her prig of a brother to pay me."

Fitzwilliam laughed. His humor was genuine, he could not help it. "Georgiana's money is tied up so tightly to her benefit that a husband, even a good one, could never touch it. Darcy learned his lesson well when you made your first attempt."

Wickham's gaze was shrewd, assessing. "Do you really believe that once we are wed, she will keep it from me? Or for that matter, that Darcy will not give everything he has to keep her safe?" He gestured carefully around the room. "He has more than he can ever spend and yet has always denied me. His father treated me like a son, and I know he must have left me more than the possibility of a living."

Fitzwilliam wanted to lunge, to plunge his sword into this contemptible creature. Wickham had been given a great deal of money from the Darcy coffers both before and after his uncle's death. He was right in that he had been cosseted. Darcy had always been held to a higher standard. However, that did not mean Wickham was owed anything. As far as

Fitzwilliam was concerned, the charlatan had already been given far too much.

He quickly explained to Maor which window was Georgiana's. She replied, *You mean the one directly above where the thunderbird waits and that I am currently watching? Yes, thank you, you have been a great help.*

Fitzwilliam refused to display any reaction to his familiar's sarcasm. He did not want to offer Wickham the advantage of observing his irritation. "If you were born to the Darcy family, George, would you have proven worthy of the Griffin Keeper's role, as Darcy has? Or would you have complained about the cost of keeping them and sold them off to line your pockets?"

Wickham eased the window up with one hand. Was he really so stupid as to believe he could flee Fitzwilliam's custody so easily?

Apparently, he was.

Fitzwilliam almost rolled his eyes. "That is a three-story drop, Wickham, and you have spent all your spells."

Really, he ought to find work in the theater. But the best way to get Wickham to jump into Maor's path was to act as though he did not believe Wickham would. The idiot sat on the sill before the opened window. He swung his legs over and moved to push himself out.

He is coming out, Maor. Fitzwilliam leaned forward, drawing a bloodless X on the back of Wickham's neck with the magic on his sword. The skin rose, puckered into a glowing mark.

Wickham howled and leapt.

Now, Maor!

The hippogriff was waiting. *He is intact,* she said, disappointed. She held Wickham in her talons and rose above the roof.

He must remain so, for the nonce. But he has been marked as a criminal.

I could just kill him now. There was a screech from outside. Maor must have squeezed Wickham rather tightly in her talons.

As much as I would enjoy that, it is too great a risk. Just take him up to a nest.

Maor chuckled darkly. *With great pleasure.*

As heavy as they were, most believed that griffin and hippogriff nests would be located either on the ground or in the low branches – and sometimes they were. When she had the opportunity to nest, however, Maor had always preferred the uppermost branches. She was heavy, but her wings easily bore the burden of her weight. Wickham would not be able to move without plunging to the ground below. It was the perfect place for him.

Maor's shout of surprise and anger, then, came as an unwelcome surprise.

Fitzwilliam raced to the window in time to see the thunderbird, his great wings flapping slowly to keep him steady, plucking Wickham from the very top of an ancient oak and making off with him.

No! *Maor, where are you?*

There was no answer. *Maor?*

He is too fast to catch, Maor told him breathlessly. *How is Miss Darcy?*

How was she? A very good question. Sleeping.

Fitzwilliam, his heart heavy with wrath and resentment, checked on the man sprawled on the floor. A tray had fallen to the ground next to him, and the bowl of broth had spilled over the floorboards. He tossed a cloth over it to sop up the liquid. There was nothing else to be done but wait. These sorts of spells soon wore off, leaving the victims thirsty and with violent headaches, but no other ill-effects. He set his sword across the top of another small table, the hilt close enough to grab in an instant should it be required.

Then, finally, he was able to turn his attention to Georgiana, pulling her covers back to scan her from head to toe. There did not seem to be any additional magic here, but the curse pulsed hot and heavy, like a fever. He took another cloth from the stack on her bedside table, dipping it in the basin, wringing it out, and placing it on her forehead. The water would be tepid, but it was better than nothing.

"Ay up m'duck," he said quietly, as he worked to cool her off.

Georgiana moaned.

"Keep fighting, sweetling," he said. "Keep fighting."

CHAPTER 9

As Elizabeth entered the public room, several eyes turned in her direction. She stopped in the doorway. She could not storm into a public space clutching her book as if she wanted to attack someone with it. She was the Librarian, and no matter how much Mr. Darcy had succeeded in riling her, she needed to maintain some dignity. They might not know who she was here, but what if someone found out? She did not want rumors circulating that she could not control her temper.

She drew back and leaned against the door frame just out of sight, taking deep breaths to calm herself. How was it that she had been in command of her feelings all these years, but as soon as Mr. Darcy appeared on the scene she turned into a bundle of nerves? Perhaps she was more like her mother than she was prepared to admit. She sincerely hoped that was not the case, especially since the Library's magic tended to reflect her emotions.

Abraxas' words came back to her. *The quest you are undertaking is one that is meant to banish pain and sorrow for Miss Darcy. Allow it to do the same for you.* Easy enough to say, when the Library griffin had no idea what she was going through. It was like removing a bandage from an injury that had festered, revealing all the rot underneath. How could it heal when she had to work with the person who had wounded her so deeply?

More to the point, how on earth was she going to complete her mission? When she first set out, she had been certain of her success. The wisdom of the Library and the voices of former Librarians were guiding her footsteps. But cut off and alone, she would have no one but herself to turn to.

She was not completely alone, though, was she? She did have someone who could talk her through this. Abraxas was still there. He had been a steady, reassuring presence for her when she had first started her training. He had never allowed her to give up hope, even when she sometimes doubted her abilities. She trusted him completely.

Abraxas?

Silence.

Abraxas?

Silence.

Then another thought struck her, chilling her to the bone. What if she did not actually have any magic of her own? What if the Lady Patronesses had been right? True, she had some unique abilities. She was able to connect to the Library when few mortals could. That did not mean, though, that she had innate magic. What if she was only able to draw on someone else's?

She cast her mind back to when she had first met Darcy. At the time, when she had discovered he was a prominent mage, she had not been intimidated. She had believed her own magic to be powerful and had convinced Darcy that was the case. Yet somehow she had failed to connect with even the humblest familiar. Doubts and certainties warred in her mind. She reminded herself that she was the Librarian, after all, but she could not extinguish her fears.

Abraxas? she repeated for the third time.

I am here.

She sagged with relief but was not fully reassured. Why had he not answered before? Was his voice fainter, or was she imagining it? Could she be losing touch with him as well? Once again, she cursed her arrogance in thinking she could exploit the Library's magic without paying a price.

Are you certain there is no way to restore my connection with the Library?

There is, but only if you come back here and re-establish it directly. First, you must complete your quest. You are magically bound to do so.

He had said the same earlier, but the words made her stomach churn. She had no choice.

What if she failed? A niggling voice answered in no uncertain terms. She would expose herself to Mr. Darcy's ridicule. To that blank, merciless expression he had turned on her when he discovered she did not possess enough magic. To the same words, spoken just a few minutes ago in his bedchamber. *I could not marry a non-magical woman.*

That was not the worst that could happen. She had already experienced that and survived. It was not the point of her quest. The outcome was far more serious than her injured pride.

She would let Georgiana down. Georgiana would die. The rest was irrelevant. She was here to save Georgiana from a heartrending, anguished death, to free her from the terrible dreams that were killing her. Elizabeth had to break the vile spell Wickham had cast on the young woman.

As for Mr. Darcy's censure, what more could he do to her? He had cast her away like a wet rag when it did not suit him. There was nothing he could do that would be worse than that. She had wanted to prove to him that she was powerful, and she would not be able to do it. What did it matter anyway? After the quest ended, she would go back to the Library and never see him again.

She had not come to the quest for him. She was doing it for Georgiana. This was not the time to wallow in self-pity. There was no time to be lost. A sense of determination and purpose rushed into her.

She stood up straight, smoothed her skirt with one hand, and grasped her book like a shield, ready to face the world again. As she turned the corner, her step firm and strong, she slammed straight into Bickerstaffe.

"There you are, Your Eminence." Bickerstaffe's tone was peevish. He wiped down his clothes fastidiously as if she had somehow contaminated them. "I hope Mr. Darcy is fully recovered and we do not need to spend another night here. I slept abominably. I am not accustomed to such disgraceful lodgings.

As if any of them had a say in the matter! Elizabeth had not asked to share a room with Darcy, either.

"You are free to complain, of course – once our mission is over and we have saved your mistress. Meanwhile, I will order food and you may take a tray up to Mr. Darcy."

Bickerstaffe's eyes bulged, and he drew up to his full height, his jaw protruding in agitation.

"May I remind Your Eminence that I do not take orders from you."

She was about to give him a sharp answer, but her irritation turned to laughter as she noted the pieces of straw entwined in the meticulous valet's hair.

"I am not quite clear what your duties are." He looked even more indignant, and she smothered a smile. "Still, you might wish to look in the mirror before you appear in public."

"What? Why?" As he ran his hands through his hair, bits of straw dropped onto his clothes, and he began to brush them off frantically.

Chuckling openly, she headed towards the innkeeper with her good humor restored. She was tired and drained, that was all. True, her situation was not ideal, but she would find a way of dealing with it.

She entered the public room. It looked like a different place in the daytime and without the noisy revelers. The spellcasters were all there, but they looked sleepy and subdued. She ordered breakfast for three, then headed for the same corner she had occupied the night before.

The young red-headed spellcaster who had been so popular greeted Elizabeth as she passed.

"Where are you bound, sister?"

How much should Elizabeth reveal? Would it jeopardize their mission in any way? Surely not. These were spellcasters. They understood the purposes of magic.

"I am bound for Faerie."

The young lady's eyes widened. "I wish I could come with you."

"You must not say such things, Rose," said the steely-haired chaperone. Elizabeth remembered her watching closely over the younger women, intent on preserving their reputations from the drunken young men around them. The older woman's brow was furrowed in disapproval. "Be careful what you wish for. We are close enough to Faerie for your wish to be granted. As you know very well, finding your way to the land of the fae is easy enough. Finding your way back is nigh impossible."

The red-headed spellcaster rolled her eyes in a gesture that reminded Elizabeth of Lydia as the chaperone turned to Elizabeth in explanation. "They say Faerie is full of mortals who have lost their way, wandering around as they try to return home, while their families age and turn to dust. Time works differently in their land." She gave Elizabeth a stern look. "I hope you have a good reason to go there and that you are not going alone."

Elizabeth started to reply that she, of all people, was not afraid of wandering the Faerie Realm. She had done so at will for many years. But now, under the scrutiny of the spell-caster, she wondered if she was indeed being foolhardy, placing herself at the mercy of the fae when she did not have the protection of the Library. Would they recognize her as the Librarian, or would they treat her as a mere mortal? If the latter, was she also putting Mr. Darcy and Bickerstaffe in jeopardy? Could she repel the fae's magic if they chose to trap them in Faerie?

Without her connection with the Library, she was not sure who she was any more, nor what she was capable of.

"I have a good reason," she replied. "I was sent by the Library."

"Ah," said the chaperone, her tone changing. "Then you will likely succeed." She regarded her closely. "I thought I detected the aroma of fae magic on you."

She had never heard of anyone being able to scent magic. She knew little about the spellcasters, apart from the fact that they traveled from village to village, earning a living by casting spells. Most of them were women from a poorer background with limited magical abilities, though some of them might be young ladies who had no real position in the tight-knit hierarchical world of society. Because the number of mages was so limited, the Patronesses ensured that they all received some basic training. This mostly consisted of learning a few practical spells, but the Patronesses kept a strict watch over them to ascertain that they did not abuse their power or try to rise above their station. They were assigned matrons to guard their reputations and to keep them in check.

She wanted to ask the matron about her ability to sniff out magic, but the steely-haired woman had lost interest and was engaged in conversation with one of the other matrons.

At that moment, Darcy appeared in the doorway. Bickerstaffe was fussing over him, trying to convince him to use a walking cane he had acquired somehow. Darcy brushed the offering aside impatiently, but Elizabeth noticed that he was moving gingerly, almost as if he did not quite trust himself. When he approached the table and sat down, he winced.

Elizabeth was determined to maintain her distance, but she could not help reacting to his pain with concern. "Is your head giving you pain? Are you dizzy? We could stay another night if necessary."

Even though the idea of another night in Darcy's company – in the intimacy of a single bedchamber – was unnerving, it would serve no purpose if he collapsed on the way. It would be very hard to find help in the wilds of the Peak District, and she did not have magic at her disposal.

"Out of the question!" Darcy spoke tersely, making it clear he would not agree to any delay. "I cannot afford to lose a single hour, let alone a whole day. As it is, I do not know how long Georgiana will survive."

At that moment, the innkeeper's wife appeared, carrying their food. "Are you eating here or upstairs?"

"We will eat here." Darcy's voice made it clear he had already argued the point with Bickerstaffe.

Elizabeth dug into her food with relish. Despite yesterday's dinner, the strong magic she had used to fight the troll and transport Darcy to the healer had depleted her energy. Meanwhile, Darcy picked at his food without appetite.

He was far from fully recovered, but Elizabeth would not argue the point. Georgiana's life was at stake.

"How much time do you estimate it is before we reach our destination?" Darcy gave up on eating entirely, tossing down his fork.

The question rattled Elizabeth, and she choked on a chunk of bread. Darcy thumped her on the back and forced her to drink some of his ale, while Bickerstaffe looked on with a smirk.

Elizabeth took her time before answering. Without the aid of the Library, she did not have a clear idea where they were supposed to go next, and she had no means of finding out. How on earth was she going to determine their direction?

They would have to rely on the poem. "The information the Library provided is not specific," she replied slowly. "You have seen the poem. The Library provides possibilities, not particulars. I will consult the spellcasters."

She stood up and walked to the table where the steely-haired woman was sitting. Judging the way they spoke, many of the spellcasters were from this region, and they would know their way around.

"I need advice," said Elizabeth. "I am willing to pay in coin. Just name the price." After all, the spellcasters made their living from requests for help.

The steely-haired matron raised her brow. "I would prefer to ask for a boon, since you are from the Library."

Elizabeth nodded and was about to set up a binding spell when uncertainty held her back. She did not know which aspects of her magic worked. What if nothing happened? She did not want to reveal her current weakness to Mr. Darcy.

Until she discovered more, Elizabeth would just have to give her word like a regular mortal. They did not know she was the Librarian, but her word as someone who worked at the Library must count for something. "Very well. If you ever need one, I will grant it."

"I am Mrs. Harriet Brown," said the matron.

"And I am Elizabeth Bennet. When you come to the Library, you may ask for me."

Mrs. Brown gave a quick nod. Their agreement was sealed.

"Miss Bennet, what is it you wish to know?"

"I am looking for the entrance to the realm of the fae."

Mrs. Brown's mouth quirked. "It was the question I expected." She looked grave. "Though I should warn you. It will not be easy to find your way. Since the strange weather events of last year, the Peaks have changed."

"In what sense?"

"There is a darkness to the daylight, and at night the sky catches fire. Farmers tell of strange creatures rarely seen in this world emerging to steal sheep or other animals. Some even say a great dragon flies over the horizon, breathing fire and destruction, but we have seen no such thing in our travels."

Elizabeth was not surprised. Last year had been abysmal, with whole harvests washed away by flooding and cold blighting the crops, spreading hunger and misery. The Year Without a Summer they called it. Elizabeth had heard talk within the Library of great balls of fire in the air and of volcanoes in another land throwing out smoke and darkness over everything. Some argued that those were the reason for the strange conditions, but why would a volcano cause such turmoil so very far away?

For common folk, of course, it was easier to explain through common lore and local tales. No wonder they spoke of dragons. For now, Elizabeth needed something practical. "That is all very well, but you must still have an idea where the entrance lies."

It galled Elizabeth that she had to ask, particularly when

Mr. Darcy was listening. The Library should have guided her.

"There is a wise woman who can help you. It is said she is part fae. Her name is Anne of the Hills."

It was not a fae name, but then, the wise woman was only partly fae. "And where can I find her?"

"It would be difficult to explain, but I know someone who can help you. Take the main path from the village upwards. Eventually, you will come across a rocky ledge called Stanage Edge that overlooks the Derwent Valley. If you look around, you will see a small packhorse road snaking downward. Follow the road down through a gap in the stone wall. There, in the shadow of rock, you will find a cave. They call it Robin Hood's Cave, but a hermit lives there now. He will point you in the right direction."

Darcy spoke up for the first time. He had been listening to every word, then. "I know the cave. It is around an hour's ride from here. I have been there a few times."

"Good," said Elizabeth, relieved beyond words that he was familiar with the location. She could rely on him that far at least. "Then let us set out immediately."

DARCY STARED out at the familiar countryside. Normally, the sight of the Peaks filled his soul with peace, but today there was no peace to be found. His head was pounding like a thousand drums, and his chest was painfully tight. He was afraid of losing Georgiana and, absurd as it sounded at this point, he was afraid of losing Elizabeth. It was more than ridiculous to think like that, of course. He had already lost her, a long time ago, and he had only himself to blame. It was he who had made the decision to leave her, and for a long time, he had accepted that.

Then today, they had quarreled. Her words had dredged up all the misery of the past and laid it open, revealing the consequences of his actions. She had shown him what he had done in all its repugnant detail. Her words had struck him with the force of a blow. *Better to destroy my life than for you to have a wife who was anything but the best!*

It was true. It was the bargain he had made, but to have it described so starkly put him to shame. Rather than acknowledge it, he had responded with an odious accusation. *You seem to be doing remarkably well for someone whose life was destroyed, Your Eminence.* As if her success justified his callous actions! It was no thanks to him that she had – amazingly – managed to land on her feet. He had never even considered what she would do, after being rejected by both him and the Lady Patronesses. The fact that she had managed to do well without him showed what a remarkable young lady she was.

All he had thought of was his duty to Pemberley and its descendants, a duty that must include marrying a young lady with powerful magic. Was it worth it? Had duty truly demanded so much of him, or had he been so arrogant that he was willing to sacrifice Elizabeth Bennet at the altar of his pride?

Well, the damage was done, and there was no use in wishing it was otherwise. He could not blame Elizabeth for her bitterness and anger. Her words had hit him hard, but he deserved every one of them. What he had done was unforgivable.

No surprise that since they left the inn, she had not spoken more than half a dozen words to him and those only for practical purposes. She had withdrawn from him completely, and it was obvious she was avoiding him. She was riding behind him where he could not see her, but he still *felt* her there, a constant presence, invading his every waking thought.

There was nothing to be gained from any of this. He turned his thoughts away from Elizabeth to Georgiana. He wondered how she was doing. Was she sinking further and further into her dreamworld? It would not be long before she was too weak to fight, and the spell would smother her. Had she succumbed already? The very thought of it made his heart contract painfully. If the worst had happened, he would know. Richard was with her. He would send word through Hespera. But Darcy could not bear even the possibility.

He had to believe that they would find the cave and do what was required before it was too late. He spurred his horse forward, pushing ahead, his eyes searching the horizon for the rock. He had come hunting in this area with his father and uncle. Yet today it looked different, somehow, and they were taking forever to reach it. The sun had risen high in the sky. They should have arrived by now.

Then finally, he spotted Stanage Edge, with the familiar rock jutting outwards, a giant platform overseeing the valley.

"There!" he cried.

He urged them upwards towards it. They followed at a crawl. Neither Elizabeth nor Bickerstaffe could ride as well as Darcy. The way down the cave on the other side was steep and only for surefooted riders. He would be better off going there alone, but he knew Elizabeth would never agree to be left behind. And considering what dangers they had encountered before, he would not want to leave her unprotected.

"We should stop before we take the path down. We need to give the horses a chance to eat and rest."

He dismounted and put his hand out to help Elizabeth down. Her hand burned into his, despite two layers of gloves between them. As soon as her foot touched the ground, he withdrew and dropped his hand to his side, resisting the temptation to check if his glove was singed. There was no magic there. She simply had that effect on him, even now.

Wondering if she felt the same, he flicked his glance towards her as she walked to the edge and stood there, staring over the valley, the bottom of her cloak fluttering like a sail in the breeze. She looked beautiful, framed by the pinks of the heather, the grey stone, and waves of frothy clouds in a blue sky.

He would have given anything for her to turn and look at him, for their eyes to meet, for her to acknowledge everything there was between them, but her gaze remained steadfast on the horizon.

It was futile to long for the past when the present demanded his urgent attention. Georgiana was suffering while he dwelled on a love he had already lost. The sooner he questioned the hermit, the sooner they would find Anne of the Hills, and they would be on their way to Faerie.

"We should go." His voice sounded harsh.

Elizabeth looked surprised, particularly since it had only been a few minutes since she dismounted, but she simply nodded. "Yes. There is no time to loiter."

They were soon back on their way, and his tension eased. Stones clattered and slipped under the horse's hooves as they made their way up towards the ledge, then down again.

He had expected to find the gap in the wall immediately, but it took up precious time. Then once they were through, the path turned treacherous, and they had to slow to a walking pace. He seethed with impatience, but there was no rushing it. It had rained overnight, and the stones were slick. The old packhorse road was worn in places, causing the horses to lose their footing. He considered dismounting and continuing on foot, but it would not necessarily be faster, and it would definitely be more tiring.

It had been a long time since he had visited the cave with

his uncle, and he had a hazy recollection of coming this way. His mind at the time was occupied with the legend of Robin Hood. He had been full of questions about the hiding place of the notorious bandit and excited about crawling through the narrow opening to reach the cave. He had paid little attention to his uncle's business with the hermit. His only recollection of the man was that he had a long brown beard that reached almost to the ground. It had reminded him of a horse's tail.

Finally, they reached the bend in the road where the cave was.

"We are here!" he exclaimed, recognizing the spot. He spurred his steed onwards as his eyes searched for the dark gap in the rock face.

A swirling mist had settled into the valley, making it difficult to see the features of the landscape, but one thing was clear. Where the cave used to be, there was nothing but a pile of sludge, rocks, and rubble.

They had reached a dead end.

CHAPTER 10

$\mathcal{E}$lizabeth stared at the cave in dismay. What were they to do now?

Mr. Darcy ran his hand through his hair. "I suppose I should have known that such a convoluted way of—"

"Halloooo!" a voice called weakly. "Halloooo! Is there somebody out there? Oh dear, oh dear."

Mr. Darcy leapt forward and rushed up to the rocks that hid the cave's entrance. "Are you in there?"

Elizabeth waited, half hoping the hermit was calling from elsewhere, but his voice was most definitely calling from inside the cave.

"Yes! Oh, please help!"

Elizabeth darted forward to help. She and Mr. Darcy stood considering the massive rockslide that covered the entrance to the hermit's cave – and now almost his tomb.

"What do we do?" she whispered. For all the Library had taught her, she had never attempted moving rocks and dirt on this scale before – and what if they caused a further cave-in that would kill the trapped man? They did not know how large the cave was or how much room he had to back away from the rockslide.

Abraxas, she called. *We found the hermit, but his cave is blocked by a rockslide. How do we move the rocks without risking his life?*

Mr. Darcy was studying the rock pile intently. "Miss Bennet, I think we may be able to help."

You will have to use your own magic, Abraxas warned. *But you should be able to lift them, especially with the help of another mage.*

Elizabeth froze. Her own magic. Her magic had been mixed with the Library's magic for so long, she did not know what was hers anymore.

"Give me your hand," Mr. Darcy said.

Elizabeth looked at him blankly.

He gave a little huff and grabbed her hand, holding it firmly in his. She stifled a gasp at the feeling of his warm hand clasped about hers. At the sensation, at once so familiar and yet so foreign, a thousand memories crowded her mind.

They had often walked together in the early morning mist, at first meeting accidentally and then purposefully. She had loved walking arm-in-arm with him, feeling the strong muscles beneath his sleeve and brushing against his side. It had sent shivers of the best kind tingling up and down her spine every time. On a few memorable occasions, he had even dared to kiss her bare hand, filling her with joy. He loved her!

"I will support the structure," he said, jolting her out of her ill-timed reverie. "You work on lifting the stones away. Start with the top, so that it does not collapse downwards."

She nodded mutely. He did not seem affected by her hand in his. Of course not. He had been the one to choose to give her up. He must never have loved her, not with that all-consuming and thrilling devotion that she had felt for him.

Forcing her painful memories away, she reached out tentatively with her magical senses. She could feel the strength of his magic combining with hers, reaching for the stones together.

"And . . . begin!"

Elizabeth reached out again, more confidently this time. She could not bear the idea of looking weak in front of Mr. Darcy, not now. She was the Librarian! And even if that meant she usually filtered magic through the Library, she did have magic of her own, and it was time she practiced using it.

She focused first on making the top layer of rocks lighter. Then she beckoned them, pulling them away from the cave and towards her. Once they were out of position, she tossed them to the side.

When the top layer was done, she moved down to the next. She could feel Mr. Darcy's magic supporting the structure of the cave and keeping it from collapsing as she moved the rocks.

The stones seemed to grow heavier as she moved downwards, and her movements grew more sluggish. She was nearing the end of her natural magic. Her grip on Mr. Darcy's hand tightened, and, to her surprise, her magic felt stronger. With renewed efforts, she lifted the last large stone and hefted it out of the way.

"Halloooo!" A dusty head popped up through the removed section of the wall. "My gallant rescuers!"

Elizabeth and Mr. Darcy released their hands and stepped forward as one. Mr. Darcy grabbed the diminutive man under his arms and hauled him up over the remaining rocks and debris and to safety.

The man shook himself, smiling brightly despite the gray dust that liberally coated him from head to toe, including his large and protuberant whiskers.

"Thank you, thank you!" the hermit said, his teeth bright

against his dirty face. "I cannot express just how delighted I am that you all decided to come to tea! If you had not, I am sure I would have been trapped until dear Anne came by, and she is not due until Thursday! So, it is to be a wedding, then?"

Elizabeth avoided looking at Mr. Darcy as he answered sharply, "A wedding? No, we came to ask your directions to find Anne of the Hills." He handed the hermit a handkerchief to wipe his face.

The hermit looked down at the handkerchief for a moment in confusion, then he brightened. He spat into it, then began to wipe the dust off his face.

Elizabeth hid a smile.

The hermit finished cleaning his face and handed the handkerchief back to Mr. Darcy with exuberant thanks. She rather enjoyed the expression on Mr. Darcy's face as he took it gingerly and replaced it in his pocket.

"Not to be married, then?" The hermit looked from one to the other. "Everybody comes to me to be married. I do a far better service than that blacksmith at Gretna Green, and my weddings are even valid among the fae! Best place for an intermarriage between a fae and a human this side of the fae kingdom! I even include flowers. Free of charge, of course. Only the best for my dear brides and grooms."

Elizabeth kept her eyes averted from Mr. Darcy's as she pressed her hand to her chest, willing the sudden sharp pain away. Neither of them needed a reminder of that disastrous day when their own plans to marry went up in flames.

Out of the corner of her eye, she saw Mr. Darcy run a hand through his hair, something he had always done when he was anxious or worried. The idea of marrying her was that concerning, then, was it?

Did you succeed with the rocks? Abraxas asked. *I could feel your energy levels ebb.*

Yes, Elizabeth sent back. *The hermit is alive and seems well.*

Although he seems under the impression that we came to him to be married, of all things.

Abraxas gave a rather griffinish snort. *Married? Is he Old Man Derwent, by chance?*

"Please, sir, may we ask your name?"

The old man smiled. "Haskins, my dear, but most people call me Old Man Derwent. Best not to ask why."

Elizabeth cocked her head. The reason seemed obvious. Was that not the Derwent Valley they were overlooking? But she would take the old man's advice.

Yes, she told Abraxas.

She could feel his rumbling and snorting still. *Oh, how delightful. I must go tell Travinius. He deserves a good laugh as well.*

"Now," Haskins – or should she call him Old Man Derwent? – said, rubbing his hands together, "shall we get started? Do you have a ring, good sir?"

Elizabeth hid her embarrassment in a laugh. She could not bear it if Mr. Darcy were the first again to remind the hermit they were not here for marriage. "That is not our purpose, sir. If you remember, we were looking for your friend, Anne of the Hills."

"Oh, old I may be, but fool I am not," Haskins said. He gave Mr. Darcy a sly smile. "I see full well that there is something between you two. Not here to get married, eh? Here to see my dear Anne? Well." He looked behind him at his cave and sighed. "I would ask you to bring her a few things, but I suppose they are lost in the rubble. We have been courting these many years, you know. Have not convinced her to marry me yet, but I get closer every year."

"Can you tell us how to find her?" Mr. Darcy said, and Elizabeth admired his calm. She was not sure whether to laugh or cry at the old man's repeated suggestions that they marry. But then, Mr. Darcy had a great deal of practice hiding his emotions, she supposed. He had always been good at that.

"She can be a little tricky to find," Haskins said, tapping a finger to his cheek. "Moves around a lot, that one. But she is very regular in her travels. Let's see, in the fae kingdom from Saturday to Monday. Today is Tuesday, so . . . I think she should be gathering woad. Or, wait, is that Wednesday? No, Tuesday, I am sure of it. It *is* Tuesday, is it not?" He squinted at the sun. "It is awfully difficult to tell the day of the week by the sun."

Elizabeth blinked. *Could* you tell the day of the week by the sun?

Travinius is still laughing, Abraxas said smugly. *Old Man Derwent is always trying to marry everybody off.*

He certainly is determined. And I do not think he is half as forgetful as he pretends.

Her chest still tightened a little at the thought of marriage, but she took comfort in the fact that Abraxas was unlikely to feel her pain through their distant connection. And after all, repeated exposure to Mr. Darcy was making things easier. It was a little like bathing at Brighton, which she had done once when she was about twelve. At first, the water was so cold that you could not breathe or think or even shiver. But after a few minutes, you became used to it a little, and you could move and paddle and enjoy the sensation of floating despite the frigid temperatures. Eventually she would be so immune to Mr. Darcy that she would be able to treat him as a common and indifferent acquaintance.

Elizabeth fought to remember what they came here for. Old Man Derwent was so odd that one could not help becoming a little befuddled during conversation with him.

"Anne of the Hills," she said. "Yes, it is Tuesday. You said she will be gathering woad today? Could you tell us where she goes?"

"Oh, you cannot miss it," he said with a grin. "It is the only woad around here. It grows where the fae magic has leaked out a bit, you know, from the fae lands. Only place you are likely to see it in Derbyshire. Just look for the yellow fields over yonder." He waved towards the north.

"You cannot give us anything more specific?" Mr. Darcy sounded dismayed. "Yellow fields? Over yonder?"

The old man squinted. Then he caught Elizabeth's eye.

"He may need some work before he is ready to marry." He leaned in close and whispered loudly, "Needs to work on his imagination. But a fine lass like you ought to be able to fix that right up. You are certain you do not wish a wedding? I do a fine ceremony. And there are some lovely caves around here if you want a nice wedding trip after."

Elizabeth laughed before she could stop herself. "No, sir," she said solemnly. "I have no plans to marry today."

"Very well." He pouted. "Do not let Anne marry you then, eh? She cannot perform proper English weddings at all, only fae. She might lie and tell you otherwise. I love the woman, but I do not trust her. She would steal all my weddings if she could, but as it is, she only gets some of the fae business. If you change your mind and decide to marry – which you should, in my opinion – everyone should marry! – you come back here and let old Haskins do it."

Elizabeth smiled. "Very well, sir. I promise we will not let Anne marry us."

Mr. Darcy gave her a look of exasperation, but she met it with a bright – if forced – smile.

A shadow flew over them, and Elizabeth looked up to see the silhouette of a dragon against the bright sky.

Haskins ducked and looked about to run back into his cave, but of course he could not.

"Is the dragon dangerous?" Mr. Darcy asked sharply.

"Not dangerous, no," the hermit said, but he was still

backing away towards his ruined cave. "It is just . . . well, you look like you are about to be married, you see. It *is* why most people come to me."

"It does not like weddings?"

"Rakover? He loves them as much as I do! But last time I had the honor of performing the ceremony, Rakover tried to bring a gift. It did not go over well. Myself, I like a gift of a disemboweled sheep now and again, but I can understand not appreciating it when it arrives unexpectedly during one's vows."

This time it was Mr. Darcy who laughed, but it was cut short as the dragon's shadow grew larger. A gust of wind almost bowled them over, and the old man grabbed Elizabeth by one hand and Mr. Darcy by the other, hauling them away from what was apparently about to be the dragon's landing spot.

The dragon landed with a great flapping of wings that sent many of the smaller rocks rolling and blew Elizabeth backwards into Mr. Darcy, who caught her before they could both be knocked to the ground.

"Greetings, humans," the dragon intoned. "My congratulations on your nuptials. Are you in need of a sheep?"

CHAPTER 11

"No," Darcy said. "But—"

"A goat then?" the dragon asked.

"No. We need—"

"A cow?"

Darcy gritted his teeth. "No! We need no livestock at all!"

"A hedgehog? A rabbit?"

Darcy strove to keep his tone level. "We need no animals. We are not getting married."

"Oh! Did you argue?" The dragon's face was quite sympathetic.

"No, we did not argue. We never intended to marry." Darcy massaged his temples, where a headache was starting to form – then realized what he had said. "Well, that is not quite accurate, but it was several years ago..."

Now the dragon appeared skeptical. "You really should make an honest woman of her."

Darcy sighed. "It is complicated."

The dragon settled its head on its front claws. "Do you want to tell me about it?"

How had he arrived at telling his romantic woes to a

dragon? Darcy glanced at Elizabeth, hoping for some assistance. Her hand covered her mouth, but her eyes were dancing with merriment. *At least someone is entertained*, he thought sourly.

Darcy took a deep breath. "We are seeking Anne of the Hills."

The dragon nodded. "It is Tuesday, so she will be gathering woad over yonder."

Was there no-one who understood directions? Darcy would give his entire fortune for a map.

"Might you tell us how far away 'yonder' is?" Elizabeth asked.

The dragon scratched his chin with one very long and sharp claw. "Well, it is not the next valley over...or the one after that...I would say, five or six valleys. Of course, Anne might be finished with woad gathering for the day."

Darcy exchanged an alarmed look with Elizabeth. They could travel for a day or more only to find that Anne of the Hills was no longer there.

"Or, if you would like to arrive in a more timely manner, it would be my pleasure to give you a ride," the dragon said.

"A ride?" Darcy echoed faintly.

"Oh, yes! What a delight!" Haskins exclaimed. "Wonderful prospects from the back of a dragon! I have some blankets hereabouts that I use as a saddle of sorts...And then ropes." The man started rummaging under some nearby bushes.

Darcy turned to Elizabeth. "What would you prefer?"

Her eyes were shining. "I have always wanted to ride a dragon! They are much faster than griffins – and they breathe fire."

"Only when necessary," Rakover cautioned. "I always get ashes stuck in my teeth."

"Of course," Elizabeth said.

"Here we are!" Haskins said, returning with ropes and blankets. Rakover lowered himself to the ground so the man could tie the ropes around his neck.

Bickerstaffe pulled Darcy aside. "You cannot possibly be considering this foolhardy scheme!" he said in a low voice. "We just met this dragon. We cannot know if he is trustworthy."

"My sister grows weaker every hour," Darcy said. "We do not have the luxury of delay."

Bickerstaffe folded his arms over his chest. "No. I refuse. Once we are in the air, the dragon could turn us into roasts. We must find another way."

His valet's refusal actually heightened Darcy's enthusiasm for the plan. "You need not accompany us. You could take the horses back to Pemberley and inform my cousin what we have learned."

Bickerstaffe's mouth opened as if he planned an objection about Darcy's cravats. Then he shot a second glance at Rakover. "An excellent plan."

Haskins had fastened ropes right where Rakover's neck met his shoulders. Under each rope was a folded blanket. "You sit on the blanket, see?" he explained to Darcy and Elizabeth. "It is like a saddle, keeping some padding between you and the spines on Rakover's back. That is more comfortable, believe me! And then you tuck your legs under the ropes, which keeps you from falling off in the middle of the flight – most unpleasant."

"Indeed." Darcy tried not to dwell on the image those words conjured. Then he helped Elizabeth climb onto the dragon's neck and position her legs under the ropes. He clambered up behind her, tucking his legs under his own set of ropes. Slowly Rakover rose to his feet. Already it was quite different from riding a horse or even a griffin; they might as well have been atop a three-story building.

The dragon bunched his muscles, preparing to leap into the air. "I thank you for your help!" Elizabeth called to Haskins. The next moment, the air was rushing past them as the dragon climbed into the sky with powerful strokes of his wings.

It was indeed quite different from riding a griffin. With only a few beats of his wings Rakover took them higher than Darcy had ever flown. The features of the Peak District below them might as well have been details on a map – and eventually they were altogether obscured by clouds. As Elizabeth predicted, they were also moving far faster than griffin speed. The wind whipped Darcy's hair around his face, and he was thankful he had thought to stow his hat in the saddlebags. Elizabeth kept one hand on her bonnet to prevent it from blowing away. But when she glanced over her shoulder at Darcy, she had a huge grin on her face. There was no doubt she was enjoying herself.

They had been flying for about fifteen minutes when Darcy heard an unearthly screech coming from above them. He and Elizabeth both craned their necks upward to find the alarming sight of another dragon bearing down on them.

While Rakover was a deep emerald green, this dragon was a shimmering cobalt blue. Darcy might have admired the other dragon's colors if it had not been about to attack them. Rakover dodged to the side just as the creature's claws would have impaled Darcy. Both of the passengers were forced to grab their ropes as Rakover dipped and then swooped away from the other dragon.

"What is happening?" Elizabeth shouted to their dragon.

"This other dragon is unfamiliar to me," Rakover rumbled back. "I do not understand why it is attacking."

The blue dragon came around for another attack, and Rakover went into a steep dive, causing Darcy's stomach to lurch uncomfortably.

This was the second unprovoked attack. Yes, the holes in the fae border allowed magical creatures to venture into the human world, but it could not be a coincidence that two of those creatures had targeted Elizabeth and Darcy. Someone did not want them to reach Faerie or find a cure for Georgiana. But who? Darcy found it hard to believe that Wickham commanded the powers to control a dragon or a troll.

The next time the other dragon came around, it belched fire directly at Darcy and Elizabeth. Orange and yellow flames came perilously close to their heads. "Fire?" Rakover muttered as he dove yet again. "How uncouth!"

The other dragon swooped downward, preparing to attack Rakover from underneath, but the green dragon was ready. Before the attacker could breathe fire, Rakover emitted his own flames, scorching the other dragon's face and neck. With a screech, it fell backward.

Rakover spat something from his mouth. "Blech! Ashes!" He then took advantage of the adversary's momentary incapacity. Flying faster, he tried to escape the other dragon. Unfortunately, Darcy soon spied the blue dragon behind them – rapidly drawing closer. "It is following us again!" he called.

"Is there anything we might do to help you fight him?" Elizabeth asked Rakover.

"I am not actually in great danger," Rakover mused. "I am fireproof after all. But I do not know how to protect you if he catches up with us."

Darcy exchanged a worried look with Elizabeth. He had no idea how to stop a dragon in flight. "I will contact Hespera," he told her.

Darcy had enjoyed a few brief conversations with Hespera during their quest. He had updated her about their progress, and she had given him information about Georgiana's health which Richard had relayed through Maor.

Unfortunately, Maor did not particularly care for Hespera and did not see fit to provide her with much additional information about the happenings within Pemberley. Nevertheless, Darcy had confidence that Richard would contact him in the event of an emergency.

Now he reached out to his familiar urgently. *Hespera!*

Darcy! What is the matter?

We are on the back of a flying dragon and another dragon is attacking us.

Hespera's mental voice was astonished. *How did that happen?*

Never mind! How can we stop the other dragon?

Hmm...Can either of you conjure a net? If you can tangle a dragon in a net, then it cannot fly and will fall to the earth.

We will try that. Thank you!

Darcy glanced over his shoulder. Rakover was tiring and the other dragon was definitely gaining on them. "Hespera suggests tangling the dragon in a net. Can you conjure one?" He asked Elizabeth.

She leaned back to speak right into Darcy's ear. "I have little experience with manifesting objects. Are you familiar with this type of spell?" He tried to ignore how good it felt to have her warm breath ghost over his neck.

"I have performed a manifestation spell, but never with a net and never at high speed. Still, I shall attempt it."

"Rakover!" he called. "Can we fly closer to the ground?" If Darcy was going to knock a dragon from the sky, he would prefer that the creature would not fall from a great height.

Rakover nodded his acknowledgement and swooped lower. The blue dragon followed suit. Soon they were only a hundred feet from the ground and dodging the tops of trees.

Darcy twisted around in his seat, staring at the pursuing dragon. He visualized a fishing net entangling itself in the dragon's legs and then pushed his will into the spell. A drain of his magical energy reserves told him that the spell had been activated. But he could not see the net. Oh, there it was, attached to one of the dragon's front claws. Unfortunately, it was the size of a napkin. Drat! Darcy had failed to specify that he wanted a *big* net.

He closed his eyes and concentrated on making the net larger, expanding it until it enveloped the entire dragon. When he opened his eyes again, the dragon was gone. Instead there was a grayish blob of net and blue dragon that was in the process of plummeting into the lake below it.

As Elizabeth and Darcy watched, the dragon fell into the lake with an enormous splash. It bobbed to the surface immediately as its claws tore at the net. Darcy was relieved he had not killed the magnificent creature, but he sent a little energy to reinforce the net, giving them a little more time to escape.

"Well done," Elizabeth whispered in his ear, sending shivers racing down his spine. He tried to quell his inappropriate feelings. *She wants nothing to do with me and rightfully so.*

But, whispered a treacherous part of his mind, *she is unmarried after all these years. Perhaps she longs for your affection, your touch.*

No, he could drive himself to distraction with such thoughts. It was best not to entertain them at all. Hope was the thing he must quash. Hope was the enemy.

He leaned away from Elizabeth and spoke loudly to Rakover. "How long until we are at the field of woad?"

"Not long!" They flew in silence for about ten more minutes, then Rakover announced, "It is below us!"

Peering downward, Darcy indeed saw a field of yellow flowers adjacent to some hills, although he did not see any people. He could only hope that Anne of the Hills had kept to her accustomed schedule and had not chosen this Tuesday to purchase new trim for her hats.

Rakover circled the field twice, each time getting lower. Finally he alighted gently on a country lane beside the carpet of yellow flowers. He lowered himself completely so that his neck was only a few feet from the ground.

Darcy freed himself from the ropes and slid down the dragon's neck, happy to have an opportunity to stretch his legs. He put up his arms to help Elizabeth dismount. Mindful of his recent resolution, Darcy immediately removed his hands from her waist and tried not to notice how fetching her curls looked when tousled by the wind.

Elizabeth surveyed the area. "Are we sure this is the right place?" she asked the dragon.

"Oh yes. Anne is here," Rakover responded.

"Where?"

"Yonder." He pointed a claw to the left, but Darcy saw nothing. Rakover chuckled. "Anne! Anne! Wake up! You have visitors."

A figure in the midst of the field of woad sat up. Her dress and large floppy hat were the exact color of the yellow woad flowers, making her indistinguishable from her surroundings. "Visitors?" she said vaguely. "How lovely." And she collapsed back down among the flowers.

Rakover appeared a bit embarrassed, although it was difficult to discern given his dragonish features. "Anne is not the most...industrious being I have ever encountered."

"Miss—" Darcy started and then realized he did not know how to address her. *Miss of the Hills? Miss Hills? Argh! This is ridiculous!* "Miss Anne!" he called. "We have need of your help!" He paused. "Quite urgent need!"

"Mr. Haskins sent us!" Elizabeth said.

This, at least, induced Miss Anne to sit up again. "Haskins? Do I know a Haskins?" she asked Rakover.

"He said he wants to marry you," Elizabeth said.

"Oh, him!" Miss Anne exclaimed. "Sweet man. Too much beard."

"He would probably shave at your request," Elizabeth reasoned.

Miss Anne waved this away. "No, no. Then I must marry him, and that would not do at all."

Elizabeth looked a little mystified at this response, but Darcy was getting impatient. "Miss Anne, we need entrance to Faerie. We were told you know where it is."

She squinted at him. "Faerie?"

"Yes. I understand there is a grotto hereabouts that provides an entrance to their land."

Miss Anne rubbed her chin thoughtfully. "I believe I am half fae."

"That is what we were told," Elizabeth said.

Darcy was beginning to doubt the woman had the wits to direct them to the nearest tree let alone the land of the fae.

Rakover made a sound like clearing his throat. "You are lucky we arrived on one of her good days. Sometimes it is difficult to have a coherent conversation with her."

"Fortunate indeed," Elizabeth murmured with a twitch of her lips.

"Miss," Darcy tried again. "If you can just tell us where the entrance is, then we will go and leave you in peace."

"What are you seeking again?" she asked.

Darcy sighed. "The entrance to Faerie."

She stared at him blankly for a minute. "Why did you not say so? It is right there." She pointed behind Darcy. He whirled around and saw an opening carved in the stone of the hill. It was recessed within a grotto, and he might have missed it altogether, but the doorway was illuminated with a faint yellow glow.

"That is the land of the fae," Miss Anne said.

CHAPTER 12

Finally, their destination! There it was, after all their meandering through the hills and asking directions of odd people who could not seem to answer a simple question. The entrance to the land of Faerie!

Darcy strode towards the opening. The faint glow, accentuated by the frame of dark purple blooms around it, so distinct from the yellow wildflowers filling the valley, drew him like a magnet.

Behind him Elizabeth bade a hurried farewell to Anne of the Hills and the dragon Rakover, but Darcy had already forgotten them. His goal was the glow, which must be the entrance to the grotto mentioned in the Library's poem, and nothing else mattered. It sang to him, called him, promised him everything.

Suddenly a hand gripped his arm. He tried to shake it off, to stop it from slowing him. Then Elizabeth was in front of him, blocking his path.

She grasped his face between her hands, none too gently, and forced him to look in her eyes. "Stop! Put your shields up. Do not let the fae song seduce you!"

What was she talking about? "Get out of my way."

"Now, William!" she snapped. "Your shields!"

It was a reflex, then, raising his shields, rather than a rational decision, but no sooner had he done so than he stiffened in shock. He was himself again. Good God, how had that happened? One moment he had been in complete control, then he had seen the glowing gate and completely lost himself. Awkwardly he said, "Ah, thank you."

She looked away, as if in embarrassment. "The siren song of Faerie can affect some people very strongly. I suggest you keep your shields firmly in place."

Keep them in place? He might never let them down again! Horror trickled through him at how easily he had been bespelled. Dealing with the strange inhabitants of these hills had helped him to put aside the seriousness of their mission, but that was no excuse. "I will not forget again."

"Good. This must be the place – yes, do you see the lily lovell blooming? Just as the spell said." He nodded, and quoted,

> *"At the mouth of the Faerie kingdom,*
> *Where the lily lovell grow*
> *In the shadow of the grotto,*
> *Those who seek must enter slow.*
> *Never bring what is familiar*
> *Lest the magic be brought low.*
> *Deep into the darkness burrow,*
> *Two speak the word the fae do know,*
> *When spoken true, both pain and sorrow*
> *From the heart away will go."*

She glanced at him. "You memorized it?"

"With Georgiana's life at stake? Of course." He stepped forward.

Elizabeth caught his arm again. "Remember, it says we must 'enter slow.'"

With a huff of frustration, he tipped his head back. "But what does that mean?"

The corners of her lips twitched. "I cannot say, except that hurrying seems unwise."

He exhaled slowly through his teeth. "You are correct, of course. We must be careful, since we will not have a second chance." But it was hard to be patient when Georgiana might be dying at that very moment. "Perhaps we should examine the opening."

But the examination revealed little, just a small shallow grotto with purple flowers, the golden glow around the entrance which still tried to tug his shields, and deep darkness within.

Hair prickled on the back of his neck. "How do we know this is not a trap? First they do not allow us our familiars, and then we must proceed in darkness."

She frowned. "The quest is designed to be difficult, but not impossible. I will go first, since I am already known to the fae."

He did not like the idea – in fact, he detested it – but he could hardly argue when he had just fallen victim to fae wiles and had to be rescued by her. Not only had he failed her in the past, but he continued to do so now. "Very well."

Darcy had followed Elizabeth through the darkness for what seemed like hours, led only by a faint glow she had conjured from her fingertips. It barely showed enough for them to be secure in their footing on the rough stone floor of the cavern beyond the grotto. At least he assumed it must be a cavern, since it was underground, but the light did not extend that far. And it would be foolish to waste their magical energy on creating additional light when they might need it more urgently later. Especially as his stores had not yet recovered from moving all those boulders to free the hermit.

And it was not only his magical stores that were depleted. The healer had managed to mend most of his injuries from the troll attack, but his ribs and the back of his skull had still ached. And that was before the ride up to Stanage Edge, the challenging climb down to the hermit's cave, clearing the rockslide, riding a dragon to find Anne of the Hills, and this long, tense, dark walk. His quarrel with Elizabeth in their room at the inn felt like weeks ago, but it had only been that morning.

Twice now they had reached a dead end, a wall of rock that could neither be climbed nor gone around, and had to retrace their steps to find another path. But now, for the first time since entering the cave, he could hear a noise other than the echoes of their footsteps, the sound of running water in the distance. Was that a smear of light far ahead? Perhaps they had finally reached their destination. Or would this be another impassable obstacle?

More endless minutes of walking, but his flagging energy revived as the distant light grew larger and brighter. Then, before he expected it, the darkness lifted, and he was standing by Elizabeth's side before a rushing river, foaming as it tore its way across a vaulted cavern. Two parallel rows of stepping stones crossed it, though he had never seen stepping stones in such a wild river before. Stepping stones were for shallow, slow-moving streams, not deep water full of wild foam. Elizabeth nodded slowly. "This is the true entrance of Faerie."

Darcy started. He thought they had been wandering in Faerie for these past hours, but he supposed the fae would not make it so easy to enter their realm.

Elizabeth caught his arm. "Wait a moment, if you do not mind. There is something I must do here before we proceed." Her fine eyes took on a distant look as she murmured some words beneath her breath. She moved her head slowly from one side to the other, as if taking in everything around them. "Hmm. Not as good as I had hoped, but not quite as bad as I feared."

"What do you mean?" he asked.

"The wall between Faerie and the mortal world. There have been unexplained breaches in it of late, and the Library asked me to examine it here. I can see some ragged spots, but the repairs Abraxas and I have made seem to be holding, at least for now."

The very idea of Elizabeth being tasked with the enormous job of stabilizing the wall shocked him. "That is quite a task."

Her mouth quirked. "It has kept me busy. But look, someone has come to meet us." She pointed across the rushing river.

On the opposite shore stood a tall, slender figure with hair that reached beyond her waist, dressed in veils of filmy silks. She had to be fae, with those pointed ears and tip-tilted eyes, and the long, narrow fingers with pointed nails. "I am the guardian of the Waters of Truth," she said in a voice that chimed, as if bells were ringing in the background. "Those who dare to cross will earn their reward."

He should not have been able to hear her over the roar of the water, but it sounded as if she was standing next to him. At least this was a concrete task. It might be a little nerve-wracking to cross that wild water on the small stones, but it was nothing he could not manage, and the river was not wide. He stepped forward to the line of stones nearest him.

Elizabeth held up her hand as if to stop him. "What is the price of crossing the river?" she asked.

The fae smiled, but it was a dangerous smile, not a welcoming one. "The price is truth, Librarian. You must cast aside your mortal lies to step into Faerie. Each truth will earn you one step."

Darcy turned to Elizabeth. "She recognizes you."

"We have met," Elizabeth said. It was not an endorsement. "A word of warning. When the fae ask for the truth, they mean the truth that is most painful to your soul. Do not try to slide by with correcting a lie you told as a child. It will not work, and the consequences may be unfortunate."

Like the test at the entrance to the Library, then, which had forced him to reveal his loss of Elizabeth. Well, that was old news now. "Very well." He walked to the right to the nearest set of stones and stepped out onto the first one. To his left, Elizabeth did the same.

Then the river changed. All the stones except the ones they stood on vanished beneath the rapids, and the river swelled behind them, making it impossible to go backwards. The fae said, "The first step is free. You must earn the next one by speaking truth. You first, Librarian. The river desires the truth of your heart."

Elizabeth closed her eyes for a moment, then reopened them, her expression stern. "Here is truth. I am proud and happy to be the Librarian, but late at night, when I am alone, I sometimes think about what I have lost to hold that position. My family, whom I see only rarely, and with whom I cannot speak of my work. The pleasure of attending an assembly with my sisters. The hope of a family of my own someday. I would make the same decision again, but there are moments when I have regrets."

A rock pushed up through the water in front of her and slid to a stop. She heaved an audible sigh of relief, stepped onto it, and turned to look at him.

The fae spoke again. "Your turn, mortal man. What is your truth?"

A truth, and he knew what it had to be, but it would not reflect well on him. Clenching his hands, he said, "When I was young, my parents determined that I would marry my cousin, Anne de Bourgh. I did not wish to marry her. She was...well, it does not matter why I hated the thought of marrying her, but I did. My parents would not listen, though, and it became an open wound between us. When Anne came of age, she went before the Patronesses of Magic, but to everyone's shock, she failed to bond with a familiar."

He paused, gathering his courage. "I saw my opportunity and broke off the betrothal, announcing that I could not marry a woman without magic. Everyone told me I was doing the right thing, putting the needs of my family first. Even my parents, who still wished for the marriage, begrudgingly agreed that I had a point. But my aunt was furious and kept demanding that I marry Anne, making my refusal a public matter and forcing me to say again and again that I could not marry her daughter because she had no magic."

He halted, not wanting to say the rest, but no stone appeared for him. The fae must not be satisfied. Somehow he had to force the rest out. "But in truth, no one would have stopped me from marrying her if I wished to. It was just an excuse I had seized upon because I did not want to marry her. It was a lie to say that was my reason for ending the betrothal, and I paid dearly for that lie. Very dearly indeed."

His face was hot, and he could not bring himself to look at Elizabeth. But the water ahead of him parted as a stepping stone appeared. He was that much closer to saving Georgiana. And perhaps, just perhaps, it might help Elizabeth understand that his refusal had not been about her.

"Your aunt," said Elizabeth in a dangerously level voice. "Was that Lady Catherine de Bourgh?"

"Yes." Obviously.

"Lady Catherine de Bourgh of the Patronesses of Magic who falsely judged me as being unable to call a familiar – and she was the mother of the woman you jilted for failing that very same test?" Her voice rose on the last words.

He winced. It did sound damning, put that way. And the stone he stood on was slowly lowering into the racing water, droplets smashing on his boots. A few inches lower, and the water would wash him away. "Yes. The very same."

The stone rose again.

Elizabeth blew out a breath through pursed lips. "I always wondered why that happened. Now I know."

He wanted to explain that his aunt would never have cheated on that test, not least because the other Patronesses would not permit it. But this was not the time, not with a raging river ready to drown them if they spoke anything with a hint of falsehood and with the cure to Georgiana's illness on the other side. If they survived this trial, he could explain it later.

If she would even speak to him then. It would be more than he deserved.

"Now you, Librarian," came the chiming voice. "Unless you no longer wish to continue."

Elizabeth straightened, not looking his way. "Here is truth. The Library entrusted me with this mission, and I have failed it because of my own weakness. My pride was injured when the Patronesses declared me lacking in magic. Instead of ignoring this obvious untruth, I have squandered the Library's power in a foolish effort to demonstrate how wrong they were. I have allowed my injured feelings to outweigh my good sense, and as a result I can no longer call on the Library." Her voice shook.

What? She was cut off from the Library? But the fae seemed to think it was true, for another stepping stone emerged from the water. Elizabeth moved to it. She was almost to the opposite shore.

And now it was his turn again, and Georgiana's life rested on his willingness to humiliate himself. "My lie trapped me, though I did not see it for years, until I fell in love with a woman who failed the same test. But everyone knew I had refused my cousin. It was still the case that it would harm my family to marry a woman without magic, but it would harm my good name far more to admit that I had been lying all those years. And so my easy excuse, my lie, cost me the woman I loved, and I have missed her every day since."

But no stone appeared. It was not enough. "Worse, my lie harmed her. I wanted nothing but to make her happy, and instead I hurt her, destroyed her prospects, and gave her reason to hate me. And I must live with that." The image of Elizabeth's face that morning at the inn, contorted in anger, flashed before him and his chest ached.

But there was the next stepping stone. He set his foot on it and moved forward with great care, as if his precarious footing on the wet, slippery surface of the rock was his greatest worry. It was easier than seeing Elizabeth's reaction.

"What is your truth, Librarian?"

Elizabeth's words were so soft that he struggled to hear them over the rushing water. "When Mr. Darcy rejected me, I could make no sense of it except that he must have been lying to me all along, pretending to love me. It hurt to lose him, very badly indeed, but what made it worse was blaming myself for being fool enough to believe him. It made me act out of anger, seeking to prove him wrong. Which I did. But the lie I told myself then was that I did not care about him anymore, that the man I thought I loved never truly existed. But love does not just stop because one wishes it would."

Now he stared at her. Could it be true? Did a part of her still care for him? But she stepped forward onto the next stone – and then onto dry land.

And turned to look at him, her chin held high and her expression unreadable.

There was only one thing he could do. "Walking away from you was a terrible mistake. Being with you these last days has only shown me how much I lost. I loved you then, and I have never stopped loving you. And that is my truth, that my heart today is even more yours than it was five years ago." He did not even need to look down to know that the next stone was there. Some truths could not be denied.

And then he was standing on the far shore, only a few feet from Elizabeth, whose fingers rubbed against her lips.

The fae held up her hand, displaying inhumanly long, slender fingers. "You have passed the test. What is your request?"

He shook himself out of his thoughts. He had almost forgotten why they were there. "My sister is bespelled by the Scottish Word. I seek an antidote for her."

Her head tilted to one side, and she seemed to study something in the far distance. "An antidote to the Scottish Word. Yes. You must go to the Field of Scarlet." She turned to Elizabeth. "And you, Librarian, what is your question?"

Elizabeth hesitated, as if she had not anticipated having this opportunity. "How do we find the Field of Scarlet?"

The fae laughed, a musical sound like the tinkling of silver bells. "Oh, no, Librarian. You must ask a question to your own benefit, not to his."

She pursed her lips and gazed around the enormous cavern, up and down and over her shoulder. In a tight voice, she said, "Then, since it is to my benefit to return to the mortal world, my question is how we can cross the river again after our quest."

Darcy looked back at the Water of Truth. All the stepping stones had vanished, and the river had swelled to at least twice its previous width. His pulse began to race.

The fae spread her hands to each side. "An easy answer – you cannot." She laughed, her hair flowing behind her as if moved by a non-existent breeze. "Did you think it was so simple, mortal? Anyone may cross and ask a question, but you cannot return the way you came. You must find your own way out of Faerie."

Darcy's heart sank. "But how?"

The fae's smile showed sharpened teeth. "You have used up your questions. Find further answers on your own." She laughed again. "Or not. It is up to you." She turned in a circle, spinning faster and faster, and vanished.

They were alone in an immense cavern in Faerie, with no map or directions. And Faerie had never been a safe place for mortals.

CHAPTER 13

General Fitzwilliam paced the length of Pemberley's grand portico in agitation, keeping his eyes to the sky. Maor had yet to return from surveying the grounds. He would be unable to rest easily until his familiar confirmed that Wickham was well and truly gone from the property.

At long last, he spotted Maor landing smoothly on the lawn. *Is there any sign of him?* Fitzwilliam asked, reaching out through the bond with his familiar.

None that I could see. And there is no trace of the thunderbird either. Good riddance, I say.

Thank you, Maor. You may return to the stables.

Maor turned her head sharply towards Fitzwilliam. *No. I shall keep watch. You should return to your charge.*

Fitzwilliam knew better than to argue with his stubborn familiar. And it would certainly be prudent to keep their guard up against Wickham.

Fitzwilliam made his way back to Georgiana's room in time to see Mrs. Reynolds emerging. The housekeeper had an expression of such bewilderment upon her face that

Fitzwilliam began to panic. "Mrs. Reynolds, what is the matter? Has Georgiana succumbed?"

The housekeeper shook her head. "She has not changed, but her familiar most certainly has. It is difficult to explain, sir. It would be better for you to see for yourself."

With that, Fitzwilliam opened the bedroom door.

Georgiana sat in her bed, propped up with pillows. At her side was not the seal familiar that Fitzwilliam was accustomed to seeing, but rather a man with pale skin, jet black hair, and golden eyes. The man was clutching Georgiana's hand and singing a strange song in a low voice. Neither had noticed Fitzwilliam's entrance.

"What is the meaning of this?" Fitzwilliam cried.

Georgiana's eyes flew to his, and her pale cheeks were stained with the deepest flush. "Richard, there is no need for alarm," Georgiana said weakly. "This is Galon, my familiar."

Fitzwilliam gaped at the pair. Surely this was impossible. Georgiana's familiar had always been an ordinary seal. Unless. . . but no. There was no record of a selkie ever becoming a familiar. Although that would explain why Wickham wanted Galon's skin – selkie skins were rumored to have fabulous magical properties.

The man stood and faced Fitzwilliam. "It is true, sir. I hope you will be able to forgive Georgiana for the deception after I have explained."

Fitzwilliam staggered to a vacant chair. This was sure to be a fascinating tale. He listened with rapt attention as Galon spoke.

"In Faerie I was a fae prince, as such I was engaged to a fae princess. It was not a love match. Fae nobles do not put much stock in such things. Life with my intended, though, was rather miserable. She was vain and power-hungry. I knew that I would never be able to be enough for her. She would always want more. Rather than face the next few centuries with such a wife, I renounced my crown. The engagement was broken off and I left for the mortal realm."

Galon took Georgiana's hand, as though drawing strength to continue. "I knew I would never be welcomed back to court after setting aside my intended and giving up my position. I was still left with my magic and my fae life-span. I had to find some way to fill my days. I never imagined that I would find it that day. But there was Georgiana, dancing in a field of woad."

"It was when I was traveling with your parents before my familiar ceremony," Georgiana explained.

Fitzwilliam nodded, remembering Georgiana describing the trip as life-changing, though no one had ever known precisely what she meant.

Galon smiled fondly at Georgiana. "I approached her, and when she offered her hand in greeting, I knew the moment I took it, that we were fated to meet. That afternoon, we conversed as though we had known each other for years. She spoke of her magic and her worries about her upcoming familiar ceremony. I told her of my past and my wish to find a purpose in the mortal realm. Her aunt and uncle called her back too soon, but Georgiana returned to the field of woad the next three days. When it was time for her to make her sojourn to London, I knew that I would do whatever it took to stay by her side."

Fitzwilliam saw Georgiana blush prettily as Galon spoke of his devotion.

"When a fae truly falls in love, it is rare and for life. I knew I needed to share mine with Georgiana." Galon said with the frankness of the fae. "So I took the form of a seal and presented myself to the Patronesses on the day of Georgiana's test. I have no doubt she could have bonded with any of the available familiars, but I was blessed when she chose me."

"As was I," Georgiana said, her voice soft, her eyes shining with affection. "I am sorry for the years of deception, Cousin. I thought that if you or my brother ever discovered Galon's secret that you would send him away. I couldn't bear the thought of losing him."

It was a sensible fear, to be sure.

"I know that humans have a strict notion of propriety," Galon said. "Allow me to assure you that nothing untoward has occurred between myself and Georgiana. It was our intention to reveal the truth to you and her brother – and then she crossed paths with that dreadful cad."

Fitzwilliam nodded. "Georgiana is a responsible young lady. If she trusts you, then I will trust you as well. You have certainly been a faithful familiar to her. But now I must ask, what does Wickham want with your skin?"

Georgiana and Galon exchanged a glance.

"I doubt that he wants the skin for himself. Georgiana has informed me that Wickham is not considered to be a powerful mage."

Fitzwilliam snorted. "I should say not. He did not even have enough magic to bond with a familiar."

"Then we are to assume that Wickham has a powerful benefactor, one who helped him curse Georgiana with the Scottish Word. I fear that the benefactor must be a fae. I am afraid that I angered many members of the fae court when I left Faerie. If Wickham delivers the skin to a fae, that fae will be able to control me. They can force me to abandon Georgiana. I am sure Wickham would be heavily compensated for delivering such a prize."

It made a good deal of sense. Wickham was far from gifted when it came to magic. And it was perfectly within his character to resort to dark magic to get what he wanted.

"Do you think Wickham would lift the curse if you gave him your skin?" Fitzwilliam asked.

Galon nodded. What little color was left in Georgiana's face drained away.

"We cannot trust Wickham. If you surrender your skin, what will stop him from fleeing without lifting the curse?" Georgiana said.

"I intend to use a fae vow to compel him to lift the curse *before* he gets the skin." Galon declared. Then with a sad look to Georgiana, he said, "It will save your life. I am willing to make the sacrifice."

"We must trust that my brother and Elizabeth will be successful in their quest for the cure," Georgiana said.

"My dear, Faerie can be a treacherous place. I know you have faith in your brother's abilities, but the longer he is gone, the less likely it is that he will return in time with the cure." Galon took Georgiana's hand in his. "I cannot help but feel responsible for what has happened to you. Please, allow me to make it right."

"No," Georgiana said, her jaw set stubbornly in a remarkable imitation of her brother. "They will return—" Her words were cut off as she suddenly convulsed in pain. Her breath became short and panting, and her eyes closed.

Fitzwilliam and Galon watched in terror as her fit continued. After a few agonizing minutes, she collapsed back against the pillows. Her breathing was still labored, and her eyes remained closed.

"Georgiana—" Galon said, his voice tinged with fear.

"I cannot open my eyes. I fear I may not have much time left." Georgiana's expression was pained, her voice terribly weak. "Richard, please, do not permit Galon to do something foolish. I would rather die than allow Wickham to get what he wants." These were not the brash words of a young girl but the words of a woman resigned to her fate. It nearly broke Fitzwilliam's heart to hear them. However, it was not a promise Fitzwilliam could make, not with Georgiana's life on the line. He said nothing.

"Galon, sing to me, so that I might rest," Georgiana said faintly.

Fitzwilliam excused himself as Galon began to sing. He waited in the hall for a quarter of an hour before Galon emerged, a determined expression on his face. "I am going to retrieve my skin, then I will find the blackguard and make a deal. Will you aid me?"

"Are you certain this is wise? Georgiana will not thank you for going against her wishes."

"I would rather Georgiana be alive and furious with me than to see her in a cursed sleep for the rest of her days," Galon said. "You need not help me, but if you try to stop me, I will be forced to use my magic to restrain you."

Years in the military had taught Fitzwilliam to recognize a losing battle. "Very well. Where is your skin?"

"It is hidden some distance away. I will require the use of your familiar."

Fitzwilliam followed Galon out of the house. *Maor, I have a task for you.* The hippogriff appeared before them only minutes later. To Fitzwilliam's surprise, Maor needed no further convincing to allow Galon to ride her.

"If Georgiana shows further signs of weakness, send word to Maor. I will return as soon as I am able," Galon said.

Fitzwilliam gave his word and watched as Maor and Galon took off into the night.

CHAPTER 14

*T*he cavern was dark and dank after the fae disappeared. For a few awful moments, there was nothing but the sound of water dripping from the stalactites and hitting the ground.

Plop. Plop. Plop.

No map, Darcy's mind tapped out in time with the drops. *Map. Map.* There had to be one, did there not? They were not the only humans to find their way to Faerie and return home again. There must be a way to do it.

Darcy chanced a glance at Elizabeth, who had at least worked her magic to light the way again. Her countenance was calm, serious, but the flicker of panic in her fine eyes nearly broke him.

Love does not just stop because one wishes it would.

Her truth rang in his ears. He had not lost her love. But he had lost her. Worse. He had abandoned her. If anything were to break him, it would be that.

Having witnessed the courage of both Georgiana and Elizabeth, Darcy could not allow himself to falter now. It was his quest to save his sister that had brought Elizabeth to Faerie. It was therefore his duty to determine a way to return her home, even if that home would never be Pemberley. Even if he could not follow her back.

He had not been worthy of Elizabeth. But he swore to himself that he would be.

Darcy studied the cave as his eyes adjusted to the dark, seeking a way out. Finding none, he made his way down to a pool of water and discovered a flat place to sit by the edge.

It was foolish to think about a map for Faerie, as the place altered completely from one day to the next. The landscape flickered, faded, reappeared. A mountain might be in the east one day and the west the next. Convenient for the fae, less so for the unfortunate human traveler.

"Elizabeth," he called, stepping back up the rocky slope to her. "Let us rest for a while and consider what must be done."

She nodded but ignored the hand he offered to help guide her down. He left it extended in case she took a false step.

Once she had safely descended, Darcy cupped his hands together and dipped them in the water. Elizabeth knelt and did likewise, lifting the cool liquid to her mouth and drinking deeply.

When they were both settled, Darcy drew his knees up and set his chin atop them. "The fae cannot cast magic without leaving a little of it behind."

Elizabeth nodded. "I am not sure whether that helps us, however, without knowing what it is meant to do."

"I was hoping that there might be some sort of magic remaining in this cavern." He turned his head in her direction.

She cocked her head to one side and met his gaze. "I suppose it might. The Fae do enjoy placing the answer for perplexing questions right under one's nose . . . but where even to begin?"

"I thought, perhaps—" he hesitated. Was he offering hope where he ought not? "I thought perhaps the spell."

"We have exhausted the Library's poem, have we not?" Elizabeth did not sound as though she disapproved of the idea, though she was certainly not convinced.

"Possibly," he said. "However, I was considering the line, 'deep into the darkness burrow.'"

Elizabeth was silent for a few moments as she pondered it. "Do you think it possible that we should go *deeper* into the cavern? I know the fae can be maddeningly oppositional, but it is possible the cavern may simply close around us. At least here we have water to drink."

He nodded. "There is that risk. Yet there is a greater risk in not acting at all." He paused. "If I could walk ahead to be sure before asking you to join me, I would, but with the way in which Faerie transforms on a whim . . ."

"No, we must remain together," Elizabeth told him firmly. "There must be a way out."

There must be. And he would find it.

"My feet hurt, and I am tired," Elizabeth said with a sigh. "I am willing to linger here a short time before we attempt to find our way outside."

Mr. Darcy nodded. "We have been setting a prodigious pace."

"I know you are anxious to free Georgiana. Your haste is understandable and necessary."

They sat in the dark, each lost in their own thoughts.

Eventually, Elizabeth determined to address the looming issue between them. They had been required, each of them, to speak the painful truth. She had suffered, and now she knew that he had, too. That he still did. She gathered her dignity around her like a cloak and began.

"William," she said, "I feel we must discuss what was said as we crossed the stepping stones."

He was silent for a time before responding to her. "What is left to say, Elizabeth? I treated you cruelly, and I will pay for it the rest of my life. I have no chance to requite my love for you or yours for me, because to do so, you would have to give up being the Librarian."

His tone was flat, indifferent. Another woman might not fathom how intricately his pain was intertwined with every word. She shared that hurt, she yearned to ease it, and yet this was not enough.

"I *need* to understand what happened that day. Not only your behavior, but also why my magic did not function as it should. You can clearly see that I have all the magic we presumed, and more. There is no *honest* way that I could have failed to bond with a familiar."

William stood and began to pace. Elizabeth held one of her hands down near the floor so that he could see where he was walking. The last thing they needed was for him to rein-jure himself.

"While I do not doubt that something was terribly wrong with your examination, Elizabeth, I cannot believe that my aunt intentionally tampered with it. She knows and respects the laws and traditions of the familiar ceremony. She always has."

Elizabeth shook her head. "You were never planning to marry a woman being tested before. A woman who was a significant threat to all her hopes of an alliance with you."

He laced his hands behind his head and looked up at the cavern's ceiling. "It would go against everything she ever taught me."

"I am sorry for your disappointment," Elizabeth said, contrite. "Truly, I am. But with the evidence of my magic, you must face the possibility that your aunt was willing to bend the law to have her way. After all, it worked, did it not? She did not wish someone like me to wed her nephew, and in fact, you did not. No one has ever accused her of prevaricating. No, the shame of that day has been my portion."

His expression was a horrible thing to witness, anguish adding years to his countenance. She could see, here in the shadows of the cavern, how terribly he would age if he did not shed the burden of his guilt.

"You did not deserve it," he told her.

"I did not," she agreed. After a moment of hesitation, she continued. "You said, 'My heart is even more yours today than it was five years ago.'"

"It is my truth."

"Then while it is true that I did not deserve the scorn heaped upon me that day, that I did not deserve to be abandoned . . ."

William's face contorted in pain.

"I am sorry, William, but I must say it. You abandoned me when you should have stood beside me and demanded another test without your aunt's involvement."

"Yes," he said hoarsely. "I should have, and I condemned us both when I walked away."

"You did," she replied. "And yet despite that, you did not deserve what has come, any more than I did myself."

His eyes rose to meet hers. "What?"

"You have not deserved to suffer for these past five years." She tipped her head slightly and said, lightly, "Although it speaks sadly of my own character, I am gratified to hear that you did, William. I should have thought less of you had it been an easy thing for you to live with. But now . . ." She pressed her lips together and stood. She dusted off her skirts, straightened her shoulders, and waited for him to turn around. When he did, she stepped close enough to hold his gaze. "Now I forgive you. And you must forgive yourself."

"Elizabeth," he said, her name lifting in the air like a song.

She sighed. "I have more to say, sir."

Mr. Darcy frowned. "More than this? It is everything to have your forgiveness, Elizabeth."

She saw no way for them to have a future together, but she could do this for him – she could help lift the blinders from his eyes, help him prevent any future attempts to coerce him. "This will bring you more pain, I am afraid, but I must ask you a question."

He waited, which Elizabeth took as an invitation to proceed. "Have you never considered that there might be a connection between what has happened to Georgiana and your aunt's behavior all those years ago?"

"What do you mean?"

She laughed quietly and shook her head. "Clearly not. Your aunt has never relinquished her dreams of a grand match for you, has she?"

Darcy pinched the bridge of his nose. "She has demanded I wed my cousin Anne now that Georgiana is ill. But even if I thought well of Anne, which I do not, I could not marry another." He turned away. "I am still in love with you."

They stood silently in the dark as they contemplated the impossibility of it all.

"William," Elizabeth said gently, "please, for your own good, at least *consider* this. If your aunt tampered with my ability to bond with a familiar five years ago and finds herself still waiting for you to acquiesce, she may not be above taking advantage of Georgiana's illness for her own ends. Your aunt has never had your best interests in mind, only her own."

"I cannot believe . . ." The words were not heated or disbelieving now, but they were still not what she wished to hear.

"Stop," Elizabeth said sharply. "How can you say you love me when you defend her and not me? I beg you to consider the evidence. She wants you to marry her daughter. She knew we were betrothed. And she was in charge of the test that I failed even though shortly afterward I bonded with Abraxas." She paused. "Were this my mother would you think it possible?"

At his incredulous look, she grunted, exasperated. "If my mother was an intelligent schemer rather than an emotional one, would it be possible?"

"It would be," he admitted at last.

Elizabeth took a deep breath to steady herself. "Then it is not impossible that your aunt has done this. Your aunt strikes me as someone who values money, but even more, she desires power – and are not those the motives of nearly every war in history?"

"Lady Catherine already has both," he responded, barely whispering the words.

"When does anybody believe they have sufficient quantities?" Elizabeth looked away. "The Lady Patronesses wield considerable power by influencing the granting of familiars. The Library watches such developments, and it has not escaped our notice that your aunt has grown in power even among the Patronesses. She has become so significant that she moves in the first circles of the *ton*. Few dare oppose her. Why is it so difficult to believe she would use her power to keep you from marrying a woman of whom she did not approve?

ELIZABETH'S WORDS rang in Darcy's ears and echoed against the walls. Why indeed? Could it be that he had fallen so neatly into a trap laid by his aunt? Had his own blood conspired against him and Georgiana? Why could he not accept that five years ago? Why did he still have such difficulty accepting it now?

Because he was proud.

That was the truth. He had been offered a choice at the familiar ceremony all those years ago. His pride or Elizabeth's hand? Tell them all he had lied for years and marry a woman without magic, or just walk away?

He had selected pride, just as his aunt had known he would. And in doing so, he had set all of this in motion.

It was too much to bear. "I need some time to consider this," he said gruffly. "Come, let us push on."

Wisely, Elizabeth did not press him, but her vexation at his dismissal was clear in the set of her shoulders. Darcy wished to speak more, he truly did. But he was not certain he could do so coherently, and losing his composure would do neither of them any good.

They picked their way down, down, down a dark, narrow, sloping path. Eventually, Elizabeth's light flickered and vanished. She was weary, but there was no safe place to stop and rest. Darcy's ribs ached and his head throbbed, but he thought about what Georgiana was suffering and doggedly placed one foot in front of the other.

It was at least two hours later when his skin began to tingle with magic. Fae magic. "There it is," he murmured, just as the narrow path they traversed dipped down into a wider, flatter space. He moved into the chamber and tipped his head back. The ceiling was as high as in a cathedral, though there were no windows to let in the light. He closed his eyes, focused on absorbing some of the magical energy remaining here, and began to draw in the air. The symbols lit up the cavern, washing over them in a blue light.

This was definitely the place.

"What is that?" Elizabeth asked curiously.

"A magic resurrection spell," he said wearily as he etched another symbol in the air.

"I thought resurrection spells were forbidden, just like love spells."

"Resurrection is a rather grand name for it. It merely allows us to see magic that has been spent."

He completed the final figure with a flourish and watched, satisfied, as the blue writing transformed itself into flames that leapt up the cavern walls, crackling with energy.

"What is happening?" Elizabeth asked, raising her voice to be heard over the noise.

"First, the flames will burn away whatever conceals the traces of magic that were used here recently," he explained. "Then, when the flames die away, we will see a shadow of what has been."

From the beginning of their journey, Darcy had been more a hindrance than a help. He had been injured straight off, and it was Elizabeth who had ultimately stopped the troll and found help. He had even required her assistance to rescue the hermit from the collapse of his cave.

No magic indeed.

He would focus on his anger about the Patronesses later. For now, it was time that he began to be of some use. And this, this he could do. The flames took longer than he had expected to cease burning, but in the end, it revealed two items: a map and a compass.

The map was not made of paper – it was glowing in a light as yellow as the sun and emblazoned upon the rough stone wall. There was a thin, straight line down the center.

Darcy stepped back so that he could read it, and he could see Elizabeth, bathed in the yellow light, stepping back with him.

He used the river they had crossed as a way to locate their position on the map and etched the entire thing into his mind.

"How are we to find our way," Elizabeth said, frustrated and in distress, "if we cannot take the map with us?"

"I will remember it," he told her gently.

He impressed the map's hills and valleys upon his mind and studied the compass closely. It was pointing true north, and as long as he recalled its orientation he could use it to help find their way.

She waved a hand at the wall. "You can recall all of that?"

He nodded. "My education required that I commit many spells to memory. I find that I can now memorize many things with ease if I purposely impress them upon my mind."

Elizabeth looked up at him with admiration.

Darcy impressed this image of Elizabeth upon his mind, too. He would have need of it when their quest was done.

"What is that?" Elizabeth asked, motioning to the ghostly item on a stone near the map.

"It is a compass," he told her. He oriented himself in that direction and wrote two words in the air. They shimmered in blue and then disappeared without the flames that the first spell required.

"What did you write?" Elizabeth inquired.

"True north," he told her.

"Another spell?"

He nodded. "We may not be able to use the compass that was here, but if we know where north is, we can use the map and the landmarks to find our way to . . ." he closed his eyes to be certain it was all there . . . "the Scarlet Field."

"But how will we use either of these things when we cannot find our way outside?" she inquired.

Darcy smiled. "Open," he wrote at the base of the wall, where the map was divided. The walls rolled back far enough that one person might walk through at a time. He offered Elizabeth a little bow and motioned her forward.

She blinked at the sudden brightness. "That was very well done, Mr. Darcy," she said teasingly. "Perhaps you have a little magic after all."

CHAPTER 15

*G*alon held firm to the belief that he would return with his skin quickly enough to save Georgiana from a tragic fate.

When he had left his life in Faerie behind, he had no idea if he would be able to find a new life purpose. But then he met Georgiana as she danced in a meadow of woad. She had unwittingly enchanted him with her beauty and generous heart. In that moment, Galon had become hers.

She had trusted him at once, though he had appeared out of a magical cave. She had confided to him about her fear of her test with a group of magical women, terrified that she would not be magical enough to create a bond with a familiar. Galon knew then that he would take the form of a selkie and create a bond with her. Since the day of her test, Georgiana had filled his life with light, love, and laughter. Not even the dangers of skirmishes at sea could make him regret his departure from Faerie.

Still, Galon could not fight the belief that Georgiana had been cursed because of one of his enemies in the fae court. After all, the Scottish Word was of fae origin. Wickham had needed help to obtain it and the other spells. Galon would force Wickham to reveal the identity of his benefactor when he saw him again.

Your heart is so heavy that I am surprised we have not fallen from the sky. Maor's voice was imperious, and yet Galon thought he could detect a hint of concern.

Georgiana would not be on the brink of death were it not for me, Galon said.

Indeed not. She likely would have perished at sea were it not for the bond and the strength she received from it. You forget that I have seen what difference a familiar bond can make in times of war.

Perhaps there was some truth to that, Galon admitted. But someone had caused Georgiana to suffer, and Galon began to wonder about the identity of Wickham's benefactor. Who would be cruel and petty enough to curse an innocent young lady? A gnawing sensation took hold of him as Galon remembered the day he had broken his engagement. Princess Alaine's vow of vengeance had been uttered with hysteric determination, but Galon had not taken it seriously, convinced that Alaine was simply raving in anger.

Because of his naivete, Georgiana might be doomed to suffer for the rest of her days. If she survived this, Galon would make it up to her. He would finally propose. There had not been a marriage between a fae and a human in decades, but Galon had already done so much to flout tradition.

Land on the cliffside, Galon silently instructed the hippogriff, who dove gracefully, her wings cutting through the night air.

Galon slid from his mount and surveyed the face of the cliff. A crack ran vertically down the middle, jagged and rough. Galon ran his fingers along it and the rock melted away to reveal an entrance to a hidden alcove.

He stepped into the gloomy hiding place, igniting the torches set into the stone with a casual flick of his hand. His selkie skin was hanging there, gleaming and safe from those who would wish to steal it. Now Galon would offer it willingly in order to save the one he loved so dearly.

A great gust of wind whistled through the small cave, creating gooseflesh on the back of Galon's neck. He turned only to see Wickham sliding off a majestic thunderbird. He entered the cave as lightning lit the sky.

"I see you have come to your senses," Wickham drawled. "Surrender your skin to me now and I will gladly lift the curse."

"How did you find me?" Galon demanded.

"I have been keeping watch over Pemberley, hoping that you would lead me to your skin. Your foolish love makes you predictable. My benefactor suspected that you would stop at nothing to save the little chit, even if it meant sacrificing yourself."

"And who is this benefactor?" Galon asked.

"Someone you never should have crossed," Wickham said with a grin. "Had you married Alaine, then little Georgiana would not be suffering."

Galon paled. So Alaine had been serious when she made that vow of vengeance. Why, oh why, had he not taken her at her word? Galon cursed himself for failing to protect Georgiana from the scorned fae princess. Knowing now who was truly after the skin, Galon could not surrender it. This went beyond the possibility of Galon being compelled to return to Faerie. If Alaine was seeking revenge, Georgiana would never be safe. With the skin, Alaine could order him to slay Georgiana. It would be Alaine's idea of justice.

"If you cure Georgiana, I can protect you from Alaine. And I will see to it that you receive a hefty sum in payment," Galon said, hoping to find a way out of this predicament.

Wickham grinned. "Very well. Let us return to Pemberley, and I will save the little chit. You can pay me what I deserve and you will never have to see me again."

Galon was desperate enough to believe him. He wrapped his skin around himself like a cloak and strode out of the cave, forgetting that one should never turn their back upon an enemy.

It happened very quickly. Galon felt the blade of a dagger against his neck. "Surrender your skin. I have more than gold at stake. If I fail to deliver your skin to Alaine, my life will be taken, which is far more important than Georgiana Darcy and her generous dowry."

Galon placed his hand against his captor and cast a conflagration spell. Wickham's tailcoat ignited, and the blade fell away. As Wickham tried unsuccessfully to douse the magical flames, Galon mounted Maor and urged her to return to Pemberley.

What of the scoundrel? Were you not prepared to make a deal with him? Maor dove from the cliffside with graceful ease.

Galon spurred her on. *There is more at play here than I realized. The one truly behind Georgiana's curse will not be satisfied with Georgiana succumbing to the Scottish Word. I must return to the fae court to see that she is punished for her crimes.*

Maor increased her speed. Galon would have to fetch his royal seal from Pemberley to return in peace to the fae court. He prayed that Georgiana could hold on long enough for Darcy and the Librarian to return. As much as Galon did not like leaving Georgiana's fate to chance, the success of the quest was now her best hope for recovery.

Suddenly, a bolt of lightning illuminated the night sky. From the strike emerged a brilliant thunderbird. Galon swallowed hard. He had underestimated Wickham.

The despicable cad, now only in shirtsleeves and

breeches, sat astride the enormous gold and silver bird and urged it to give chase.

I will not be outstripped by a creature from the Americas. Maor's tone was disdainful as she dove closer to the trees that dotted the land. Maor wove through the rugged Derbyshire landscape with surprising agility. Galon was forced to cling for dear life. His selkie skin protected him from magic, but he could still lose his seat and suffer grave injuries.

Lightning struck one of the tall trees, causing it to crack and fall. Maor dodged it by mere inches. Wickham's curses sounded in time with the thunder that followed.

This will not do. I will have to attack. Maor declared after several failed evasive maneuvers.

Galon thought this a foolhardy notion, but he was unaccustomed to airborne skirmishes. He would have to yield to Maor's greater knowledge of battle.

Maor flew higher, rising into the clouds until Wickham and his thunderbird were barely visible. Then, without warning, Maor dove. The hippogriff struck the thunderbird with incredible force. The beast cried out as Maor's razor talons dug into the flesh of its back.

Wickham was unseated from his mount. He screamed indecipherable orders to the thunderbird as he plummeted to the ground below.

Maor, however, did not emerge unscathed. Lightning lit the sky again, and the thunderbird disappeared. The lightning struck Maor's flank, causing the hippogriff to plunge toward a craggy cliff. Galon acted fast and caused foliage to erupt from the cracks of the cliffside, cushioning their landing.

Galon was thrown from Maor, colliding with the springy foliage dangerously near the edge of the cliff. On shaking legs, he made his way back to the hippogriff. He stroked the colorful feathers of her neck and murmured the words of a healing spell. She would need to rest for a short time before returning to Pemberley. But Wickham had not bested them.

~

FITZWILLIAM WAS SLUMPED in the chair by the fire watching over his young cousin as she murmured incoherently in her sleep. His eyelids drooped with tiredness, but he would not fall asleep at his post.

Lightning flashed, illuminating Georgiana's darkened bedroom, followed by a nearly deafening rumble of thunder. Georgiana whimpered in fright but still did not stir.

Fitzwilliam reached out through his mental connection with Maor. *Where are you?*

We were detained by Wickham. We will return shortly. Meet us on the lawn.

Fitzwilliam gazed at his cousin, who had begun to cry out for Galon. Fitzwilliam prayed that she would have the strength to fight the curse a little longer.

True to her word, Maor and Galon landed smoothly on the lawn a quarter of an hour later, looking ragged and beaten down. Fitzwilliam ran to meet them. "What happened to you?"

Galon winced as he dismounted. "Wickham followed me to my hiding place. He pursued us and his beast attacked Maor when I would not surrender my skin."

"Do you mean to tell me that you forfeited Georgiana's chance to be cured?" Fitzwilliam accused.

Galon's expression was grim. "I discovered the identity of Wickham's benefactor. Even if Darcy and the Librarian return with a cure, Georgiana will not be safe until the threat is dispatched. I must return to Faerie. Alaine must be punished."

"Who exactly is this Alaine?" Fitzwilliam asked.

"The powerful fae princess whom I was supposed to marry. It appears that she has never forgiven me for setting her aside. Even now, she might be trying to thwart Darcy and the Librarian."

"We cannot leave Georgiana unprotected," Fitzwilliam declared. "Maor and I will go."

"But I must report Alaine's crimes to the Faerie court. They would not consent to meet with a human."

"Allow me to be your emissary, Galon. Georgiana would not want you to leave her. She was crying out for you as she slept."

Galon appeared torn, but eventually nodded. "I will write a letter for you to take to Faerie. My royal seal is in Georgiana's room. Present my sealed letter to a fae and you will be brought to the king."

Fitzwilliam, Galon, and Maor made their way back to Georgiana's room. Fitzwilliam was the first to notice the change. The fire had died in the hearth and the room was icy. Georgiana was no longer muttering in her sleep. Instead, she resembled a masterfully carved statue. The color had drained from her complexion.

Galon ran to her side and uttered her name with heartbroken urgency. Georgiana made no reply.

CHAPTER 16

*M*r. Darcy stopped short, his brow furrowed.

"What is wrong?" Elizabeth's stomach clenched. Were they lost already? Every other time she had been to the Faerie Realm, it had been with the Library to guide her and Abraxas at her side. Could she and Mr. Darcy possibly do this on their own?

"This outcropping was not on the map." Mr. Darcy cocked his head as he examined it. "We will need to go around it, but the shape of the rocks beyond it means it will push us too far to either the left or the right. Leaving the path marked on the map makes me nervous."

Elizabeth suddenly remembered her last trip through the realm. Abraxas had sometimes told her to close her eyes as she walked along the path. Abraxas!

Abraxas? she called.

There was no response. Was he busy? But he always responded, even if it was to tell her he could not speak at the moment.

Abraxas! she called again, on the verge of panic. And then . . . she remembered.

They were in Faerie. And Faerie was a realm unto itself. The wall that protected the human world from the world of the fae also kept the two realms separate. It must also block Abraxas from being able to speak with her.

Fighting off fear and the searing pain of being cut off from her dearest partner, Elizabeth tried to focus on their task ahead. Abraxas had asked her to close her eyes sometimes as they walked through Faerie . . . perhaps it was because her sight would have misled her.

"I think we go straight through."

"Straight . . . through?"

She took a breath and nodded. "It is the Faerie Realm, after all. Things are not always as they seem."

"Very well, then."

He held out his arm, and Elizabeth reluctantly took it, although walking arm in arm seemed more suited to leisurely walks through the garden than hiking through the Faerie Realm.

Elizabeth held her breath as they strode forward directly into the wall of rock and dirt, wincing as she half expected to slam into it. But it dissolved as they stepped through like cool mist on a foggy day, and then they were on the other side.

They gasped in unison.

"Well." Mr. Darcy turned to look over his shoulder, shaking his head. "I suppose I should have expected such things in the Faerie Realm. No wonder humans rarely make it out alive."

At that sobering thought, Elizabeth took a steadying breath and straightened her back. They would make it through. They had to. Georgiana was counting on the cure, and the world needed Elizabeth to return to her role as the Librarian. And Mr. Darcy . . . she could not think of that now.

A sudden deep rumbling came from her left. Elizabeth clung to Mr. Darcy's arm while they both stumbled, as much to help him as to keep from falling. The quaking had not come from the land beneath them, though, but from the side. The wall!

"What was that?" Mr. Darcy asked once the shaking stopped. "Should we stop, do you think?"

"No, but . . . I will let you guide me as we walk for a few minutes. I'm concerned that that came from the wall – the human side showed some damage, as I expected and as Abraxas and I have been fighting to fix, but I would like to see how it looks from the Faerie side.

"Of course." He supported her arm and took a slow step forward.

Trusting in Mr. Darcy to lead her straight, she muttered a few words under her breath and blinked slowly, allowing her vision to blur as she changed her focus to see the ambient magic around her.

The realm practically sparkled with magic, which was not unexpected. But it was the wall she needed to see, and so she swung her gaze back and forth, trying to catch a glimpse of it at the edge of her vision.

And there it was. The sparkles coalesced into something far more ethereal and less defined than the wall appeared on the human side, but a wall it was.

This section of the wall showed more weaknesses than she had seen on the part she had examined when they first arrived in Faerie. *Oh, this was not good!* There were stretches where it was almost gossamer thin, and others with small rips and tears. In some places, the tears were large and gaping, torn almost as if something had forced its way through.

She swallowed, realizing just how large some of those tears were, and the size of the creatures that must have made them. That dragon, the one that had chased Rakover . . . had one of these tears been from it? And what about Rakover himself? Kind as he seemed, surely he could not have always lived in the human world undetected. That troll that had attacked them on the road? Had he, too, pushed through a weak spot?

She could see some of the patches from the human side, her attempts at repair with Abraxas's and the Library's help. There were many patches, but even she could see how futile they were compared to so very many holes. Was it an impossible task?

Mr. Darcy sucked in a quick breath, and Elizabeth realized that she had tightened her hold on his arm in her worry and frustration. She relaxed it quickly, glancing up at his serious face as he looked ahead.

There was nothing she could do about the wall now. She and Mr. Darcy had made it to the Faerie Realm. Surely they would find the cure soon, and then she could return to her work. She would have to find a way to patch faster. If only she and the Library could figure out what was destroying the wall and make it stop! She might never catch up at this rate, not alone.

But for now, she had to keep her mind on their quest. The Faerie Realm was too tricky a place to allow herself to be distracted, and only by finishing this quest could she return to her duty. They had to find the cure – and quickly.

The path ahead meandered off to the left, but Mr. Darcy continued straight, following the directions he had memorized. From the crunching beneath their feet, they continued along a packed dirt path, although it looked as though they were cutting straight through a field overgrown with tall grasses.

"This may be the oddest experience of my life," Elizabeth mused, trying to distract herself from her worries. "I have walked along lochs in winter and batted away monstrous insects in jungles at the Library's bidding, but I have never walked through rocks that do not exist or followed a path that can be felt but not seen." Her stomach gave a sudden lurch. "Or perhaps I did, and the Library concealed it from me. I have been here before, but Abraxas was with me and the Library acted as guide."

"I would not be surprised if the Library could call even the Faerie Realm to order." Mr. Darcy's smile was fond. "It is a powerful force in itself."

Elizabeth smiled. "That it is. I am glad you have the talent of memorizing maps. As we both know," she said, giving him a sly look, "I never had a governess, and my father never taught me to read maps. Probably he worried I would attempt to follow one for an adventure and find myself in Essex."

"Knowing you, I would not have taken the risk." Darcy patted her arm, and she laughed.

"I see! I thought you were being gentlemanly in offering your arm, but now I see you are just trying to avoid my wandering off."

Darcy smiled at her, but his eyes were ahead of them, and the crease in his brow had reappeared.

"What is wrong?"

"Well, it has occurred to me...the next landmark we are to see is a hollow tree, at least according to the map. But after that outcropping that was not really there . . .What if the hollow tree does not really exist, or if it is masked by some magic to look like a pond or mountain or field?"

Elizabeth bit her lip. In the Faerie Realm, anything was possible. Was it not?

But wait. If the landmarks could change, how could a map be any use at all? Was it nothing more than a prank by malicious fae?

Before she could speak, Mr. Darcy was already shaking his head. "No, it cannot be. The hollow tree was one of the landmarks on the map, and the outcropping was not. I believe that the map marked only those things that do not change, otherwise what good would the map be? We go directly from the cave through the hollow tree and turn left at the rock that looks like a bull. Then the Field of Scarlet should appear on our right after we pass a few hills. There may be other things along the way, but I believe those landmarks will hold firm."

Elizabeth had her doubts, but she kept silent. The Library would not have sent her on an impossible quest, and therefore it made sense that there was some way through it . . . and a map that did not seem to fit the landscape was just the sort of thing the fae would enjoy.

It was a relief to find the hollow tree exactly as described – a massive tree as tall as the redwoods the Library had once shown her in New Spain. The bottom of the tree was split, leaving an opening wide and tall enough for a carriage to drive through, although the split was so natural that it was as if it had grown that way. Of course, this was the Faerie Realm. Perhaps it had.

The bull-shaped rock and hills were similarly straightforward, and it seemed almost impossibly easy that they should find themselves standing before a field of scarlet pimpernels glowing as brightly as an orange sunset.

"This must be it," Elizabeth breathed. "Are these the cure?" She reached for the Library's book but recalled at the last moment it was useless. *Abraxas, I think we are almost at the cure!*

He did not answer. Elizabeth remembered with a pang that her connection with him was gone.

Darcy pointed mutely. There was somebody in the field. "Pardon me!" he called.

The fae stood up and turned to face them. His bright blue hair contrasted starkly with the field of orange before him. His clothes shimmered despite their muted hues of soft greens and browns. Gardening clothes for a fae, perhaps.

"Ah," he said mildly. "Visitors! Illustrious visitors! Your Eminence." He bowed his head slightly in Elizabeth's direction. "Come, ask me anything you wish!"

Elizabeth bit her lip. Questions, then, would come at a price.

"My sister lies dying of the Scottish Word curse," Mr. Darcy said boldly. "We seek the cure."

Statements, not questions. Good, he was clever.

The fae raised his eyebrows. They were pink to match his hair. But had his hair not been blue a moment ago? "You have been sent to the right place. You must have gained favor with the fae." He tilted his head. "These flowers are the only known cure to the Scottish Word. You need one, and here they are. Simple. And yet not."

"There are thousands of them here. It does seem simple." Too simple, really. But Elizabeth did not dare ask a question. The spell had led them to the Faerie Realm and the cave, but not beyond. Was that because the way the curse was cast dictated the cure?

The fae laughed, shaking his yellow-green hair out of his eyes. Elizabeth was sure that it was changing color before their eyes, but she could not see it doing so. "Thousands? Hardly. A dozen, perhaps." He cocked his head, his hair now a gleaming orange. "I must away. I shall leave you to find your cure. Good luck. Perhaps."

∾

DARCY STARED at the field of flowers. Thousands upon thousands stretched across the field, and they were to find just the right one? No, there were perhaps a dozen, but how were they to know which ones were real? Were the rest false in some way?

He took a cautious step and touched a flower. It felt authentic. The petals were soft, the leaves firm. It did not feel like the silk flowers he had seen ladies wear on their hats. But perhaps the fae had more realistic artificial flowers?

Elizabeth gasped, and he turned to see. She bent low over one of the flowers, examining it closely. "I think I know what he meant!" she said excitedly. "They have six petals!"

He looked at a nearby flower, puzzled. "Yes, they do." But what did that mean?

"Scarlet pimpernels have only five!"

He shook his head, bemused. "Are you certain?" He had seen the flowers before of course, mostly on trips to his Scottish estate, but he had never considered the number of petals before.

"Yes. I think these flowers are the false ones, and the true flowers have five petals."

"But . . . is it possible that these are not scarlet pimpernels at all, but some other flower of the Fae Realm?" He thought back. "I do not recall the fae giving them a name."

"That in itself may have been a clue," she said thoughtfully. "But, look. Do you see the shape of this leaf? It has many veins that branch off a single thicker vein. My father has a book called the *Genera Plantarum*, and it describes plants as one of two types. Plants with leaves like this are dicotyledons, which have petals in multiples of four or five. It should not have six petals. These are wrong."

Darcy was not sure he followed, but he believed her. Not for the first time, Darcy thought the Library had chosen well. Elizabeth loved to learn more than anybody else he knew.

The petals were wrong, therefore the plants were wrong. They were not true scarlet pimpernels.

"So all we need to do is to scour this field for a flower with five petals?" He shaded his eyes as he looked across the field.

Miss Elizabeth drooped. "An impossible task. Or, rather, it is possible, but we do not have much time. We must find it quickly."

Darcy blanched. Georgiana! What if, after all of this, they returned to Pemberley to find they were too late?

They could not be too late.

Elizabeth's movements were jerky, frantic, as she looked from one flower to another, and Darcy felt a sudden sympathy for her. They had to hurry, but the task was best accomplished with a clear mind and a cool head.

He spoke softly as he began, his eyes moving quickly from flower to flower. "I am rather good at this." It might sound like boasting, but he also felt comfort in reminding himself of the fact that this was something he could do. "When I was a child, my nurse told me that four-leaf clovers are good luck, but I despaired of the impossibility of finding one in a field of three-leaf clovers." For one heart-stopping moment, he thought he glimpsed a flower with five petals, but a closer examination proved him wrong.

He sighed and went on. "My father told me that four-leaf clovers are rare, but not as rare as most people think. Almost any reasonably large patch of clover will have at least one, sometimes several. It only requires a careful eye to spy it out amidst its friends."

"At least the flowers do not grow in bunches. Or imagine if we needed to find daisies with one more or fewer petals? It would be impossible." Her voice sounded stronger, and Darcy was pleased to think that he had encouraged her in some small way. "I am glad that one of us is an expert, then."

"I have found many four-leaf clovers in my day," he

assured her with a smile. But what good luck had they brought him?

Darcy had to force himself to keep his mind on his task and not let it wander to Pemberley, worrying about whether Georgiana had slipped deeper into sleep, whether Richard was protecting her, whether Wickham would attempt to attack her again. He dreaded the moment when he and Elizabeth would have to part. Because once they found the cure – and they would, he was determined – he would return to Pemberley, she to the Library. And the chance of ever meeting again in this life was almost nothing.

Blinking, Darcy looked again at the flower he had just passed. Had he seen . . . yes! It had only five petals!

"Elizabeth!" he called, almost shaking in his excitement. "Elizabeth, I think I have found it!"

He was about to pick it and hold it aloft in triumph when a voice cried, "Stop!"

His hands dropped to his sides, and he spun to see the odd fae back again, this time leaning on a walking stick, his hair an unnatural red.

"You have found it, then," the fae said, his eyes on the flower. "That shows you have a good eye." His gaze moved to Elizabeth. "And a good mind, although that is to be expected from one called by the Library." He turned back to Darcy. "But there is a price for picking a flower from my field."

Darcy held back a sigh. Of course there was. Everything had a price with the fae.

Before he could think of the right approach, the fae spoke again. "The Librarian cannot leave the Library," the fae said, his eyes again flicking to Elizabeth. "The result would be utter disaster, Your Eminence, especially as you have no master or apprentice."

Elizabeth bowed her head solemnly.

The fae's furrowed brows and hair were violet now. "She

is bound to the Library, and you are bound to your estate. I have seen the affection between the two of you, but it cannot be. And so my price is more of a gift."

He dug through the pockets of his shimmering robes and held aloft a bottle of clear liquid. "While you searched my field, I made a little journey of my own. This bottle contains waters from the River Lethe."

By Elizabeth's gasp, Darcy knew that she, too, knew the mythological reference. At least, he had always assumed it was mere mythology.

"The waters of forgetting," the fae said, silvery eyes now boring into Darcy's. "You will take a drink, and all memories of Elizabeth Bennet, formerly of Longbourn in Hertford-shire, will be erased from your memory." He smiled, and his teeth showed. A little too numerous and a little too sharp, they were a reminder that the fae were not to be trusted for all that they could not lie.

"You will, of course, remember your quest, but you will remember only that Her Eminence, the Librarian, aided you in your quest. Any more . . . personal details will be forgotten. That is the price of picking the flower."

Darcy turned to Elizabeth. Her face was white and pinched, but she met his gaze steadily. "You must do it," she said, her voice husky. "Georgiana's life depends on it. And . . . and it is not as if we can have a life together even if we could bring ourselves to . . . to start anew."

Pain ripped through Darcy's chest at the thought. No. It was impossible for them to be together. He had Pemberley and his responsibilities there, and Elizabeth had the Library.

But if he had to force himself to give her up, must he give up his memories of her, too? It might make it easier, but it would be like cutting off a limb. Would he not always be haunted by the wisp of something missing, something as important as his own life, something he could never quite remember but would always long for?

Georgiana needed him. She needed the cure. Even now she was on the brink of death, and the cure might be too late. It was selfish to want to hold onto his memories of his beloved Elizabeth – a woman he was destined to leave again – at the expense of his sister's life.

He opened his mouth to answer, but he could not.

Elizabeth was looking at him now, her dark eyes warm and sympathetic. She knew, she must know, what this would cost him.

"I give you leave to forget me," she whispered. "It will be better, really. You can move on. Marry. Live the life you were meant to live. It would comfort me to see you happy, even if we must be apart."

He recoiled at the thought – marry another? His heart pounded in agony. She would not forget *him*, though. She still loved him. She loved him enough to give him up and wish him joy in a life without her.

"No," he said, the words bursting out without further thought. "I cannot – I cannot. Not even to save Georgiana, not even . . . I cannot. Please, please, there must be another way."

"Darcy!" Elizabeth cried. "But Georgiana—"

The fae held up a hand. A peculiar smile crossed his face. "So be it," he said, and he tossed the bottle far into the air. They watched as it reached the top of its arc and fell, hitting the ground with a tinkle, the water trickling into the soft earth between the plants.

The fae smiled. "You have proven yourself true, Fitzwilliam Darcy. You once abandoned your love with very little effort, but now . . . now even at great personal cost and heartache, even when that love is doomed, you still chose not to abandon it. And you, Miss Elizabeth Bennet.

You once had your love torn from you, and you were embittered for it. But now you have also proven yourself true, willing to forgive and to love unselfishly, to give up your love when it would cost him all." He bowed to each of them in turn. "More I could not ask for. I will give you the cure."

He reached out with long fingers tipped with sharp nails and plucked the five-petaled scarlet pimpernel.

"I cannot allow you to pick the flower without paying in forgetfulness," he said, his smile devious. "But I can pick it for you in exchange for this afternoon's entertainment. After all, the truth delights us fae. Truths told to cross on stones, true flowers found in a field of lies, and true hearts that love completely. Mind you, you have not chosen the easy path, but you have chosen the true path."

"Thank y—" Darcy almost breathed, but he remembered at the last moment that it would be disastrous to thank the fae. What was the phrase his father had once taught him when warning about the dangers of the Faerie Realm?

"I am pleased with the flower," he said cautiously. He tucked it into his inner coat pocket, delicately arranging the petals as he did to avoid crushing it more than was inevitable. It would be foolish to attempt to carry it in hand out of Faerie.

The fae's smile grew wider. He turned as if to usher them from the field, but Elizabeth cleared her throat. "The rhyme given to us by the Library also mentions a word of power we must speak to trigger the cure." She gave the fae a pointed look.

He raised an eyebrow, a spark of mischief in his eyes. "Does it?"

"You know very well that it does," Elizabeth said. Darcy realized it was another trick. The fae had hoped they would forget they needed to obtain a word from him.

He shrugged. "Very well. The word is—" He repeated a sound in the liquid fae language.

Darcy frowned. "I do not know if human throats can make such a sound."

"When you need to say the word, you will be capable of it," the fae assured him. Darcy had misgivings but he supposed they were accepting the fae's word on a number of things.

"We do not know the meaning of this word," Elizabeth said. "Uttering it might cause harm to befall us or those around us." Darcy realized that was as close as she could come to asking if the word was dangerous.

"It will not," the fae assured her. "You have everything necessary to cure Miss Darcy."

Darcy reminded himself that the fae could not lie. "Very good." He nodded to show his appreciation.

The fae man gestured for them to join him. "Now, my little humans, I will escort you to the edge of our realm and there we will part. Your cursed one does not have much time, so we will take the shortest route."

The fae grasped both Elizabeth and Darcy by an arm and propelled them forward. Each step was like a leap, and as the air rushed by, Darcy had the odd sensation that he was riding on Hespera.

They found themselves in a wood, and the fae slowed and released their arms. The forest was dark around them, but there was an odd shimmer ahead. Trees from both sides of the path leaned in and twisted overhead, making an arch.

Darcy blinked at the arch. The air within seemed to shift and move like smoke or fog, and it gleamed as if it had its own light source.

Taking Elizabeth's arm, he stepped cautiously towards the passage.

"Oh, you humans," the fae said with a laugh. "Always so

careful. But there are times when caution is the more dangerous choice. Now go!"

A hard shove at their backs knocked Darcy and Elizabeth through and broke them apart. Darcy landed on his hands and knees, feeling as though all the breath had been knocked from him. A heavy fog filled the air, blinding him and making him cough.

He was about to call out for Elizabeth when the fog lifted and he saw her crouched beside him, gasping.

They had done it. They were out of the Faerie Realm. Only now did he realize how strange the colors had been there, how thick the air had felt. He breathed in the fresh air of his native Derbyshire. They were back where they had started, in front of the grotto where Rakover had left them.

A sudden thought had him glad he was already on his knees. He had the cure. They had escaped the Faerie Realm.

This was where they would have to part. She would return to the Library and he to Pemberley. He would save Georgiana's life. And then . . . what then? How could he ever return to life as it had been before?

"Elizabeth," he said, reaching for her hand. "I have to tell you—"

But she was not looking at him. She was staring upwards, her eyes wide.

Tamping down his fear, he followed her gaze to see what threat now loomed.

CHAPTER 17

A winged shadow crossed the ground.

"It's Rakover," said Elizabeth in relief. "It means we will not have to walk back to the inn." She squinted towards the sky as her eyes adjusted to the bright light in the mortal world. "Haskins must have been watching for our return and sent the dragon to help us. I feel strangely drained from our time in Faerie."

Darcy shaded his eyes. He could not see it clearly against the glare of the sun, but apart from its giant wings, the creature coming towards them did not resemble a dragon. The shape was wrong. Darcy stiffened as it circled above them like a giant hawk intent on its prey.

"It does not look like Rakover. We need to take cover." His voice grew urgent as the hairs on the back of his neck bristled in warning. Next to him, he could sense Elizabeth come to full alertness as she reached the same conclusion.

A strange cry from above confirmed his suspicions. The winged shadow was swooping towards them with murderous intent.

There was nowhere to escape but the grotto. In front of

them was open moorland, with no trees to hide them. Behind them, the rugged slope was too steep for them to scale.

"Head for the grotto," cried Darcy.

He turned and ran towards it, but his legs did not quite obey him. He felt sluggish, his body heavy and constrained. Their visit to Faerie must have taken its toll, and he had not yet adapted back to the human world. He tried to set up a protection spell, but his magic barely responded. It worked, but it was too weak to hold off an attack.

"I cannot summon my magic," said Elizabeth, panic in her voice.

He tugged at her hand and pulled her towards the grotto. He felt as if he was wading in water. Above him, he heard the ominous beating of wings. The shadow grew larger until it surrounded them, a monstrous shape swallowing the sunlight.

The grotto was close, very close, but they would not reach it in time.

"I will stand and fight," said Darcy, struggling to breathe. "You take shelter in the grotto."

"I will not hide away while you are left to fend for yourself." Elizabeth's voice was grim and determined. Why must she always do things her way?

"What is the point of both of us being killed?" he said in frustration.

"Save your breath for the fight, Darcy," she muttered.

He gritted his teeth. If they survived this, they would have to have a serious discussion about her obstinacy.

There was no more time to argue. His heart sank. He could only hope his magic would revive when he most needed it.

The shadow solidified into an enormous gold and silver bird. Lightning skirted the span of its wings, and the sound of thunder rumbled around it. A thunderbird. Darcy had read descriptions of the creature. It was a dangerous predator, more dangerous even than a dragon. Dragons could be reasoned with, but thunderbirds operated on instinct.

He could now make out a form on its back. It was too slight to be human. At a guess, he would say the rider was fae and possibly female. Why in heaven's name was one of the fae attacking them?

The thunderbird gave a screech that pierced through his skull. He shuddered, trying to focus on drawing his magic instead of covering his ears. It was close enough now for Darcy to see its talons. They were longer than Darcy's arm. Those claws could tear through him like butter.

If he and Elizabeth did not do something now, it would soon be too late.

"Ready to strike?" he said.

"My magic is not reliable," said Elizabeth, "but I will do what I can."

Darcy directed a shard of ice towards the thunderbird. At the same time, Elizabeth lifted a rock from the ground and sent it in the direction of the creature's head. Neither spell reached its target. The rider raised her hand and the two objects bounced back, as if from an invisible wall. Darcy ducked as the deadly ice headed straight for his head.

A tinkling laugh came from the fae. "Spare me your puny human spells."

The thunderbird landed a few feet from Darcy. Lightning flashed off the bird's feathers and hissed as it charred the ground. The odor of burnt heather filled the air.

The rider was a graceful, beautiful being, but she filled Darcy with unease. Her clothes swirled around her, turning silver, then gold. Her ever-changing fae eyes shifted to a blue that was so pale it looked like frost. As her gaze locked onto

Darcy's, her eyes gleamed. He shivered at the cold intent in her eyes.

"Well, Mr. Darcy. Is that all you are capable of? You are more of a disappointment than I expected. I was looking forward to engaging in battle."

She had come for him, then. But why?

"I see that you know me," said Darcy, hoping somehow it was all a mistake. "May I enquire who you are, and why you have intercepted me?"

"You may. I may decide to tell you. Or I may not."

Darcy's eyes narrowed. How dare she toy with him at a time like this, when his sister's life stood in the balance?

He took a step towards her, but Elizabeth put a hand on his arm.

"Leave me to deal with it," she murmured. "Your sister is waiting. When I give you the signal, I will distract her."

As if he would ever leave her alone with a dangerous fae. He grunted in response, not willing to make any promises he would not keep, then turned his attention to the thunderbird and its rider.

The fae hissed at Elizabeth.

"*You* should know better than most that fae ears are more sensitive than those disfigured blobs humans call ears. So you are willing to sacrifice yourself for your lover? How positively delightful."

She clapped her hands with glee. Her child-sized teeth were razor sharp.

"She is not my *lover*," said Darcy, outraged at the impropriety.

"You humans have such quaint notions. Since you love her, you should bed her. It is simple. But no. You must suffer instead. How long has it been? Five years? How ridiculous!"

How did the rider know so much about him? Who was

she? He was at a complete disadvantage. He had no idea what she had against him and what she was doing here.

"And to think you believed that the love of your life had no magic! That she could not summon a familiar! You believed everything your aunt told you."

What did the fae mean? How did she even know about Lady Catherine?

He gasped as a thought struck him. Was this his aunt's doing? Did she want to separate him from Elizabeth again? "Did my aunt send you?"

The fae scoffed. "Do you really think I would take orders from a *human*?"

No, of course. His aunt would not be capable of this. "Will you at least tell me your name?" he asked.

"I will not give my name to *you*, human."

"Then if you have nothing more to say, I suggest you go on your way. I have no time for riddles."

A high-pitched laugh filled the air like dissonant bells. The fae spun towards Elizabeth, her clothes catching the light, iridescent like crystals.

"Are you just going to stand there and stare?" the fae woman taunted. "Will you not do anything? I thought a Librarian would be more plucky than this."

She was goading them, Darcy realized in a sudden moment of insight. She was trying to hold them back, to distract them. He and Elizabeth were not here to discuss Lady Catherine, nor to fight. Their goal was clear. They needed to get the flower to Georgiana. That was all that mattered. For some unclear reason of her own, this fae was trying to stop them from leaving.

"Ignore her," he whispered to Elizabeth. "Don't take the bait."

Elizabeth gave a quick nod to indicate she understood.

The fae shifted positions, and the thunderbird reared up

and spread out its giant wings, encircling the fae in streaks of lighting. "You cannot ignore me. I am Princess Alaine of the Fae Summer Court."

Darcy realized she had revealed her name, despite saying she would not. Her arrogance was her undoing. Perhaps if he could keep her talking, she might reveal why she was here.

"Surely a Princess of the Fae Court would not concern herself with the affairs of mere mortals," he said.

"I am here to ensure that you fail in your mission. I already sent two of my creatures to stop you earlier in your journey. It was sheer luck you were able to escape. You will not get away the third time, I can assure you."

She raised her hand and sent a flash of lightning into the ground in front of Darcy. The grass sizzled and a dark acrid plume of smoke rose to fill Darcy's nostrils. His mind was spinning as he struggled to understand the fae's intentions. So it was she who had sent the troll and the dragon to attack them.

Darcy had no idea what she wanted, but he sensed she was more interested in him than Elizabeth. He was stronger now, and the languid feeling that had followed him from Faerie was fading. He did not care what the rider wanted, as long as the flower reached Georgiana.

He would hand the flower to Elizabeth, then battle the fae princess and distract her while Elizabeth escaped back to Faerie. Surely the fae would help her go out another way if she explained what had happened.

Moving inch by inch, he stealthily slipped the flower into Elizabeth's hand and indicated the grotto with the minutest of gestures, hoping she would understand his intent.

Another flash of lightning crackled through the air. It landed barely a finger's width away from Darcy's foot. He jumped back.

The fae laughed. "I saw that, you know." Her disconcerting eyes had turned violet. They were full of mockery. "I did not come all this way to talk about your aunt, however satisfying it might be to see you at each other's throats." Her dark locks rippled and swayed, turning orange, then deep purple. Her eyes were suddenly empty pools of darkness. "I have come for the cure to your sister's curse."

Darcy's heart skipped a beat, and his throat went dry. Any hope that she did not know about the flower was lost.

"The cure is intended for my sister. Why would you possibly want it?"

"I have my reasons, and I will not share them with a mortal."

She stared at him, then, with a whimsical fae shift, her mood changed. Her voice turned silky, almost seductive. "Why don't you give *me* the flower, Mr. Darcy? I have a thunderbird, but you will have to walk across the valley, and then climb a peak to reach civilization. You stand no chance of getting to Pemberley before the flower shrivels and dies. With my thunderbird, I could reach your home in a few minutes."

If he did not know better, her innocent and helpful expression might have tricked him. Instead, Darcy noted that she had not said anything about taking the cure to Georgiana. Fae were incapable of lying, but they could twist their words in deception.

He chose his own words carefully. "If I give you the flower, will you take it to Georgiana and administer the cure to her, so that she recovers fully?"

"I will take the cure to Georgiana. I promise." The look of cunning was unmistakable.

"That is not good enough. I will hand you the flower, if you promise you will use the flower to ensure my sister recovers fully."

The fae's face twisted. "I *will* have the flower, one way or the other. I will crush your life rather than allow you to save the woman who stole the man I love."

Darcy stared at the princess. Who was this man she was talking about? This had to be a mistake. "But my sister has done nothing."

"Your *sister* – " she spat out the word " – has lured away my prince. She has him in her thrall." Her face contorted with hatred.

Any hope he had that he could bargain with her for his sister's life disappeared. She was either mad, or Georgiana had done something by accident. But what could she possibly have done? Georgiana was bedridden. Which left only one alternative. The fae princess was mad.

"I will give you one more chance" said Alaine, tossing her hair back. "Hand over the flower, and in return, I might allow the Librarian to go unharmed."

She had certainly not earned his trust. "I am not so foolish as to bargain with a fae, especially one who has already resorted to trickery. And I will certainly not bargain with the life of my sister."

"I think you will find you have no choice," said Alaine, baring her teeth. "Foolish mortal! Do you really think you can stand against me? A princess of the Fae Court?"

Suddenly, a powerful force tugged at him, drawing him towards the princess. Darcy struggled to dig in his feet and to draw the symbols of a spell at the same time as he lurched forward. The fae was – literally – trying to sweep him off his feet. His own magic kept him on the ground, just barely, but he knew he would not be able to withstand the princess for very long, not when he was not at his full strength. If he failed at this, then Georgiana's life would be forfeited.

If only Elizabeth would take this opportunity to escape! It was their only hope. Alaine did not know that Elizabeth had the flower, and by the time she discovered it, Elizabeth would be far away. If only he could resist long enough.

Just then, another force took hold of him, pulling him backwards, fighting Alaine's control. Elizabeth's magic was returning. He was grateful, but he did not want her help, not now. He threw a beseeching look at Elizabeth, willing her to understand. It was now or never. She had to go back to Faerie to save the flower. There was no other choice. He tried to communicate the idea with his eyes.

To his astonishment, Elizabeth shook her head, smiled, and brought her finger to her lips. There was a hint of mischief in that smile, and his heart tripped at the sight of it. She had a plan, another way to save the flower. As hope returned, all the love he had felt for her in Faerie came flooding back. Not for the first time, he marveled at her resourcefulness.

The fae princess was looking at him suspiciously, and he realized he, too, was smiling. His love for Elizabeth was making him foolish. Quickly, he schooled his expression and prepared to do whatever it would take to save them all.

He had no idea what Elizabeth intended, but he trusted her with his life.

CHAPTER 18

*E*lizabeth's grin widened as Hespera and Abraxas flew into sight over the crest of the hill.

I am very happy to see you! She told her familiar. Only a few minutes ago she had realized that they could accept the familiars' help because the quest had been completed. But when she contacted Abraxas, she discovered that he and Hespera were already on their way.

And I am happy to help you, Abraxas responded, but his mental voice was tinged with anxiety. *We must return you to the Library soon. The situation with the border is unstable.*

Elizabeth took a deep breath. *One emergency at a time.*

When the man beside her turned his head and caught a glimpse of the two griffins, he actually laughed at the sight. "Well played!" he exclaimed. She realized she was coming to think of him as William – again. Their journey had been too intimate to continue calling him Mr. Darcy in her own thoughts.

Alaine cursed but then laughed. "Those puny creatures are no match for my thunderbird!" She jumped onto the thunderbird's back. They leapt into the sky to meet the griffins. It was true that each griffin was only a quarter the size of the thunderbird, but Elizabeth was not ready to count them out.

As the thunderbird wheeled away and the princess focused her attention on the griffins, Elizabeth could sense Alaine's magic loosen its grip on William. He was quickly able to muster his own magic to shake it off entirely. Thank goodness!

But they were hardly out of danger; it was only a momentary respite.

Trying to escape from the two griffins, the thunderbird swooped upside down in a huge loop. When the thunderbird came close to the ground, the princess leapt from its back with the preternatural grace of her kind, landing lightly on a stony outcropping. Alaine gave them a cold smile as she climbed down from the outcropping as easily as she might descend from a flight of stairs. "Those blooms do not last very long, Darcy. I only need to delay you a little while and it will be too late to save your sister."

"Why do you hate Georgiana?" William asked, bewildered. "She has never hurt a soul in her life."

"That is what you think," Alaine hissed.

She had reached the plateau where Elizabeth and William stood. Elizabeth's stomach clenched. They faced a fae mage – who were known to be the most powerful mages in the world. A glance upward showed that Abraxas and Hespera were quite busy fighting the much larger thunderbird.

Alaine raised her hand and shot a bolt of blazing white lightning at William. He dived to the side, hitting the ground with some force before taking shelter behind a cluster of boulders. Elizabeth hurried to join him. Alaine directed another bolt at William, but he managed to raise his shields, glowing a bright blue when the bolt struck them.

Peering out between two boulders, Elizabeth watched Alaine very deliberately place her hand in the sky with her fingers splayed. Standing still, she closed her eyes. With her magical senses, Elizabeth could discern that Alaine was drawing power straight from the faerie lands through the holes in the border. This gave Alaine a huge advantage; she could fuel far more powerful attacks than Elizabeth and William could hope to muster. They could never survive a battle of attrition. The human mages would need to find another way to fight, and they would need to find it quickly.

If only they could combine their magic! But human mages found that notoriously difficult. On the other hand, William was a skilled mage and Elizabeth was the Librarian....

William turned to her. "Elizabeth," he said urgently. "I will create a diversion so you might take the bloom and ride Abraxas to Pemberley."

She shook her head. "I refuse to tell Georgiana that I abandoned her brother to fight a fae princess by himself."

"But—"

She forestalled his objection with a raised finger. "Would your sister want her life to come at the cost of yours?" When he had no immediate response, she spoke again. "I have another idea. Please give me your hand."

William placed his hand in hers. Elizabeth tried not to think about the impropriety of the touch...or how wonderful it felt. She closed her eyes and accustomed herself to the shape of his magic – its texture and weight. Fortunately, the feeling of his magic had grown more familiar over the course of the journey.

She had merged her magic with Abraxas's many times; it was a common way for familiars to augment their mages' power. But where Abraxas's magic felt like the ripples of a soothing bath, touching William's magic was like plunging her hand into a typhoon. It ebbed and flowed in great jagged waves, moving wildly and unpredictably. How could she ever merge her magic with something like this?

Elizabeth tried to keep a calm mind; if she panicked now, they would never form a successful link. She imagined her magic as a placid river trickling into the raging sea of William's magic, a little at a time – like a stream of warm water would mix into the colder sea. She pictured their magic mixing together.

Eventually their magic combined to produce something like ocean waves: powerful, but regular and predictable. She had done it! She had established a link between their magics.

She opened her eyes to find William staring at her. "I did not think it was possible," he said. "Why could you create a bond when so many others have failed?"

She gave him a small smile. "I know that you love me."

He huffed a soft laugh. "How could I not? You are amazing." They were under attack and yet his eyes focused on her with an intensity that suggested there was nobody else in the world but her. His gaze drifted to her lips. Would he kiss her? Every part of Elizabeth yearned for increased intimacy with him, wanting to take advantage of these moments before they had to go their separate ways.

Of course, these were not ideal circumstances for a kiss.

A lightning bolt crashed noisily into William's shield, making them both flinch and jerk apart. He spun around and poured more power into the shield, but it was wearing thin in places.

His forehead furrowed with concern. "What you have accomplished is marvelous," he said. "However I am not certain that even our combined powers will be enough to defeat a full-strength fae mage."

"Ah, but I have another trick up my sleeve!" she said with

a smile. She reached out mentally to Abraxas. *Can you and Hespera spare a little power?*

The griffins had landed on a lower plateau after forcing the thunderbird to the ground with an injured wing. The griffins had a distinct advantage on land. Four legs gave them great maneuverability while their opponent could only hop around, dragging its injured wing in the grass.

Yes, Abraxas answered. *Take the power you need. It is yours. We do not need magic to bring this creature to heel.* Power and renewed energy flooded into Elizabeth, as if she had partaken of several cups of coffee. The expression on William's face suggested he had received a similar gift from Hespera.

"*Now* I think we are ready to do battle," Elizabeth said to him. "Will you take the lead? You have training in combat magic. It is not something that Librarians usually require."

Darcy nodded, happy that he could finally be of some use. He grasped ahold of the four threads of magic – two human and two griffin – now entwined into one sturdy rope. But it was a rope with a mind of its own. In fact, holding such a strong force of magic was like riding a bucking horse. It was wild and powerful and not sure it wished to bend to his will.

He had never before held so much power. No doubt few human mages had. It was heady and terrifying at the same time.

I cannot fail. Georgiana is depending on me, he reminded himself.

He jumped out from behind the boulder to launch a fire spell, easily the most powerful spell he had ever created. It burned a path from his fingertips across the air and splashed against the shield covering Alaine. She had not bothered to take shelter behind any boulders; instead, she stood in the open, protected only by the glowing red dome of her shield. Darcy was not sure whether to admire her confidence or consider her foolhardy.

He fed more power into his fire spell, but it could not penetrate the shield. Alaine returned jets of green fire in Darcy's direction, forcing him to hide again.

When Darcy next emerged from behind the boulder, he tried a shatter spell. A wave of kinetic energy designed to burst anything in its path crashed into Alaine's shield with a loud bang. Then he tried to bind the fae with enchanted ropes, but the shield foiled that attack as well. His next choice was a telekinesis spell which hurled hundreds of rocks at the fae princess. He was making progress. He could sense Alaine's shield weakening, but none of the rocks penetrated it.

Darcy barely refrained from swearing. Despite commanding massive magical power, he could not penetrate Alaine's shield. Apparently she was justified in her confidence. Meanwhile they had Darcy pinned down with no hope of escaping to Pemberley and Georgiana.

Elizabeth had been observing the battle from a space between two boulders. "Alaine's shield falters when she is distracted," she noted.

"What do you mean?"

"She must be fueling the shield directly from her mind rather than casting it as an independent entity – as you did with your spell. When her attention is directed away from the shield, it flickers and weakens."

"Thank you," Darcy said, grateful that Elizabeth could perceive magic so clearly. "My magical combat professor would have given her poor marks for such an amateur mistake." If Alaine loosened her hold on her shield, Darcy might be able to pierce it with a spell.

But how could he make use of that information? Darcy would need a powerful distraction to disrupt her concentration.

Fear could divert her attention, but what did Alaine most fear? Perhaps an illusion of a dragon? No, some fae were capable of commanding dragons. An illusory army of orcs? No, she would not believe such a thing was possible.

Unfortunately few things could threaten a truly talented fae mage except *another* fae mage. *Ah! Now there was a possible illusion that might distract Alaine!* Surely the princess's activities were not condoned by others in the fae court. A group of fae would not be a welcome sight for the princess.

Darcy conjured in his mind every fae he had ever met, even including the woman by the side of the Faerie river and Anne of the Hills. It amounted to half a dozen fae. Then he put the fellow with the ever-changing hair color at the front of his illusory crew. Finally, he positioned the illusion at the approximate location where he and Elizabeth had emerged from Faerie. The door had disappeared from inside the grotto, but he would wager the entrance to Faerie was nearby –merely concealed from human eyes.

Taking a deep breath, he prayed that the ploy would work and released the illusion. Elizabeth gasped as half a dozen fae emerged from the grotto and marched purposefully toward Alaine. The fae man in the front looked particularly grim despite his colorful hair. Darcy could only hope that he would not turn out to be Alaine's best friend.

Alaine's face paled at the sight, and she scrambled backward. "Malus!" she exclaimed to the man in the lead. "What are—? I can explain myself!"

"Her shield is almost completely gone," Elizabeth whispered to Darcy.

Dividing his attention – and his magic – was one of the most difficult things Darcy had ever attempted. It would not have been possible without the power borrowed from Elizabeth and the griffins. He continued to feed power into the illusion while commanding the "fae" to stop and stare imperiously at Alaine. But he had to act quickly. She would not be fooled for long.

At the same time, Darcy cast a strong sleep spell, one that should quickly render the fae unconscious. He stuck his head up above the boulder just long enough to hurl the spell at Alaine – before ducking down again. "It penetrated the shield!" Elizabeth cried. Darcy allowed himself a small triumphant smile.

He waited in suspense for a few seconds. "She is asleep!" Elizabeth said.

Darcy was exhausted; every muscle in his body hurt. Practicing magic was far more physically taxing than many people assumed. He almost envied Alaine's nap.

He emerged cautiously from behind the boulder, but the fae princess was slumped in the grass–with no signs of stirring. The illusory fae had disappeared the moment Darcy no longer needed them.

Well done, Darcy, Hespera greeted him as she landed in the field a few yards away. Abraxas was not far behind.

The thunderbird? He asked Hespera.

It lives, she answered. *But it is injured. It will not be able to fly without healing. The fae know how to care for such creatures. Perhaps we can find one since we are so close to their realm.*

Care for the thunderbird would have to wait. "We must leave for Pemberley," Darcy said to Elizabeth.

Before Elizabeth could reply, she was startled by a shriek emanating from the sky. *Not another threat*, she thought wearily. *Surely we have done enough fighting for one day.*

William must have had the same thought. He placed a hand on Hespera's shoulder as if preparing to leap onto her back and fly into battle. Then the source of the shriek came into focus and he sagged with relief. "It is Richard and Maor!"

Now that they were close enough, Elizabeth recognized William's cousin and his hippogriff familiar. When they had landed, William hurried over and gave his cousin a hearty handshake. "Richard, you are a welcome sight indeed! How did you find us?"

The general laughed. "Blind luck. I was searching for the entrance to Faerie when Maor said she spied two griffins and a thunderbird in the distance. That is a collection of creatures you do not see everyday. We thought we would investigate."

"How fares Georgiana?" William asked.

"She lives," the general said, his expression grim. "She still fights the curse. But I do not know how much time she has left."

"We have the cure," William said. "We must reach Pemberley."

Elizabeth produced a miraculously unbruised flower from her pocket even as she was striding toward Abraxas. But she was startled by a crash so loud it nearly knocked her off her feet. They all whirled around to find that the grotto itself had split into two pieces. Elizabeth took a moment to marvel at the power that could cleave solid rock.

Then a figure emerged from the darkness between the two rocks. It was the fae with the changeable hair whom Alaine had called Malus. He wore a rich silk shirt and matching breaches – all covered by a high-necked cape that fell to his feet. On his head was a solid gold crown in the shape of vines and leaves, and in his hand he held a naked sword. Elizabeth could easily imagine why *this* Malus would frighten Alaine.

When he spoke, his voice rumbled like distant thunder. "I am Malus, Summer King of Faerie. Who has dared to use my likeness?"

Behind him, fae warriors, carrying spears and swords, poured out of the cleft in the rock.

CHAPTER 19

*W*illiam stepped forward, holding his head high. But Elizabeth noticed a bead of perspiration trickling down the side of his face. It could not be easy to face dozens of armed fae warriors. This powerful army could delay them long enough that the cure reached Georgiana too late. And they would never win a battle if the king and his warriors chose to fight them.

"My deepest apologies for the trespass," William said. "I was trying to distract Princess Alaine." He gestured to where she slept on the grass.

How was Princess Alaine related to the king? Was he fond of her? Would he demand the return of the flower if he was displeased?

Malus crossed the field and stared down at Alaine. "What have you done to my daughter?" he thundered in a voice that shook the earth.

Elizabeth's blood froze, and she exchanged a stricken look with William. Daughter? How could they have had the bad luck to make an enemy of the fae king's daughter?

She edged closer to William and General Fitzwilliam as

the fae warriors marched around the edge of the plateau, encircling and entrapping the humans.

"Alaine was attempting to kill me and Elizabeth." He cleared his throat. "The princess wanted to prevent us from taking the cure to my sister."

"We have reason to believe the princess helped Mr. Wickham to poison Miss Darcy in the first place," General Fitzwilliam added.

The king gave them a piercing look. "Why would she do such a thing? I cannot imagine Alaine has ever met her."

William shook his head. "I do not know why. She did not explain her reasons to us."

Malus glared at them imperiously. "Why should I believe such an absurd story? Fae do not involve ourselves in the affairs of mortals. It is far more likely that you attacked her."

"Sir," the general crossed to Malus. "I have a letter for the Faerie Court that will help explain some of this confusion."

Malus's brows drew together. "Who is this letter from?"

The general gave William a sidelong look. What was that about? "A member of the court whom I recently encountered. He describes how Princess Alaine's actions violate the laws of Faerie." He pulled the letter from the pocket of his coat and handed it to Malus.

The fae king examined the seal before breaking it and scanning the letter, growing more sober the more he read. He shook his head. "These are grave crimes. Interference with mortal mages is forbidden. I knew Alaine was impulsive and prone to fits of temper, but this…I have no choice but to punish her." He regarded Alaine almost sorrowfully.

Elizabeth said, "It must be difficult for you to pass judgment on your own daughter."

Malus's features settled into a blank mask as he shrugged. "I have 28 other daughters. Perhaps some of the others will not disappoint me."

He clapped his hands. Instantly two fae, wearing the helms and armor of guards, stepped out of the circle. Malus gestured and the men picked up Alaine, none too gently, and slung the sleeping fae princess over their shoulders. They carried the captive through the cleft in the rock and disappeared into the darkness.

"I hope she will get a fair trial," Elizabeth said pointedly.

"Mortals do not tell us how to conduct our business," Malus said imperiously, staring down his nose at her. "However, trials are the custom of our people. In any case, you need not concern yourself. Your family will never be bothered by Alaine again. She will be imprisoned for at least a hundred years."

"There is also a wounded thunderbird in the field over there." Darcy pointed.

"Yet another crime to lay at Alaine's feet," Malus grumbled. "Thunderbirds should never be treated in such a careless manner." He gestured and a contingent of fae warriors was soon making its way to the thunderbird.

The king gave Elizabeth a sharp look. "I expect that you will be returning to the Library now that the quest is concluded?" The question emerged almost like a command.

She was a bit taken aback. "I do not believe the quest is truly concluded until Georgiana is cured, but then I will return to the Library."

"You are running out of time," he said darkly.

"What do you—?" Elizabeth started to say, but the king had pivoted and was striding back toward the opening in the cliff. The warriors followed him, moving far more silently and gracefully than men in full armor should.

Once they were gone and the entrance to Faerie had rumbled closed, William turned to his cousin. "We must get the cure to Georgiana without delay." He cast a look at Elizabeth. "You need not accompany us. I daresay I can administer the cure by myself, and no doubt you would be happy to get some rest."

Elizabeth shook her head. "The poem that sent us on this quest suggested we were both needed to affect the cure. And I care about Georgiana too." And, in case they were too late, William might need a shoulder to cry upon.

He gave her a wan smile. "I must confess, I was hoping you would join me."

Elizabeth climbed on Abraxas's back. They followed Hespera into the sky with Maor and Richard trailing behind.

Darcy managed to stay relatively calm during the flight. He only urged Hespera to hurry three…well, perhaps four…very well, five times. The journey seemed to take forever, although he knew it was a short distance in the air. But eventually the two griffins landed in front of Pemberley's grand front entrance. Darcy leapt from Hespera's back and stormed through the doors, ignoring surprised exclamations from his butler and one of the maids in the front hall. He was vaguely aware of the sound of Elizabeth's footsteps behind him.

He hurried up the steps and turned right, pounding along the hallway until he reached Georgiana's room. He did not even stop to knock but threw the door open and rushed to her bedside. For a moment he feared he was too late; she was so still. But then he saw the slight, shallow movement of her breathing. Thank God! He pulled the flower from his pocket and only then realized he did not know how to administer the cure.

He stared wide-eyed at Elizabeth, on the other side of the bed. "Should she eat it? Smell it? Perhaps it should be in a tincture of some kind?"

Elizabeth shook her head. "Nobody gave us any instructions. But I daresay the fae eat flowers all the time, so placing it in her mouth would not be untoward. She may not need to swallow it."

Darcy opened his sister's mouth and positioned the bloom on her tongue before pushing her chin gently to close her mouth again. He took one of her hands; on the other side of the bed, Elizabeth held the other.

They looked at each other and uttered the fae word in perfect synchronicity. Malus had been correct. They were capable of saying it when necessary.

They waited, staring at his sister's face. Nothing happened.

"Perhaps we should have prepared a tincture," he said to Elizabeth.

Then Georgiana's eyes blinked. His heart pounding in his chest, Darcy leaned forward. "Georgie?" Her eyelashes fluttered. Her eyes opened, focusing on him.

"William?" Her voice was thick and sluggish, but the sound was music to his ear. His heart swelled with joy that almost could not be contained by his chest.

"How are you feeling, dearest?"

"Better." She struggled into a seated position and then made a face of disgust before she spat out the flower. "Did you put a weed in my mouth?"

Elizabeth laughed.

"It is not a weed," Darcy explained patiently. "That is the cure. We went to Faerie to obtain it."

Georgiana glanced from him to Elizabeth. "All the way to Faerie?" Elizabeth nodded. His sister looked back at him. "You truly are the best of brothers. I could not ask for a better one." She embraced him and gave him a kiss on the cheek. Then her eyes searched the room. "Where is Galon?"

Darcy did not see the seal. "I do not know. Perhaps he went to the lake" Since seals needed water, her familiar often spent time in the small lake on Pemberley's grounds. "Can you not speak with him in your mind?"

Georgiana shook her head, biting her lip. "Sometimes I cannot hear him. Not when he is in that form...." her voice trailed off as she stared at something at the end of her bed.

Darcy looked as well and jumped in startlement. A strange man had just entered the room.

"There you are!" Georgiana said with a tone of relief.

"I apologize. I was under an invisibility spell," the man said to her.

"Who are you?" Darcy demanded. "Who is this?" He asked Georgiana. "Why is a total stranger in your bed chamber?" Darcy turned to the man. "This is most inappropriate. Leave immediately!" He pointed at the door.

"William! William!" Georgiana caught his arm. "This is Galon."

Darcy blinked at her and then reexamined the man. He was tall and well made with dark hair and green eyes. He definitely was not a small sea mammal. Had Georgiana's struggles with the Scottish Word made her delusional?

The man bowed to Darcy. "My name is Galon. I am a prince of the Faerie's Winter Court. I fell in love with your sister three years ago and disguised myself as her familiar so that I might be close to her."

Darcy realized his mouth was hanging open and closed it with an audible snap.

"You have been living with Georgiana and courting her in secret?" Elizabeth asked.

"I assure you that nothing untoward has occurred," Galon said hastily. "I never spent the night in her room...until she became ill. Most of the time we acted as mage and familiar. I wanted Georgiana to grow accustomed to me."

"Accustomed?" Darcy asked in a low and deadly voice. "Why? What designs do you have on my sister?"

"I assure you my intentions are entirely honorable," Galon said stiffly. "I love her."

This was all happening far too quickly for Darcy's taste. "You want to court my sister? *Marry* my sister? She is a Darcy! And who are you? Do you even have a surname? You – You are a sea mammal who can shed your skin!"

"William!" Georgiana gasped.

Galon's expression darkened. "I am also a prince of Faerie. Surely that is assurance of my good breeding."

Darcy clasped shaking hands behind his back and made an effort not to shout. "We have recently encountered some very ill-behaved fae royalty. I—"

Elizabeth placed a hand on Darcy's arm before he could work himself into full-throated anger; it had an instant calming effect. "Have you considered all the implications?" she asked Galon. "Humans and fae do not intermarry often. Would the courts of Faerie be displeased? Where would you live?"

Galon's expression was grave. "We must live in the human world. Faerie is not a place for humans, and I would be exiled if I married Georgiana." Darcy's sister looked distressed at this news. "But," Galon added, "that would be a small price to pay."

"Surely that would put her in danger from the fae," Darcy growled.

Galon's brow furrowed. "Princess Alaine is the only fae who presents any danger to me or Georgiana. She was angry that I refused to marry her and is responsible for attacks upon both you and Georgiana."

Despite his anger, Darcy was impressed with the young man for confessing such information. "She is no longer a threat," Darcy said. "Alaine was taken into the custody of King Malus, who also is in receipt of a letter delivered via General Fitzwilliam – which I assume you wrote." Galon inclined his head. "Malus assured us she would be locked away for a long time."

Galon blew out a sigh of relief. "That is excellent news indeed!" He walked to Georgiana's bedside and took her hand, gazing at her adoringly. Love was nearly a palpable force flowing between them.

Darcy could not help a twinge of envy. He may not have given his consent for Georgiana to marry the fae prince, but they were free to love each other in a way that he and Elizabeth were not. Glancing up, he caught Elizabeth's melancholy expression and guessed her thoughts were similar.

Galon turned to Darcy and regarded him steadily. "Will you give your consent?"

Darcy scowled. "I have barely made your acquaintance, sir. I know nothing of your family, your prospects, or your plans for the future. Being a selkie is hardly a means of supporting a family."

"Surely my dowry is enough!" Georgiana said.

"Perhaps your dowry is the feature he finds most attractive about you," Darcy suggested.

"William!" Georgiana cried indignantly.

Galon advanced toward Darcy. "I assure you—"

"I believe we should leave this discussion for the time being," Elizabeth said in a loud voice, interposing herself between Darcy and Galon. "Georgiana has recovered from a long illness, and we have returned from an exhausting journey. Now is not the time for life-altering decisions."

Darcy drew back, acknowledging the wisdom of Elizabeth's words. "It *has* been a long day. Perhaps it would be best to retire for the evening. We may speak of this further in the morning."

Galon nodded, but Georgiana folded her hands over her chest. "Very well, but I will remind you, brother, that I do not require your permission to wed. I am of age."

With a jolt, Darcy realized she was correct. He was not accustomed to thinking of her as a woman past the age of needing a guardian.

He nodded an acknowledgement. "I will send Mrs. Reynolds to you. No doubt she believes you need some cosseting," he told Georgiana with a smile. "And we will retire for the evening." Darcy gestured for Galon to precede him from the room.

The fae prince took his time, kissing Georgiana's hand in farewell before strolling through the door. Elizabeth followed Darcy from the bedchamber.

Once they were in the hallway, Darcy asked Galon stiffly. "I assume you have been given a room?"

The fae colored. "Yes, I have been assigned a room in the guest wing."

Darcy gave a curt nod, satisfied that he had done his duty to his "guest." He signaled a passing maid. "Could you have a room made up for Miss Elizabeth? She will be staying the night." The maid curtseyed and hurried away.

"One more word, sir!" Galon called before they departed. "Was Wickham with Princess Alaine?"

Darcy glanced over his shoulder. "Wickham? No, I have not seen the man."

Galon pressed his lips together. "I do not like that. Wickham has been doing Alaine's bidding, and he is still free to wreak havoc."

"Indeed," Darcy agreed. "Tomorrow we must search for him." He cast a glance at Elizabeth. "But tonight, we will rest."

He bid the fae goodnight and then offered Elizabeth his arm as he escorted her toward the guest wing. "Would you like a tray brought to your room?" he asked.

"Perhaps later. For now I would dearly love a bath," she said.

"I will have the maid draw one."

Elizabeth's grateful smile fell aways as she got the abstracted expression Darcy associated with her talking to her familiar.

"What does Abraxas say?" he asked.

Her hand clenched his arm convulsively. "I cannot stay. Abraxas needs me in the Library immediately. I have been away too long!"

CHAPTER 20

*D*arcy placed his hand over Elizabeth's where she was clutching his arm. Her fingers relaxed their hold.

"I shall assist you," he blurted before a little shake of her head told him that he could not. His business with both the Library and its Librarian were now concluded.

Their parting had always been inevitable, but it was a shock to have it arrive so abruptly. After all they had been through, he had hoped for the time to at least offer her a proper farewell.

Elizabeth's eyes clouded over. It was as if a heavy fog had descended, a damp and chilling mist that tore at Darcy's heart. This time with Elizabeth had been terrible and wonderful, a break in the grief he had never shaken.

She had forgiven his cowardice, and what a gift that was. But it did not erase all that they had lost, and he would carry the pain of the consequences forever. He could only pray that she would not. Elizabeth might never wed, but as the Librarian she could live a fulfilled, purposeful life. More than anything else, Darcy desperately wished that happiness for her.

She slid her hand out from beneath his. "I must leave, Mr. Darcy."

What could he say when so much had already passed between them? He took a breath to steady himself. "I will walk you out."

She nodded.

"You must be careful," he told her quietly as they moved towards the stairs. "Wickham is still about somewhere, and your magic – you are not yourself." Darcy had drawn a great deal of Elizabeth's remaining power to defeat the princess – he could not have done it alone. When they returned to Pemberley, his own magic had begun restoring itself, but his home would not offer the same respite for her.

It might have, once.

"I will be well when I reach the Library," she replied.

Of course. The Library would restore her, because that was her home.

Elizabeth glanced up and met his gaze, her fine eyes shining with tears he knew she would not allow to fall. He dared not look away, filling his vision with her, committing to memory the curve of her jaw, the perfect outline of her lips, the little nose, the eyes that told a million tales. It was but a moment until she offered him a faint smile and gave him the promise he sought. "I will be careful."

Darcy offered Elizabeth his arm. She took it, and they descended the steps, crossing the hall towards the front door. Each step took her closer to removing herself from Pemberley, from the place he ought to have brought her as his bride, and out into the fading light of the day.

∼

Despite all the time they had recently spent in one another's company, there was still much more to say. Unfortunately, they were out of time.

Elizabeth was in a hurry to return to the Library, to discover what was happening and what was to be done. But her urgent need to confer with Abraxas was secondary to her desire to remain with Will— Mr. Darcy.

She wanted to be the Librarian, needed to be the Librarian. She had a purpose in life now that could never again be fulfilled by becoming merely the mistress of an estate, even one as magnificent as Pemberley.

It did not stop her from loving the master of Pemberley with a ferocity that lit her heart afire.

When she had been forced to admit the truth of her feelings on the fae stepping stones, it was as though she had breathed truly, deeply for the first time in five years. When she had connected her magic to his, allowed him to draw from her own stores and to feel the raw power in his own, it was the sort of partnership she would never be able to replicate with anyone else. Nor would she ever be able to forget it.

None of that mattered.

The Librarian who preceded her had betrayed The Library. Elizabeth had been chosen as the Librarian to restore it, and she had accepted the charge. It had required years of training to prepare her for the role, and she had barely had a moment to use the powers that her position had bestowed before she had started out on this mission with the last man in the world she had expected to see again.

"I know you cannot stay," Mr. Darcy said quietly as they approached the front door. "But I would never have you doubt the first desire of my heart. Had I my way, we would never be parted again."

"I feel the same," she said. "However, I cannot abandon

the Library or those who need it. What would happen to all those who depend upon its knowledge?" She touched his hand lightly. "What would have happened to Georgiana had it remained closed for even another fortnight?"

He nodded once. "Were it possible, I would give everything I own to be by your side. I simply wish you to know that. To believe it."

She squeezed his hand. "I do."

He leaned down, his warm lips brushing a kiss on her forehead. "Should you ever require aid in any way, Elizabeth, call on me."

It was all she could do to respond. "I shall."

"That is all I ask." He held her hands a moment longer, and then released them to step back. "Safe journeys, Your Eminence."

Elizabeth lifted her eyes to Mr. Darcy's face. His expression was not haughty or stony or entirely shuttered—all masks she had seen him wear when his feelings ran the deepest. Instead, it was open and vulnerable. She could see, in the tortured depths of his steady gaze, how difficult it was for him to let her go.

He wanted her to see him at his weakest. He trusted her enough to show her.

Elizabeth would never love another man as she loved him. Yet she smiled and turned away.

WHEN ELIZABETH SLID down from Abraxas's back and took her first step inside the Library, the warm embrace of magic welcomed her as softly as the beginning of spring. The building itself was just as she had left it. Even Travinius still sat at his perch, impervious to whatever great alarm had been sounded.

She stood in the doorway for a moment, reveling in the sensation of her magic returning to her. Reestablishing the connection not only allowed her to access the Library, it also sped the recovery of her own magic.

When Abraxas followed her into the grand reading room, he stared at her balefully. *You have made your peace with him.*

Made her peace? She never would, not completely. "I am not sure that I have. But it does not matter. I have promised my life to the Library, and I mean to honor that pledge."

Sacrifice is required. You always knew that.

"I did. I do. Why have you called me back?"

The final battle with Princess Alaine was only the greatest tax upon your strength. You have not been a part of the Library's magic for long. Were you to remain at Pemberley in such a state you would have drained your magic entirely, and that could be catastrophic. The wall to Faerie is weakening more rapidly. We need you at your full strength to help repair it.

Although Abraxas was informing, not scolding, Elizabeth was ashamed of herself. The griffin did not issue warnings with no cause. Had she not learned as much when she misused and ruined the book the Library had sent with her on their quest? They were fortunate indeed that Mr. Darcy's memory was so precise. If he had not been able to memorize the map, they would never have found their way home.

It had been very difficult to leave him at Pemberley. She had not wished to do it at all, and Abraxas must have sensed as much, for he had understood better than she that her magic was waning. He was entirely correct to call her back. Without a fit Librarian, the Library could not function properly and would have to be shut up again.

"Thank you, Abraxas. I do not deserve you. But I shall try to do better."

You have made mistakes, but you have been strong and brave. You shall have to be those things again. Are you ready?

Elizabeth was not ready. She was exhausted and heart-sore. "I am."

~

THE DOOR CLOSED SILENTLY behind the retreating figure of Galon. The man had withstood Darcy's interview – interrogation, really – and Darcy had to admit that he admired his sister's intended. He poured himself a brandy and dropped heavily into a seat by the fire.

Georgiana was to be wed. To a fae prince, no less, not that his title would mean anything to them. He would have to give it up to wed the woman he loved. Darcy sipped his drink and tried not to acknowledge the sickening jealousy that pooled in his chest. If only such a sacrifice on his part could gain him Elizabeth's hand.

Galon valued Georgiana over his birthright. He was willing to live as a human, so long as he could marry the woman he loved, and therefore, he deserved her. When Darcy had been faced with a similar choice, he had made the wrong one, and therefore he did not deserve Elizabeth.

It did not keep him from wanting her. And so, despite how busy life had been at Pemberley since his return, his thoughts were often more than a hundred miles away in Oxford.

He stood to return to his desk and glanced at the marriage articles for Georgiana and Galon. It was all for form – Galon had nothing to give other than himself. And in any case, as a fae, he did not consider himself bound by contract or promise to a human. No human other than Georgiana, that is. For when Darcy was able to observe them without being noticed himself, it was clear that Galon held himself bound to her. That he had so selflessly loved Georgiana all this time without any hope of it being requited did soothe Darcy's concerns a bit, and, as his sister had been sure to repeat, she did not require his permission.

She did, however, ask very earnestly, very prettily for his blessing. It eased the sting considerably.

Georgiana was now legally promised to Galon, and soon both would return to the oceans. When they did, Darcy alone would remain resident at Pemberley. It was not a new sensation for him, but after his disappointment five years ago, he had just thrown himself into his work. It had helped distract him; for when he worked himself to exhaustion, he could not think too much about Elizabeth.

Elizabeth, who was gone.

Now working was not enough. Darcy knew what all of society had gained in having her as a Librarian because he knew what he had lost.

The house was still full of people. Richard, Georgiana, Galon. Loneliness gnawed at him anyway like a starving rat.

Darcy closed his eyes so that he could feel the magical connection that still existed, a remnant of sharing Elizabeth's magic to defeat Alaine. It was tenuous, fragile, but it was there. One day, he supposed, it would be severed when they had been apart for too long or she simply wished the memory gone.

"I was not worthy of her," he said quietly. The words seemed to echo off the walls of his study, but perhaps that was his imagination. "But I will live my life in a way that she would approve."

The door to the study opened suddenly. Fitzwilliam stepped inside, his nose wrinkled in distaste.

"Remind me," he said, "never to be caught in a room with your sister and her betrothed ever again. They are shameless."

"They are young," Darcy replied with an affection that ached.

Fitzwilliam walked to the brandy and poured himself a glass. He held the decanter and glanced at Darcy, then put the spirits down without offering to pour a second glass.

"You look like hell, cousin," he said blithely. "And you have cloistered yourself here to hide away from the cause, I suspect?"

"Sadly, I was rather shocked to find that while I have been moldering away in my anger at the world, my younger sister has become a rather formidable woman." Fitzwilliam sipped from his glass, the amber liquid glinting in the sunlight. "Galon has answered my concerns. Georgiana will be well looked after, not that she needs it anymore."

"You remain in your study to grieve, then," Fitzwilliam told him. "And Georgiana is not the cause, though her happiness does throw your own state of mind into rather sharp relief. You are missing your Elizabeth."

There was no point in denying it. Richard had been witness to Darcy's despair the first time he had parted from Elizabeth. He was well aware that Darcy had never recovered from it. "What of it?"

His cousin's gaze was sympathetic, but his words were not. "We still have a job ahead of us, Darcy," he said quietly. "Wickham is still out there somewhere. His attack on Georgiana may have been at Alaine's behest, but he must still be made to answer for it."

His cousin was correct. Darcy took a deep breath and with some effort, shook his melancholy away. It would return, eventually. It always did. It would not, however, keep him from his duty. He stood, lifted his drink to his mouth, and finished the brandy.

"Then let us begin."

❧

"I AM WELL, ABRAXAS," Elizabeth said with some pique. "Perfectly well." She chanted a quick incantation and several books appeared on the table next to her. "Can you not see?"

Then why do you spend so much time inquiring about this Mr. Wickham?

Elizabeth's cheeks warmed. "He is still a danger, and I would not have him casting love spells on any other woman. It is forbidden."

And yet, enforcing such laws is not within the responsibilities of the Library.

Elizabeth slumped into the nearest chair. "It is the last thing I might do for Mr. Darcy," she said softly. "I know it is self-indulgent, but . . ."

You are correct. And we have more important work to complete, Your Eminence. Work that protects the entire human realm, not only one family in it.

Elizabeth was silent for a moment. Abraxas had been kind to say that it was the family she was protecting. They both knew it was the man and not his sister in her thoughts. She would ease Mr. Darcy's burden if she could, but it was not her place.

She closed her eyes and touched the last remaining bond between her and Mr. Darcy. She ought to sever it, but she could not. It brought her comfort in a way that nothing else could. That nothing else ever would. If it was to be cut, he would have to do it.

"Very well, Abraxas," she said, standing. "What is happening that threatens the Library?"

It threatens us all. The wall between the fae lands and the human world is growing ever more porous.

Elizabeth had seen the holes in the wall when she visited Faerie. The ease with which Alaine had sent creatures from Faerie demonstrated how dangerous those gaps were. When

Elizabeth returned to the Library, she had resumed regularly patching the holes.

The holes in the wall are multiplying at an alarming rate, Abraxas said. *Even newly repaired holes have broken open. Unsurprisingly there are more accounts of fae creatures in England and strange weather events.*

The griffin's thoughts were tinged with something Elizabeth had not felt from him before. Trepidation. Fear?

Elizabeth felt helpless. *I do not know what else we might do. Perhaps I can patch the holes more quickly. But we are no closer to finding the cause of the wall's deterioration. If the Library had a book with the answer, surely we would have found it by now.*

Perhaps we could— But Elizabeth never learned what Abraxas planned to say.

The ground trembled beneath her feet. A rumbling sound was followed quickly by a rolling sensation, as though the ground had somehow formed into ocean waves, and they were bobbing along atop the surface. She threw her arms around Abraxas, whose solid weight held her upright. Soon enough, the movement ebbed and ceased. She thanked the griffin and released him.

"Was that an earthquake?" She had experienced them in her training, but she had never known one to occur in England. She called up the ancient book of Aohwah Aihpid, the last fae to live entirely among men. Such shaking indicated . . .

Oh, no.

What is it? Abraxas inquired anxiously.

Elizabeth looked up from the book. "It appears that the walls are not only porous." She swallowed nervously. "They are collapsing."

CHAPTER 21

"If you *taught* me, I would have less to fear," Georgiana said, hands on her hips. Her imperious gesture was made a little less severe by a sudden jolt of the ship that tipped it briefly towards the starboard, forcing Georgiana to fling her hands out to maintain her balance.

Galon grabbed her wrist to steady her. "Easy," he said softly.

Georgiana looked down at the deck of the ship, which had resumed its natural movement. The sea had been increasingly odd lately, even more mercurial than it usually was. The sky was gray and heavy today, but there was no rain yet.

She and Galon stood at the bow where they could be out of the way of the sailors but still able to stand ready for danger from the sea.

"We know Wickham will come," she insisted, returning to the topic of discussion. "Fitzwilliam and Darcy are looking for him on land, but I think we are his greater targets. He may come for your skin, perhaps, or he may consider me an easier target to attack first. But at this point, he will want revenge on both of us."

"And I have promised to keep you safe," he said in his solemn voice, his green eyes steady on hers. "I would die to protect you, my dear girl. You know that."

"I do." She softened, looking at his earnest expression. Since her illness, he seemed determined to wrap her in cotton wool and protect her with all of his strength. But that was not who she was, and that was not who they were. "But you cannot protect me all of the time. No," she said when his mouth opened in protest. "You cannot. Even you must sleep. You must sometimes take more than a few steps from me. You must sometimes return to the sea."

That last was the one that frightened her the most. As a selkie, he could not stay out of the sea forever. He had been far from it for too long during her time at Pemberley. Returning to the ship had helped him some, but he would have to go into the water soon or he would begin to suffer. And there she could not follow him.

"I will delay it as long as possible."

"No!" She clenched his wrists. "You must! Galon, I love you. I could not bear to see you suffer. And you know that the longer you are away from the sea the weaker you will become. Do you not see? This is the only way."

He looked out across the water, his brow furrowed.

"Why are you so resistant?" Georgiana asked at last. He had often seen her fight in sea battles. He had fought by her side in his selkie form. Why was he concerned now?

He sighed and pinched his brow. "I suppose . . . I suppose because teaching you physical combat acknowledges that I cannot protect you. And the idea sends chills down my spine. If something happened to you—"

"I wish I could say that nothing will happen to me. But if it does, would it not be better if I was able to protect myself?"

Galon nodded reluctantly. "Very well. I will have to set aside my fears. But you will forgive me if I occasionally forget and hold you like the precious gift you are?"

She laughed. "Of course. And Galon . . . thank you."

～

SHE WAS NOT QUITE AS thankful on the third day of their lessons. The storage room under the second deck was their chosen site for their mock battles, as they were out of the way of the sailors and did not have to worry about flying off the deck when the ship rocked or jolted unexpectedly. Here, they would only fly into barrels or crates which were tied onto rails to keep them from rolling about.

Fighting in the storage room meant that she could not use much magic, for fear of damaging the supplies. She was determined to learn how to fight even without her magic, so that Wickham could not take her by surprise again.

"Again," Galon said, gripping Georgiana from behind. This time, he grabbed both of her arms at the elbow.

Georgiana tried to elbow him, but his grip was too tight. She went to reach for her magic, but she held herself back. There could be times when she could not use her magic for fear of hurting bystanders, or Wickham might find another spell to block it. She had to learn to fight without it.

Remembering what Galon had taught her, she threw her head back, but she was much shorter than Galon and her head only hit his chest.

So she let her legs go limp, yanking her weight downwards. Simultaneously, she used his grip on her elbows to pull him forward, throwing his weight off-balance until he was forced to release her or fall.

"Excellent!" Galon said, taking a step back.

Georgiana smiled, rubbing her elbows.

"Are you well?" He was watching her movement with concern, so she stopped quickly, even though his grip had hurt. She was not about to let him end their lessons so early.

"Yes!" She grinned. "Can we try the one where I throw you next?"

He laughed. "Does your brother know how bloodthirsty you are?"

"Not in the slightest."

They faced each other and she prepared, keeping her weight balanced and ready. As he stepped forward, she pulled him, planting her left foot to throw him off balance, then hitting his leg from behind while shoving him hard.

Galon fell. Of course, with his height, the fall was rather dramatic. It was made more so by the fact that Georgiana forgot to let go of him at the end and so she tumbled with him. Not just with him but directly onto him.

"Oof!" he gasped as he landed hard.

"Oh no! Are you hurt?" Georgiana frantically wrapped her hands around his head, feeling behind it for blood. Had his head hit the ground?

"Georgiana." She ceased her panic over his potential head injury when she realized how close his face was to hers, and the look in his eyes was certainly not pain.

Well, maybe a certain kind of pain.

She gave him a tentative smile, and he took that as all the permission he needed. His hands wrapped around her head, pulling her even closer to him as his mouth met hers.

With a sigh of pleasure, she sank into him, forgetting everything but how much she loved this loyal, kind, clever man who had always been there for her. He was the reason she wanted to learn how to protect herself – because she could not bear the idea that he might be hurt trying to protect her and because she wanted a long, happy life by his side.

He groaned, and she smiled and deepened the kiss. Her fingers played with his silky hair.

As if she had issued an invitation, his hand was suddenly buried in her hair, pins flying as he pulled her ever closer.

For a moment, Georgiana felt dizzily that she had forgotten which way was up, until she realized that he had rolled them over so that he was on top, his mouth plundering hers as he hovered over her on his elbows. She was bereft when he finally pulled back and smiled down at her.

"My dear, we—" His face suddenly froze, and the light in his eyes darkened.

"Galon?"

He pushed himself backwards onto his knees. "Georgiana, get behind me."

She obeyed immediately. Whatever the threat was, he recognized it while she did not, and she would trust him to stand before her.

Galon crept forward towards one of the crates. When he reached it, he flung the crate over, sending its contents flying.

A metal plate flew out, hitting the opposite wall of the storage compartment with a clang. A small lantern followed, rolling a few feet across the floor. Georgiana frowned at the remaining contents. Several loose blankets, a pair of pants.

With horror, Georgiana looked to where the plate had landed. Several large crumbs of bread and a small chicken bone lay near it.

"A stowaway," she whispered, realizing what it all meant.

Galon's gaze went sharply to hers. His face was pale, his eyes dark in the gloom of the compartment. "Not just any stowaway," he said grimly, picking up a familiar whetstone.

Georgiana sucked in a quick breath as she recognized it, not only from her past but from her dreams.

"Wickham."

⁓

THERE HAD BEEN no other sign of Wickham in the storage compartment. Perhaps he spent his nights there. Perhaps he had abandoned it when they had first begun their practices in the room. Perhaps, perhaps.

Galon had spoken to the captain, who had ordered the ship searched. The sailors had grumbled, but they had searched. However, it was a large ship. Most of the sailors had no magic, and Wickham was adept at those tricks he knew. Nobody had found him.

"Galon," Georgiana said patiently yet again. "You must go into the sea."

"I cannot leave you while Wickham is here."

"I will be well protected." She looked back at the captain. Captain Wentworth was a powerful magic user in his own right, and he had invited her to stand next to him at the helm while Galon spent a little while in the sea. "And you know that I would rather fight by your side than hide in your shadow."

"But—"

"You will be of no use in my protection if you do not recover your strength," she said, pushing his skin at him. "And we will need to fight. It is not just Napoleon anymore. You have heard the reports. Strange creatures, cyclones, fuming water. I will need you at full power, at my side. Please, Galon."

Galon turned to Captain Wentworth. "Please," he said softly, "do not fail to guard her. She is my heart."

"I give you my word," the captain said, the solemnity in his eyes backing his promise. "None will harm her under my care. I know what it is to have one's heart in another's keeping."

And finally, finally, Galon slipped into his selkie skin and dove into the sea.

Georgiana kept her own promise. She stood next to Captain Wentworth and split her attention between the sea, watching for Galon, and the ship. She would see Wickham if he tried to approach her. Even invisibility spells could be spotted if one were diligent and if the wearer was moving. The ripples were always there to see.

But there were no ripples, and there was no disturbance on the ship.

The sky was blue and almost cloudless, the wind just brisk enough to keep the sails filled without heralding an approaching storm.

Georgiana took a deep breath. The salty air refreshed her in a way that even the cool air of her native Derbyshire no longer could. This was her home now, her duty, her purpose. She smiled to hear the shouts of the sailors as they adjusted sails and manned their posts.

There. Was that Galon in the distance? Yes, she could just see him darting among the waves. He was moving towards the ship, in fact. Was he done already? She might have to scold him if his color was not better. She was well, safe, and he could afford to spend longer in the water.

Several of the sailors had spotted him, and she could hear them calling to each other and pointing to him. But she frowned.

He was coming far too fast. This was not Galon returning to the ship after taking a revitalizing swim. Something was wrong.

One final dive, and Galon leapt up as a seal and transformed into a man just in time to grab hold of the rope ladder with one hand and his selkie skin in the other.

"Something is coming!" he yelled. "Port side! Something is wrong with the sea!"

Just as he threw himself over the deck and Captain Went-worth sounded the alarm, there was a deep rumble. The ship shuddered as if the ocean itself had split, and the waves suddenly became rough in a strange circular pattern, as if someone had dropped something very large and heavy into the water some distance away.

The sailor in the crow's nest yelled, "Sea monster!" It was cacophony on board.

Galon leaped up the stairs towards Georgiana. For a moment, she thought he was injured from how he clutched his side, but then she realized he was holding his selkie skin. He shoved it into a corner under a pile of ropes before hurtling to her side and taking her hand in his.

She clutched the railing on one side and Galon on the other, but she stood, chin raised, ready to meet this threat with the magic that flowed within her.

A dark shape was visible under the water on the port side. It disappeared under the keel of the ship, and Georgiana held her breath. Would it butt the ship from underneath? She had heard of sea monsters upending entire ships in the past from such a move.

Suddenly, it surfaced on the starboard side, and Georgiana gasped and clutched at Galon's hand.

It was not the massive flippers that kept it afloat that terrified her, although the monster could capsize the vessel in one blow. It was not even the sharp teeth in its massive mouth or the vicious look in its lizard-like head that made her tremble.

It was the long, long neck that allowed it to reach its head up over the ship like a swan before darting its head in like a bird snatching prey, a screaming sailor trapped in its maws.

Georgiana fought to control her terror and keep her stomach from revolting as she threw out her magic, reaching for the sea. She could feel Galon next to her, his own magic flying forth to wrap around the monster's gargantuan neck. Captain Wentworth and several of his lieutenants sent forth winds to buffet the monster, loose its jaws, and release its captive.

Georgiana pulled hard on the monster from beneath, sucking it down into the waves, trusting that the others would free the man in time.

The sea was now a raging maelstrom, and Georgiana fought hard to keep the ship from being sucked in along with the monster as she grappled with its mighty form.

There were cries of relief from the men as the sailor dropped out of the monster's mouth and was blown gently onto the deck, but she kept her focus on the monster. Now that the man was freed, it was time to push it away from the ship and destroy it.

It was easier, she found, to push the ship away from the monster. She shoved, and the ship sailed through the water as if propelled, far enough away to simplify her job of controlling the whirlpool.

She could feel it when Galon's focus shifted to the ship, keeping it steady and afloat in the still raging waters, taking the pressure off her to mind both things at once. She released it into his care.

The captain and his men worked with her, their magic spinning around hers, all of them attacking the sea monster from different angles, twisting and pulling. It writhed and groaned, but finally they twisted its neck until it broke.

The sea monster, its body still undulating, slowly sank into the sea.

Georgiana kept her hold on the sea, which still roared with the magic she had pushed into it. Slowly, she settled the sea back to its natural state, careful not to becalm it, otherwise she would have to answer to Captain Wentworth.

She released her magic and staggered, exhausted.

Fighting the maelstrom to keep the monster trapped but the ship safe had taken a massive amount of her energy.

She had never seen a sea monster like that in all of her time at sea. And what had Galon seen or felt that had alerted him? She could have sworn there had been an undersea earthquake, but would they have even felt such a thing on a ship?

The oceans had been strange for the past few years, but this was beyond strange. This was dangerous. Something was very, very wrong.

What was that?

There was an odd ripple to Georgiana's side, and suddenly she was wrenched back against someone.

"Galon!" she managed to gasp before a sharp pain at her neck and a warm trickle of blood blocked her speech.

Mr. Wickham! He had used the distraction of the sea monster – or was the sea monster his doing? – to grab her.

She frantically reached for her magic, but Mr. Wickham was already dragging her backwards.

"Your skin!" Mr. Wickham called, and Georgiana recognized the fear and fury in his voice. He knew this was a last desperate effort. He knew he would not likely succeed. The thought gave her courage. "Your skin for your beloved!"

"No!" Georgiana wanted to shout, but the knife was already cutting into her neck. Mr. Wickham had misjudged his strength, and if she did not stop him, he would kill her before he even intended to.

Galon took a step forward, murder in his eyes, but Georgiana acted first. She used the last of her magical strength to yank water from the sea, hurling it into Mr. Wickham's eyes and the deck around his feet. He cried out at the salt in his eyes, and Georgiana used a move Galon had taught her, hooking her leg behind Mr. Wickham's and pulling.

He fell backwards onto the deck, and then Georgiana was

in Galon's arms. He hugged her fiercely, then put her behind him.

Mr. Wickham was gone. But Captain Wentworth was blocking the stairs, and there! There was a ripple at the coil of rope—

"I have it!" Mr. Wickham crowed, reappearing. He held something aloft.

To Georgiana's horror, she recognized it. Galon's selkie skin.

He moved forward, but Mr. Wickham held a knife to the skin. "Ah, ah, ah!" he said, waving the knife at Galon. "One move, and I will tear it to shreds."

"Very well then," Galon said to her shock.

"I am not bluffing," Mr. Wickham said, but Georgiana could hear his uncertainty. He would never dare destroy Galon's skin. Galon would kill him, and he knew it. The skin was worth nothing if it was destroyed.

Movement behind Mr. Wickham caught her eye, and Georgiana stifled a gasp. One of Captain Wentworth's sailors was creeping up behind Mr. Wickham.

Whether it was her reaction or whether Mr. Wickham felt the man's presence, she did not know. But he spun around just as the sailor reached for the knife.

Mr. Wickham cursed and fought viciously. But it was too late. The sailor had yanked downwards to take control of the knife, and the sharp edge tore into Galon's skin, tearing it almost into two.

Georgiana cried out in anguish. "No!" Galon released her, and she dropped to her knees, her heart breaking. Not Galon's skin! If he could not return to the sea, he would die!

Quick as a wink, Galon dove forward. Before Georgiana could blink, he had kicked away Wickham's knife and was kneeling on his chest.

"Galon!" she cried. How long did he have to live? With his

skin destroyed, would he wither away instantaneously, or would he die more slowly as he could not revert to his selkie form to recover?

Galon turned back to look at Georgiana for only a moment, but his look glowed with love and ...triumph?

"You are done, Wickham," he said loudly.

Wickham was staring at the skin, his face pale and waxen. "I have failed," he whispered, his voice barely audible. "Alaine will not forgive this." He closed his eyes, then opened them again, fixing them on Galon. "If I must die, at least I have taken you with me. And through you, *dear* Georgiana. And through her, my old enemy Darcy!"

"I could destroy you now," Galon said. "But I wanted you to know this first." He leaned in close, but Georgiana could still hear every word. "That was not my skin."

Wickham tried to laugh again, but his laugh withered and died as he looked up at his enemy.

"You lie," he spat out, but his retort was weak.

"I do not lie. I knew you were coming for my skin. We fae are good at disguise. You should know – that invisibility spell you use was one of Alaine's, was it not? My true skin also hides under a charm. As for that . . ." He reached out and grabbed the shredded skin. "Shall I show you its true nature?"

Georgiana's heart burst with delight and amusement when the guise faded away, revealing a torn burlap sack.

"I anticipated that you might use a moment of distraction to steal my skin, so I have kept it close to me all the while. Even my beloved Georgiana was not aware." He glanced back at her a with an apologetic look. "The only one of us who will be destroyed today will be you."

Mr. Wickham struggled frantically, fighting against Galon's weight until his face was bright red. "You will regret this!" he gasped. "She will come after you and destroy you!"

"*She* has already lost," Galon told him. "She is a prisoner of the fae and will receive their punishment."

Mr. Wickham sagged as he looked up at his captor, his face wracked with shock and horror.

"Will you kill him?" Captain Wentworth asked.

Galon looked up. "I should."

"He is a menace. We do not dare keep him prisoner on the ship. We know how dangerous he is. Even with Alaine imprisoned, he may have spells she gave him before she was captured." Georgiana had not realized Captain Wentworth knew so much, but it made sense that Galon had told him everything in order that he might be on guard.

"Much as I hate to stand as judge, jury, and executioner, I think I shall have to. But I shall give him one element of mercy. I shall not kill him directly. Instead, my magic of the sea shall force Wickham to take the form of the sea creature he most resembles."

There was a burst of magic, and suddenly a huge flounder flopped on the deck beneath Galon's knee. Galon shook his head, grinning broadly. "A flounder. I should have known. Carnivorous, highly predatory, and a bottom feeder."

Georgiana smiled. Horrifying as the past hour had been, seeing Mr. Wickham transformed into a fish was worth it all.

With a laugh, Galon hauled it up, still flapping, and hurled it off the ship into the dark waters below.

Georgiana ran to the railing, looking down as the fish disappeared beneath the waves.

"Is he—"

"He is alive for now," Galon said as he too looked down. "But he has only the mind of a fish. Even if someone were to fish him up, he would not know who he had been or be able to ask for help." He grinned. "The more bloodthirsty part of me hopes that somebody *does* fish him up. After all, I mentioned the negative attributes of a flounder, but not the most positive one."

"What is that?"

"They are delicious."

CHAPTER 22

*T*he world convulsed around Elizabeth. The floor bucked beneath her and tossed her from her bed onto the rug.

Elizabeth's pulse raced and her hands shook. She had only returned to the familiar and secure confines of the Library a few days ago. And now it was feeling decidedly unsafe.

She staggered to her feet and lit the room's lamps with a thought. Books had dropped from the shelves and a few trinkets from her dresser had broken on the floor, but otherwise the damage from the earthquake was not severe.

She feared the same was not true for the rest of Oxford. Bells rang in alarm and people screamed outside the Library's walls. Elizabeth rushed to the window and pushed back the curtains. People were swarming into the street in their nightclothes, fearful of being in buildings that might collapse. She could only see one building that had been reduced to a pile of rubble, but no doubt there were many more. Was the earthquake centered on Oxford? Had there been parts of England that experienced even greater shocks?

Elizabeth was not concerned about the solidity of the Library; it was built with fae magic. But the rest of the country was not so fortunate. What was happening in Hertfordshire? In Pemberley?

An ache of pure longing made her gasp. Why must everything remind her of him? Even an earthquake took her thoughts to Darcy. It was not fair.

Still, if she had stayed with Darcy, the wall between the mortal world and Faerie would have already collapsed completely. Elizabeth had made the right decision; she just had to learn to live with it.

If only we could fix the wall permanently! She had devoted hours to repairing it, but there seemed to be no end to the amount of damage they faced. Now she needed to address the cause of the earthquake.

She threw on a dressing gown and raced to the Library's main reading room, where she knew she would find Abraxas. Unsurprisingly, he was consulting with Travinius, whose face was pale and grave.

"Do we know what caused such a violent earthquake?" she asked them.

Abraxas rustled his wings, the human equivalent of nervous pacing. *We believe the wall is about to fall.*

"Fall?" Elizabeth echoed. "Disappear completely?" The thought was inconceivable.

Travinius nodded solemnly. "My fae brethren have reported that parts are so tattered and fragile that it cannot hold itself together much longer."

Fear raced down Elizabeth's spine. If the wall fell, then all the creatures of Faerie would flood into the human world. Humans were not equipped to handle them. Death and destruction would follow.

"But our repairs—"

Something is unraveling them as fast as we create them. And the pace is increasing, Abraxas said.

Elizabeth's heart plummeted into her stomach. This was a disaster.

"King Malus has been studying the situation," Travinius reported. "He believes a human mage is using a Forbidden Spell which is destabilizing the wall."

Elizabeth gasped. Forbidden Spells were very powerful and could be shaped for many different purposes, but they always came at a high cost – which was why they were forbidden. However, all Forbidden Spells were locked away in a Library vault. Elizabeth herself had never so much as looked at them. "How would a human mage have gained access to a Forbidden Spell?"

We do not know, Abraxas said. *One was stolen from the Library years ago, but we retrieved it. We know of no other breaches of our security.*

"There is one piece of good news," Travinius said. "Malus's warriors have been patrolling the wall and have pinpointed the area of greatest weakness. They believe that is where the magic is being drained."

"That is good news!" Elizabeth replied. "So they can stop the miscreant, whoever it is."

Travinius shook his head. "The mage is definitely a human using a Forbidden Spell. Malus cannot act against a human who remains on our side of the wall."

Elizabeth's anxiety spiked. "Who can stop him? Perhaps we can get word to the Mages' Council? They could send a few of their top people."

We have no time, Abraxas said. *This villain must be stopped now.*

Elizabeth straightened her spine. "Then I must go. I have the use of the Library's magic once more. Hopefully that will be sufficient to stop this mage."

Travinius scowled. "You just returned! Librarians are not supposed to leave the Library willy nilly!"

"This is not a holiday at Brighton!" Elizabeth exclaimed. "We cannot stop this mage if we remain here. Someone needs to visit the wall, and I am the best equipped."

The fae crossed his arms over his chest. "I do not like it. It violates many of the Library's protocols."

I do not like it either. Abraxas's mental voice was deep and regretful. *But Elizabeth is correct. No one else can arrive in time. The Library will allow her to go.*

Elizabeth's shoulders sagged slightly. Even while she had argued with Travinius, she had hoped another solution could be found. This promised to be an unpleasant journey – with no Darcy to keep her company. "Very well. I will change into traveling clothes." She had thought that her days of magical quests were behind her. Apparently one more remained.

Abraxas's mental voice rumbled in her head. *But you will not be alone. I will be with you.*

It was early morning by the time Abraxas landed near the section of wall the fae had identified. The sun was beginning to peek out over the horizon. The area was a field of grasses and plants surrounded by hills and craggy cliffs. King Malus believed whoever was using the Forbidden Spell would be found in the vicinity.

Elizabeth slid from Abraxas's back and peered at the wall with her magical senses. She gasped. It bore no resemblance to a solid structure–more like a torn dish rag. It was worn thin in many places, so that she could even catch glimpses into Faerie. In other places there were great rents and gaps. This section of wall appeared ready to collapse at any moment.

The only saving grace was that no creature or fae lurked on the other side waiting for a chance to escape into the human world. Elizabeth had sent word to King Malus asking him to keep the denizens of Faerie away from the border, and it appeared that he was doing so.

The field glowed with golden light as the sun rose in the sky. Elizabeth scanned the area but could see no one who could have perpetrated the damage. *Do you see the mage who has done this?* She asked Abraxas. The griffin's eyesight was better than hers.

No, he replied.

Are we certain the mage is still here? In a way, it would be a relief if the mage had departed, although it would only prolong the problem.

Abraxas's head swiveled back and forth. *Yes*, he said. *I sense...a strong magical presence.*

A mage?

I cannot be sure...the magical signature is...distorted....

Elizabeth started when she spied movement on the other side of the field. But it was only a pig...No, a boar. A wild boar? Here? It was not behaving as a wild animal should, either. It was moving toward the wall as if hoping to slip through a jagged hole near the ground. But it only managed a few steps of drunken staggering before it stumbled and fell.

The boar is a familiar! Abraxas said.

Elizabeth pulled up her skirts and raced across the field toward the creature. *Can you speak with it?* she asked Abraxas.

I am attempting to, but he is not responding. I do not know why.

Elizabeth was nearing the boar when her attention was distracted by movement in the sky. A hawk had swooped low, nearly brushing her forehead as it soared toward the wall. At first Elizabeth flinched, thinking the bird might attack, but then she noticed the wobble in its flight. The hawk pumped its wings, trying to stay aloft, but it was a losing battle. The creature managed to land without breaking anything, but it was an ungainly and graceless process. Once on the ground, the hawk sank miserably into the grass.

Elizabeth asked Abraxas, *Is the hawk a familiar too?*

Yes, the griffin answered instantly. *But she will not talk to me.*

Elizabeth had reached the prostrate boar, which rested on its side, panting rapidly. She could see nothing obviously wrong with it – no wounds or signs of disease. She rubbed its snout reassuringly, wishing she could do something.

"Can you tell me what happened?" she asked the familiar. "What is wrong with you?"

But the boar only watched her with suffering eyes.

If we have two sick familiars, does that mean that there are two injured mages nearby? Elizabeth asked Abraxas.

That is one possibility, he replied. *But...there is something odd about these familiars. They want to return to Faerie, which they should not do unless their mages are dead. And I do not understand what saps their life force...* The griffin jerked up his head. *Oh my!*

A tiger had just emerged from behind the trees. Elizabeth's heart beat a little faster despite knowing that she had her magic and a griffin familiar to protect her. However, like the other animals, the tiger moved sluggishly. It weaved on its feet, barely managing to remain upright as it made its way to the wall.

It is another familiar, Abraxas said.

Elizabeth frowned. *Abraxas, do you know of any mages who have called a tiger familiar?* She asked.

Not in Britain, he replied. *It happens in India and nearby countries, but it has never happened here.*

That was what I thought. How had a mage managed to call a tiger familiar without anyone knowing? Such a feat would be a crowning achievement for the Lady Patronesses. They would be crowing about it for months.

Is there anything we can do to help the familiars? She asked Abraxas.

No. I do not understand what is ailing them, so I do not know how to help. I do not believe they are in imminent danger. They are simply exhausted.

How? And where are their mages?

Abraxas stared at the tiger very intently. *The three familiars are tied to each other somehow.*

How is that possible?

I do not understand it. Abraxas's mental voice was puzzled. *Unless they are....I do not see how....But I believe that they are all familiars for the same mage.*

Elizabeth's mouth dropped open. *I did not believe that could be done.*

I did not either. But surely their mage must be nearby. Elizabeth searched the area but could not see anyone.

Suddenly the three animals exclaimed at the same time. The hawk screeched. The tiger roared. And the boar moaned. It was quite eerie.

What is happening to them? Elizabeth asked Abraxas.

Her griffin examined the other creatures intently. *Their mage is drawing power from them.*

How horrible! The mage is making them suffer!

Elizabeth, the wall! Abraxas cried.

She whipped her head around and saw that the wall had torn a few new holes – which were allowing a unicorn, a wyvern, and a great snowy owl to leave Faerie, although none of the animals looked very happy about it.

Familiars! Elizabeth realized. *The mage is summoning animals to become familiars. Who would do such a thing? Who was even capable of doing such a thing?* A suspicion was beginning to form in Elizabeth's mind, but she had no proof at the moment.

We must stop this mage! she said to Abraxas.

The new creatures from Faerie were marching toward the east, so Elizabeth followed them. They passed through the field into a densely wooded area where Abraxas could not follow. *I will remain here,* he told Elizabeth. *Call if you need me.*

I will.

The creatures did not travel far before they reached a clearing ringed by pine trees. Elizabeth stood behind a tree to survey the scene. In the center of the clearing was a fire. But it was no ordinary fire. The flames twisted of their own accord, forming various magical sigils – one after another. Elizabeth had never seen magic like it. Could that be part of the Forbidden Spell?

She was unsurprised at the identity of the mage standing by the fire. If a human mage would twist the summoning of familiars for their own end, Elizabeth had one candidate in mind: Lady Catherine de Bourgh.

Indeed Darcy's aunt was chanting the words of a spell and throwing herbs into the fire.

How did Lady Catherine obtain a Forbidden Spell? Elizabeth asked Abraxas.

His mental voice was troubled. *Philip, the previous Librarian, had a weakness for her. He would have been a fine librarian otherwise. He was the one who arranged for the Lady Patronesses to assign familiars. He stole a Forbidden Spell and was dismissed after returning it. But he must have given a copy of the spell to Lady Catherine. I never thought he would violate his oaths in such a way!* Of course, Abraxas had been Philip's familiar as well. No wonder he was disturbed.

The new creatures from Faerie had arrayed themselves in

a semicircle around the fire. Lady Catherine regarded them with a wide smile. "Yes. Yes! You will do very nicely! The Duke of Barrington's son will summon one of you, no doubt. And, of course, Lady Amelia...her mother will be so pleased."

Elizabeth shuddered. All this suffering and horror so that Lady Catherine could obtain prestigious familiars for the families of the *ton*! No wonder Elizabeth had failed to summon a familiar. Lady Catherine had been manipulating who received familiars and what kind of familiar they received. No doubt dozens of wealthy mages possessed familiars they were not entitled to, and any number of mages from more modest families had likely lost a chance at a familiar altogether.

Elizabeth's blood boiled. Lady Catherine's success at matching mages with familiars had made her very wealthy and allowed her to move in the highest circles. She even attended St. James Court and visited the Prince Regent in Brighton. She was flattered and cossetted wherever she went. Everyone took care to avoid angering her. And all the while she had been building her conquest of society by tearing down the fae wall and endangering the entire population of Britain.

Elizabeth could only imagine how much power Lady Catherine commanded with the Forbidden Spell. *How can I fight her? If only I could summon the help of other mages!* But they could not afford the delay. The wall could collapse at any moment – particularly if Lady Catherine summoned additional familiars. Elizabeth needed to stop her now.

The mistress of Rosings Park had finished gloating over the new familiars and resumed chanting with her hands outstretched toward the fire. *I must stop her, and I must stop her now.*

Elizabeth slipped out from behind the tree and strode

toward Lady Catherine. "Stop!" she commanded. "You must cease the use of the Forbidden Spell immediately!"

Lady Catherine started at Elizabeth's sudden appearance. But then she drew herself up to her fullest height and affixed a sneer to her face. "You cannot tell me what to do!"

"I can and I am," Elizabeth replied.

Lady Catherine laughed. "You are a nobody. That little chit that my fool of a nephew was once enamored with. You could not even summon a worm!"

Elizabeth smiled. "True, I could not summon a worm, but I could summon a griffin."

Abraxas timed it perfectly, landing behind Elizabeth at that precise moment.

Lady Catherine's eyes went wide. "No. That cannot be your familiar. You are borrowing someone else's!"

Abraxas laughed at that, making a strange clacking sound with his beak.

"I assure you that Abraxas is my familiar," Elizabeth said.

"Abraxas? But that is—"

"The name of the Library's griffin? Yes. I am the Librarian." She gave Lady Catherine her most amiable smile – showing lots of teeth. "And the Library is open again."

Lady Catherine paled. No doubt she had counted on the Library's closure to help conceal her activities. But in the next instant she managed a show of nonchalance, shrugging and returning her attention to the fire. "The Library is nothing to me."

Elizabeth stalked closer. "It has everything to do with you. You are using a Forbidden Spell to grant familiars to undeserving mages. And the spell was given to you by the last Librarian."

Lady Catherine sniffed. "Ridiculous."

Elizabeth rolled her eyes. "You cannot deny it. The proof is right here." She waved to the creatures from Faerie. "But your crimes are greater than you realize. Every time you use the Forbidden Spell, it thins the wall between Faerie and our world. Soon it will disintegrate completely."

Lady Catherine lifted her chin. "It could not possibly do any such thing."

Elizabeth sighed. "Did it not occur to you that there is a reason the spell is *forbidden*? Your spell is the cause of the recent earthquakes, the odd weather, and crop failures. It has allowed fae creatures to roam freely into our world."

A flash of guilt crossed Lady Catherine's face. Elizabeth gaped. "You knew! You knew you were weakening the wall and yet you continued to do so!"

The other woman looked away. "The wall repairs itself. There is no harm done."

Elizabeth laughed bitterly. "It does not repair itself. I repair it with the help of the Library. And the wall has reached a point where we cannot fix it."

"Nonsense! You are just jealous of what I can do and you cannot. *I* have summoned three familiars for myself!"

"You have, but have you looked at them lately? You are draining their magic. They are dying."

Lady Catherine shrugged. "I can find more."

Disgusted with the other woman's callousness, Elizabeth was done debating her. "You must stop what you are doing. Now."

"No," the other woman said with a sneer. "Now be on your way." As she made a shooing motion, her magic pushed Elizabeth back toward the edge of the clearing. Taken by surprise, Elizabeth needed a minute to draw on the Library's power and unravel the spell.

When she glanced back into the clearing, Lady Catherine was again chanting and causing sigils to form in the fire's flames. In her mage sight, Elziabeth could see the line of power as the other mage drained magic from the wall. Each second the wall was closer to collapse.

I think we are finished negotiating, Elizabeth said to Abraxas.

I agree. The griffin flew across the clearing, claws outstretched to grab Lady Catherine. But when he drew close, he was repulsed by a blue glow that surrounded the woman. *She has erected a shield,* he reported.

Elizabeth wanted to swear. They needed to stop Lady Catherine *now*! How could they do it if they could not touch her?

She took a deep breath and forced herself to examine the situation rationally. In addition to the power Lady Catherine drained from Faerie, three fainter lines also connected her to familiars. Of course! The wall provided enormous amounts of energy that had to be directed and controlled. The other woman had summoned additional familiars not just to demonstrate her magical capabilities but also because the familiars helped shape the magic to her will.

What would happen if Lady Catherine were cut off from her familiars? Elizabeth asked Abraxas.

She would lose control of the power.

That might be a death sentence for the other woman, but better her than the rest of the world.

Elizabeth focused her mage sight on the threads of power connecting Lady Catherine to her familiars. Then, in one quick movement, she used a severing spell to cut those threads.

The effect was instantaneous. As soon as the familiars were no longer connected, the spell flew out of Lady Catherine's control. Magical energy crackled and whipped through the air around her. The woman screamed and struggled to cut herself off from the spell. After a moment of agony, she succeeded. The spell dissipated and the fire died. Lady Catherine collapsed onto the grass.

Elizabeth hurried toward her. The other woman's shields had disappeared, and Elizabeth had no difficulty finding her pulse. Lady Catherine was still alive.

Elizabeth was both relieved and chagrined. She did not want to be the instrument of the woman's death, but now she would be required to decide the mage's fate.

Elizabeth, look! Abraxas directed her attention to the sky.

King Malus was approaching them, floating through the air as if standing on an invisible magic carpet. *I did not know he could do that!*

He landed with perfect grace right in front of Elizabeth. "I see you have captured the miscreant who has been causing so much trouble for your land and ours."

"Yes. Although I could have used your help ten minutes ago," she grumbled.

He smiled. "We are forbidden from fighting human mages outside Faerie. It is one of many rules Alaine violated."

"You threatened me and Mr. Darcy with a cohort of fae warriors not long ago!" Elizabeth said indignantly.

He shrugged. "That was a bluff. We would not have fought with you."

It would have been nice to know that then, Elizabeth thought.

Lady Catherine blinked and groaned as she began to awaken. Malus gazed dispassionately at her. "This woman has done damage to Faerie. I demand that she be punished."

Elizabeth rubbed her forehead wearily. "She will be." Judgment of wrongdoers was one of the Librarian's duties – seldom performed. It was only necessary when a human violated one of the Library's laws, and few humans even had that opportunity.

Lady Catherine staggered to her feet. She was a pathetic figure. Her dress was streaked with mud and her hair was in disarray. Moreover, she appeared to have aged 20 years in the past few minutes. Malus conjured manacles and chains around her hands before she could attempt to escape or cast spells.

The laws of the Library required Elizabeth to render judgment. She turned to Abraxas. "Will you create a courtroom?" He flapped his wings once, and she immediately felt a surge of power. Suddenly she, Lady Catherine, Malus, and Abraxas were standing in a room with marble floors and dark wood paneling. Elizabeth knew they had not actually left the field. Abraxas had created an illusion – a recreation of a room in the Library. But the illusory courtroom bounded this space to ensure they would not be interrupted and gave Elizabeth's words the force of law. She swallowed. She had never wanted to be in this position.

The punishment for using a Forbidden Spell was death. Lady Catherine had used it repeatedly, more than earning that fate. The judgment should be clear. But Lady Catherine, despite everything she had done and the pain she caused Elizabeth by tearing her from Darcy five years ago, was still Darcy's aunt. His own mother's sister. He had believed her to be honorable and incapable of such selfish acts. Darcy would be furious and sad if he heard of his aunt's death. It would give no opportunity for her repentance or their reconciliation.

And he would learn that her death was at Elizabeth's command.

Then Abraxas's words echoed in her head – *Philip always had a weakness for her.*

No. She could not allow her love for Darcy to stand in the way of her duty to the Library. The thought made her heart ache. He might hate her for it, but Elizabeth's path was clear.

"The Library is prepared to pass judgment upon Lady Catherine de Bourgh." Elizabeth's words echoed as if bouncing off a real marble floor. The lady started to speak, but Elizabeth held up her hand.

"The law of the Library forbids the use of Forbidden Spells on pain of death." Lady Catherine blanched as Elizabeth continued. "Moreover, the Forbidden Spell lives in her memory, and nothing but death can prevent her from casting it again. She must be executed to protect both the fae and the human worlds."

"Darcy will never forgive you!" Lady Catherine cried to Elizabeth.

Elizabeth gritted her teeth. "I must live with that."

"At least I prevented you from marrying him, you social climbing chit! You may have a familiar, but you can never marry him now!" The other woman cackled.

Elizabeth swallowed the bitter taste in her mouth and reminded herself that Lady Catherine's words had nothing to do with the justice the Librarian was required to mete out. She said, "For use of a Forbidden Spell and for attacking a Librarian, you are hereby sentenced to—"

"One moment, Your Eminence," Malus interrupted. "I can offer you another option."

He pulled out a small leather pouch and handed it to Elizabeth. Opening the pouch, she drew out an oddly familiar-looking small bottle of clear liquid. She had seen one like this before, when Malus had offered it to Darcy in the Field of Scarlet: his memories of Elizabeth in exchange for the cure for Georgiana. "The waters of Lethe?" she whispered.

The king nodded. "But if she accepts your offer, she must live in Faerie as a servant – as a way of atoning for her crimes."

It could be a way out for Lady Catherine. Elizabeth could use it to strip Lady Catherine of any memory of the Forbidden Spell, and not have to execute Darcy's aunt, no matter how much she deserved it. Even if Elizabeth could never have Darcy, she still ached for his good opinion.

But when given the choice, Darcy had refused the easy answer of the waters of Lethe.

Elizabeth weighed the bottle in her hand. "Lady Catherine, I offer you a choice. If you drink the waters of Lethe, it will remove your memory of the Forbidden Spell. But for your crimes you will be exiled to Faerie, no longer the powerful Lady Catherine de Bourgh, but merely Catherine, a servant who must earn her bread. Or you may choose death."

Lady Catherine's eyes narrowed. "Mortals in Faerie are often mistreated."

Elizabeth's spine stiffened. "You have mistreated a great many people in your life." Herself among them.

"Never! You cannot expect me to do manual work, subject to the whims of the fae!"

Elizabeth took a deep breath. "Then you choose death? Beware, I shall not ask you again."

"I will die as an earl's daughter, not a drudge!" She spat the words at Elizabeth, as if daring her to do it.

Elizabeth slid the bottle back into the pouch and handed it to Malus, giving Lady Catherine one last moment to change her mind.

Then she nodded to Abraxas.

With his claws extended, the griffin leapt forward at an impossible speed, so fast Elizabeth could barely see the motion. A moment later, Lady Catherine slumped to the floor, her neck at an odd angle, her eyes empty as blood welled from a tear in her throat.

There was a long moment of silence, and then King Malus said, "It was more merciful than she deserved."

Elizabeth averted her gaze from the body. She had done her duty. Hopefully she could live with the consequences.

"The Library has passed judgment!" she announced. "The court is adjourned."

Abraxas flapped his wings and the courtroom disappeared. Once again they stood in a clearing.

Her mouth dry, Elizabeth turned to Malus, "I must arrange to return her body to her daughter." That way Darcy could at least have the comfort of a funeral.

And he would know what she had done.

"Allow my people to do so," the king said. "You have performed a great service for us today. Please let us be of service to you."

"Gladly," she said.

Malus snapped his fingers. In a blink both he and Lady Catherine's body disappeared.

Elizabeth sank down into the grass where she was standing.

She had ordered a woman's death.

Abraxas touched her mind softly. *You had no other choice.*

He meant to be comforting, but it was not the comfort she longed for. She wanted Darcy's arms around her, Darcy telling her she had done the right thing. Telling her he would forgive her. But she would never have that. Hot tears slipped down her cheek.

A thought crossed her mind. "What happened to Philip?" They had never told her the previous Librarian's name before.

Abraxas sighed. *As soon as he was discovered to have taken the Forbidden Spell, he requested death. At the time I thought he did not want to drag the process out. Now I wonder if he was trying to protect Lady Catherine and make certain we never found out she possessed the spell.*

You knew about his feelings for her? She could hardly believe any man, much less a Librarian, could find Lady Catherine lovable.

From the beginning. He came to us, not out of love for the Library but because the woman he loved had chosen a richer, more powerful man. He was not an ideal candidate, but the old Librarian was tired and wanted to retire to her studies. He seemed to do well enough at the beginning...We only discovered the spell had been used because of the first breach in the wall. By the time it was repaired, we had bigger problems.

What do you mean? Not that it mattered now.

The retired Librarian stepped up to mend the breach, but she was old and it was too much for her. She fixed it, but died in the attempt, leaving us with no Librarian. We closed the Library and began the search that led to you.

His words left a bitter taste in her mouth. *And ended up with yet another lovelorn Librarian.*

Abraxas gazed at her. *You have done well. You have not allowed your feelings to interfere with your duties.*

Elizabeth stared at the pine trees ringing the clearing. No. She had put her duties before everything else. As had William. They could be proud of themselves for that. Abraxas's words should have made her feel proud, but she was only numb.

Mr. Darcy will know I killed his aunt, she told Abraxas. *He will hate me.*

I doubt it, Abraxas said. *And if he does, why does it matter? You will probably never see him again.*

There were times when griffins simply did not understand human emotions. *I cannot explain it,* she told her familiar. *It should not matter, but it does.*

*I*n her youth, Georgiana Darcy had been a thoroughly nervous and fretful creature. Galon becoming her familiar had changed that, or rather, he had given her the strength to cast off her cloak of reticence and become the strong young woman she was always meant to be.

In her years at sea, she had faced countless battles and skirmishes. She had come into her magic and defended her country against ruthless enemies. She had been placed under one of the most dreadful curses known to humans and survived it.

Despite all this, on her wedding day, her nerves had returned in full force. She paced the confines of her small ship cabin, wringing her hands as she waited for her brother to come.

It was not that she was afraid of becoming a wife. She loved Galon dearly, and their relationship had flourished beautifully over the years. Taking him as her husband seemed natural. It was not even the prospect of leaving home, as she had spent much of the past five years away.

In truth, Georgiana Darcy was scared to leave her brother.

In the weeks since he had returned with her cure, he was decidedly altered. His disposition was gloomy; he was withdrawn, and Georgiana could count the times he smiled on one hand. He had not changed in essentials, but it was as though his spirit and heart were somewhere else.

What would he do when left to his own devices? Georgiana did not want to see her brother lose himself in his heartbreak. So she asked to see him before she walked down the aisle to begin her new life.

Darcy came, as he always did whenever she needed him. He was a devoted brother.

"Georgiana, you look beautiful. Mother and Father would be so proud if they could see you now."

Georgiana smiled and took his hand. "Thank you, Brother. I am so grateful to have your blessing."

"Would it have stopped you had I withheld it?" Darcy asked earnestly.

Years ago, it would have, but Georgiana was a grown woman now. "No," Georgiana answered truthfully, "But I am glad I have it. In many ways, you have been more of a father to me than a brother. I do hate to disappoint you."

"There is not anything you could do to disappoint me, sweetheart," Darcy said. "You have become a remarkable young lady and mage. I am so proud of all you have accomplished. And now, you have found your match. I know you will be safe with Galon."

"I will be, and happy as well, but…" Georgiana trailed off, her courage momentarily failing her.

"But what?"

Georgiana had called him to her cabin for a purpose, and she would see it through. "I worry about leaving you alone at Pemberley."

"I will hardly be alone," Darcy said.

"I do not mean the servants, tenants, or even Hespera. You have not been yourself since you returned from your quest with Elizabeth."

Though her brother tried to hide it, Georgiana saw his composure slip. She saw the flash of grief in his eyes. "I am no longer a child, William. You can confide in me. Tell me the truth. Are you still in love with Elizabeth?"

Darcy was silent for a long moment, but he finally said, "I do not believe I ever stopped loving her. But it will come to nothing. She is the Librarian. She cannot marry or leave her position, and I cannot leave Pemberley. Sometimes, one must sacrifice happiness for duty and responsibility."

"Surely there must be some way for you to be together," Georgiana said.

Darcy shook his head. "There is not, but today is not about me. It is about celebrating the love you found with Galon. We should not keep him waiting."

Georgiana longed to press him, but her brother's tone brooked no argument. She nodded, and he kissed her forehead before leaving her to finish her preparations.

Galon was well versed in the traditions of the fae and the Library. Perhaps he would know of some way that would allow her brother and Elizabeth to reunite. She vowed that she would broach the subject with him in the coming days.

～

"She looks so much like your mother," Fitzwilliam whispered as Georgiana marched down the length of the ship, her lovely face framed with golden ringlets. Galon stood with Captain Wentworth at the bow of the ship with a moon-eyed expression on his face.

The crew, all of whom greatly admired Miss Darcy and

her beau, stood assembled and adequately washed for the special occasion. It was not often that a wedding ceremony was performed in the middle of the ocean.

Fitzwilliam and Darcy had arrived on their familiars. Darcy envied his sister. She was fortunate enough to wed the person she loved against reason, station, and laws of magic. A union between a fae and a human was practically unheard of.

The ceremony was brief and solemn, ending with a chaste kiss. Georgiana was glowing as Galon led her to the middle of the ship to accept the well-wishes of the crew.

And so, a rather peculiar wedding breakfast began. Three crewmen produced two fiddles and a drum and began playing lively music. Georgiana and Galon moved through the steps of a reel, joined by pairs of sailors.

Some other crewmen brought out casks of fine wine and ale and poured out generous measures.

Darcy crossed the length of the ship to where Hespera stood, her feathers rustled by the sea breeze. She looked particularly annoyed with her circumstances. *How long must we remain on this wretched vessel, Darcy?*

Darcy stroked her neck. *Only for a little while. Then we will return to Pemberley.*

The dear girl deserves such happiness. I only wish they could have married on land.

Georgiana and Galon did not deem it prudent to leave the ship. Not after the troubles they faced last week.

It was troubling that the border still seemed unstable. Hespera told him there had been an earthquake in Oxford that very morning. Darcy wondered how Elizabeth was faring. Surely she was safe in the Library, but he longed to assist her with the seemingly impossible task of mending the wall.

Darcy was resigned to the fact that he was doomed to a

CHAPTER 23 | 249

life of bachelorhood. Pemberley would go to Georgiana and Galon's first born, and the Darcy legacy would continue.

Darcy watched as the celebration grew more raucous. Toasts were given in honor of the bride and groom. Stories of their heroism were traded and reenacted.

Fitzwilliam was happy to participate in the festivities, but Darcy could find little joy in them. Truthfully, he found little joy in anything. Without Elizabeth, he was hollow and aching. He prayed it would get better with time, but he was not certain it would. How did one recover from losing the love of his life?

It will get better, Darcy. Hespera's words startled him. He idly stroked her soft feathers.

Perhaps.

After the tale of Wickham's fate had been recited, ending with one of the men flopping on the deck in a bizarre imitation of a flounder, Darcy decided it was time to depart. He had a long flight ahead of him, and if he did not leave soon there would not be enough daylight to see him safely home.

Galon and Georgiana were still surrounded by the crew, blissfully happy in their newly wedded state. Darcy made his way to them. "Georgiana, I am afraid it is time for me to depart. Please accept my heartfelt congratulations. You and Galon will always be welcome at Pemberley."

Georgiana embraced him tightly. "I wish you would stay longer. Richard is staying aboard. The night is young. Mr. Edwards has composed a poem in my honor. And his words are not to be missed."

Darcy saw one of the burlier sailors flush a deep crimson.

"I am sorry, my dear, but I cannot linger. Pemberley needs me."

Georgiana nodded. Galon shook Darcy's hand. "I will look after her, Darcy. Your sister will always be safe with me."

"I do not doubt it. Thank you, Galon."

Darcy returned to Hespera and climbed on her back. The griffin took off into the clear sky. Darcy idly thought of directing Hespera to make her way to the Library, but quickly banished the notion. He had to return to Pemberley and attempt to make the most of his lonely life.

～

IT HAD ONLY BEEN two days since Georgiana's wedding, but Pemberley felt emptier than ever. Perhaps Darcy should visit London. At least at Darcy House he could be lonely surrounded by diversions like theater and concerts. And there were a few people in London whose company he could stand. Three. Perhaps four.

Darcy had just opened his ledger book when he heard the swift pounding of feet in the hallway outside his study. He was immediately alert. Was there an emergency on the estate?

He was already standing when his cousin Richard threw open the study door and stormed into the room. "Aunt Catherine is dead!"

"What? No!" Darcy's legs turned to water, and he fell into his chair.

Richard nodded grimly. "As you know, I was with Anne at Rosings. Aunt Catherine's body simply appeared on a fainting couch in the south drawing room. I have seen that before. It's a fae trick; I know of no human mage who could teleport an object that big."

"Good Lord!" Darcy buried his head in his hands. It was true that he had not seen eye-to-eye with his aunt in recent years, but he owed her an enormous debt of gratitude. He and Georgiana would not have survived the period after their father's death without Aunt Catherine's help and advice. Darcy had been too mired in grief and overwhelmed by his new responsibilities to manage Pemberley and raising Georgiana by himself. Their aunt had taken them under her wing until he was capable of managing on his own. At times he had considered marrying Anne simply out of a sense of gratitude.

Darcy collected himself and glanced up at Richard. "How did she die?"

"I can tell you little. She had been away from Rosings. Anne does not know where her mother went and knows of no dealings with the fae. But you know Aunt Catherine. I doubt she confided much in Anne."

Darcy's hands clenched into fists on the top of his desk. "Did you see her? How did she die?"

Richard took a deep breath and then turned toward the table where Darcy kept his brandy. He poured a generous helping for himself and brought another to Darcy. He swallowed a measure of the brandy and seated himself opposite Darcy before speaking. "When I saw the state of the body, I would not allow Anne to view it." Darcy gaped. Had his cousin examined his aunt's body himself?

Richard stared into his glass. "She had been in the woods. There were twigs and leaves in her hair and dirt on her half boots. Her clothing was torn and burned as if she had been in a magical fight. But that was not what killed her." He raised his head, meeting Darcy's gaze. "She had been attacked by claws. A creature had savaged her, right across the chest and neck. It knew exactly how to kill. At least her death would have been quick."

Darcy gasped. Of all of the ways for his aunt to die! He would never have expected her to be killed by a creature with claws. "Perhaps an attack by a wild animal?" Darcy mused, but then answered his own question. "Then why would the fae return her in such secrecy?"

"Indeed," Richard said. "There is some secret they are keeping. But they did not do it. They do not have claws and they are forbidden to interfere with human mages."

Darcy gulped his brandy. "If only we could get them to tell us. But how can we force the fae to reveal anything?" He did not relish the thought of another journey to Faerie to demand something the fae did not want to give.

"There is more." Richard spoke as if the words were forced from him. "I have seen that pattern of attack before. It is very distinctive. There is only one creature that attacks in that way – with claws that size. Napoleon's army had two and they wrought destruction."

"What creature?"

"A griffin." The word went through Darcy like a lightning bolt.

"No—" There were only two griffins in Britain. Darcy knew that Hespera had not killed his aunt. That only left Abraxas, but it was unthinkable.

"Perhaps it was one of the griffins from France," he suggested.

Richard shook his head. "They were both killed in the war. It would be a long and wearying flight for any griffin to come here from the continent – and for what purpose? There are far easier ways to kill an elderly lady."

"Perhaps a griffin from Faerie," Darcy said.

"You know that no griffins live in Faerie. Only human mages can be griffin keepers."

Darcy did not want to accept the obvious conclusion. "Perhaps it was a dragon or that thunderbird!"

Richard shook his head slowly. "Their claws are much larger. Only a single claw would have been required to rip out her throat."

"A hippogriff?"

Richard gave him a cool look. "I have the only hippogriff

familiar in Britain. I assure you that Maor has been with me this whole time. Darcy, you must face the possibility that Abraxas killed our aunt."

Darcy stood and started pacing. "But why? Why would he do such a thing?" He reached out to Hespera who had been drowsing outside in the sun. She came fully alert when he explained the situation. *Why would Abraxas kill someone?* He asked her.

Hespera's mental voice was shocked. *He would only do so if he felt he had no other choice. If he had to defend himself or Elizabeth or the Library.*

Darcy could not imagine how his aunt could be a threat to a griffin or an august institution like the Library. Although she had led the Lady Patronesses, her magical powers had not been great. He could imagine her threatening Elizabeth. Aunt Catherine was no Alaine – shooting bolts of lightning from astride a thunderbird.

However…Elizabeth had been convinced that Aunt Catherine had deliberately sabotaged her familiar summoning. In his own mind Darcy had conceded that Elizabeth's theory was possible but unlikely. His aunt would never do such a thing, and the other Patronesses would have stopped her.

But what if Elizabeth had undertaken an investigation of the event and things had spiraled out of control? Had Elizabeth and his aunt engaged in a magical battle that Abraxas had ended with a swipe of his claws? No, Darcy did not want to believe it was possible.

"Darcy?" Richard was staring at him.

He realized he had frozen in place with the brandy glass halfway to his mouth. Darcy set it down on the desk.

"What are you thinking?" his cousin asked.

"I am thinking I must go to the Library and ask Elizabeth if her familiar killed my aunt."

CHAPTER 24

*T*he next morning, Hespera and Darcy landed in front of the Library just as they had that fateful day when he first re-encountered Elizabeth. Hespera never liked being indoors, so she declined to join Darcy. The stone griffins admitted him as before. Darcy strode through the courtyard, completely focused on reaching his goal. He swung open the door to the long hallway and marched down it to Travinius's desk. The fae looked up, giving no sign that he recognized Darcy.

"I wish to see the Librarian," Darcy announced.

"Welcome to the Gallery of Librarians." Travinius opened his ledger book. "Why do you wish to see the Librarian?"

"I need to talk to her."

Travinius blinked and laid down his quill. "The Librarian is not available for casual visitors."

"This is not casual. I have a matter of utmost urgency to discuss."

"Do you have a request for the Library?"

Darcy ran his hands through his hair. He could think of no way to frame his mission so that it pertained to the

Library. It would not contain a book describing what had happened to his aunt. "No. I must see Elizabeth."

The fae's eyes narrowed at Darcy's use of her given name. "Her Eminence is not available."

"Will you at least tell her I am here and need to speak with her?"

"No. She is busy with supplicants. I must ask you to leave."

Darcy slammed his hands on the table. "No! I will not leave! I must see the Librarian now!"

Travinius flinched backward. But then his expression hardened. He waved his hand imperiously and Darcy found himself being propelled backward out of the gallery – as if pushed by a giant invisible hand. The sensation was not uncomfortable, but it was inexorable. The double doors flew open just in time to deposit Darcy back on the cobblestones of the courtyard and then slammed closed again.

Of course when Darcy scrambled to his feet and tried to open the doors, they were locked.

What happened? Hespera inquired.

They will not let me see Elizabeth. Could you speak with Abraxas and tell him that it is urgent I see her?

Of course. After a few moments, Hespera said, *How strange. Abraxas is not replying.*

Perhaps he is not at the Library.

No. I can sense his presence. He is simply ignoring my attempts to contact him. How rude!

Ignoring Hespera? Darcy sat heavily on one of the courtyard's stone benches. He could never think of a time when Abraxas had not responded to Hespera's inquiries. Perhaps Travinius was not simply being officious. Perhaps Elizabeth really did not want to see Darcy.

His heart sank. It was a damning suspicion. He and Elizabeth had parted on good terms. There was no reason for her to avoid him…unless she had taken part in his aunt's death and was experiencing guilt over it. If that was true then Elizabeth was not the person he had taken her to be. Grief for that Elizabeth piled upon his existing grief for his aunt.

For a moment Darcy feared his heart would break under the weight.

But, he reminded himself, he did not know how his aunt had died. Perhaps Elizabeth was completely innocent. Unfortunately he would never know unless she spoke with him – which she apparently did not want to do.

Well, to hell with that.

Darcy stood and faced the main Library building. There were first- and second-floor windows overlooking the courtyard although he did not know which rooms they belonged to. He planted his feet wide and looked up at the windows.

"ELIZABETH!" he bellowed so loudly that Hespera started. "ELIZABETH! Come down here to talk with me!" He paused. Nothing happened. He had not expected an immediate response. So he bellowed again. "ELIZABETH! Come down and talk with me!" No response. Darcy repeated his demand.

How long do you intend to do this? Hespera asked.

Until Elizabeth comes or my voice gives out, he replied.

After ten minutes, he alternated shouting her name with throwing pebbles at the various windows. He knocked on the door, not really expecting a response. An hour later Darcy had Hespera fly him to the second story windows so he could knock politely. He saw no way to open them, and he drew the line at breaking a window to enter the Library – yet.

After three hours, Hespera was thoroughly bored, and Darcy's voice was growing hoarse. He had seen no faces at the windows, no signs that anyone had noticed him. Perhaps, he conceded, he would need a different approach.

Then the door opened, and a slim figure slipped out, closing the door behind herself. Elizabeth gazed at him solemnly. "I am here, Mr. Darcy. What do you want to discuss?"

∾

WILLIAM – Mr. Darcy – stared at Elizabeth for a moment as if a little shocked that she had finally appeared. Elizabeth was a little shocked herself. Abraxas, Travinius, and the voices of past Librarians had all been against the idea of her speaking with Mr. Darcy.

Travinius had found the man's demands to be impertinent and inappropriate. The Library had decreed that nobody should know about the Forbidden Spell or the damage Lady Catherine caused to the wall – and therefore believed Elizabeth had no reason to speak with Mr. Darcy. Abraxas had reminded Elizabeth that she was not allowed to receive guests who were not supplicants, although he obviously had difficulty not responding to Hespera's inquiries.

At first Elizabeth had resolutely ignored Mr. Darcy's increasingly desperate pleas. But it grew harder to concentrate on her work as he persisted. Eventually she had suggested to the others that the best way to make Mr. Darcy leave was for Elizabeth to speak with him. They had disagreed. Arguments had ensued. Their stance had not softened, so eventually Elizabeth had given up the fight – making them think she conceded the point, although Abraxas had remained suspicious.

But even he had not been quick enough to stop her from slipping out through the door when the others were distracted. Now that she was outside, she doubted they would try to stop the conversation.

After all, they knew there was little that Elizabeth could say to William – Mr. Darcy. She was the Librarian. She must speak with him as the Librarian, not as Elizabeth Bennet. And there was not much information the Librarian could share with him.

He had regained his composure but still stared at her. "My aunt – Catherine de Bourgh – is…dead."

"She is." There was no point in pretending ignorance.

He seemed nonplussed by her matter-of-fact response.

"I am sorry for your loss," she said in a gentler tone.

He nodded, a jerky up-and-down motion. "Do you know how she died?"

"I do, but I cannot tell you."

His voice rose. "Why not?"

"I am bound by my oath as a Librarian."

Mr. Darcy stared up at the sky. "So she was killed as part of some business having to do with the Library?"

There was no harm in answering that question. "She was."

"Not because you suspected her of manipulating your familiar summoning?"

Elizabeth gaped at him. How could he think such a thing of her? "I would never kill someone for revenge— Why would you believe—?" she spluttered.

His shoulders relaxed fractionally. He had actually believed it was a possibility. Elizabeth tamped down her indignation, reminding herself he was grieving.

Mr. Darcy spoke again. "Richard – General Fitzwilliam – thinks Lady Catherine was killed by a blow from a griffin."

Elizabeth could not control her flinch – as good as an admission of guilt. Mr. Darcy was watching her closely and his face hardened.

"Why would Abraxas do such a thing?" His voice was

pleading with her, begging for an answer. "Was it an accident? Were you fighting someone else and she got in the way? I would understand."

Elizabeth closed her eyes. He wanted to find a way to absolve her of this responsibility. How she wished she could say yes!

"No." She shook her head regretfully.

You may not tell him about the Forbidden Spell or the effect it had on the Faerie wall, Abraxas reminded her.

Yes, I know! Her response was emphatic enough that Abraxas instantly withdrew from her mind.

But Elizabeth refused to leave Mr. Darcy in the dark about everything. "This much I may tell you: Your aunt *was* manipulating the assignment of familiars, not just for me but for many mages. High-ranking mages received familiars they were not entitled to and low-ranking ones often received no familiars at all. The Library has notified the Mages' Council that the Lady Patronesses will no longer have the privilege of assigning familiars. In coordination with the fae, we will develop a new process."

Mr. Darcy's mouth had fallen open. "How is that possible? How could one woman do that?"

"I cannot tell you how it was accomplished."

"Then how can you be sure she did it?" His tone was belligerent.

"I know how she did it, but I cannot share the information with you," Elizabeth clarified. "There is no doubt as to her guilt. I saw the evidence with my own eyes."

Mr. Darcy drew himself up. "Still, manipulating familiars is hardly grounds for death."

Elizabeth sighed. Perhaps it had been a bad idea to come out to the courtyard. "That was not the reason for her death – or not the only reason for her death."

Mr. Darcy advanced on her. "You must tell me the whole of the story."

She stood her ground. "I am forbidden to."

He was only a few feet away. "I must know!"

"It is not your business!"

"She was my AUNT!"

Elizabeth tried not to take it personally that he was shouting in her face. She stepped back toward the door. "I am sorry for your loss, William." At that moment he looked so haggard that she wished she could give him a hug. "But I have told you all that I am permitted to tell you."

She put her hand on the doorknob.

"No, don't leave!" There were tears shimmering in his eyes. "Don't leave me out here believing that somehow the woman I love had a hand in my aunt's death."

Elizabeth wondered how much pain a heart could take before giving out altogether – and whether it would be her heart or William's that would break first.

What comfort could she give him? That his aunt's death was quick? That she deserved it? That she had chosen death over servitude?

She took a step toward him but managed not to touch him only through a great effort of will. "I am very sorry. I knew her death would hurt you. But, if you believe nothing else, please believe this: I had no other choice."

Quickly, before he could ask another question, she turned and slipped through the door into the Library.

DARCY IMMEDIATELY TUGGED on the door. Locked again. Of course.

His knees were giving out. Darcy staggered to a bench,

narrowly avoiding the indignity of crumpling on the cobblestones of the courtyard. Well, he had gotten his wish. Elizabeth had spoken with him. Little good it had done him. This was like losing Elizabeth all over again. How often could he withstand it? He never believed she could have a hand in something so...ruthless. He understood she must keep secrets, but not from him.

And she had been so cold, so stiff. She even seemed taller. She had wrapped the cloak of the Librarian around herself, concealing any glimpses of the woman he loved.

He did believe Elizabeth. His aunt had been manipulating who received familiars and what kind of familiars they received. He did not like to think about it, but looking back he could see that Elizabeth's assertion was likely true. Certainly the *ton* was awash in unusual and high status familiars. The Duchess of Warden had a unicorn! And he had heard rumors that the Earl of Longley's heir had called a phoenix. The children of people who had crossed Lady Catherine had called slugs, hedgehogs, or no familiar at all.

And, certainly, Aunt Catherine's star had risen as members of the *ton* were pleased with their familiars. His aunt had been invited to every ball and luncheon. The other Lady Patronesses had become nearly irrelevant. Lady Catherine had practically operated the organization on her own.

Darcy slumped into the back of the bench. How had he not seen it before? Elizabeth had suspected, but he had dismissed her suspicions. Aunt Catherine had been kind to him. He had not wanted to believe she could be cruel to someone else.

But that alone could not be the reason for her death. Elizabeth had strongly implied that it was not – that his aunt had violated other laws concerning the Library. What could they be? In all his years as a mage, he had never heard of anyone running afoul of the Library's strictures. Most mages never dealt with the Library at all.

Well, if Elizabeth would not answer his questions, Darcy would see what he could learn by other means. With a plan coming together in his mind, he strode across the courtyard and past the griffin statues. Hespera had been sunning herself on the street outside the entrance – and enjoying how the people of Oxford gawked, stared, and hastily turned to walk down other streets.

She lowered herself so that he could climb onto her back. *Are we returning to Pemberley?*

No. To Rosings Park.

Why?

I have a few things to investigate.

An hour later, Hespera landed in front of Rosings' main entrance. The de Bourgh's butler was startled to find Darcy unexpectedly on the doorstep but took him immediately to see his cousin Anne in the blue drawing room.

Anne was wearing black, but otherwise looked healthy and in good spirits. Darcy had no patience for social niceties, so he got straight to the point. "Cousin, I need access to your mother's magical studio and all of her books."

DARCY SPENT the next day shuttling between his late aunt's magical studio and her library, cobbling together an understanding of what she had been doing with her magic. The following day their family gathered for a solemn funeral as his aunt was interred in the graveyard at the small village church.

Darcy said nothing to anyone about what he had found among his aunt's papers, but suspicions were beginning to form in his mind. He continued his research, emerging only for meals or to ask if they had past issues of London news-papers. Five days later he asked Richard to return to Pemberley with him, saying only that he wanted to discuss a few things.

They settled in Darcy's study the day after their arrival. Darcy handed his cousin a glass of brandy and took a seat by the fireplace, although it was too warm for a fire. "I apologize for keeping you in the dark, but this is a delicate situation."

With a sigh Richard sank into the opposite chair.

"First, I must have your vow that you will not say anything to anyone about what we will discuss here. It touches not only on the honor of our family, but the safety of Britain."

Richard's eyebrows shot upward. "Of course."

Darcy stared at the empty fireplace. "I have been investigating Aunt Catherine's death. I do not have all the facts, but I have a good working theory."

Richard nodded for him to continue.

"First, Eliza – the Librarian told me that Aunt Catherine was using her position as a Lady Patroness to advance her position in the *ton* by procuring exotic familiars for 'worthy' mages while punishing those she considered 'unworthy.' By examining our aunt's papers, I have confirmed the truth of this accusation."

Richard's jaw dropped open. "That is why Miss Elizabeth failed to summon a familiar?"

"Yes. Aunt Catherine wanted me to wed Anne, so she arranged for Elizabeth to fail."

"That—That is heinous!"

"Indeed. If she were not already deceased, I would have reported Aunt Catherine to the Mages' Council and recom-mended imprisonment and trial. However, when I spoke with the Librarian, she implied that Aunt Catherine's crimes were even greater."

Richard swirled the brandy in his glass. "I am not sure I want to know."

"I wish I did not. But our family must take responsibility for her actions." Darcy pointed to a stack of newspapers by the side of his chair. "Over the past few years there have been a series of strange events. The Year Without a Summer, earthquakes, magical creatures appearing without warning, crops failing for no reason…"

"Yes, that is well documented."

"However, I have been looking through the papers. England has experienced none of these things since June sixth."

Richard rubbed the back of his neck. "I suppose that is right."

"Aunt Catherine died on June sixth."

His cousin frowned. "Are you saying that she had something to do with those events? That would be bizarre. Surely her magic was not that powerful."

"When I traveled with Eliz – the Librarian, she occasionally examined the wall between our world and Faerie because something was tearing holes in it. Most people do not know that was the cause of the weather, the earthquakes, and the random magical creatures. She and the Library have been working to repair those holes, but they did not know what was causing them. I thought little of it at the time. It had no direct bearing on our quest."

"But, Lady Patroness or not, how could our aunt have caused such holes?" Richard asked.

"Familiars come from Faerie. They are supposed to appear when needed by the appropriate mage, but somehow Aunt Catherine managed to manipulate the system to compel particular familiars to do her bidding. That is powerful magic that nobody should have access to. I believe she tore holes in the wall in the process. That is why the strange incidents ceased – the wall has stabilized since June sixth."

Richard nearly dropped his glass. "Good Lord! Do you know what you're saying?"

"Yes. Our aunt caused all that suffering. Either she did not know, or she did not care. But either way she was using magic that she knew she should not use – for her own selfish gain."

"And *that* led to her death."

Darcy nodded. "I am guessing that Abraxas needed to kill her in order to stop her from causing more damage – or perhaps her death was necessary to repair the wall."

Richard blew out a breath. "And here I was believing Abraxas was the villain of the piece. I should not have been so quick to judge."

Darcy gave a rueful laugh. "That is nothing. Think of the size apology I owe Elizabeth. I all but accused her of killing my aunt because she suspected sabotage in the familiar ritual."

"You…did? That…That is even worse than when you insulted her family."

Darcy gave a dark laugh. "You would think I would learn." He sipped from his brandy. "I wrote Elizabeth a letter of apology saying that I guessed what my aunt had done. She sent a gracious note saying there was nothing to forgive since I was grieving. Of course she said nothing that confirmed my suspicions."

"You are very fortunate she has forgiven you."

"Well do I know it – which only reminds me of how much I have lost." He tossed back the rest of his brandy.

Richard cleared his throat. "You said our family had some responsibility. What do you mean by that?"

"I have told the whole to Anne. She would like to make amends to the people her mother hurt when she tore the wall. Some of the victims may require healers and others will need money. We have identified several farmers in Sussex whose crops were burned by a dragon and a shepherd in Romney Marsh who was mauled by a manticore. But that is just the beginning. There must be hundreds of people our aunt wronged through her callous and selfish actions. I was hoping you would help convey Anne's compensation to these people."

"Of course. It is a noble endeavor and the least our family can do." His brows knit together. "But, speaking of Anne, why did her mother never obtain a familiar for her?"

Darcy chuckled. "Anne answered that question before I could ask it. She has no magic at all."

"None?" Richard nearly fell out of his chair.

"None. It sometimes happens to children of mages. But Aunt Catherine did not want anyone to know, so she told everyone Anne was sickly and never presented her at court. She merely said Anne failed to summon a familiar – never admitting that Anne could never have done so."

"I had no idea!"

"Nobody did. Anne was forbidden to discuss it. I must say that she does not seem very distressed about her mother's death. She is planning a lot of changes to Rosings – modern crop rotation and repairs to tenant cottages. And apparently she's been secretly engaged to the son of a local squire for two years. So she was just as happy that I do not intend to wed her."

"So everything is working out for her," Richard said with a disbelieving laugh.

"Yes," Darcy said. He had never thought there would be a time in his life when he would envy his cousin Anne, but there it was.

CHAPTER 25

*G*eorgiana Darcy had never thought much of marriage, despite society's expectations for young ladies. But after three days of being Galon's wife, Georgiana found that marriage was more than agreeable. She now had a true partner by her side. Someone to love her at her best and at her worst. And she loved him fiercely in return.

On the fourth morning after her wedding, Georgiana woke abruptly, her heart racing. The spot beside her was empty, and muffled shouts and scuffling footsteps could be heard overhead.

Georgiana rose to dress only to be thrown from her feet as the ship heaved drastically.

The bizarre storms and encounters with fae creatures seemed to have stopped in the past days, but there were still other sea creatures to contend with.

When she arrived on deck, she saw a glimpse of a pod of whales. The sailors were in awe and trying to stop the ship so they would not harm the majestic creatures. Galon stood at the edge of the ship, about to don his selkie skin.

Georgiana hurried to meet him. "Galon, what are you doing?"

"I am going to guide the whales away from our course. I will return shortly, my love." He kissed her cheek and transformed, his first transformation since their wedding. The beautiful selkie jumped off the side of the ship, landing in the water with a great splash.

Georgiana watched as her love led the whales to the east and was once again impressed by Galon's uncanny way with sea creatures.

Knowing that Galon was well, Georgiana returned to her cabin below deck. She sat at the small desk that was nailed into the wall and removed a sheet of paper and quill. No matter what he might have said, Georgiana still worried about her brother. Galon had suggested a way to reunite the wayward pair, but there was no telling if his idea would be successful. Perhaps Elizabeth had already come to terms with the separation and had fully devoted herself to her duties, to the exclusion of any romantic considerations.

Georgiana suspected that her brother would not move on any time soon, if ever.

It would be a couple of days until they made port and she could post the letter that may help her brother. Georgiana left half of the page clear in case she needed to make any additions. Then she took up her needle work, intent upon embroidering a set of handkerchiefs for her new husband.

Several hours later, Mr. Edwards was pounding on her cabin door. "Madam, you are needed above. Something is wrong with Galon."

Georgiana threw her embroidery hoop aside and hastened to follow Mr. Edwards.

Her heart clenched when she saw Galon, still in his selkie form, collapsed and in pain. Galon had once shown her how to help him transform in times of duress, but she never imagined she would have to use that knowledge.

Georgiana knelt beside Galon and placed one hand on his head and one hand on his sleek body. She whispered an ancient fae incantation. Galon cried out, and though no words came, his cry conveyed sheer agony.

But the transformation came. Galon's handsome face was bloodless and pained. One hand moved to her cheek. His voice was weak. "My love, all is not well. The holes in the border between Faerie and this world have been repaired, limiting my ability to transform. If I take my selkie form again, I will not be able to live in this world as your husband."

Georgiana clutched his hands. They were icy and stiff. "Then what are we to do?"

"There is little that can be done. I will write to King Malus for assistance, but I do not expect he will offer any. The answer may be found at the Library, but I fear we cannot be the ones to make the request. We need your brother."

Captain Wentworth approached them. "What would you like to do?"

"We must make port as soon as possible."

Captain Wentworth nodded and began shouting orders to his crew.

Georgiana pressed a kiss upon Galon's forehead, for he had collapsed in her arms, exhausted from the pain of transforming. "Do not worry, my love. All will be well." And though she said the words, she scarcely believed them herself.

DARCY SAT at his large desk, perusing the ledger books. The instability of the wall had impacted the annual profits, as Darcy had to oversee repairs to several tenant homes and reimburse several others for crops that had been lost in bizarre natural phenomena.

All the instabilities seemed to have resolved. Darcy could only guess that Elizabeth and the Library had fixed the wall. However, he still surveyed the grounds daily for any residual problems. It was an excellent way to distract himself, if only for a few hours. At night, his heart still ached for Elizabeth. He was not sure the aching would ever stop.

Someone knocked on the door, jarring Darcy from his gloomy thoughts. The butler entered, his expression oddly grim. "Mr. Darcy, your sister has returned to Pemberley. She and her new husband are in the sitting room."

Wondering what could possibly bring Georgiana home so soon after her wedding, Darcy hurried to meet his sister. Upon entering the room, Darcy understood his butler's odd manner.

Georgiana was pale and still dirty with dust from the road. Galon slumped against the brocade of the settee. His skin was almost colorless and his eyes shifted from brown to grey.

"Georgiana, what has happened to Galon?"

"He is fighting against transforming, and it is taking all the strength he has to do so," Georgiana said, her voice shaking, and her eyes glistening with unshed tears. "Cut off from Faerie, if Galon takes his selkie form again, he will be unable to return to his true form. We must go to the Library and hope that Elizabeth can help."

The thought of seeing Elizabeth again was tempting, and Darcy almost agreed for that chance alone. But going there himself might do more harm than good to his already aching heart.

"You need me to accompany you? I am not sure what my presence there would accomplish. You are more than capable of clearing the trials to gain an audience with the Librarian."

Darcy had complete faith in his sister, and joining her in this venture would surely lead to further heartbreak.

Georgiana took his hand, her eyes beseeching. "I need you, William. The Library does not grant requests for fae."

"But Georgiana, you are human. Can you not make your own request?"

"Not in the eyes of the Winter Court. Since I married Galon, Faerie considers me to be one of their own."

Galon raised his head and opened his mouth, his voice was weak and hollow. "We need you, Darcy. You are the only one who can make such a request from the Library."

"Please, Brother," Georgiana said. "I cannot lose him."

Darcy's heart clenched. He had never been able to deny his beloved sister any request that was within his power to fulfill.

"Very well. I will arrange things with Hespera. We shall depart for the Library in the morning."

SOMEHOW, Galon survived the long journey from Pemberley. It was nothing short of a miracle, and sheer force of will on Galon's part. Georgiana helped the fae prince dismount from Hespera, her face tight with anxiety. They were running out of time. Hespera flew up to perch on top of the stained-glass rotunda in the center of the building. Darcy supposed she was communicating with Abraxas, but it would not help them gain entry any faster.

They had to go through the proper steps. Darcy was grateful he knew what the process involved.

As Darcy answered the questions, he recalled his first encounter with Elizabeth in the Library and squirmed. He had been so dismissive of her, so certain that her magic was weak. How could he have been so wrong? Even worse, how could he have allowed his aunt to poison his mind against her? He was appalled at his own arrogance and blind acceptance of the Patronesses' verdict.

But this was not the time to consider the past. He needed to concentrate on giving the correct answers.

Georgiana was hovering anxiously. "Is there no way to gain access any quicker, William? Galon is fading fast."

Galon was leaning heavily on her shoulder, his breaths were short and shallow.

Her situation was like his when he last came here, fearing the worst for Georgiana and hoping he would be allowed to meet the Librarian. He understood exactly what she was going through.

"Unfortunately, we cannot rush the Library. We must pass each of the hurdles or risk being refused admission. The Library does not have favorites." He pressed Georgiana's arm in reassurance. "Have faith in your brother, Georgie. I know what I am doing."

She gave a resigned nod and did not argue further.

He must have said all the right things because great stone griffins with their menacing swords moved apart to allow him entrance. Next, it was the turn of the clerk painstakingly checking a list of items. Darcy was relieved to see a new face behind the desk; after their last encounter, seeing Travinius would be awkward – to say the least. Then finally, they were inside, waiting in the courtyard for Abraxas to take them to the Librarian.

Elizabeth. Now that they were through, he could afford to think about her. In a few minutes, he would be seeing her again. Darcy's heart pounded in anticipation. It was both exhilarating and terrifying.

Time passed, and the sense of anticipation turned into frustration. The classical columns were elegant and graceful, but the courtyard felt hemmed in. He felt like a child called to the headmaster's office. He kicked at the marble benches instead of sitting, ran his hand along the bark of a twisted olive tree that had no business growing in the cold English climate, and paced up and down. When would he see her?

"I wish you would sit down, William. This is not helping anyone," Georgiana said.

He perched on the edge of a marble seat. It was cold and damp. He jumped up and began to prowl around the courtyard again. More time passed. He had nothing else to do but wait. He looked around for Hespera, but she had disappeared, and he could not sense her presence.

Where are you?

There was no answer.

At long last, the great door swung open with a high-pitched squeal. Then Abraxas and Travinius came out, and Darcy sprang forward. Hespera appeared, landing in front of Abraxas, and the two griffins greeted each other with a gentle nudge of the head. Only then did Abraxas turn to him.

I apologize for the delay. The Librarian will see you now. Travinius will take you in. I need to confer with Hespera.

Darcy's heart skipped a beat. He knew what the two griffins would be discussing. But there was no time to question them now. He had more pressing matters to deal with.

Travinius gestured for them to follow.

Georgiana and Galon moved slowly forward. The fae prince was barely able to progress. He was hobbling on legs that were no longer meant for walking. He had removed his shoes, and his feet were already fully webbed.

"May I help?" Darcy had offered before, but Galon had refused.

Galon shook his head. "I can manage."

The fae prince was proud and disliked depending on anyone else. Darcy knew that the fae did not like to owe favors, but Galon was in the mortal world now, and those rules did not apply any more.

"Georgiana, will you let me know if you need me?" His sister would be more reasonable.

"Of course." Her voice was terse and tight, and Darcy could guess her frantic thoughts. What if there was no solution? The griffins thought there might be one, but they had expressed uncertainty about the outcome.

They followed the clerk inside. Once again, Darcy's pulse quickened. He gave only a cursory glance at the high arched windows and the bookshelves that lined the walls. There was a world of wisdom to be found here, but he was already looking for Elizabeth. Last time he had picked the door on the right out of the three possibilities, but this time Travinius led him to the left one.

Travinius stopped just in front of the open doorway. "Wait here. I need to inform Her Eminence of your approach."

Elizabeth was absorbed in her work and did not notice his arrival. Darcy had thought himself prepared to see her again, but he still felt a jolt when he spotted her familiar figure. He closed his eyes briefly, holding back the onslaught of emotions, then opened them and let himself revel in the sight of her. She was sitting on an elevated platform with three steps leading upward, her arm draped over the arm of a carved chair. The light, twisting sculpture above the chair was exquisite, produced by fae artisans. It glowed with an eerie light, reminding him how otherworldly Elizabeth had become. She was beautiful.

He was interrupted by a gurgling sound beside him. Georgiana gave an exclamation. With a flash of guilt at neglecting her, Darcy tore his attention away from Elizabeth and back to Galon, who was doubled over. His skin was transforming into a mottled stone-like grey. He was doing everything he could to hold onto his fae form, but he was losing the battle.

"Help me," whispered Georgiana, her eyes fearful.

Darcy quickly moved to Galon's other side and wrapped his arm around Galon's shoulder. The fae's legs were squeezed together. Darcy suspected they were already transitioning.

"Do you have my skin, Georgiana?" Galon rasped.

He had spoken aloud rather than communicated with her mentally as her familiar. It did not bode well.

"I have it," she said softly. "Try to hold on a bit longer, my love."

Despite his anxiety, Darcy knew the exact moment when Elizabeth became aware of his presence. She sat up straight in her chair, her gaze seeking him out. Across the wide space that separated them, her dark eyes caught his and his breath hitched.

"You may approach Her Eminence now," intoned Travinius.

Darcy had to tear himself away from the sight of Elizabeth to help Galon. At that moment, Abraxas appeared at his side, his conversation with Hespera apparently over. Darcy wanted to ask the Library griffin about the outcome, but now was not the time.

"I will assist His Highness, while Mr. Darcy makes his request." He inclined his head to Darcy and Georgiana and put his taloned limb forward for Galon to lean onto.

With Galon taken care of, Darcy offered his arm to Georgiana. They made their way swiftly to the front of the room. Darcy's boots drummed on the marble floor, echoing the wild beating of his heart.

As he approached, Elizabeth cleared her throat. Her eyes glimmered like the surface of a lake, dark and deep and impossible to decipher.

As he reached the bottom of the steps. He halted, released Georgiana, and bowed. "Your Eminence."

It was impossible not to be distracted by Elizabeth's presence. It was torment, standing here, unable to do anything when every impulse was driving him to go up to her. Chiding himself that the young lady before him was the Librarian, not Elizabeth, he focused on the task at hand. At this point in time, he was here as a supplicant, and he had to play that role to save his sister's husband.

He drew a steadying breath.

The tightening of her hands on the chair was the only indication she had noticed him. Otherwise, she was as distant as a monarch, her feelings carefully controlled. The irony did not escape him. Their roles had been completely reversed. When they first met, she was the spirited one, and he had been one who was proud and distant.

"Mr. Darcy. Georgiana." The Librarian did not stand up. "Tell me what you wish to know, and I will do what I can to fulfill your request. How may I help you?" There was a sing-song lilt to her voice, and he could hear the resonance of other voices behind it.

"I am here on behalf of my sister Georgiana," Darcy said.

"Before you continue," interjected Travinius, "may I remind you, Mr. Darcy, every creature may ask for the Library's assistance a total of three times in their lifetime. You have already done it once, on behalf of your sister. This would be your second time, also on behalf of your sister. This means, no matter what the circumstances, you will have only one more opportunity. I would like you to consider that you have already made two requests in the space of a few months."

By his side, Georgiana made a strangled sound. "There must be some way for *me* to make the request. Or surely, Prince Galon, considering the circumstances—?"

"Neither you nor the prince may submit a request." Travinius' answer was unequivocal. "Galon has no right to appeal to Her Eminence. She is the mortal face of the Library. As fae, if he wishes to ask for the Library's help, he must travel to the Fae Court. But with the wall closed, there is no guarantee the door would open for him. In this particular case, however, it would not avail him. He and Georgiana are bound together in a magical vow that cannot be reversed. Only someone else – someone whose love is not motivated by self-interest – can ask for their bond to be broken, and even then, dissolving the bond can only be granted in exceptional circumstances."

There it was. Hespera had already told him as much, but Darcy had hoped there might be a way around it. Georgiana looked defeated.

Darcy turned to Travinius. "I am more than happy to give up my second request."

"Your willingness to sacrifice one of your remaining requests affirms your affection for your sister." He ticked a box on his list, then wrote something down in an unintelligible scrawl. The letters moved across the page and disappeared. Travinius looked up. "I have entered it into the records. Once you have made your formal request to the Librarian, you cannot withdraw it."

"I understand," Darcy smiled at Georgiana. "I will do what is necessary to protect those I hold dear."

Georgiana glanced back towards Galon. Darcy followed her gaze. The fae was sitting on the ground, leaning against Abraxas' flank. He was sweating profusely with his eyes tightly shut.

There was no time to waste.

"I have come to the Library to ask for Prince Galon of the Winter Court to be released from his role as a familiar to my sister Georgiana, and to be granted the right to remain in the mortal realm to live as husband to my sister."

He deliberately did not pause until the end. When he was finished, he held his breath. Technically, those were two separate requests. If the Library declared he had used up all his requests, so be it. His pulse thundered as waited for Travinius to break in and declare that Darcy had used up all three of his chances.

Travinius' eyes settled on him. They were fae eyes, shifting color and drifting with unfathomable emotions. Darcy stood rock still, hardly daring to move as the clerk assessed him.

"Very well, Mr. Darcy." It was Elizabeth, speaking in the voice of the Librarian. "The Library will now consider your request."

It was still possible that the Library would proclaim that Darcy had asked for two things, but he was heartened by the fact that Elizabeth had said "request," not requests. He began to breathe again, allowing himself to hope. There was so much at stake here, on so many levels.

He had seen Elizabeth at work before, so he knew what to expect. Still, he could not help looking on in awe as she raised her hands in an elaborate dance, and the Library around her swirled and danced in response. Shelves packed with books appeared and disappeared, drawing closer, then spinning away, books upon books, some of them ancient and well-worn, others much newer. What must it be like to be able to command so much through her magic? To have so much knowledge at her fingertips?

The swirling stopped as suddenly as it started, and Elizabeth put out her hands to receive a large leather-bound book. A short lectern appeared in front of her. Setting down the book on it, she began to turn the pages.

As he waited, he could hear gasping noises behind him.

Galon was struggling to breathe now. He would soon need to be immersed in water or he would die.

Hespera, we need water, a pail of water, quickly.

I will see to it.

He returned his attention to Elizabeth. He could not afford to let his attention drift. Everything rested on Elizabeth's decision. *Everything.*

The unworldly light that flickered around Elizabeth made her seem almost angelic. He caught that thought and once again, considered the irony. *Angelic?* Elizabeth had never been the angelic type.

She continued to flip the pages, reading at a speed that should not be possible, the pages turning one after the other while she searched. Meanwhile Darcy memorized her features. The way her lips puckered in concentration. The way her eyelashes fluttered like wings while she was reading. The way her soft hair hovered above her brow until she pushed it back with an impatient finger. These were the little things that assured him she was still the same Elizabeth as she always was.

What would happen if she did not find a way to do this? Would Georgiana and Galon be condemned to Darcy's fate? To the same hollowed-out existence where he was no more than a ghost of his former self?

Please find it, he willed her. There had to be a way.

Then, abruptly, she snapped the book shut and rose to her feet. Elizabeth was expressionless, but he could feel the temperature in the room dropping. He knew through experience that her sadness would cause a frost that could freeze him in minutes. He was filled with dread.

"There is a way."

Darcy's shoulders slumped in relief. There *was* a solution.

Please let it not be a poem. Or a quest. Galon would not last long enough.

"The bond can be severed, but only if there are no other options available. And dissolving the bond requires a sacrifice from each of the partners."

"I am willing to give up whatever is needed." Georgiana's voice rang out firm and strong.

The Librarian nodded and looked towards Galon, who did not answer.

"The prince must be able to say the words to seal the magic. If he turns into his selkie form and can no longer speak, it cannot be done. You must hurry."

Elizabeth turned to Abraxas, communicating silently with him. The griffin raised a paw and tapped Galon on the head three times. It must have been a healing spell, because Galon twitched and sat up, his round selkie eyes shifting color from silver to brown. Georgiana ran to him and rapidly explained what needed to happen.

"Georgiana, you must hold the prince's hand," Elizabeth said.

She took Galon's hand. It was webbed and crusted.

"To stay in the mortal world, Prince Galon, you must agree to relinquish all rights to return to Faerie for as long as your wife lives. Quickly, say it three times to seal the bargain." Elizabeth's voice was urgent.

Galon's voice grated like rock upon rock, but he somehow managed to form the words. He repeated them three times.

"And you, Georgiana, must relinquish all possibility of having a familiar."

Darcy gasped. What would that mean for her? Would she still be able to live on the high seas and engage in battle?

Georgiana did not hesitate. She nodded quickly.

"Are you certain you want to do this?" Darcy said.

"There is no time. It must be done." Georgiana turned to

Elizabeth. "I accept the terms." She uttered the phrase three times.

Elizabeth wrote the words in the air. They glowed, then vanished. A sharp light, like the blade of a sword, appeared in her hand. She cut the air between the newlyweds, severing the bond.

Galon gave a harsh cry and slumped down, unconscious. Georgiana staggered, then righted herself.

"Are you in pain?" Darcy gripped his sister's arm in concern.

"It is nothing compared to the pain I experienced with the Scottish Word." She stood up straight and addressed Elizabeth. "Is it done, Your Eminence?"

"It is done."

"Will Galon recover fully?"

Abraxas bent his head and probed at Galon with his beak. "The prince is weak. It will take time. But he will be well, and he will retain his fae form."

"Thank you, Your Eminence." Georgiana's voice echoed through the room. Darcy marveled at how strong his little sister had become.

He looked towards Elizabeth. He owed her so much. What had he ever given her in return but pain? He had rejected her. He had taken her on a dangerous quest. He had all but accused her of murder. "Thank you," he said to her, his heart full. He could not hope to convey the depth of his gratitude with those two words.

"You are welcome, Mr. Darcy. It is our duty."

He was seized by a strong urge to reach out to her, but he knew better than to do so when she was still connected to the Library.

Travinius stepped forward. "Let us all adjourn to another room to give the young couple a chance to recover from their ordeal. I have prepared a room. Prince Galon may need to sleep for several hours to recover his strength. Meanwhile, you may enjoy the hospitality of the Library while you wait. This way, please. The Librarian needs to meet with other supplicants."

"No!" The word burst from Darcy's mouth.

Elizabeth was already starting to walk back to her chair, but she turned when she heard him. "Mr. Darcy. I am the Librarian. I—"

"It is not what you think. I know you cannot—"

He took a deep breath, his heart quivering, his throat dry. This was it. This is what he had been hoping for.

"I have a third request to submit to the Library."

CHAPTER 26

*D*arcy was leaving, and Elizabeth's control was shattering. He was talking, but she could not listen to what he was saying. She had to detach from the Library first. She could not afford to let her feelings manifest in the ordinary world.

Very carefully, making sure there would be no unexpected consequences, she withdrew her magical connection. As her magic began to shrink, the other Librarians receded to the background and reality came rushing in – along with the pain.

Mr. Darcy was leaving again. Seeing him had cut into her, through and through, threatening to strip her of all her defenses. And now her heart was shredding into tattered ribbons on an old scarecrow, weathered and bleached of all color.

She shut her eyes, willing herself to keep an iron control. She did not want to feel anything anymore. Over the last few days she had been working like an automaton, her body an empty shell, a mere imitation of herself. If she stopped to think about her loss, it would be very difficult for her to find the strength she needed to do her work.

Her only consolation was that she knew it would pass. She had gone through all this before and knew that it would get easier. It would never go away completely, but the impact would dwindle. The wound would turn into a scar, itching and tugging, constantly reminding her of what she had lost, but with time, it would fade.

Though she was sorely tempted, Elizabeth would not go to him. She had bid farewell to Mr. Darcy already. She fought against the tightness in her chest, the bile that burned in her throat. The books stirred in response, and she had to ruthlessly shut down all thought. She distracted herself by dwelling on irrelevant things, like the oranges she received as a thank you gift from a supplicant who had a hothouse. They were a rare luxury. She had meant to send them back but had been too caught up in Library business. Just as well. In a few minutes she would go and peel an orange, slowly and carefully. She imagined the sting of the juice on her tongue.

Anything rather than think of Mr. Darcy.

But how could she not think of Mr. Darcy, when he was still in front of her? He was looking at her, waiting expectantly. Suddenly the words he had uttered broke through her haze. She snapped her attention back to him. She stared at him, blinking, wondering what he could possibly have to say.

"Another request?"

What was Darcy thinking? In the entire history of the Library, only one person had used up all three of his requests, and that person had come to rue that day. Having that last request might have prevented his life being cut short. It deprived the world of a brilliant philosopher.

She had not fully completed her withdrawal from the Library. It responded to her worry by creating a whirlwind.

Books rose in the air in agitation and came hurtling towards her.

Your Eminence. Stop this immediately. Abraxas's voice broke through the turbulence and steadied her.

She raised her hand in time to stop a book from striking her in the face and took a long, measured breath. She had to rein herself in. She was not Elizabeth. She was the Librarian.

As the Library settled back down, the books lining up neatly on the shelves again. She glanced towards Darcy to make sure he was not injured. He had backed himself up against the wall but appeared unharmed. Abraxas was standing in the doorway, radiating disapproval.

She took refuge in ritual. Mr. Darcy had a request. She needed to answer it. Returning to the familiar chair, she opened her mind to the ancient wisdom of the Library and to all the knowledge passed down the generations. Once she was certain she was back in control, she uttered the traditional words.

"Tell me what you wish to know, Mr. Darcy, and I will do what I can to fulfill your request. How may I help you?"

Darcy took a deep breath. "There is a great deal of work to be done, and it is my understanding that many Librarians train a curator to help them in their research and to—" he paused and swallowed before continuing, "—take over in case of unforeseen circumstances. My magic is strong. I can be an asset to the Library. I am willing to undertake the training to take up such a position. I want to dedicate my life to the work of the Library. I have come to ask for the position of Curator. That is my request."

The moment Darcy stopped speaking, Elizabeth cut off her mental connection to the Library. The sudden withdrawal brought an agonizing pain stabbing through her head. She pressed her fingertips to the side of her temple, trying to ease it. Her emotions reeled drunkenly as she tried to grasp the enormity of what he had just said.

He wanted a position in the Library. It had to be the most foolhardy, irresponsible thing she had ever heard in her life.

She stood and strode over to him, ignoring the pain piercing her head.

"What in heaven's name do you think you are doing, Mr. Darcy? Have you lost your mind completely? Did your time in Faerie rob you of your senses?"

"William," he answered, serenely. "You should call me William now." He took up both her hands in his.

She pulled them away. "No."

"No? You do not want to call me William? Very well, we will use one of my middle names."

How could he joke in such a supremely flippant manner?

"I will *not* allow you to do such a foolish thing."

His eyes flashed. The careless façade dropped. He looked hurt and angry. What did he expect? That she would sing his praises for such a singularly rash decision to throw away his whole life?

"I am sorry to disappoint you, *Your Eminence*, but I have already done it."

"You have not yet received a response."

He raised his brow. "I may be mistaken about this, but I was under the impression the Librarian cannot refuse a request once it has been entered into the records."

She did not deign to answer. There had to be a way out. She tried to concentrate through the pounding of her head. True. His question had already been submitted. Even if she did find some reason not to take him on as a Curator, he would still have used up his third request.

She spun and walked away from Mr. Darcy – out into the courtyard. The sun glinted at her, blinding her after being indoors for so long. Her head throbbed. She squeezed her eyes shut and breathed heavily, trying to make sense of what had just happened.

Why did Mr. Darcy have to do such a stupid thing? She shook her head and tightened her fists in sheer frustration and dismay. Foolish, foolish man! How on earth was she supposed to repair the damage now?

"Elizabeth?"

She had not heard his footsteps as he approached. Twisting her body away, she refused to look at him. Something warm and damp trickled down her cheek. She wiped it with the back of her hand. Tears.

She was crying.

"Elizabeth?"

His hand settled on her arm. The touch was light, but it rippled through her body. She shrugged it off and wrapped her hands around herself, folding her shoulders forward and leaning away from him.

"Elizabeth."

It was the third time he had said her name. There was something binding about it. It forced her to turn around and confront him.

"You should not have done it." Her voice was heavy.

"It is done."

"Not yet."

But she knew it was inevitable. He was right. She could not refuse what he asked. She had no reason to, nothing that would convince the Library, at any rate. He was a good candidate for a Curator. He had all the necessary qualities. He was perfect.

The fight went out of her. Instead, she began to imagine what it would be like to have him here, by her side. "But how can we live together here, day after day, and—"

"—not marry? That would be very improper." Darcy looked at her tenderly. He reached out and hooked a strand of her hair behind her ear. "It seems Abraxas has found a solution."

Elizabeth looked towards the old griffin, her eyes narrowing on him. *You knew about this. You planned this,* she said. It was not a sudden impulse on Darcy's part, then.

We were not certain until today.

Who is we?

Hespera and I. There was a smugness to his voice.

Hespera? So you did not plan this with Darcy?

There was a rumble of amusement. *We kept him informed of our progress.*

She did not know how to feel about any of this, so she focused on what was important. *Are we allowed to marry?*

There is a requirement for the Librarian not to marry, of course, and that cannot be overcome. However, we have found a loophole. The rule is stated in a complicated manner. I will not go into the details, but what matters is that the rules mentions the word outside *the Library. I have researched the matter thoroughly, and the wording is always the same. Hespera consulted with King Malus, and we just received confirmation. He has agreed that the stipulation only applies to marrying outside the Library. It is irregular, of course. But you must consider that there are few people who would wish to live within the confines of the Library. Mr. Darcy is sacrificing a great deal to do so.*

I know.

Darcy was watching her, his eyes grave. "Has Abraxas explained to you that it is possible?"

"He has, but I am not yet convinced." Even as she spoke the words, a strange sensation spread through her body. A sense of buoyancy and lightness she had never experienced before. A lifeboat on a gray, raging sea. She held it back. She could not allow herself to believe such happiness was possible, not at the expense of everything he held dear. And yet….

"You cannot give up everything for me." She whispered

the words, because, even though it was the thing she wanted most in the world, she could never ask it of him.

"I am giving up nothing. Pemberley is an edifice, a building. I will not deny that I love it, but I cannot love a building more than I love you. For me, it is nothing more than an empty husk if you are not there."

The words shuddered through her, tempting her, urging her to accept. She stood firm against their allure.

"But who will take care of it? Who will inherit it? You cannot simply relinquish it! It has belonged to the Darcys for generations."

"And it will continue to do so. Georgiana will need somewhere to live now that she no longer has a familiar. Between her and Galon, the estate is in excellent hands. As for the future, we shall have to see."

There was a promise in the depth of his eyes and her heart lurched. *Children.* It had never been a possibility for her, not since she had come to the Library.

"But what about your position in society? Your power?"

"Power? How can you ask me this? You have seen what the pursuit of power has done to my aunt. It created a monster."

"*You* are not a monster, just because you have power."

"I am glad you do not think so." The corner of his mouth curled.

She pursed her lips, refusing to laugh. She had to convince him.

"What about your family?"

He frowned. "It is a loss, I agree. I do not know when I will be allowed to see Georgiana again. I will miss her sorely." He smiled. "But do you really think I would be willing to give you up so I can spend time with my sister?"

She shook her head. "You are making light of it. I know

what it means to be confined to the Library. I have missed my family more than I can say."

"Would you give it up to return to Meryton and live at Longbourn? Do you long to join society? To dance at a ball and wear fine dresses?"

Female vanity raised its head. "Are you hinting that my dress is not fine?" It was a ridiculous question, given the circumstances.

His eyes skimmed across her, examining her with a boldness that made her flush. His gaze was intimate, brushing across her skin like a physical touch. She shivered in response, her senses tingling.

"Your dress could not be more perfect."

She could not doubt his sincerity. His eyes held a strange warm light. Flustered, she took a step backward, trying to hold onto some measure of rationality. She would not let him distract her. It was up to her to prevent him from making a huge mistake.

She tried to recall what they were talking about. Ah, yes. He was asking her if she wanted to join society.

"I have no interest in London society." She considered the things she did miss. Dancing. She loved to dance. "When I first came here, I was obsessed with proving myself. I wanted to demonstrate that Lady Catherine was wrong – that despite what had happened during the familiar ceremony, my magic was powerful. Since then, I have realized that I can make a difference in the world. There will be Librarians after me, but I know that while I live, I want to do everything I can to help others. I could never give that up for a few dances and events in London."

She paused and looked at him intently. "I know no one there apart from my uncle, but you have lived part of your life there. You have many friends and acquaintances. One day you might even want a seat in Parliament. You can have your fill of social engagements – clubs and theaters and dances. How could you give all that up?"

"As you know very well, I am not particularly fond of dancing, and I do not feel comfortable around strangers."

He crossed his arms and planted his feet, waiting for more questions from her. She tried to think of objections, but she had run out of possibilities. The tension left her body and she trembled.

She had never even allowed herself to dream they could be together. It was too overwhelming to take it all in. Desperate, she clutched at one of the fears that had kept her awake at night.

"I thought you would hate me for—" Her voice cracked. "—for what happened to Lady Catherine. I thought you would never forgive me for what I did."

She looked down, hiding her face, afraid to see his expression.

Darcy put his finger under her chin and tilted her face up.

"I could never hate you, my love." The truth shone out of his eyes. His voice was deep and tender. "If anything, I admire you for your courage to do what had to be done. My aunt created devastation and chaos in her wake. She decimated crops, caused earthquakes, and destroyed the livelihoods of thousands of people, and all for nothing beyond her personal gain. She destroyed *us*. Those years she stole from us can never be replaced."

Still, Elizabeth felt she owed him an explanation. "King Malus offered her the choice between the waters of Lethe and death. She chose death. I tried my best to convince her to drink the waters, but she did not wish to suffer the indignity of losing her power and position."

Elizabeth needed him to understand how it was, that she would not have condemned Lady Catherine to death if there had been another choice.

"Aunt Catherine was a fool, and you were far too merciful."

A sob made its way up her throat as a terrible weight of guilt was lifted from her.

"Are you sure you want to spend your life in the Library? Will you not grow tired of it one day and regret it? You cannot leave once you take your oath."

"It is no ordinary library, you know. It is an enchanted library. I would be delighted to spend the rest of my life exploring what it has to offer – with you." He paused and stared at her, his gaze humble and open. "If you will have me."

The walls she had set up to protect her crumbled. She had wished for this possibility for so long, she was afraid to wake up and discover it was a dream.

"I have longed for those words for five whole years," she replied. "My answer is yes, yes, and yes. Three times."

The words inscribed themselves in a warm light in the air between them.

Darcy reached out and crushed her to him. She buried her face in his shoulder, reveling in his scent of cedarwood and bergamot and something bluntly masculine, and wished she could stay there forever.

Abraxas spoke into her mind. *Have you resolved things between you?*

She stiffened. Darcy felt the change in her body and released her.

Abraxas. Go away.

Not until you answer.

Very well. We have resolved things.

Then you had better grant him his request.

She could not possibly turn into the Librarian, not when her feelings were so raw. Not when she was ready to soar with joy.

Give me a few minutes.

"Is there anything the matter?" Darcy examined her intently. "Did you think of something else to object to?

"No. It is Abraxas. He wants to know what is happening."

He groaned. "Will we never have a moment's peace?"

"It is the price we will have to pay. Are you—"

"Do not ask me again if I am prepared to pay it."

"Very well, I will not. Besides, there are compensations to giving up your life outside. You may have given up Pemberley, but you have gained the world. Come with me and I will show you."

She took his hand, leading him out of the courtyard, through a dark passageway, and down a worn circular stair into an octagonal room full of doors. Doors on every wall, sometimes two or three of them. Stone doors, wooden doors, doors in every style, ancient and modern. She took him to one decorated with ornate curls of filigree. There, she came to a halt.

"Are you certain you want to come with me?" she asked, with a hint of mischief. "How do you know where I will lead you?"

"You hold my life in your hand. Just being with you like this, breathing the same air as you, is a treasure beyond my dreams. I want to luxuriate in your presence and never let you go. And to do so, so much more with you."

He ran his fingertip along her palm. She gave a little shiver and he laughed, pleased to see her reaction.

A blush stained her cheeks as she opened the door and was met by a climate that could not be England. They stepped through, hot, dry air meeting them. Loud sounds and unfamiliar scents filled the air. As she leaned back against him, surveying the scene, she could feel his heart pounding.

"Where are we?" he asked in a hushed voice.

294 | MR. DARCY AND THE ENCHANTED LIBRARY

"Alexandria," she said with a touch of pride. She pointed around her. "This is the site of the old library that existed in the third century BC. It was burnt to the ground, but the fae managed to salvage many of those ancient tomes and hold them underground in structures that rival the burial tombs of the pyramids."

She stepped away from him, wishing they could stay. "We cannot linger today, but we will return." She tugged at him, pulling him back through the doorway and up the spiral stairway. "When we have time, I could show you worlds you cannot imagine. From the Library, we can travel to many lands. We could visit the ruins of Babylon, take a stroll beside the Taj Mahal at dusk, explore the steppes of Russia, or visit Pompeii any time we choose. We can even step into Faerie if we have permission. Maybe we can visit that glowing field of flowers again."

They had reached the top of the stairs. Darcy grimaced. "I would prefer not to face any questions by King Malus ever again."

Elizabeth's mouth curled upwards. "At least he gave us your sister's cure."

"He did, and because of him, I discovered the depth of your love. I do not regret a moment of our time there. If we had not gone on that quest," he whispered, "I might never have known this happiness. You say you are giving me the world, but you are the world to me."

He trailed his thumb along her jaw. "Besides, there are other ways for us to entertain ourselves."

"Are there?" She meant to be playful, but his earnest gaze drove the laughter away. She did not know whether to be terrified or exhilarated.

"There are," he murmured, his lips suddenly so close she could feel his breath on her cheek. "Would you like an example?"

"I would." Then all words dried up as his lips moved to touch hers. It was a tentative touch, a question so full of tenderness that her tears welled up with joy. Her knees weakened and she took hold of his collar to steady herself. Her fingers found the rapid drumming of his pulse at the corner of his jaw. Encouraged, he deepened his kiss.

Sometime later – a long time later – she emerged from the warmth of his arms into the light of reality.

"I have to return. There are supplicants waiting for me," she said, her voice full of regret. "And I have not yet approved your request."

"You will." His voice was deep and soothing. With a special smile meant only for her, he pressed her gently back into his arms. She snaked her fingers to the spot where his dark curls met the sinews of his shoulder and gave a sigh of contentment.

This was the true meaning of happiness. She had everything she could ever want, right here at her fingertips.

EPILOGUE

"*D*o not touch – Mr. Darcy, I implore you, do not touch your cravat!"

Darcy's new valet, Grimes, part of the Library staff, held up his hands in a warding gesture. Darcy had already ruined two beautifully knotted cravats by absentmindedly worrying them with his fingers.

Darcy liked the man already. He was far younger and more flexible than Bickerstaffe, who had chosen to remain at Pemberley and be a valet for Galon.

"Never fear," Richard assured Grimes with a grin. "I shall keep him too distracted to ruin another of your constructs." He noticed Darcy fiddling with the cuff of his coat. "Although I may have to tie his hands behind his back."

Darcy snorted at his cousin. "I would like to see you try."

"I do not understand you at all," Richard said. "You have faced a troll, a dragon, a journey through Faerie, fae warriors, and a vengeful fae princess, but the prospect of a wedding ceremony makes you anxious?"

Darcy reached up to touch his cravat, remembered just in time not to, and dropped his hands. "Before I only faced death then. Now I will have to face..." He shuddered. "...an audience."

Richard laughed. "Perhaps you are well suited to life in a Library after all. When you first told me about the Curator position, I thought you had taken leave of your senses. But I must say that you seem to be settling in well."

"It is glorious, Richard. You could not imagine the things I have learned and the places I have visited." His position as Curator allowed Darcy to indulge his curiosity and love of learning in a way that he had never been able to satisfy before. The master of Pemberley had little time for learning and leisure.

"And you do not miss Pemberley?"

Darcy regarded himself in the mirror, brushing a wayward curl into place. "Of course I miss it, and I miss seeing the people there. But I hope I may go to visit soon." In the month since he had joined the Library, Darcy had been speaking with the fae who set the rules for the Librarians.

He thought he had them mostly convinced to relax the rules around Librarians contacting the outside world. He had pointed out that greater awareness of events in Britain might have helped the Librarian prevent dangers like the weakening of the Faerie border.

One sign of their softening was that the fae had already bent some of their rules, allowing outsiders to attend Darcy and Elizabeth's wedding. When Elizabeth learned that she might invite her family to the ceremony, she had wept in a way that Darcy had never seen before.

She had been tearfully reunited with her family the previous night at the inn where the Bennets were staying. Over dinner, she and Darcy had met Jane and Bingley's two little ones and been introduced to Kitty's new husband, a clergyman.

Today's service and wedding breakfast would be held in

the Library's courtyard so that the wedding guests would not need to prove themselves worthy of entering the Library. To distract himself, Darcy strode to the window of his sitting room and gazed down at the space where people were gathering. Fortunately, the day was beautiful and sunny but not overly warm. Everyone was dressed in light and colorful clothing, lending the occasion an even more festive air.

Mr. and Mrs. Bennet sat with Mary while Jane and Bingley chased their children up and down the aisles. Lydia flirted with one of King Malus's warriors, who seemed impervious to her charms.

Darcy and Elizabeth had been unsure about inviting the fae king as the fae approached marriage quite differently. But Abraxas had gently hinted that the ruler would feel slighted at not being included, so they now hosted a contingent of a dozen or so fae, including Anne of the Hills and several of Malus's daughters, who were all quite lovely.

A small group of humans clustered to one side. They were part of Elizabeth's new spellcaster program. Miss Carteret and Mrs. Brown inhabited a small house not far from the Library and guided a program that invited spellcasters to Oxford to match them with familiars. Now that Lady Catherine was no longer interfering with the familiar magic, many of the spellcasters had bonded – although some had declined the invitation and happily practiced their magic as they always had.

Mrs. Brown's protégé Miss Rose Tilden had bonded with a seal (apparently one who was not secretly a fae prince) and had taken over Georgiana's duties keeping ships safe on the open sea. Miss Carteret's familiar was a phoenix, truly a glorious bird; Darcy was secretly a little envious – although he would not trade Hespera for anything.

The widowed Mrs. Brown had stunned them all by summoning a magical crocodile. The creature's appearance had created quite a stir; nobody knew where it had come from since such animals were not native to Britain. The spellcaster's house had to be hastily renovated to accommodate a low-slung reptile, and they could only hope that the neighbors would accustom themselves to the sight of the creature making its way to the river for a swim. Mrs. Brown pronounced herself delighted with her familiar, and it was true that nobody in the town would dare to offer her a word of disrespect.

Georgiana was having an animated conversation with Kitty, a sight that gladdened Darcy's heart; his sister had been so isolated in recent years. Galon spoke seriously with Kitty's husband. The former selkie had fully recovered his health and was settling into life as a land-dwelling human. In her letters, Georgiana had confided to Darcy that Galon sometimes seemed melancholy but that he enjoyed the challenges of helping his wife run the Pemberley estate. She had also shared the not-yet-public news that they were expecting a child in seven months.

Darcy could not wait to be an uncle; the news had prompted thoughts about what it would be like to raise his own children in the Library. But he and Elizabeth would cross that bridge when they came to it.

Behind the altar, Haskins the hermit was talking with the Archbishop of Canterbury; they would co-officiate the ceremony. Mrs. Bennet had been horrified at the thought that an unconsecrated hermit would perform her daughter's wedding ceremony – even if he was authorized to perform fae weddings. She had spoken to the Meryton parish priest who had written to his bishop.

Unbeknownst to Elizabeth and Darcy, the church hierarchy had decided that the Archbishop himself was the only person who could sanctify the first recorded marriage between two Library staff members. The recent events regarding the boundary with Faerie had thrust the Library into the consciousness of even the non-magical population of Britain, and Parliament was obviously eager to establish good relations with the Library and the fae.

The Bennet and Darcy families had been compelled to refuse many hints and outright requests from members of the *ton* and the government who saw invitations to the wedding as highly desirable. Darcy shuddered at the thought of a larger audience for his wedding. This crowd was big enough for him. They had no intention of turning the Library into a political institution and would be happy when it once again faded from everyone's awareness.

Darcy scanned the courtyard but was unsurprised that he did not see Hespera. In the weeks since he had moved into the Library, she had become somewhat distant. It saddened Darcy, and he did not know what to do about it. He had assured her that his marriage to Elizabeth would not lessen his affection for her. She had agreed, and yet he had seen less of her. He hoped she was merely giving him space to grow accustomed to his new life. Nevertheless, once the wedding and honeymoon were past, he planned to seek the griffin out and have a long conversation with her.

"Darcy," Richard's voice recalled him to the task at hand. "It is nearly time to start the ceremony. Let Grimes inspect you one more time before we go downstairs."

Darcy turned away from the window, reminding himself that his anxiety over the audience did not matter. Today he would be marrying the love of his life.

ELIZABETH SIGHED. The ceremony had been everything she could have hoped for, although truthfully she mostly remembered the expression of incredulous joy on William's face. She could understand that feeling. Neither one of them had believed this day would be possible.

Now the ceremony was behind them, and all that remained was enjoying the good company and delicious food of the wedding breakfast. Travinius and the Library staff had outdone themselves. The food was magnificent, if somewhat unusual: blue tea, orange grapes, fruit with spikes, and tiny apples that grew in bunches. Loaves of bread shaped like dragons and mushrooms and oak leaves, all the color of woad. And, of course, a wide selection of faerie cakes.

But she supposed it was a fitting accompaniment for a ceremony conducted by an archbishop and a hermit. Fortunately Haskins had restrained some of his wilder impulses. Elizabeth had persuaded him to wear shoes and not to use animal bones to bless the union. However, he had insisted on performing his ritual dance and sprinkling them with lavender water.

She gave William, sitting beside her, a fond look. He noticed her attention. "Did you need something, my dearest?"

She smiled. "You are my husband."

"I am."

"I thought it would never happen."

"Nor did I. I was in a very dark place for a long time."

Elizabeth wiped away a tear from her cheek. "I am happier than I ever thought I was capable of being."

"I know exactly how you feel." William leaned forward to give her a quick kiss that soon turned into something deeper and more passionate. The taste of his lips was more intoxicating than the finest wine, and Elizabeth did not want to deprive herself of their touch for a single second.

Someone whistled and someone else laughed. "Now, Darcy, save it for tonight!" Richard's voice chided. Blushing, they separated, although Elizabeth refused to relinquish

William's hand. She could not say that she wholly regretted such a public display of affection. They had waited long enough.

As the meal was winding down, King Malus marched into the open area in front of Elizabeth and William's table and announced that he would bestow presents on the new couple – in keeping with fae tradition.

"That is very kind of you," William said. Elizabeth, more familiar with fae customs, was a little more concerned. Ten minutes later it was clear she had reason to be. The first "gift" had been a traditional dance by a troupe of what the king assured them were the most elite pixie dancers in all of Faerie. The dance had started graceful and ethereal and quickly turned bawdy, baring body parts that Regency society always kept under wraps and ending in a pantomime of the marital act itself. The fae were laughing, the Bingleys had covered their children's eyes, and the newlywed Darcys were red in the face.

Unfortunately, that was not the only gift the king had in store for them. He also gave them a painting that showed a very realistic and lovingly rendered portrayal of Princess Alaine, her face frozen in a rictus of horror and hatred in the moment she was imprisoned. The king was under the impression he had given them a great treat. Elizabeth managed to act delighted while privately vowing to bury it in the bottom of a trunk and never look at it again.

Other guests produced gifts as well. Haskins brought a large boulder – Elizabeth had no idea how he had carried it – and placed it in the center of the courtyard. Anne of the Hills gave them a bouquet of woad, which was already wilting. Rakover, who had perched on the Library roof for most of the festivities, swooped in to present them with a sheep. Fortunately, Haskins had managed to convey to the dragon that the new couple would prefer a live animal. The creature proceeded to run around the courtyard in confusion, but William drew Galon aside and made plans for it to join Pemberley's flock.

Despite the occasionally bizarre cultural differences, everyone seemed to be enjoying themselves. As Elizabeth and William walked about, greeting their guests, she overheard snatches of some unlikely conversations.

Her mother was lamenting to King Malus, "You do not know what a trial it is to have five daughters and wanting to see them all well married!"

"Five!" he scoffed. "I have twenty-eight, and each one lives a thousand years…."

Elizabeth stifled a laugh as they continued to walk, and she overheard one of the king's daughters speaking with Richard. "Prince Galon seems very happy in the human world."

"I believe he is," Richard replied.

The fae woman leaned closer to him. "Because humans live shorter lives, I hear they are more vigorous lovers."

Richard choked on his glass of wine. "I have no basis for comparison."

Her hand caressed his arm. "I would be very interested in finding out…."

Elizabeth and William hastily turned away, giving the couple some privacy and nearly tripped over Haskins presenting Anne of the Hills with a necklace of river stones.

"Do I know you?" Anne asked him.

He looked affronted. "I am the man who wants to marry you. I have asked thirty-seven times."

"Oh yes," she responded with a vague smile. "How did I respond the last time?"

Haskins did not seem in the least dismayed. "Have you seen my gift to the newlyweds?" He tucked Anne's hand under her arm and took her to admire his boulder.

Elizabeth laughed softly. "There are some people I believe I will never understand," William said in a low voice.

"Indeed." But there were two beings Elizabeth did not see. "Where is Abraxas?" She asked William. "Or Hespera for that matter?" She had seen them at the ceremony, but they had been absent for most of the breakfast.

He shook his head. "It has almost been as if Hespera has been avoiding me these last few weeks."

Elizabeth had not seen as much of Abraxas either, but she had believed the griffin had been busy preparing for the rare occasion of hosting a public event at the Library. She reached out to her familiar. *Abraxas, where are you?*

She did not receive an answer in words but a mental image: a room not far from the courtyard. She looked at William. "He seems to be somewhere with Hespera."

He nodded. "I got the same message from her." He surveyed the crowd of happily chatting wedding guests. Nobody appeared to need them at the moment. King Malus, who apparently liked to live dangerously, was now flirting with Mrs. Brown. "We might as well solve this mystery," he said.

Elizabeth took William's arm, and they hurried out of the courtyard and down a short hallway to the room in the image. It had once been an unused storeroom, but when William opened the door, they found it was now painted in rich blues and greens. There was no furniture. Instead, Hespera sat in the center of the room on an immense pile of feathers, scraps of fabric, and twigs – almost like a –

"Nest!" William said.

The heads of both griffins turned toward their humans.

"What is happening?" Elizabeth asked them. "Have you been keeping secrets?"

If it was possible for a griffin to look abashed, Abraxas was. *Well, you two were so busy with the wedding plans...*

Hespera's voice added. *And it happened faster than we expected....*

"*What* happened?" William asked in a choked voice.

Hespera stood and moved off the nest. In the center was a large golden egg.

There will be a new griffling in three months, Abraxas said, every inch the proud father.

"Oh!" Elizabeth clapped a hand over her mouth and tears welled up in her eyes.

"Congratulations," William managed to say, although he sounded quite stunned.

"You two are sly," Elizabeth said. "I suspected nothing."

Hespera managed to shrug her wings. *We said nothing of our feelings...even to each other.*

We did not believe it would be possible to live in the same place...until Darcy became Curator, Abraxas added.

William put his arm around Elizabeth's waist as they watched Hespera settle gently onto the nest again. "The new griffling may be a familiar. It might need someone to bond with...."

Elizabeth laughed. "We certainly have the bloodlines for it. But, Mr. Darcy, will you please allow us to enjoy our honeymoon before we plan for the next generation?"

"Gladly, Mrs. Darcy." He took her hand and kissed it. "Because, truthfully, as enchanting as this Library is, it is not nearly as enchanting as you are."

The End

ABOUT THE AUTHORS

Monica Fairview, a former literature professor living near London, is a confirmed Jane Austen addict who is now having fun writing novels that combine magic, bonnets, and handsome gentlemen in cravats. She loves to chuckle, read, and visit historical places. She firmly believes her cats have telepathic powers.

Abigail Reynolds ought to be embarrassed to admit she's been writing Austen-inspired novels for over 20 years, but as a retired doctor, she's immune to embarrassment. She keeps her retellings of the beloved story of Elizabeth and Darcy fresh by taking them in new directions with magic, Faerie, and alternate history.

Melanie Rachel has a Ph.D. in English and enjoys convincing her business-minded college students that reading is magical. She believes the love story of Darcy and Elizabeth transcends time and place, so writes them in many worlds: regency, modern, and fantastical. Melanie lives in

Arizona with her husband and their rescue dogs, who would rather chew books than read them.

Lari Ann O'Dell made the fatal mistake of picking up a *Pride & Prejudice* variation in a bookstore closing sale. It must have had a magical curse on it, since it compelled her to drop everything and start writing them herself – and including paranormal characters and magic. Now a nurse, Lari strives to keep her sanity by working on her next magical story.

Victoria Kincaid has written more than 16 *Pride & Prejudice* variations, has a Ph.D. in English literature, and runs the annual JAFF Reader/Writer Get Together. She is a full-time writer/editor who specializes in subjects like IT and crime and justice. On weekends she immerses herself in Austen and magic. She lives near Washington DC with her husband, who fortunately is not threatened by Mr. Darcy.

Sarah Courtney loves to read fantasy, fairy tales, and *Pride & Prejudice* variations, so what could be more fun than combining them? She currently lives in Virginia where she homeschools her six children and still manages to write books, which has to be proof that magic exists!

Find out more about us at Magical Austen or our Facebook group, Fantasy Reads for Austen Fans!

DANGEROUS MAGIC

BY MONICA FAIRVIEW

Pride & Prejudice with a magical twist.

Elizabeth Bennet is defiant when she is plucked from her familiar life at Longbourn and commanded to marry a powerful mage -- Fitzwilliam Darcy. She has always dreamed of marrying for love, and an arranged marriage with an arrogant stranger was never part of her plans.

Fitzwilliam Darcy is equally disapproving. A little-known young lady with no official training is hardly worthy of his noble lineage -- even if she has unusual abilities.

But Darcy and Elizabeth have no choice. Uniting their two forms of magic is the key to repelling Napoleon's invasion. They may dislike each other on sight, but the kingdom is doomed if they do not work together. Fortunately, it is not long before the sparks begin to fly between them.

Join us in this award-winning, enchanting Regency fantasy featuring Jane Austen's beloved characters, a whiff of Harry Potter, and a sweet slow-burn enemies-to-lovers romance.

Dangerous Magic was awarded Readers' Choice 2021 on *Austenesque Reviews* and Favorite Book 2021 on *From Pemberley to Milton*

Excerpt:

"Haven't I sacrificed enough? What more do they want of me?" He cringed at the note of despair in his voice.

Bingley was watching him, his eyes full of sympathy. "You have the consolation of knowing that you are doing your duty."

Darcy drew in a breath, trying to compose himself. "There is only so much a man can take in the name of duty!"

"You must go on, for the sake of King and Country," said Bingley. "Look, I know things have been more difficult for you than for anyone else, but you have to put the past behind you."

Everyone mouthed the same empty words. *Put the past behind you.* As if the past was an overcoat that could be shrugged off at will.

Darcy rose impatiently and went over to the window. The river looked so peaceful in the last rays of the sun, the rigging of the boats outlined against the orange sky. He wished he could sail with them down the river, away from all this.

Except that, when he looked more closely, he could see they were not moving. There was no wind to fill the sails today. Even the boats were at the mercy of other forces, just like he was. Freedom was nothing but an illusion. There was no escape.

The frustration began to ebb away, leaving behind a smoldering sense of resentment.

"Maybe it won't be as bad as you think, Darcy," said Bingley. "Maybe Miss Bennet will prove to be a good sort of wife."

Even Bingley could not come up with anything more reassuring than that.

"An insignificant young lady, from an insignificant family, and an even more insignificant village? I hardly think so."

Darcy turned from the window to look at Bingley. The setting sun cast a garish light on his friend's face.

"All I can hope for is that she is at least tolerably pretty," he said, bitterly, "or do you think that would be too much to ask?"

The way his luck had been going lately, he did not believe even that tiny wish would be granted.

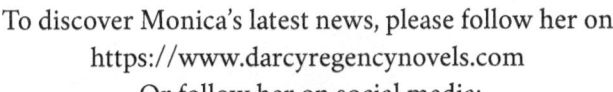

To discover Monica's latest news, please follow her on
https://www.darcyregencynovels.com
Or follow her on social media:

facebook.com/MonicaFairviewAuthor
bookbub.com/authors/monica-fairview

A SEASON OF MAGIC

BY SARAH COURTNEY

Everyone knows Elizabeth and Jane's parents were magical murderers. But blood isn't everything.

When the girls are forced to reveal their elemental magic, it does not matter to the Mage Council that they did so only to save lives. Their parents were traitors, and the entire magical community is simply waiting for them to descend into evil themselves.

The Council reluctantly admits Elizabeth to the magical university (and unofficial marriage market) called The Season, where she will learn how to control her powers. If she can keep her head down and avoid drawing any untoward notice, she might be able to graduate and finally be accepted as a fire mage.

But fading into the background will be difficult. Mr. Fitzwilliam Darcy, nephew to Lord Matlock of the Mage Council and a student himself, is assigned to observe her and report any misstep. One mistake could send her back to her foster parents, the Bennets—or worse, to prison. Yet when that mistake inevitably comes, he stands up on her behalf. Could he be an ally instead of an enemy?

When pranks between classmates become something more dangerous—and potentially deadly—Elizabeth will be forced to depend upon her friends—including Mr. Darcy.

There's something terrible lurking beneath the surface of the Season, and it will take everything Elizabeth has to survive it.

Excerpt:

"Miss Bennet," Miss Bingley said with a sneer, "while you may have nothing better to do than to pour over your books day and night, you may wish to see to it that you do not create enemies in the process."

"Oh, I apologise," Elizabeth said with false contriteness. "For some reason I was thinking that we were here to learn about magic."

"How to use our elements, yes," Miss Bingley hissed. "It is not as though history will be of any use. You had best be careful. You would not want to be thought a bluestocking." Her eyes flickered downwards for a moment, and there was a gleam in them when she again met Elizabeth's eye. "Or some country girl raised by foster parents who has never had a proper dress fitting in London."

Suspicious, Elizabeth looked down. Her dress was no longer the simple green calico she had donned that morning. The green was light, almost grey, as if it had faded. The dress sagged at the waist and shoulders as if it had been made for someone larger and clumsily altered to fit.

"Goodness, does your maid not have time to alter your clothing, Miss Bennet?" Miss Bingley taunted. "It is just too, too bad. I suppose it takes her so long to remove the mud from your gowns and make you presentable that there simply is not enough time for adjustments."

Elizabeth clenched her fists as she felt her face heat. "I warned you," she said, controlling her fury.

Miss Bingley squealed and jumped back as her necklace fell from her neck and poured itself onto the floor in a little puddle of melted silver, the small emerald floating rather pathetically on top.

"My necklace!" Miss Bingley cried. "That was a gift from my brother!"

Elizabeth wondered what Mr. Bingley would think of the fate of his gift. "And I created many such necklaces to earn enough for my gown." There was no point in hiding her metalwork or her connections to trade, as Miss Bingley already knew all about it. "If you are going to destroy someone else's belongings, you had best look to your own."

"How dare you!" Miss Bingley's face was almost purple. She took a quick step towards Elizabeth, hand raised.

Elizabeth stumbled backwards when a man appeared behind Miss Bingley and grabbed the woman's extended wrist. It was Mr. Darcy. He must have been watching them from the shadows.

"Miss Bingley," he said firmly, using his hold on her wrist to place it on his arm. "Would you do me the honour of walking with me to ethics class?"

Miss Bingley gaped, her mouth opening and closing a few times before she snapped it shut. "Very well," she said after a moment. Her eyes blazed at Elizabeth as she turned to go. "Clean up that mess, girl," she called back just before they turned down the next passage and out of sight.

Elizabeth held out her hand. The metal leaped into her palm, and she stroked it with her finger, guiding it back into the shape of the necklace as it had been before as best as Elizabeth could remember of it. She had to bend down to pick up the emerald, as her metal powers did not affect gems, but she placed it into its original spot in the necklace before hardening the surrounding metal.

Perhaps she would leave it on Miss Bingley's desk the next chance she got. Perhaps.

Or perhaps not.

～

You can sign up for Sarah's newsletter here:

https://landing.mailerlite.com/webforms/landing/w7v6p8
Or on her website at:
authorsarahcourtney.com

facebook.com/author.sarahcourtney.1

SPELLBOUND AT PEMBERLEY

BY ABIGAIL REYNOLDS

Fitzwilliam Darcy is a powerful mage and master of illusions. His abilities make him the perfect man for a dangerous mission to end the devastating war with Napoleon – a mission that would leave him little chance of returning alive. When he meets the enchanting Elizabeth Bennet, whose magical Talents are as deep as they are inexplicable, he knows he needs her help. And there's only one way to get that – marriage. Immediately.

Elizabeth wants nothing to do with his plan. Marrying Darcy would mean breaking her strong and beloved magical bond to Longbourn and giving up the use of her Talent forever. Then dragons enter the war in Europe, and England's survival hangs in the balance. And Elizabeth must make the ultimate sacrifice.

In this first book of the Fitzwilliam Darcy, Mage trilogy, dragons are already watching their newlywed journey to Pemberley, and a shocking discovery will force them to question everything they believe. Can they learn to trust each other and work together to save their country--and their lives?

Experience a thrilling, magical twist on Jane Austen's classic Pride & Prejudice in *Spellbound at Pemberley*, the first book of the Fitzwilliam Darcy, Mage trilogy!

Excerpt:

Darcy rubbed his hands over his face as he turned his

thoughts inward, the open field around him fading away. He focused, inhaling strands of power from the autumnal air. Then he drew the magical forces together and flicked his wrist.

To all appearances, a herd of cattle charged across the pasture towards him.

He eyed the illusion critically, but there were no telltale flaws, at least none that he could spot. When the nearest animal was a dozen feet away, he blew out a breath to dismiss the vision. The cows vanished.

Not a bad performance. Of course, that was the easy part.

Beside him, Bingley mopped his forehead, his eyes bulging. "By Jove, Darcy, I was certain we were about to be trampled. I could see the flecks of foam flying from the bull's mouth!"

Darcy grimaced. "From this view, yes, but watch this." He gathered fresh energy, plaited it into a bundle, and cast. This time, though, the cattle ran beside them instead of at them, giving a spectator's view of the running herd.

His breath hissed between his teeth. The same problem as always. The sound of thumping hooves, the cloud of dust rising around them, the bodies of the cows bobbing as they ran, all of those were adequate. But the damned legs!

Bingley's brow furled. "Oh, dear. I see what you mean. Too many knees, or perhaps not enough?"

"And they do not move properly, either. The cows are only convincing from the front. From any other side, it will not fool even a casual observer." Worse, it would draw attention to the existence of the illusion, just when he needed people to believe in it.

"Perhaps it will be easier when you move on to horses," Bingley said brightly.

Darcy snorted. "Given that the whole point of practicing with cattle is because their legs are easier than horses, I doubt it." He bent forward, his hands on his thighs, breathing deeply. He had to find a way to do this. The price for his failure would be counted in thousands of innocent lives.

"I say, adding fire is an excellent thought!" Bingley exclaimed, pointing. "I hardly notice the legs now."

"What are you talking about?" Darcy straightened, staring. Flames billowed in the distance ahead of the illusory cows. "That is not my work!" A tenant must have ignored the message to stay away from these fields. It would not harm his casting, but someone might be frightened by the sight of cattle charging through fire, so he pursed his lips to dispel the illusion. But the cows were already veering away.

Veering away. Impossible. Illusions had no minds of their own. He had set the herd in motion, and they should have run straight ahead unless he directed them otherwise.

Had he lost control somehow? No, the connection still pulled at him, but there was something else, something pushing at his cows.

This was unheard of. Illusions might lack strength, but nothing should be able to interfere with them. Or at least nothing he knew of.

His eyes narrowed. "Bingley, I did not tell the cows to turn away, and I can sense something out there, a presence of some sort. Is there anything in your books about a power that can alter an illusion?"

"Not a thing. Illusions are immutable, except by their creator. Are you certain? Perhaps you were just distracted."

Darcy glared at him. There was no question he had been distracted of late. Distracted by a bewitching combination of fine eyes, sparkling wit, and lively intelligence, but that did not affect him now. Casting took every ounce of his concentration.

This was something different, and he had to discover what had interfered with his casting. Even if nothing could save his own life, so many others depended on his ability to create a convincing illusion. "Stay here," he told Bingley brusquely.

He released the illusion, and the cows disappeared. Cloaking himself in shadows, he strode off towards the smoke.

~

Buy Spellbound at Pemberley -
https://books2read.com/u/mdP6ky
Abigail's website:
https://www.pemberleyvariations.com/
Abigail's social media:
https://linktr.ee/abigailreynoldswrites

INTERWOVEN

BY MELANIE RACHEL

England's best mages are called to Pemberley in their youth. Elizabeth can't understand why she's always left behind.

Not only does her father neglect to correct what must be an oversight, he won't allow her to use her most powerful magic at all. Each year, he further restricts Elizabeth's movements. She can no longer wander beyond Longbourn's boundaries, and he locks her chamber door at night with magical charms.

She allows her father to believe that his efforts are enough to keep her home. But when first her elder sister and then her youngest sister are called, Elizabeth is finished pretending. On the last day of the fifth moon, she defies her father's edicts by following her sisters through the portal to Pemberley.

Not everyone is pleased to see her.

Since the attack five years ago that left Fitzwilliam Darcy in charge of hundreds of young mages, he and his cousin have been keeping a dangerous secret. The last thing he needs to add to his crushing number of responsibilities is training an uninvited mage—even a pretty, intelligent one— whose magic is unusual and unpredictable. The portal is closed, however, so he cannot send her back.

He is not an easy master. She is not a compliant pupil. Still, Elizabeth is determined to find her place at Pemberley, something Darcy admires. Her talents are a puzzle, though, and her strength often falters. Perhaps there was a reason she was never called.

Yet Darcy has no choice but to continue working with Elizabeth. For the secret he's been keeping is beginning to unravel, and Elizabeth's unique magic may be the only way to keep Pemberley from unravelling with it.

Excerpt:

May 1798

"Why is it the fifth moon of the year, Papa?" Elizabeth asked.

Her father murmured a spell and manipulated a tiny whirlwind of dust. It spread and formed itself into a model of the Egyptian pyramids. Elizabeth climbed onto the chair next to his desk so she could see better.

She still recalled when Papa had created a model of the Erechtheion in Greece. And a few years ago, when she was very small, he had favoured Carpenter's Hall in Philadelphia, not because he found the structure beautiful, but because it had been a gathering place for Englishmen who wished to be independent of the king.

"Because the month of the fifth moon is when the most powerful magic of the old year and the most powerful magic of the new combine."

"Why is it not the sixth?" She waved one hand at the dust, and it fell into a heap beneath her father's hands. He frowned at her. "That would be exactly halfway."

Papa rearranged the dust into the form of a bear, then a giraffe, and finally a hound. Elizabeth clapped her hands in delight.

"There is more power in the push to the top of the mountain," he said, "than there is in having achieved the peak."

She nodded as though his words made sense.

He smiled at her. "Only when magic is forcing itself to its height is there enough power to open the portal; only then are we able to pass over the bridge from our world into the circle of Pemberley, where the magic is so thick it slows time."

"Slows time?"

"Even mages live longer than the non-magical, child. It is the faerie blood, you see. Those in Faelond live longer still."

"I want to live longer!"

"Living longer is not always a blessing."

"Can I see the portal? Can I go to Pemberley?"

"No, my dear. Only the mages who receive a call have the sort of magic that allows them to see the portals to Pemberley open and close."

Elizabeth pondered that. "What is *in* Pemberley?" she asked curiously. Papa would know. He knew everything.

"It is a village for the most powerful of mages: warriors, healers, artisans of every kind."

"Artisans?" she asked, forming her mouth around the unfamiliar word. She used her hands to shape the dust into an intricate castle with a boy trapped in a spiral tower. A small spark from her finger had the figure calling for help. Another spurred a tiny dragon with a female rider winging to his rescue.

"Those who have magecraft like us," he told her. "But they are mostly from the oldest of families, those who have a bloodline from both parents that extends back to the time when faeries lived among us. Some still command great magic, and people fear them."

"Should we fear them, Papa?"

Her father did not answer her question, but that was not unusual.

"You and I have useful magic, Elizabeth, but we are not powerful enough to be sent to live in Pemberley." He removed a book he was illuminating and opened it on his desk. Indigo blue began to seep into the paper, forming an S, the first letter on the page.

Elizabeth pressed her lips together, waiting for the letter to be complete. Papa would be angry if her interruption spoilt his work. When he finished, she spoke again.

"But I *am* powerful, Papa!" she insisted. "I can make it so much bigger! Look!" Elizabeth positioned his hand and her own before sending an electrical current between them. She concentrated on weaving the threads of light together so tightly that there was no air between the strands. Then she hopped down from her chair and stepped back, lengthening the stream, making it grow. The windows shimmered and began to bend outwards. The wooden frames around them began to unravel.

Her father closed his hand into a fist and severed the link so suddenly that she blinked with surprise. The windows returned to their proper place.

Papa breathed heavily, as though he had run up the stairs, but his wide eyes never left her face. "Do not ever do that again, Elizabeth," he said, his thin eyebrows lowering until they formed a sharp V above the bridge of his nose. "Do you understand?"

Elizabeth did not understand. But she nodded anyway.

https://www.melanierachelauthor.com

facebook.com/melanierachelbooks

instagram.com/melanierachelbooks

MR. DARCY'S PHOENIX

BY LARI ANN O'DELL

A phoenix brings them together. Will a curse keep them apart?

When the hauntingly beautiful song of a phoenix lures Elizabeth Bennet to the Netherfield gardens, she has a vision of an unknown gentleman. He whispers her name with such tenderness that she wonders if this man is her match. Unfortunately, her gift of prophecy has never been exactly reliable.

Mr. Darcy is a celebrated fire mage, the master of Pemberley, and the man from her vision. But he is not tender; he is haughty, proud, and high-handed. His insult of her during the Summer Solstice celebration makes her determined to dislike him in spite of her love for Dante, his phoenix familiar.

After Mr. Darcy is called away by his duties, Elizabeth's magic runs wild, and it is only their reunion at Rosings that offers her any hope of controlling it. They are drawn together by their love of magical creatures and their affinity for fire. But Elizabeth soon has another vision about Mr. Darcy, one that may portend a grave danger to his life.

Can Darcy and Elizabeth overcome misunderstandings, curses, and even fate itself?

Excerpt:

Elizabeth picked up the pace once she was out of sight of her home. The song drifted over the trees, and she briefly wondered if a siren had taken up residence in the pond a short distance away from Longbourn. Elizabeth quickly dismissed the notion as ridiculous. According to the histories she had read, sirens had rarely been seen in England. And there were no merfolk in Hertfordshire, miles from the sea as it was.

As if to remind her of her quest, the song grew louder, more insistent, pulling her toward the winding lane that led to Netherfield Park. That was peculiar, for Netherfield Park had been vacant for the past six years. When the back garden of the grand estate came into view, Elizabeth could hear the song more clearly. It touched her heart in a way she had never experienced before.

Elizabeth pushed on the back gate, which creaked open to allow her entry into the overgrown garden. The bushes to her right rustled. A wizened gnome poked its head out from the shrubbery and hissed, likely unhappy to have its slumber disturbed by the sound. Elizabeth ignored the tiny shaking fist. In truth, gnomes were quite harmless.

Elizabeth sucked in a breath when she finally spotted her quarry. Perched regally atop a silent fountain was a swan-sized bird with gold and scarlet plumage. A phoenix.

Elizabeth had always been enamored with magical creatures but had only ever seen pictures of phoenixes in her beloved books. Her heart began to pound with excitement at the prospect of interacting with one. Phoenixes were rare in England, and were said to bring good fortune. What on earth could such a magnificent creature be doing in the garden of a vacant estate?

The beautiful singing stopped suddenly as the phoenix turned its large amber eyes upon Elizabeth. She stood rooted in her place, not daring to move lest she frighten the bird away. Her skin tingled in anticipation. The phoenix seemed to study her for a long moment before deciding to come down from its perch, its brilliant plumage glistening in the early morning light, and landing on the stone bench beside her.

For a moment, neither of them moved again. Dark eyes connected with amber ones, and Elizabeth somehow understood that the creature had been singing for her. She reached out her hand to stroke the soft feathers of its neck, and as soon as she did, her legs grew weak and she collapsed.

The world around her disappeared, replaced with a vision of a gentleman standing beside the phoenix. His back was to her, but she was certain she had never seen the man before. The phoenix nuzzled its head against the man's palm, and Elizabeth felt the urge to reach out and touch his shoulder, hoping to catch a glimpse of the stranger's face. The ends of his dark hair curled slightly at the nape of his neck. He was dressed far finer than the inhabitants of Meryton, and she could hear the low timbre of his voice as he spoke to the phoenix. It made her heart flutter.

The vision faded away, leaving her head spinning. As the Netherfield gardens came back into focus, Elizabeth looked up to find the phoenix watching her with a shrewd, intelligent gaze. "Will I meet your master, then? Is that why you sang for me?"

It inclined its regal head, which Elizabeth took as confirmation. She would meet the man from her vision. And soon.

The sound of approaching hoofbeats invaded the awe of the moment. It would not do to be caught skulking around the Netherfield gardens uninvited. She hurried through the open gate, ducking behind the low garden walls for cover, and then crept toward the standing stone situated near the edge of the property.

It was a large, towering object, unused for transport these last six years, but it would bring her home quickly. She pressed her palm against the cool, moss-covered stone and thought of home. As her body faded into the stone, she could just catch the sound of two male voices conversing.

Fitzwilliam Darcy dismounted with grace, unlike his companion Charles Bingley, who had nearly leaped off his horse in excitement to see the house and grounds of the property he had just decided to lease.

Despite being vacant for the past six years, the estate was well cared for. The grounds were carefully maintained by elves, nymphs, and gnomes, and the house and furnishings were as pristine as could be expected under the housekeeper Mrs. Campbell's watchful eye. The staff seemed trustworthy, polite, and duly deferential. When the tour was complete, Bingley eagerly turned to Darcy for affirmation.

"Netherfield should suit you very well, Bingley," Darcy said, though he secretly believed his friend could have looked at a few other properties before leasing the first he had viewed.

Bingley's grin was large and bright. "And shall you consent to spend the summer here as my guest?"

"Certainly. But first I must return to London. My cousin is due to return from the Peninsula."

"I read of his honorable discharge from the militia in the paper. He must join us as well. I am sure a few months in the country shall hasten his convalescence."

Darcy's cousin, Colonel Richard Fitzwilliam, had been injured in the war by an Iberian wyvern. His physician cautioned that he might never again have functional use of his left leg, and there was still danger of him needing amputation. Darcy agreed that the putrid environs of London could hamper his cousin's recovery. In any case, Colonel Fitzwilliam had been born and raised in Derbyshire with him and surely missed the countryside after three years in a warzone on the Continent. "I thank you for your offer. I shall extend the invitation."

"My sisters and Hurst will be arriving next Thursday," Bingley said.

"Then you may expect me to arrive Thursday as well," Darcy promised, "but I really ought to return to London."

"This property has a standing stone at its edge. I will show you."

"Thank you," Darcy said, following his friend through the front gates. It was far preferable to make the return to London via standing stone. The ship carrying his cousin would arrive at port on the morrow, and Darcy wished to be well rested for the reunion.

Darcy's phoenix, Dante, was soaring elegantly overhead. Darcy smiled at the creature and called to him. The phoenix swooped to the ground in a regal manner before landing gently by Darcy's side. "We shall travel to London shortly, Dante," Darcy said.

The bird acknowledged its master with a dip of his scarlet head.

Bingley observed the pair. "Dante seems at peace here."

"That he does," Darcy agreed. He could not say why, but Darcy did as well. His emotions were closely linked with Dante's. The phoenix had been with the Darcy family for generations, burning and rising from the ashes when each new master of Pemberley was born.

"I believe the season shall be a happy one," Bingley said. As if to emphasize his point, some of the closed buds on the nearby trellis bloomed. Bingley had never been able to completely control his affinity for nature, and when his emotions were strong his magic seeped out in unexpected ways. The tips of Bingley's ears turned red under Darcy's scrutiny. "It is fortunate I was not blessed with an affinity for fire. I am not in possession of your impossibly strict regulation."

Darcy privately agreed. If Charles Bingley had been given Darcy's own abilities, there would be spontaneous fires everywhere the man went.

Darcy and Bingley shook hands after Darcy promised to return the following week. Dante followed close behind his master on the path to the standing stone. The bird kept a wary eye upon him as Darcy touched the mossy stone and vanished. The phoenix began its clear song before flying in the direction of London.

Three miles away, Elizabeth Bennet heard the melody and smiled.

❧

Find Lari at
Facebook Author Page
GoodReads

SPELLS AND SHADOWS

BY VICTORIA KINCAID

As a secret agent for the Mages' Council, Mr. Darcy investigates a necromancer who is leading his followers down a dark path. When they discover him, a fight and a chase drive Darcy—injured and close to death—into the river. He is rescued and healed by Elizabeth, a talented mage at the Longbourn estate. Darcy cannot help developing feelings for her, but he dares not reveal his true identity while the necromancer's creatures search for him.

Elizabeth Bennet is intrigued by the family's new guest as he recovers at Longbourn. But mystery surrounds the man, and strange happenings plague the neighborhood while he visits. Elizabeth herself harbors a secret that she cannot share with the handsome stranger.

When Darcy's enemies come calling, the Bennet family is caught in the crossfire. Worse, Elizabeth's magic draws the necromancer's particular interest. Darcy is falling in love with her and believes she returns his feelings, but the secret of his true identity could destroy their budding relationship —if they survive the upcoming danger.

Excerpt:

Darcy was aware of moving between periods of waking and sleeping, unsure of what was real and what was a dream. When his eyes finally opened, Darcy was more alert. He noted some details of his surroundings: a wholly unfamiliar room with blue striped wallpaper and well-made but worn oak furniture. The chamber was bathed in lemony yellow sunlight from two open windows that were framed by lacy curtains blowing in the breeze.

Awaking in a strange room should have been frightening, or at least disconcerting. However, Darcy found it difficult to experience anything other than pleasure that he was alive. He had no idea how he had arrived at this place, but he had expected to awaken cold, wet, and in pain. He could not possibly object to his situation. Surely nothing terrible threatened Darcy in such a room. He could not imagine that the necromancer decorated his house in blue stripes and lace.

Endeavoring to sit up provoked the discovery that Darcy was strong enough to only lift his head, but he could survey the room. Only then did he realize he was not alone.

A dark-haired young woman was laying down a book and uncurling herself from a chair in the far corner. She was familiar from his intermittent periods of semi-alertness.

A maid assigned to watch over the patient? No, her dress was too fine; she must be a gentlewoman. What was she doing alone with him? Perhaps she was married. Although if Darcy had a wife that pretty, he would not have left her alone with a strange young man. *On the other hand, I am not much of a threat to her virtue.*

She crossed to his bedside. "Would you like some water?"

Following his nod, she held a glass and supported his head while he drank eagerly. Nothing had ever tasted as good as that tepid water. Exhausted from that slight exertion, Darcy allowed his head to sink gratefully onto the pillow while she returned the empty glass to the bedside table.

"How are you feeling?" she asked in a soft voice—so rich it was almost musical to Darcy's ears.

"Where—" He coughed and cleared his throat. "Where am I?"

"Hertfordshire."

Hertfordshire? He had never been in that part of the country. "How— How far from Luton?"

Her eyebrows shot upward. "Is that where you were? We are quite a ways."

What had happened while Darcy was insensible? How long ago had he fallen in the river? What had Richard thought when Darcy had not reported in? He yearned to leap from the bed and order a carriage for London, but he was patently incapable of travel.

The people in this house had taken care of him, kept him alive. But could he trust them?

"Will you tell me your name?" the woman asked.

"D—" Darcy stopped himself. The enemy would be searching for him. "You can call me...William."

She chuckled, a low and lovely sound. "Surely I cannot be so informal! For all that you are in my home, we have not actually been introduced." Playfulness in her tone suggested she took the dictates of propriety rather less seriously than Darcy did. What kind of a woman was she?

"I am Mr. D."

"Mr. Dee?" She gave him a quick, ironic curtsey. "I am pleased to meet you. I am Elizabeth Bennet, and you are a guest in my family's home of Longbourn."

She was altogether charming. Many other women would have peppered him with questions, retreated into shyness, or fussed about his health. Her directness was refreshing, helping him bear his current weakness. "I must thank you for your hospitality," he said formally.

"It is our pleasure. Is there anyone we should contact on your behalf? Where is your family?"

"I have a house in London." That was true enough. "My family raises sheep and sells wool." That was also true; Pemberley had a lively wool trade, although it was hardly the chief source of income. Thoughts of home recalled Darcy to his duty. "I should send a note to my cousin...." However, the mere thought of attempting to write was exhausting.

"Perhaps when you are improved," Miss Bennet suggested. He must have appeared as tired as he felt.

"How long have I been asleep?"

"More than a day. You arrived here yesterday morning, and it is now evening."

As long as that? Richard must be frantic with worry. Fortunately, Georgiana was at Matlock with family and believed Darcy to be in town. Richard would write her a letter to account for Darcy's lack of correspondence. "Arrived? How did I arrive?" The last thing Darcy recalled was diving into the river with the expectation that he would drown.

"Via a most unconventional means. You were traveling in the River Lea without a boat, which does not have much to recommend itself by way of transportation. My sister and I found you along the riverbank."

Darcy was amazed at his good fortune. He had a vague recollection of being pulled out of the water but regarded her skeptically. "You and your sister pulled me out of the river? Perhaps with the help of your husband?"

She regarded him blankly. "I am unmarried, sir. My sister and I took you from the river with some effort. My father and a footman transported you here." Perhaps she was unaware of how much she revealed. Not only was she unwed, but her family was wealthy enough to keep a manservant.

"Your father allows you to be in a bedchamber with an unknown man?"

To his amazement, she laughed. "You are hardly in a position to do me harm. Even if you managed to stand, I could easily push you over."

He coughed, imagining that he still had river water in his lungs. "All too true, I am afraid. But propriety…." Clearly this was a family wealthy enough to care for the reputation of an unwed daughter.

She leaned forward and spoke in a low voice. "I shall not tell anyone if you do not."

Darcy found himself smiling despite the circumstances.

"Do you wish me to leave?" she asked.

"No," he said hastily and found he meant it. Apparently recovering from a near-death experience was far more pleasant if one had company. "I enjoy your conversation."

She did not simper and blush as he expected. Instead, she gave him a look of mock disapproval. "Now, sir, you are not yet strong enough to expend energy upon compliments to a lady. Conserve your strength."

This elicited a chuckle from him. "It was not intended as a compliment; it was simply the truth."

Now a faint blush did stain her cheek, and she averted her eyes. "Are you in pain?"

He attempted to sit up in bed and was rewarded with an ache in his side. *Oh yes. I was stabbed.* Touching the skin over his ribs, he discovered that the area was covered by a bandage, but the pain was not nearly as sharp as he expected.

"That wound and the one in your leg are mostly healed, but there is still a chance you may develop an infection," Miss Bennet said.

"Mostly healed?" How was that possible? It had only been two days.

"We did what we could to heal them and reduce the swelling from the blow to your head and the ankle injury. But everything will require additional time and rest."

Darcy gingerly touched the bump on the back of his head, wincing at even light contact. And how did she even know that his ankle was injured? Surely he had not attempted to walk?

"How long does the doctor suppose I must remain in bed?" he asked.

"The doctor has not examined you."

No doctor? The thought alarmed Darcy. "Who treated me then?"

"I did." Miss Bennet colored slightly. "I have a bit of healing magic."

Oh. A few puzzle pieces fell into place. Magical healers were rare outside of large cities. Darcy had been exceedingly fortunate indeed. No doubt she was being modest, and she was the reason for his unexpected survival.

"We can send for the doctor if you wish," Miss Bennet said.

"That is not necessary. I believe your care has been quite beneficial."

She wagged a finger at him. "Now you are wasting strength on compliments once again!"

www.ingramcontent.com/pod-product-compliance
Lightning Source LLC
Chambersburg PA
CBHW020932260626
47169CB00006B/1687